Praise for
CINDI MYERS

"Real life for the sandwich generation."
—*Paperback Swap* on
The Birdman's Daughter

"An engrossing read about family, marriage and love."
—*Curled Up with a Good Book* on
The Birdman's Daughter

"Lyrical...the father is a memorable character."
—*RT Book Reviews* on
The Birdman's Daughter

"A very emotional, heart-wrenching story."
—*The Ratmammy Reviews* on
The Birdman's Daughter

"Delightful and delicious...Cindi Myers always satisfies!"
—*USA TODAY* bestselling author Julie Ortolon

"Myers's ability to portray true-to-life sympathetic
characters will resonate most with readers of this
captivating romance."
—*Publishers Weekly* on
Learning Curves

Dear Reader,

Nothing shapes our personalities and lives like our families. Whether our family relationships are good or bad, they influence us throughout our days. The stories in this volume look at those family relationships from different angles. In particular, they look at the relationships of two grown daughters with their fathers.

I was close to my own father. He taught me a lot and we shared a love of history, gardening and nature. He passed away suddenly on the eve of the original publication of *The Birdman's Daughter* and I was always sad he didn't get to see it, for he took pride in my writing. He would buy copies of my books and give them away to new people he met.

The daughters in these stories aren't always as close with their fathers as I was with mine, but those difficulties have made them stronger. Through the course of these stories each discovers a kind of healing that I hope readers will find uplifting.

I love to hear from readers. You can look for me on Facebook or MySpace, or e-mail me through my Web site www.CindiMyers.com. Or write to me in care of Harlequin Books, 225 Duncan Mill Rd, Don Mills, Ontario M3B 3K9, Canada.

Cindi Myers

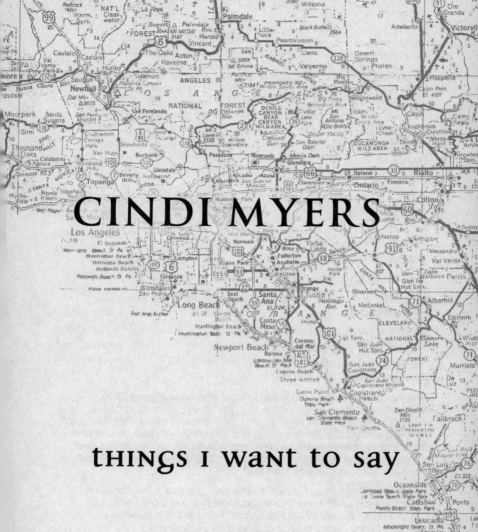

CINDI MYERS

things i want to say

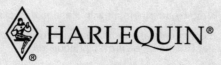

HARLEQUIN®

TORONTO • NEW YORK • LONDON
AMSTERDAM • PARIS • SYDNEY • HAMBURG
STOCKHOLM • ATHENS • TOKYO • MILAN • MADRID
PRAGUE • WARSAW • BUDAPEST • AUCKLAND

Recycling programs
for this product may
not exist in your area.

ISBN-13: 978-0-373-23083-9

THINGS I WANT TO SAY

Copyright © 2010 by Harlequin Books S.A.

The publisher acknowledges the copyright holder of the individual works as follows:

THINGS I WANT TO SAY
Copyright © 2010 by Cindi Myers

THE BIRDMAN'S DAUGHTER
Copyright © 2006 by Cindi Myers

This edition published by arrangement with Harlequin Books S.A.

For questions and comments about the quality of this book
please contact us at Customer_eCare@Harlequin.ca.

® and TM are trademarks of the publisher. Trademarks indicated with ® are registered in the United States Patent and Trademark Office, the Canadian Trade Marks Office and in other countries.

www.eHarlequin.com

Printed in U.S.A.

contents

tHINGS I want to say

In memory of Lyle Sterling, 1933–2006

Prologue

Frannie Lawrence believed in secrets. The things you didn't talk about couldn't hurt you the way words said out loud could. Words made the bad things too real sometimes. Better to keep silent, with the hurt locked safely away.

She took one last look around at the room where she'd spent most of her nineteen years—a room that had held so many secrets. The beds were made, the clothes they were leaving behind folded neatly in the dresser. In the kitchen she'd covered and put away the last of the funeral food and watered the potted ivy sent over by her boss at Weisman's Drug Store. Everything was as orderly as she could make it. When she thought of this place at all, this was how she wanted to remember it.

She turned to her sister. "Are you ready?"

Ellen looked around the room, as if searching for something she'd left behind. She was still wearing the black dress she'd put on for the funeral. It was too tight across her chest and in the arms, the seams straining at her rib cage. Three years younger than Frannie, Ellen still had the soft look of a child. Frannie's heart ached when she looked at Ellen and thought of how vulnerable she was, in a way Frannie, as the oldest, had never been.

Ellen's eyes met Frannie's, worry making a slight V over the bridge of her nose. "I guess I'm ready," she said.

"Come on. The taxi will be here soon."

"All right." Ellen picked up her suitcase and followed Frannie into the living room, where their mother sat in a faded chintz armchair.

"I'm going to California and I'm taking Ellen with me," Frannie said. She'd kept this plan a secret until now, too, to lessen the chance of anyone trying to stop them.

Confusion clouded their mother's eyes. "He's dead now. Why do you need to leave?"

"We'll both be happier out there. I'll find a job, and I'll make sure Ellen finishes school. You won't have to worry about us."

Their mother didn't look alarmed or even particularly distressed. "California? Why California?"

"The weather's good. I hear there are good jobs out there. And it's as far away from here as I could think of."

She looked at Frannie a moment longer, the puzzled expression never leaving her eyes, then she sighed, like steam escaping from a soufflé, collapsing it. "I suppose it's for the best," she said.

"Yes, it's for the best." Frannie and Ellen would be better off separated from all the things that had happened here. They would never talk about them again.

1

Memories are a lot like men. Some of them look best when viewed from a distance.

Unfortunately, the only way to separate the dreamboats from the duds is to move in for a better inspection. I'd been keeping my distance for a lot of years when I finally decided to take a chance and see what a closer look would show me. My twentieth high school reunion seemed as good a time as any to examine the men and the memories I'd left behind.

"Why would you want to go back for the reunion when you didn't even graduate from the class?" My sister, Frannie, stood in the bedroom of my condo, which sat next door to her own in Bakersfield, California, and watched me pack for the trip back to Ridgeway, Virginia, home of the Ridgeway Rebels, Markson's Manufacturing and, once upon a time, Frannie and me.

It was true I hadn't graduated from Ridgeway High School—we'd moved away when I was sixteen—but I had grown up as part of the class of 1986. I felt a lot closer to them than to my actual graduating class at Hollywood High. "They were nice enough to ask me, so I'm going," I said.

"You never wanted to go before." Frannie's tone approached a whine. "Why now?"

"I never wanted to go before because I was fat." Not "plump" or "chunky" or even "heavy" but fat. Such an ugly word. I hadn't wanted to hear my old friends use it to describe me. "Now I'm not fat anymore and there are a lot of people there I'd like to see again." I mean, how could I pass up the chance to impress my old friends with what a hot item I'd become?

Frannie's expression didn't soften one bit. "Such as?"

"Well…" I tucked a pair of sandals more securely along the side of the suitcase. "Marc Reynolds is going to be there," I said.

In high school, I'd been sure Marc was the most perfect boy I'd ever known. He'd been tall, with a strong jaw, thick brown hair falling just so across his forehead and eyes the color of Little Debbie fudge brownies. One smile from him in the hallway and I'd be floating all day.

So when I found out he was still single—and that he was on the committee planning the reunion—I took it as a sign. I'd spent most of my life as a dumpy plain Jane and figured I had, at best, only a few prime years left. I had to take advantage of them while I could.

"As I remember it, Marc Reynolds wouldn't give you the time of day in high school," Frannie said.

"That's because I was on my way to being fat then." I held up two dresses, both with tags still attached. "Which do you think looks better on me—the blue or the pink?"

"The blue brings out your eyes. And you were not that fat in high school."

"Not as fat as I got later, you mean." I studied the dresses again. "Are you sure the blue looks better? The pink is a size eight." Probably mismarked since it fit me, but it was the only size eight I'd worn in my life.

"Take them both if you can't decide." Frannie came all the way into the room and sat on the side of the bed. "Ellen, I know you've worked really hard, and I'm very proud of you, but you can't think losing a few pounds is some magic trick that will suddenly get you everything you want."

"One hundred pounds. I lost one hundred pounds." I added both dresses to the suitcase and turned to face her. "One hundred pounds is another person. People look at you differently when you weigh two hundred and forty than when you weigh one hundred and forty. *Men* look at you differently."

"And you think Marc will look at you differently?" The twin worry lines on her forehead deepened.

"I know he will. And more important, I look at myself differently now. I know any man would be lucky to have me." I said this with more conviction than I actually felt, but all the self-help books I'd read had assured me if I kept faking it, the actual feelings of self-confidence would eventually show up. "Marc's not going to know what hit him," I added.

"Maybe he's bald and has a beer belly now," she said. "Maybe he's nothing like you remember him."

Have I mentioned that my big sister hates to lose an argument? "I saw his picture on the reunion Web site," I told her. "He looks better than ever. A few lines around the eyes, a touch of gray at the temples. Sexy as hell."

I glanced at my own reflection in the dresser mirror. My hair was the same rich auburn it had been in high school, thanks to Frannie, one of the best hairdressers in the state of California. She does hair for movie stars. Going to her salon for my monthly cut-and-color was like a trip through the pages of *Soap Opera Digest*. You never knew who you'd find under the dryer next to you. Once I'd been at the shampoo sink beside Susan Lucci!

"You look great," Frannie said, catching me in my moment of vanity. "That new cut makes you look five years younger, and those highlights I put in really draw attention to your eyes. You've always had such great hair and eyes."

This is the kind of thing well-meaning family and friends say to try to cheer up fat people. If I had a dollar for every time I'd heard "she has such a nice face," I could retire now. But I guess I was glad I hadn't ended up with limp, mousy hair and a big schnoz, in addition to having a big butt and thunder thighs.

I did a half turn to check the rear view. I still couldn't quite get used to seeing my much smaller caboose. Thanks to the millions of hours I'd spent in the gym—and the tummy tuck I'd had last spring—I had a pretty decent figure. And before anybody makes cracks about plastic surgery being cheating, let's see *you* lose almost half your body weight and not end up with a ton of loose skin with nowhere to go.

I left the mirror and went back to packing. "Yolanda has everything she needs at the shop, but I gave her your number for emergencies." I own a flower shop—The Perfect Posie. I specialize in flowers for movie sets. That gorgeous arrangement sitting on the piano in your favorite sitcom? I did those. The flowers for that big TV wedding extravaganza a few years ago? That was me. Yolanda's been my right hand at the shop for five years, so I was confident she could keep things going while I had my fun.

"Bring me some postcards for my scrapbook," Frannie said, apparently resigned to the fact that she wasn't going to talk me out of this.

I smiled. "Of course." Frannie has dozens of scrapbooks devoted to every facet of our lives. Not that we have very exciting lives, but Frannie documents every minute bit, as if collecting evidence that we really do exist.

Evidence for whom I haven't decided. We're both single and childless, though I'd like to change that.

"How long are you going to be gone?" Frannie asked. She was still frowning. I ought to tell her how bad that is for her face. The plastic surgeon I'd seen had offered Botox but since I don't have very many lines yet, I'd decided to pass. All that fat under my skin had been good for something after all—not as many wrinkles. That, and I have redhead skin. I can burn on a cloudy day, so I'd worn sunblock out of self-defense a long time before everyone preached about it.

"The reunion is over the long weekend, but I wanted to get there a little early and look around the old hometown." I closed the suitcase and leaned on it, struggling to pull the zipper shut.

Frannie came over to help me. "So how long? A week?"

"At least. I booked an open return on my ticket, in case I decide to stay longer." I tried to keep my expression casual, but Frannie knows me better than anyone.

"You mean in case things get hot and heavy with Marc Reynolds." She punched my shoulder. "Ellen! You haven't seen the man in over twenty years and you're already planning to sleep with him."

Another thing about redheads is that we blush easily. At least I do. Right now my cheeks felt as if they were on fire. "Not *planning*. I'm just leaving the possibility open. Is that so bad? Jeez, I haven't had sex with anybody but myself in so long, I'd like to think it's a possibility, you know?"

She put her arm around me and hugged me close. "I know. I just don't want to see you get hurt."

"Life hurts, sis. You know that."

She nodded. "I know." We'd been through some times, Frannie and I. I'm not going to talk about them now, but suffice it to say I'd gotten through them with food, and Frannie had focused on worrying about me. I'd given up my food addiction, but Frannie couldn't let go of worrying. I don't think there's a twelve-step program for that one.

"Just tell me this." She straightened and looked me in the eyes. "What happens if you meet up with Marc and you two don't hit it off? You're not going to get all depressed again, are you?"

"I promise I'm not going to drown my sorrows in chocolate

doughnuts." I held up one hand, Scout's honor—though I was never so much as a lowly Brownie. "Maybe I'll meet someone else. Or maybe I'll decide they're all a bunch of losers and I can do better." I patted her shoulder. "It's okay. I'm not a fifteen-year-old who cries if you look at her wrong anymore. I'm going to visit the old hometown, maybe spend a day at the lake, see a few old friends and have a vacation. It'll be fine."

She didn't look convinced. "You couldn't pay me enough to go back there."

"Maybe you should go," I said gently. "I think part of getting over things is proving they don't have power over you anymore."

She shook her head. "I'd just as soon forget."

I understood that. No one likes bad memories. I'd tried to bury them for years under food, but it hadn't worked. I hadn't even realized what I was doing until a therapist pointed it out. And I hadn't even told her everything.

I still saw the therapist, just as I still went to the gym. Part of my maintenance plan. Frannie preferred fussing over her customers and her silver standard poodles, Midge and Pidge.

Neither of us had ever married. Frannie said she had no interest in being tied down to anyone. She rarely even dated and seemed fine with that.

I wasn't so satisfied being alone, and I hoped in the near future I could change that. Thirty-eight years is a long time to be single, but I'd spent at least twenty-five of those years behind my wall of fat, insulating myself from the opposite sex and everything else. So I figured in relationship years, I was closer to my early twenties.

I had plenty of time left to meet Mr. Right. Time to try for a different life than the one I'd had so far—a life in which I could really be *happy*.

★ ★ ★

My flight touched down at the Richmond airport at three o'clock the next afternoon, and I collected my bags and went to find my rental car. Today was Thursday. The official reunion started Saturday, which gave me a little time to get my bearings.

Like almost every other small town on the East Coast, Ridgeway had succumbed to urban sprawl. As I headed toward my downtown hotel, I passed acres of houses lined up like Monopoly playing pieces and shopping centers full of the same big-box stores and restaurants you could find in every state in the Union.

Closer to downtown, though, things began to look familiar. I passed the Elks Lodge where Frannie had her junior/senior prom, and Monroe's Department Store, where Mom worked for a while. I read street signs and remembered which friends had lived on each block.

Frannie and I had both been back here five years ago, when our mother died. We hadn't seen much of Ridgeway then, since we'd spent most of the four days cleaning out her house and planning her funeral. We'd agreed to sell the place to a cousin and then left town as fast as we could, relieved that we'd never have to come back here again.

But this time was different, I told myself. This time I wanted to be here. I wasn't the same person I'd been five years ago or twenty-two years ago, when Frannie and I had headed to California. I could come here and enjoy myself.

It was after six by the time I checked into the hotel. I unpacked my suitcase, freshened up my hair and makeup, then went downstairs to the bar.

I'm not much of a drinker normally, but I was determined not to hole up in my room the entire weekend. Ordering room service was terribly tempting, though. I've always felt so conspicuous eating alone in a restaurant—one of those holdovers from my fat days, I guess, when I was sure people were judging every bite I put in my mouth.

Anyway, I figured a drink would take the edge off my nervousness. And maybe they'd have popcorn or nuts set out, so I wouldn't show up at the restaurant famished.

The bar was a typical hotel "lounge"—tucked into a corner, one side open to the lobby, a television with the sound turned down suspended over the bar. A baseball game was on, and I pretended to watch it while I waited for my glass of white wine. After the drink came, I got up the nerve to look around.

That's when I realized I was the only woman in the place. I took a big swallow of wine. Coincidence? Or was there something I didn't know about this place? Would the other customers think I was a hooker or something?

This is what comes of not socializing much for twenty-two years. I was ignorant of the unwritten rules and silent signals that applied to dating among adults. A man in a brown suit at the other end of the bar caught my eye and smiled. I looked away, and resolved to finish my wine and get out of there as soon as I could.

Brown suit had another idea. He picked up his drink and moved onto the stool next to me. "I hope you don't mind if I join you," he said, "but I hate sitting at the bar by myself. It makes me feel so self-conscious. And well, more alone."

Since this was exactly what I'd been feeling myself, I nodded. "I know what you mean," I said.

He offered his hand. "Mitch Brannon."

"Hi, Mitch. I'm Ellen." I knew enough not to give a stranger my full name. I was naive in some ways, but not dumb.

"So, are you in town on business?" Mitch asked.

I shook my head. "Class reunion."

"No kidding? Tenth?"

I knew he was flirting then, and couldn't hold back a pleased smile. "A lady never tells," I teased.

"And a gentleman wouldn't dream of pressing the issue. Can I buy you a drink?"

I realized my glass was empty, and started to say no, but Mitch had already caught the eye of the bartender and signaled for two more drinks. I pulled a basket of snack mix toward me and started to eat. The salt would make me all puffy and bloated tomorrow, but without something in my stomach I was afraid I'd get tipsy and stupid fast.

For the next twenty minutes, we made small talk. I found out Mitch was from Pittsburgh, a salesman in town to call on Markson Manufacturing, which was still Ridgeway's largest employer. The plant made parts for hospital dialysis machines and other medical equipment. Unexciting but necessary, and apparently quite profitable, stuff.

When Mitch offered to buy me a third drink, I had the sense to refuse and switch to water. I thought about excusing myself to go get something to eat, but to tell the truth, I was enjoying myself too much to leave just yet. I couldn't remember when a good-looking guy had sat and flirted with me like this. Working in the flower shop, most of the people I came in contact with were set designers for television shows and movies, and most of them were women or gay men.

Mitch was most definitely flirting with me. For all I knew, he had a wife and six kids back in Pittsburgh, or a mistress in every town between here and Pennsylvania. I told myself it didn't really matter. Nothing was going to come of this. But I looked at it as a chance to brush up on my own technique before I saw Marc again.

Mitch had a third drink. Or maybe a fourth. I didn't know how long he'd been in the bar before I showed up. His face was a little flushed, his conversation a little more garrulous, but I didn't have the sense he was really drunk. "I love your hair," he said at one point. "It's so beautiful." He leaned forward, his tone confiding. "I've always had a thing for redheads. You caught my eye the minute you walked into the room."

I refrained from pointing out that, since I'd been the only female in the bar at the time, I naturally stood out. There were a few more women in the place now, but Mitch had stuck with me. It was flattering, in a superficial way. But sometimes superficial is all I need.

By the time Mitch finished his drink, I was overdosed on snack mix and in need of real food. I slid off the bar stool. "It was nice talking to you," I said, "but I have to go."

"No," he protested, standing also. "We're just getting to know each other. Let me take you to dinner."

I shook my head. "No. Thank you, but I have an early morning tomorrow. Thanks for the drink." I headed for the door before I could change my mind.

He followed, making a few more feeble protests, but was enough of a gentleman to take no for an answer finally. Still, I was worried if I headed for the hotel restaurant, he might spot me in there later and try again to persuade me to further our acquaintance.

Call me old-fashioned, but picking up a traveling sales-man in a hotel bar wasn't my idea of the start of a wonderful relationship. I'd had a good time, but wasn't interested in taking things to another level, which I was pretty sure was what Mitch had in mind.

As I said, I may be naive, but I'm not stupid.

So room service it was. I called in my order, then decided to check in with Frannie.

She answered on the third ring. I pictured her in her living room, piled on the sofa with both dogs at her feet, the TV tuned to that night's lineup of sitcoms and crime dramas. "Just thought I'd call and let you know I got in okay," I said.

She turned down the volume on the television. "How was your flight?"

"Fine. I would have called earlier, but I went down to the hotel bar for a drink right after I got here."

"You were in the bar for what...two hours?"

It annoyed me that she'd bothered to do the math. "A guy bought me a drink."

"You picked up a man in a bar?" She couldn't have sounded more horrified if I'd told her I'd done a strip tease in the middle of the hotel lobby.

"I did not pick him up. We were both sitting there and got to talking and he bought me a drink. Nothing else happened." Although it could have, if I'd wanted it to. The knowledge gave me a quiet thrill.

"Was he cute?"

I laughed. "Forty-year-old men aren't cute! But he was nice-looking. It was good practice for the reunion."

"So you still think you and Marc are going to hit it off after all these years?"

"I don't know that. I'm just open to the possibility."

"When are you going to see him?"

"I'm going to call him tomorrow."

"He's liable to get the wrong idea."

I rolled my eyes. "This isn't high school. A woman can call a man without having him think she's fast."

"You be careful."

Frannie had repeated this advice so often there was a recording of her voice saying these words that automatically played anytime I did almost *anything,* risky or not. "I'll be careful," I reassured her. As I always did.

I imagined husbands and wives had these little verbal rituals, too.

"The reunion doesn't start until Saturday, right?" Frannie said. "What are you going to do in the meantime?"

"I don't know. Look around. Maybe I'll see some old

friends." I hadn't planned a detailed itinerary, too nervous to think that far ahead.

"Did you go by the house yet?"

Her voice was strained, and her tension carried over to me. "No. I don't intend to," I said. "It's not ours anymore."

"It's not even cousin Lou's anymore," she said. "I heard he sold it."

"Maybe they tore it down." The house hadn't been in that great a shape when we lived in it. By the time Mom died, it was pretty run-down.

"I'd have burned it down if I could get away with it," Frannie said.

After all these years, I didn't react to her anger anymore. Her words just made me tired.

A knock on my door saved me from having to reply. "Room service."

"I have to go now," I said. "I'll call you tomorrow and let you know how it goes with Marc."

I ate dinner while I watched the news, then got ready for bed and stretched out on the floor and did sit-ups. I hate to exercise. I mean really hate it. I feel like a sinner doing penance, which I guess isn't too far off. But I'm scared enough of gaining back the weight I lost to keep at it. That's probably a different kind of neurosis, but one I'll keep.

I said my prayers and climbed into bed. I don't think of myself as an overly religious person, but I believe in a higher power, and he-she-it has helped me out a lot over the years. You don't know what faith is until you've spent an hour praying you won't go into the kitchen and eat a whole tub of frozen cookie dough from the freezer.

I fell asleep thinking about Mitch from the hotel bar, who dissolved into Marc and the memory of a game of spin the bottle we'd played at a birthday party when I was in sixth grade. Six of us had knelt in a circle on the rust-red shag carpeting of the Kincaids' family room and Marsha Kincaid had spun an empty Coke bottle.

Even then I'd been a chubby girl, the waistband of my yellow dotted Swiss minidress digging into my sides, the bands of the puffed sleeves cutting into my thick arms. I'd held my breath as the bottle spun, praying it wouldn't land on me, hoping at the same time it would.

The first spin landed on Rachel Mayfield, who grinned and took her time choosing a boy to kiss. I hoped she wouldn't choose Marc, though he was, in my eyes at least, the handsomest boy there.

But Rachel chose Scott Ruston as the object of her favor. He made a feeble protest, but when Rachel leaned forward and pressed her mouth to his, I noticed he didn't seem to mind all that much.

By the third spin, I could feel the carpet making crosshatch patterns on my bare knees, and one foot had fallen asleep. I forgot to focus on the bottle, so was startled when everyone began shouting my name. I looked down and saw the bottle pointing right at me.

I swallowed hard, and my face felt hot. "Who you gonna kiss?" Rachel teased.

I glanced up at those in the circle. Every boy there was looking away from me or down at the carpet. They seemed to have physically recoiled at the idea of kissing fat Ellen Lawrence.

At other times, in similar situations, I'd have made a joke. Maybe I'd try to skip my turn. But that year, when I was twelve, I'd begun to feel the first longings to be like other girls—thin and pretty and *normal*. And I was in love with Marc, even if he never looked at me.

Reasoning I couldn't be any more miserable than I already was, I sat up straighter and smoothed out the skirt of my dress. "I choose Marc," I said.

To his credit, he didn't flinch or protest. He merely sighed, then closed his eyes and waited. Hands on my knees, I leaned toward him, aware of the giggles and smooching noises the others were making. But all my attention was focused on Marc.

I thought he had beautiful lips—pale pink and not too full. When I got close enough to be sure of my aim, I closed my eyes and pressed my mouth gently to his. I held the pose as long as I dared. It was the first time I'd ever kissed a boy and I wanted to remember it.

When I did finally pull away, I opened my eyes and smiled. The kiss had felt good. Right. And now I knew a secret. Not only was Marc the handsomest boy in the sixth grade...

He tasted like chocolate cake.

2

The next morning after breakfast I called Marc at the number I'd gotten from the reunion Web site. A woman answered the phone and I froze. Was it his wife? Girlfriend? "May I speak to Marc Reynolds?" I managed to get out.

"One moment please."

"This is Marc." His voice was deeper than I remembered. Sexy. I pinched myself and remembered the script I'd come up with in my head. "Hi, Marc. I don't know if you remember me, but it's Ellen Lawrence. I'm in town for the reunion and wondered if I could do anything to help."

"Ellen!" His voice had all the heartiness of a used-car salesman. Or maybe that was merely my inner cynic butting in with her opinion. "Great to hear from you. We can always use volunteers."

"I'm happy to lend a hand. How have you been?"

"Great, great. Let me see here...." I heard the rustle of papers. "All right! We could use help with the cleanup committee."

Garbage detail? Not the glamorous image I was hoping to project. "I...I'm not sure I'll be able to stay after everything's over," I said.

"Oh. Well then, we could use help with child care."

Child care! Stuck with a bunch of squalling babies and fussy toddlers who wouldn't appreciate my stunning transformation in the least? I searched frantically for an out. Saying I didn't like children wasn't very attractive. "Um, I hate to admit this, but I'm allergic," I said.

"You're allergic to children?"

Okay, maybe that didn't come across quite right. "Not children," I said, a nervous giggle escaping. "Baby powder. Oh, and that sunscreen little kids wear. Something in it makes me break out in a rash."

"Oh. Well, what *did* you want to volunteer to do?"

Be your personal assistant, I thought. "Is there anything *you* need help with?" I asked. "Maybe I could stop by your office and make phone calls or something."

"No, that's all taken care of."

I sensed he was ready to hang up and fought to keep the conversation going. All those articles I'd read in *Seventeen* as a girl about getting a boy to like you came back to me. *Ask him about his interests,* they all advised. "What are you up to these days, Marc?" I asked.

"I sell real estate. You were lucky to catch me in the office—I'm usually out showing properties."

His office. Of course. So that was his secretary who'd answered. "Really? I've been thinking of buying a place." A lie, but I was desperate to keep the conversation going.

"Hey, maybe we could get together while you're here." The car-salesman heartiness returned to his voice. "I could take you to lunch."

"I...I'm not free for lunch. How about dinner?" Dinner was so much more romantic. I'd wear the blue dress, and my highest heels—when I walked in he wouldn't know what hit him. He'd kick himself for ignoring me in school and vow to make up for his past neglect.

"Let me check my calendar." I heard him flipping through pages. "Sure. I could do that. Could we meet at the Captain's Table around six this evening?"

"That would be great. I'm looking forward to seeing you again." I tried to add an extra sultriness to the words.

"You, too."

I hung up the phone, then did a victory dance around the hotel room. I was a little out of breath by the time I stopped in front of the mirror. "Not bad for a middle-aged spinster," I said.

An ugly word, *spinster*. Not dashing like *bachelor*. *Bachelorette* made me think of silly game show contestants. *Old maid* was even worse, conjuring up memories of the ugly crones depicted on children's playing cards.

Just as there are no attractive descriptors for overweight women—men can at least be *stocky* or *solid*—single females get short-changed in the language department.

I glanced at the bedside clock. Nine-thirty. A long time to kill until six.

I grabbed my purse and headed for the door. Time to see if any of the old Ridgeway I remembered still existed.

When you've lived with a picture of a place fixed in your memory for so long, it's a shock to the system to find out how different reality is from that image—similar to the feeling when you first discover your parents have actually had sex.

In my memories, Ridgeway was a little town, with only one real shopping center, one grocery store, two banks, a feed-and-seed store and half a dozen churches. Markson Manufacturing was the biggest building in town, and several seedy bars lined the highway leading out to the Markson plant.

I guess I'd been too insulated by grief and worry to notice all the changes when Frannie and I had visited five years ago. Now I had the disorienting feeling of having landed in a giant fun house, where nothing looked the way it should. The Markson plant was still there, but now it was old and shabby, dwarfed by a new office complex that sprawled beside it.

The bars still lined the road to the plant, but there were more of them now, along with *adult* bookstores and "theaters" that advertised *XXX* shows.

The shopping center had been replaced by a mammoth Wal-Mart. I counted three other grocery stores and at least six banks. This modern version of my hometown was definitely more prosperous than the one in my memories, but I couldn't say it was more attractive. Acres of woodland where the men and boys I'd known spent fall weekends hunting had been wiped away, replaced by strip malls and apartment houses.

Road construction on the south side of town had replaced large chunks of whole neighborhoods—houses and churches and playgrounds had been knocked down and paved over. A sign announced they were building a bypass around town. A detour took me around the back side of the cemetery where my parents were buried, and I thought about stopping, but couldn't bring myself to do it.

I found Ridgeway High School, but it was a sleek, modern building, not the redbrick structure I'd attended. A stadium big enough to host a pro football game rose behind the school, and the whole complex sat in a sea of black-topped parking lot.

If not for the blue smudge of mountains in the distance, I might have thought myself in suburban Bakersfield.

Driving all those streets with unfamiliar names, where nothing fit the pictures in my head, I became disoriented. So when I finally did spot something I recognized—the old ball fields off Green Dairy Road—relief surged through me. I turned the rental car onto the narrow paved street and soon was back in our old neighborhood.

There was the little store where we'd exchanged empty soda bottles for nickels, which we used to buy more pop.

There was the park where I'd scuffed the rubber off countless pairs of Keds, dragging my toes in the dirt beneath the swings.

There was the street where we had lived: Amaranth Avenue. A fancy name for a short row of almost identical cinder-block houses, each with a brown patch of front lawn and a short gravel driveway leading to a detached one-car garage.

I hesitated, then took a deep breath and turned onto the street. I'd come this far; I couldn't leave without taking a look.

I slowed the car to a crawl and craned my neck, looking for the green-shingled house where we'd lived. I really was hoping it had been torn down, but no such luck.

I pulled the car to the curb directly across the street from the house and studied it. It's such a cliché to say it looked smaller than I remembered, but it was true. It had diminished in more than size; it had diminished in significance.

It was a cramped, square building with a small stoop in front and a screened porch along the back. Inside, it was divided into a living room, kitchen, two bedrooms and a single bath. We had eaten at a table at one end of the living room. Our parents had had the front bedroom, across from the living room, while Frannie and I had shared a smaller room that opened onto the screened porch.

Someone had added a green metal awning over the front stoop, and at some point the shingles that covered the exterior had been painted gray. The color did nothing to improve the house's appearance. Looking at it, a big knot of sadness formed in my chest and began to swell like a balloon inflating.

Why the hell hadn't I listened to Frannie and avoided coming back here? It wasn't as if seeing the place again was going to conjure up a slew of happy memories.

I started the car again, drove to the end of the street and turned around, driving too fast in my haste to get away.

If I didn't already know my love affair with food was deeply ingrained, the fact that I ended up at the old hamburger stand, like a pigeon homing in on its coop, should have told me something. How many summer afternoons and crisp autumn evenings had I spent at this low square building with the red-and-white-striped awning out front? My friends and I rode our bicycles here after swimming lessons or after football games and shared root beer floats and chili cheese fries while flirting with boys who sat in booths across the way. There was no childhood sorrow that couldn't be made better with a chocolate shake and a double cheeseburger with extra ketchup.

The gnawing in the pit of my stomach urged me to order that double cheeseburger now, with onion rings and a triple chocolate malt. I stared at the menu over the order window, my nails biting into my palms.

The window slid open with a snap. "What can I get you?" asked the freckled girl inside.

"A Diet Coke and a junior burger," I said resolutely.

"Would you like fries with that?"

Yes. My mouth watered. "No, thank you. But could I have an extra pickle?"

"Sure."

She took my money and, after parking the car, I walked over to one of the outdoor picnic tables and sat down. I took deep breaths, trying to center myself. *It's just an old house,* I told myself. *It can't hurt you. Don't let it.*

"Ellen? Ellen Lawrence, is that you?"

I turned and saw a nice-looking man in a Markson's work shirt striding toward me. He had thinning light brown hair and a wide smile. Definitely familiar, but I drew a blank on his name.

"Hi," I said, manufacturing a smile. "I'm amazed anyone remembers me after all these years."

"I wasn't sure, but that hair is hard to forget, and those blue eyes reminded me of Frannie." He held out his hand. "I bet you don't remember me, though. Walt Peebles."

"Of course I remember you, Walt." I did now. He'd been Frannie's date to her senior prom. A sweet, gawky guy who had tried hard to make that evening the best of Frannie's life.

Walt sat across from me at the picnic table. "How is Frannie?" he asked.

"Good. She's a hairdresser in Bakersfield," I said. "She's made a real name for herself, has a lot of famous clients."

"That's great." He nodded. "I'm glad she's doing well. I guess she's probably married with a bunch of kids, too."

"No, she never married."

"Really?" One eyebrow shot up. "A pretty girl like her?"

"Well, you know Frannie. She's always been particular." I tried to laugh off the comment, as if my sister's choice to isolate herself from everyone was a big joke. Ha, ha.

"What about you?" I asked. "Are you married?"

"Was. We divorced a couple years ago. But I have two great kids." Before I could say anything else, he pulled out a wallet and flipped it open to a couple of head shots—the kind that come in packets of school pictures—of a boy and a girl. They had their father's thin hair and brown eyes.

"How adorable," I said. "How old are they?"

"Sybil is eight and Jeremy's seven." He closed the wallet and replaced it in his pocket. "They live with their mom, but I see them every weekend."

"Order up."

He stood. "I gotta go. It was good seeing you."

"You, too."

"You tell Frannie I said hello. Maybe she could give me a call sometime. I'm in the phone book."

Frannie would never call. I should have given him her number, then he could have called her.

Of course, if he was so interested, why hadn't he asked me outright for Frannie's number? He was probably just being polite, making conversation about the only thing the two of us had in common.

Though I wanted to believe this nice man had been carrying a torch for my sister for twenty years, I knew better. He had been her prom date, for goodness' sake. Why would he be interested in Frannie now?

Of course, why was I so intent on hooking up with Marc Reynolds after all these years? Not because I was in love with him.

But maybe because I thought I was capable of falling in love with him.

Frannie says I'm a romantic, but she doesn't mean it as a compliment. To her, it's a synonym for *delusional,* to which I counter that I prefer my delusions to her version of reality any day.

"Your order's ready, ma'am," the freckled girl called.

I carried the paper bag back to the picnic table and unwrapped my food, telling myself that a burger without cheese is just as good as one with cheese, and that greasy fries were bad for my complexion.

I've always been a terrible liar.

A slender woman with close-cropped silver hair walked up to the window and ordered a chicken finger basket. She stood with one hip cocked, her fingers drumming on the counter in a way that was eerily familiar. I had a flashback to ninth-grade chemistry class, and those same drumming fingers on the lab counter.

I blinked. What were the odds of running into two people I knew from school, here at our old hangout? Coincidence?

Or one of those weird metaphysical tricks my new-age acquaintances in Bakersfield believed in?

"I'll have that right out, Alice," the freckled girl said.

Memory confirmed, I half stood. "Alice Weston?"

The woman turned toward me. "No one's called me that in years."

She didn't remember me. The realization made me feel as if I'd swallowed rocks. Alice Weston had only been my best friend in the world from the time we met in sixth grade until I left town. "It's Ellen," I said. "Ellen Lawrence."

Alice's smile could have lit a stadium. "Oh my God, Ellen!"

She ran to me and threw her arms around me. The first thing I noticed was how strong she was. Her hug squeezed all the breath out of me. The second was how skinny she was. I could feel the ridge of her ribs outlined beneath her shirt.

She pulled back first and held me at arm's length. "You look fantastic," she said, shaking her head. "Almost good enough for me to forgive you for running out on me all those years ago."

I hung my head, shame engulfing me. "I'm sorry. I meant to get in touch, but it never happened." We'd left town so quickly, and Frannie had said it was best to make a clean break. I felt terrible about that now.

"Come on. Let's talk." She slid onto the bench on the opposite side of the table. "Here's your chance to tell all, and I'll think about forgiving you. But first you have to tell me—did you have the baby or not?"

"Baby?" I stared at her, suddenly having trouble breathing. "What makes you think I had a baby?"

She shrugged. "The last time I saw you, you were puking your guts up in the funeral parlor ladies' room. When you and Frannie hightailed it out of town after that, I thought for sure you were pregnant."

I almost laughed out loud, the idea was so absurd. I shook my head. "No. Just...stressed, I guess."

"Losing your daddy when you're only sixteen will do that, I guess." She patted my hand. "I forgive you. Life's too short for grudges, right?"

I nodded weakly. This was the Alice I'd known and loved. Older for sure, with fine lines around her eyes and her brown hair all silver. I bet it wasn't a half inch long all over her head, but it looked good on her. She had three piercings in one ear and four in the other, with silver rings in each hole, more on each finger and a dozen bracelets on her wrists. Her pale blue T-shirt and denim capris were faded and comfortable, just like the woman herself.

"If your name isn't Alice Weston anymore, what is it?" I asked.

"Alice MacCray. Are you back in town for the reunion?" she asked.

I nodded. "And you? Are you here for the reunion, too, or do you still live here?"

"I live here, but not for much longer. After the reunion, I'm going back to California."

"I'm from California. I mean, Frannie and I both live there now. Bakersfield."

"I'm in Ojai. Or was for ten years. I've been out here for the past ten. I came home to take care of my mama when she got sick. She got better, but then I ended up with breast cancer and she took care of me."

She said it so matter-of-factly, I almost missed the meaning behind the words. My gaze drifted to her short, short hair.

"Oh yeah, it's grown back in now. I had a mastectomy, chemo, the works. The one thing I got out of it was a good hairstyle. Easy to take care of." She ran her fingers through the cropped locks and smiled.

It was the smile I remembered from when we were girls, a look that welcomed you into Alice's corner of the universe, a place where curfews were restrictions to be gotten around, homework was a ten-minute inconvenience and dessert was always to be eaten first. Amazing after all she'd been through she still had the same attitude.

My own life seemed a picnic in comparison.

Alice's food was ready, so she retrieved it and joined me again at the table. "So what have you been doing with yourself?" she asked, pointing a chicken finger at me.

"Not all that much." I sipped the last of my Diet Coke. "I own a flower shop in Bakersfield. I do flowers for movie and television sets. I went on a diet last year and lost a hundred pounds."

"A hundred pounds? Holy shit, that's amazing." She grinned. "And you look amazing. Really great."

I sat up a little straighter, the dark mood that had threatened earlier gone altogether. "Thanks. What have you been up to?"

"Besides being sick?" She swabbed a French fry through a pool of ketchup. "Not much. I ran the snack bar at the bowling alley until a couple of weeks ago. Took my vacation time to pack up the house."

"So you're really moving?"

She nodded. "Are you married? Any kids?"

I shook my head. "Not yet, but I'm still open to the idea. If the right man comes along."

"Yeah. Well, I've had two husbands and I'm not so sure the right man exists." She pushed her half-eaten lunch aside. "You're going to be at the reunion tomorrow, right?"

I nodded.

"Great. We'll talk more then. In the meantime, I have to go see about renting a moving truck."

I reached over and impulsively took her hand. "It was so good seeing you again," I said. "Really." The plane ticket from California had been worth this moment alone.

"It was good seeing you again, too." She flashed another brilliant smile. "See ya."

I stared after her, an odd mix of hope and regret churning my stomach. Alice. I'd avoided thinking of her for years—feeling guilty over the way I'd left town without saying goodbye. I'd never had another friend like her, one to whom I felt so close. Closer at times even than I felt to Frannie.

Seeing her today, finding out she was moving to California, not all that far from where Frannie and I lived, opened up the possibility of having that kind of friendship once more. I could actually come away from this reunion with a new man *and* a new best friend in my life. And Frannie thought coming here was a bad idea!

I checked my watch, amazed to see it was already after two. I had time to get back to the hotel, exercise, shower and get ready for my date.

A date. I almost giggled at the word. After talking with Alice, I felt young and beautiful and more carefree—more ready for *romance*—than I had in years.

To think I could feel that way in Ridgeway, Virginia.

It was proof that anything really is possible.

I spent a ridiculous amount of time getting ready for my dinner with Marc that evening. I checked my appearance from every possible angle, all the while imagining how blown away he would be by my stunning self. Of course, an annoying little voice in the back of my head reminded me that perhaps I only seemed stunning to myself, based on the fat version of me that had stared back in the mirror for so many years. I told the voice to shut up and applied another coat of mascara, slicked on lip gloss and told myself the poor man wouldn't know what hit him. I was going to get lucky this weekend or sprain something trying.

When we met in the lobby of the Captain's Table, he clasped my hand firmly and shook it. I didn't miss the way he subtly checked me out, and the extra wattage added to his smile when he was done. I figured all those hours of exercise were worth that look alone.

"So, Ellen, it's great to see you," he said when we were seated at a table for two near the back of the dining room.

"You, too, Marc."

Marc was as good-looking as the photograph on the reunion Web site had indicated; the classic features hinted at in boyhood had matured into true handsomeness. Big sigh of relief on my part. I would have hated to find out the picture he'd posted was a lie and I'd wasted all my effort for nothing.

I tried not to grin at him like a Cheshire cat, though a ridiculous smile felt in danger of bursting forth at any moment. "I can't wait to hear what you've been up to."

It was an innocent enough remark, the prelude to any number of pleasant conversations. This, unfortunately, was not to be one of those.

"As I told you on the phone, I'm in real estate." He unfolded his napkin and spread it across his lap. "I don't like to brag, but I have the biggest agency in Ridgeway. I was named Realtor of the Year in 2001. If you're serious about buying a house in town, you'd be smart not to waste your time with anyone else. Now, what kind of place are you looking for?"

"Place?" I blinked, having already forgotten the pretense of wanting to buy property that had lured him here. "Oh yes. Well, I'm not really sure. I mean, if the right house came along..."

"You've got a home in California, right? Prices out there are ridiculously inflated. You cash out your equity in that and you could buy a mansion out here. I just listed a perfectly restored antebellum estate on the north side of town. Three other Realtors were fighting for this listing, but of course, I ended up with it. You wouldn't believe the competitiveness in this town. Everyone is jealous of my success...."

He continued in this vein through our drink order, the salad and on through the entrée, alternating descriptions of houses he thought I'd like (all sounding outrageously expensive to me) and his own accomplishments. I learned about his marriage to a beauty queen—*Miss Virginia 1995. Every man I knew would have given his right arm to be in my shoes when we tied the knot*—that had ended in divorce. *She couldn't stand that I was more successful than her. Plus, as she got older she started losing her looks and there wasn't much else there, if you know what I mean.*

The torrent of words spilled forth like lava from a volcano. I stared at him in sick fascination. Nothing more was required of me than an occasional nod.

So much for my fantasies of wowing him with my looks, charm and wit. Clearly the hot sex and instant romance I'd envisioned were not going to happen.

As pleasing as he was to look at, the man I'd carried the torch for all these years was a deadly bore. I couldn't believe my luck. I fought to keep from yawning and spent most of the meal with fake interest painted on my face. As the waitress cleared our entrées, I excused myself to go to the ladies' room, and thought about walking right out to the parking lot and driving back to the hotel.

I might have done it, except I knew I'd see Marc the next day at the reunion, and I figured explaining my behavior would be worse than enduring a few more minutes of his company tonight.

By the time I made it back to the table, I had manufactured a suitably ill expression. "I don't know if I ate something bad or if it's just jet lag catching up with me," I said, "but suddenly I feel awful. I'm afraid I'm going to have to cut our evening short."

"But I haven't finished telling you about the Delaney

estate," he said. "I know you're going to love this place. And only seven hundred and forty-nine thousand."

Dollars? Did he think I had that kind of money? Or maybe just that good a credit rating. "I'm sorry, I really do have to go. We'll talk more tomorrow." Only if he saw me before I saw him, though.

By the time I got back to the hotel, my annoyance at Marc had morphed into anger at myself. I must have been nuts to think I could hook up with a high school crush and create instant grand passion. Who was I kidding? Even if Marc hadn't been a bore, why would he have been interested in me—a woman he hadn't seen in twenty-two years, a girl he'd scarcely said ten words to in high school?

I'd wasted all this money and time on a fantasy. How could I have been so stupid?

As I sat alone in my room, my stomach felt empty and hollow. Despite the meal I'd just had, I was ravenous. I sat on the edge of the bed and took deep breaths. *You don't need to eat,* I told myself.

The cravings grew stronger. Not just for food, but for sugar. Chocolate.

I looked around the room, hoping in vain to spot some suitable substitute—an after-dinner mint or a single truffle on my pillow.

But this wasn't that kind of hotel. Desperate, I grabbed my key and hurried out the door and down the hall to the vending machines.

The soft drink and ice machines hummed a low tune and gave off a greenish glow. I bypassed them and headed for the snack machine that squatted in the back corner of the alcove. With shaking fingers I inserted my change, then pulled the handle for the six-pack of cookies. Three hundred and twelve calories. Fourteen grams of fat, forty-six grams of carbohydrates.

I knew the counts by heart, but reciting them didn't do anything to beat back the hunger gnawing at me now.

I tucked the cookies into the pocket of my jacket, like a convict hiding contraband, and scurried back to my room. Once there, I sat on the edge of the bed and took more deep breaths. After a minute, I slid the cookies out of my pocket and set them on the nightstand.

I stared at them a moment, then started bargaining. *I'll eat them after I've gotten ready for bed.*

I'll eat them after I've done twenty-five—no, fifty—sit-ups.

I went into the bathroom and began to take off my clothes. The memory of the way Marc had looked at me when we first met came back to me. He'd liked what he'd seen. So why had an evening that had started so well turned out so badly?

I sat on the toilet, pondering this question. Marc had spent most of the evening bragging about his own accomplishments. Could it be that he was trying to *impress* me?

I laughed out loud at the thought. But maybe the idea wasn't so far-fetched, after all. Though I didn't always feel like it, I wasn't fat Ellen anymore. I was a sexy, attractive woman. One any man might want to impress, especially one who hadn't seen me in over two decades. Maybe all that bragging had been Marc's attempt at *flirting.*

If nothing else, he'd certainly wanted to impress me enough to sell me a house.

I slipped on a nightgown, removed my makeup and brushed out my hair. My earlier panic had been replaced by Zen-like serenity. Maybe it *had* been a little silly to entertain the idea of a romance with a man who was really a stranger to me. Maybe other people would laugh if they knew I'd come all the way across the country to fulfill such a fantasy. But who said anyone would ever know?

I returned to the bedroom, where the sight of the Oreo

package on the nightstand surprised me. I'd already forgotten about them.

I grabbed up the package and stuffed it into my suitcase. Emergency rations. Then I locked the suitcase, stowed it in the closet and climbed into bed.

I turned out the lights and lay back, my eyes still open. Here in the darkness, I could admit that Marc was not the real reason I'd returned to Ridgeway. He was a convenient excuse and a pleasant fantasy, but he alone would never have been enough to convince me to leave my safe, if not always happy, haven in California and come back to the place that had been the source of no small share of pain for me.

No, I had come back to Ridgeway because, after losing a hundred pounds, I needed to find the part of me I'd left here—in the green shingled house on Amaranth Avenue, in the redbrick school that no longer existed and in the cemetery that held the graves of both my mother and father, but where I had never been able to bury the truth.

3

The Ridgeway High School reunion barbecue was held at City Park, in one of those huge open-air pavilions with dozens of picnic tables and a barbecue pit large enough to roast an entire cow.

I did not arrive early and had abandoned all intentions of "helping out," figuring Mr. In-love-with-the-sound-of-his-own-voice could handle things by himself. Still, when I turned into the park I was astonished to see cars filling the lot and overflowing onto the side streets. Everyone associated with the class of '86, plus all their relatives, must have showed up for this party. Obviously the reunion was the social event of the season in Ridgeway, maybe even more of a draw than the Lions Club annual Turkey Shoot.

I had to park several blocks away and hike back to the pavilion—not a comfortable proposition in the high-heeled sandals I'd worn. But what were a few blisters compared to all the suffering I'd already done in the pursuit of beauty?

The pavilion itself was packed with men, women and children from teens to toddlers to babes-in-arms. I couldn't remember when I'd seen so many children. Obviously my classmates were a particularly fertile bunch, present company excepted.

Sometimes it hurts watching children run around. I'd never had any—never been with a man long enough to even think about it. And Frannie hadn't wanted children. She hadn't wanted anyone in her life but me.

I suppose at thirty-eight I wasn't too old to have a baby, but I was definitely older than most of my peers had been when they'd had children. Some of them had already moved on from parenting to grandparenting.

The first person I recognized in the crowd was none other than Rachel Mayfield—spin-the-bottle Rachel as I'd come to think of her. "Hello, Rachel," I said as she handed me a blank sticker on which to write my name.

She looked puzzled for a moment, then recognition—and surprise—lit her expression. "Ellen? Ellen Lawrence?"

"That's me." I stuck the name tag over my right breast.

"You look wonderful," she gushed. "I didn't know it was you for a moment."

I nodded. "I guess I have changed a little." Say, by at least sixty-five pounds since I'd last lived in Ridgeway.

"Well gosh, what are you up to these days? Have you moved back to Virginia?"

I shook my head. "California. I own a flower shop in Bakersfield."

"Your own business. That's fantastic. And California!" She looked wistful. "That must be great."

"What about you?" I asked. "What have you been doing?"

"I married Scott Ruston. You remember him, don't you? He was in our class."

I almost laughed out loud, remembering the earnest kiss Rachel had laid on Scott at that long-ago birthday party. So the seed of love had been planted early for her. "Of course I remember Scott. Do you have any children?"

"Debby and Scott, Jr." She pointed out a pair of towheaded preteens who were wrestling over a Frisbee. "You two play nice!" she shouted over the din of conversation.

Scott and Debby paid no attention. Then again, for all they

knew, some other adult was yelling at some other children. There were certainly enough to choose from beneath the pavilion's roof and scattered about the adjacent grounds.

"It was great to see you," Rachel said. "I'd better get back to work on these name tags."

I helped myself to a diet soda from a cooler and began circulating among my former classmates. Most of them didn't recognize me at first. When they did, their reaction was similar to Rachel's—shock, then glee, then a kind of wistful envy. The last surprised me. Why would these people who, for the most part, had grown up to be productive, stable adults with families and houses and roots in their hometown or nearby towns be jealous of me? Were they confusing Bakersfield with Hollywood, and my small flower shop with some glamorous profession that required regularly rubbing elbows with movie stars? (Yes, I did provide flowers for movies and television, but I almost never saw an actual star. I worked with set designers and people in charge of props. Not very glamorous, really.)

Or is it merely that whatever we already have becomes so routine that whatever anyone else has looks exciting by comparison?

I was surveying the buffet table for something safe—read low-cal—to munch on when I spotted Marc. He was standing a few feet away, his arm around a bird-thin twenty-something with straight blond hair that fell to her waist.

Before I could move out of range, he turned and spotted me and headed over, bringing the blonde with him. "Are you feeling better?" he asked.

"Oh, yes." I smiled brightly and avoided his gaze, focused on readjusting the paper napkin I'd wrapped around my can of soda. "I think maybe I was a little overtired from traveling."

"I'd like you to meet my girlfriend, Sandy. Sandy, this is an old classmate of mine, Ellen Lawrence."

Your girlfriend? I thought maybe she was your daughter. I didn't say it, but I definitely thought it. Sandy No-last-name had *trophy wife* practically tattooed on her forehead. "Nice to meet you," I said with a nod.

She nodded back, but didn't say anything. She looked bored out of her skull. Why shouldn't she be? Most of us were closer to her parents' age. She'd have fit in better with the teenagers who were playing basketball across from the pavilion.

Marc tapped my shoulder, reclaiming my attention. "Call my office Monday and we'll make an appointment to see some properties I know you'll love," he said.

"Right." So much for my thinking he'd been flirting last night. His mind had been on a big fat commission, not romance.

I know, I should have told him I wasn't interested in buying anything, but I didn't want to have to endure ten minutes of him trying to change my mind.

He and Twiggy walked away. I made an ugly face at the two of them behind their backs. Even if Marc hadn't been the bore of the century, I obviously wasn't thin enough, or young enough, for him.

"Don't they make a cute couple?"

I turned and saw Alice standing behind me. She sidled closer and lowered her voice. "I don't get it. What does a man his age see in a girl that young? I mean, besides the obvious. It's not as if you can have sex *all* the time. What do they talk about over dinner?"

"I can answer that one. I went out with him last night. I didn't have to say anything. Marc spent the whole evening talking about himself."

Her eyebrows rose. "You had dinner with Marc Reynolds? Last night?"

"It wasn't a date. He thought I was interested in buying

property in Ridgeway. And apparently he assumed I had money and thus was a hot prospect."

She laughed. "Oh my. And to think I once had a crush on him."

"*You* had a crush on him?"

Her eyes met mine, the laughter still there. "We all did, didn't we?"

I smiled. "Guess we did." Alice and I had shared so much growing up, including, apparently, a crush on the same guy.

Alice took a long drink. I detected the juniper odor of gin. "Did you say you'd never been married?" she asked.

I shook my head. "Never."

"Smart woman." She held up her glass. "I need a refill. Come with me?"

I walked with her to the bar and waited while the bartender made her a gin and tonic. I accepted another diet soda. "You don't drink?" Alice said.

"Not this early." Alcohol is full of calories and besides, I've never held my liquor very well.

Someone announced the barbecue was ready and everyone began lining up for food. Alice and I got in the queue, then ended up at a long table with Rachel and Scott, Marsha Kincaid (now Frisch), and some of the others we'd hung out with in school.

Looking down the table at these familiar-yet-not-familiar faces, I was struck by how odd it was we should all be here together like this. We were years and miles away from the birthday party I'd remembered in my dream last night, yet deep down, we were still those children. Scott had the same high forehead and perpetually quizzical expression I remembered, Rachel still fidgeted like a fourth grader and Marsha, even in adulthood, had the same nervous giggle that had punctuated every gathering of our childhood.

In some ways, it seemed I was the only one who had

changed. All my friends had stayed in our hometown and grown into the lives I'd pictured they would have—marrying, having children, working at Markson's or other local businesses. I was the only one who'd left the fold.

I looked at them all as they ate and talked and wondered how they saw me. I was a foreigner now, single and childless. The one with the exotic job in the fantasy world of television and movies. I was no longer the chubby girl who chewed my fingernails or ate every cookie in sight, but I was sure something of the girl I'd been remained in me. Something one of them might recognize—maybe Alice? She had known me the best. Was I a stranger to her now, or still her old friend?

"I was sorry to hear about your mom," Scott said when we'd polished off our ribs and chicken and sausage links and had settled into the malaise that only full stomachs and a warm summer afternoon can bring. "I saw the funeral notice in the paper and thought about you and Frannie."

"Thank you," I said, touched that he remembered. "She'd been sick for a while, so it wasn't entirely unexpected."

"I heard later that you and Frannie came back to town for the funeral," Marsha said. "I would have come to the visitation, but there wasn't one."

"Frannie didn't want one," I said. My sister had insisted there was no one in town she wanted to see and that holding a visitation at the funeral home was pointless. "We only stayed a few days. We had a lot to do, going through Mama's things and arranging the services and everything."

"Oh, I understand. But it would have been nice to see you both. It's been such a long time." She pushed her empty plate away. "You both left town so suddenly back in high school, we never really got a chance to say goodbye."

I shifted on the bench. I'd been hoping no one would bring up my sudden departure, and searched for some way to turn the conversation.

I didn't think fast enough, though. "Why *did* y'all run off like that?" Rachel asked. "None of us could believe it when we heard your mama was still here, but you and Frannie were gone."

"Oh, you know how it is when you're that age," I said breezily. "Frannie heard of a great job opportunity out West and when she invited me to come along, I thought it would be a fun adventure. I mean, what sixteen-year-old doesn't want to see Hollywood?" *And no, I wasn't pregnant,* I wanted to add, but didn't.

After my father died, our house was a sad, tense place and the thought of staying behind without Frannie terrified me. When she'd insisted I come to California with her I'd been only too happy to agree.

"I really envied you both," Bill Moreland said from the end of the table.

I blinked, startled. "You did?"

"Sure. You were sixteen and you were going off to California with your sister who was only nineteen. No parents. No school if you didn't want to, nobody to answer to but yourselves." He grinned. "I would have given my left arm to get away like that."

"Frannie made me go to school," I said, but the rest of it had been true—no parents, and no one to answer to but ourselves. That had been the idea, after all. From my perspective of twenty-two years later, I could see what an audacious idea it had been.

"I can't believe your mother let you go," Rachel said. "Mine certainly wouldn't have."

I tried not to look as self-conscious as I felt. I wasn't used to being the center of attention like this. When you're the fat girl, you're usually more invisible. "She knew Frannie would look after me," I said. "Plus...she was pretty broken up about my dad. I think she was relieved not to have to worry about the two of us, too."

I didn't remember that Mom had raised any objections at all to us leaving. Or maybe it was only that my sister hadn't given her a chance to object. Frannie had bought two tickets to California with Mama's credit card and withdrawn all the money she'd saved from her job at Weisman's Drug Store and hadn't even mentioned the trip to Mama until our suitcases were packed and waiting in the front hall.

When the taxi came to take us to the airport, Mama didn't even bother to get up out of her chair. Frannie and I kissed her goodbye, one daughter's lips pressed to either cheek, but she didn't look at us or say anything.

Every time we talked on the phone after that, I pictured her sitting in that same chair, in the same gray-and-black dress she'd worn to my father's funeral. Even when the call came that she was dead, I half expected to walk into the house and find her there, fixed in place, perhaps in need of dusting.

"My mother died two years ago," Marsha said. "A heart attack. She was only fifty-nine." She shook her head. "Losing a parent like that is always a shock." She looked around the table at the rest of us. "It's one of those things that makes you realize how old we're all getting."

"Speak for yourself," Alice said. She drained the last of a bottle of beer and set it down on the table with a thunk. "Haven't you heard forty is the new thirty? If we wait long enough, forty will soon be the new twenty-five. We'll never have to get old."

"Does that mean my kids will never grow up, either?" Bill shook his head. "Give me old age over perpetual teenagers any day. Or else just take me out back and shoot me."

We all laughed at that, and the talk turned then to children and grandchildren—whose son played football and whose daughter had won a prize at her dance recital. Someone set a wine cooler in front of me and I accepted it, letting the murmur of conversation and the buzz of the alcohol wrap around me like a soft blanket.

Just before sunset, a band began setting up at the end of the pavilion. The caterers carted away the leftovers from the barbecue and a different crew draped the picnic tables with white cloths and set out hurricane lamps every two feet down the middle of each table.

Mothers and fathers began corralling children and sending them off with relatives or babysitters. Some people left altogether, but most stayed, drinking and talking and watching the transformation from family picnic to adult reunion.

A woman in a white chef's coat moved around the pavilion, lighting the lamps. Other white-coated helpers filled the buffet table with trays of hors d'oeuvres. The band stopped the random twanging that had constituted tuning their instruments and played the first chords of "Glory Days" and the party began.

Bill surprised me by pulling me onto the dance floor. "I don't know how to dance," I said, raising my voice to be heard above the music.

"You don't have to," he countered. "Just move."

Ordinarily I wouldn't have dared, but no less than three wine coolers had stripped me of my normal reticence. I raised my arms and gave an experimental shimmy. It felt good. Smiling, I began to move in rhythm with the music, my moves somewhere between tai chi and aerobics.

I caught sight of Alice across the dance floor. She was partnered with Scott, doing an energetic jitterbug that had the people around them clapping and whistling. I smiled. That was Alice—the life of any party.

After Bill, I danced with Scott and Paul and some other man I didn't even know until sweat ran down my face and made my dress stick to my back. "I've got to rest," I finally pleaded.

I found the ladies' room and applied a wet paper towel to

the back of my neck. I stared at the woman in the mirror—
my face was flushed and my bangs were plastered to my forehead by perspiration. But my eyes shone with happiness.

I couldn't help but wonder how different things would
have been if Frannie and I hadn't left for California, if we'd
stayed and I'd graduated with my class. Would I have married one of those men I'd just danced with? Would I have
children now, and the deep friendships that come from years
of shared experiences?

Frannie would say no, that only by going away could we
have made our lives better, that if we'd stayed we'd have
been trapped and probably miserable, but I wasn't so sure.

When I returned to the pavilion, Alice found me. She was
flushed, too, but she looked more exhausted than ecstatic.
"Want to take a break from all this?" She waved a hand at
the full dance floor.

Not really, but something in Alice's face—the anxiety in
her eyes, or the tight lines across her brow—worried me.
Without words, she was pleading for me to come with her.
"Okay," I said.

I followed her to the parking lot and her car. "God, it's
hot out," she said, turning the air conditioner up full blast
as soon as she started the car. She glanced over to me. "Let
me know if you get too cold. Since the chemo, my internal
thermostat is all haywire."

I nodded. "Are you feeling all right?" I asked.

"Yeah. I just needed to get away. I don't handle crowds
that well anymore."

She exited the park and pulled onto the highway. "Where
are we going?" I asked.

"Want to drive out to the bluffs? There's a beautiful view
up there this time of night."

"All right." The suggestion made me only a little nervous.
Back when we were in school, the bluffs were a popular
make-out spot. Not that I'd personally ever been up there,

but I'd heard stories. I hoped Alice wasn't going to take me up there now and make a pass at me. She hadn't struck me as a lesbian, but one thing I'd learned living in California was that you could never be sure.

Turns out the bluffs these days were the parking lot of a shopping mall. Alice drove to the far end of the lot, which looked out over the river, with the lights of houses glowing like fireflies between the trees on the opposite bank. She shut off the engine and stared out the front windshield. "I come up here sometimes when I need to think," she said.

"What do you think about?" I asked.

"Life. Love. Everything." She glanced at me. "I know it's a cliché, but having cancer made me reexamine everything. I had all that time lying in bed trying to recover from one round of chemo and bracing for the next. My head hurt too much to read. After a while you realize how inane ninety-nine percent of television is, so I ended up reviewing everything I'd ever done in my life and wondering what I would have—or should have—done differently."

A half smile flashed across her face, then was gone. "When I started wondering what I'd do differently in the future, I figured that was a sign I was going to live after all."

"I'm glad you made it," I said. I meant it. I was glad Alice was a part of my life again. Finding her was like finding part of my childhood, a good part I didn't want to give up.

"Losing weight made me think about my past and my future, too," I said. "Being fat isn't the same as having cancer, but being normal size after all those years felt like I was getting a second chance."

"I've made some bad choices in my life." Alice was looking out the windshield again, her hands gripping the steering wheel. "I've done some bad things."

My stomach knotted. What could Alice possibly have done that was so terrible? "We've all done things we regret," I said.

"Do you ever think about going back, making up for some of the badness?"

I hesitated. "You mean...like restitution?"

"Something like that." She looked at me again. "Do you think about that?"

I shook my head. "What's done is done. You can't take it back."

"But sometimes you can. Or at least ask forgiveness."

Could you really? I cleared my throat. "Anything in particular you have in mind?"

She shrugged. "I don't know. But it's why I'm going back to Ojai. I've rented a moving truck, but I could use some company and another driver. Are you in a hurry to get back to Bakersfield?"

I shook my head, my stomach fluttering with excitement. "Not necessarily."

"What about your business?"

"My manager will look after it." Frannie wouldn't be happy if I didn't come home right away, but that couldn't be helped. Frannie often wasn't happy. I'd long ago stopped trying to change that.

"Then, will you come with me? Or at least think about it?"

I didn't have to think about it. "I'll come with you," I said. I leaned over and squeezed her arm. "It'll be fun."

"Then we're set." She hugged me, squeezing me so hard I couldn't breathe. "We're going to have a great time."

I'm not an overly superstitious person, but every once in a great while I do get premonitions. Not visions or anything, just...nudges. A sense that I should or shouldn't do something. One of those nudges had led me to send in my reservation for this reunion.

Another one was telling me now to go with Alice, to make this trip. As soon as I said yes to her, I felt lighter, the happiness of earlier in the evening returning.

When I lost all that weight, I'd had to acquire not only new clothes, but a new way of dealing with people, who looked at me differently now. The life I'd lived for years didn't fit me any more than the bags of clothes I'd given away to Goodwill. I'd returned to Ridgeway hoping to find some clues that would lead to a new kind of life—one that would fit better.

So far I hadn't found much to help me here. Except Alice. I'd found her, and maybe she was *exactly* what I needed. She'd known me better than anyone way back when. Alice could help me figure out how to get my life back on track.

And maybe I could help her a little, too. I sensed she needed a friend now after all she'd been through. This trip could be a fun time for both of us—a chance to unwind and catch up and take a break from the tough things in life. We'd be two carefree travelers with no responsibilities.

No worries. The way things ought to be but seldom are.

4

While I am not exactly bursting with self-confidence, I've come a long way in the past few years. But my stomach was knotted up like the tangle of chains in the bottom of my jewelry box when I called Frannie Sunday morning.

She answered on the second ring, as if she'd been waiting by the phone. "How was the reunion?" she asked.

"It was fun. I saw a lot of friends and danced more than I've danced in years." Which wasn't saying much. A big evening for me consisted of stopping for ice cream on the way home from work. Occasionally I went to the horse races with a couple of set designers I knew. We had a good time together, but I doubt there were a lot of people wishing they were in our shoes.

"Did they remember you?" Frannie asked, as if the idea surprised her.

"Of course they remembered me. Well, some of them didn't recognize me at first, but they all remembered me. They remembered you, too."

"I don't know why they'd do that." I could picture her face, her mouth pursed in an expression of skepticism.

"Ridgeway was a small town when we were growing up," I reminded her. "The school was small, too. Of course people remember you. And I almost forgot—I ran into someone Friday who remembered you very well."

"Who was that?"

"Walt Peebles. He asked about you, said to tell you hello."

"Walt?" She was silent for a moment. Was she trying to place the name or did she remember him too well? "How's he doing?" she asked after a moment, her voice taking on an uncustomary softness.

"Good. He's working for Markson's. He's divorced, but he has a son and daughter. He showed me pictures. He said you should call him."

"Oh, I couldn't do that."

"Why not? You're both single. He really cared about you once."

"When are you coming home?"

"I could give you his number," I said, ignoring her attempt to change the subject.

"No. And don't you give him my number, either. I don't want to hear from him. I don't want to hear from anyone in Ridgeway. Now when are you coming home?"

I sighed. "Not for a week or so. Maybe a couple."

"A couple of *weeks?*" Her voice rose at the end. "What are you talking about? Don't tell me you picked up one of those men you were dancing with. What were you thinking?"

"Thanks for thinking I'm such a slut," I snapped. "This doesn't have anything to do with a man."

"Then what? What could possess you to stay in that town one more minute than necessary?"

"There's nothing wrong with the town."

"So you love it so much now you're staying there?" She was talking fast, not even pausing to breathe, the words running together. "I still don't believe this doesn't have anything to do with a man. Now that you've lost weight you can't wait to run off with the first male who'll look twice at you."

"Stop."

To my surprise, she fell silent.

I took a deep breath, trying to get a grip on my emotions. Anger was fast overtaking fear. What was with this sudden indictment of my character? "Just because you have some grudge against half the population of the world doesn't mean I do." I twisted the phone cord around my wrist. "If I had found some man and fallen in love—or lust—why couldn't you just be happy for me?"

There was a long silence. I heard a sniffing noise. "Are you crying?" I demanded. Frannie almost never cried. When I teared up at the movies she rolled her eyes and frowned at me, embarrassed.

"I miss you." She sobbed. "It doesn't feel right here without you. Why can't you come home?"

"I'm coming home," I said, torn between exasperation and guilt. "But instead of flying, I'm helping Alice Weston move to Ojai."

"Alice Weston? She was at the reunion?"

"Yes. She's been living in Ridgeway, but now she's moving back to Ojai. She needed somebody to go with her, to help her drive the moving truck. I offered to go with her."

"Why would you do that? You haven't seen or spoken to Alice in years."

"Too many years. This will give us a chance to catch up." I didn't add that it would give me some time to think about what I wanted to do with the rest of my life. Seeing other parts of the country and meeting new people might give me some ideas about what I should do next.

Now that I was thinner, life held more possibilities than it had before. I wasn't as eager to return to Bakersfield and the routine of my life, which felt more limiting every day I stayed away.

"I don't like the idea of you driving across the country with another woman," Frannie said. "Someone who's practically a stranger,"

"A minute ago you were upset because you thought I was

shacking up with some man." I tried to disguise my lingering annoyance with teasing.

She didn't bite. "I don't trust Alice. I never have."

"How can you say that? She was my best friend."

"She's too loud and brash and nosy."

Yes, Alice was loud sometimes, and some people might call her brash, but that was part of the reason I liked her. Alice wasn't afraid of anything, and when I was with her, I was less afraid also. "Nosy? I don't remember her being particularly nosy."

"She was always coming around, wanting to know what we were doing and stuff."

"That's called being interested in other people. Being a friend." Alice had cared enough to come knocking on the door on the days I missed school, and she'd been the only one who'd had the nerve to question why the Lawrence sisters wore the same dresses to school two days in a row. The fact that I never answered her questions didn't stop Alice from asking.

"You haven't seen each other in over twenty years," Frannie said. "How are you going to spend all that time on the road together?"

"I guess we'll find out."

"I'm going to worry."

She said this in the same tone of voice she'd once announced—when she was nine—that she intended to hold her breath until she passed out if Mom didn't buy her new sneakers. She'd done it, too, and when I'd revived her, she still didn't get her sneakers. I started to remind her of the incident, but decided against it.

"I'll be fine," I said. "And I'll check in from the road. It's only an extra week or so."

"What about your shop?"

"I already talked to Yolanda. She's fine with it. This isn't a particularly busy time of year." Yolanda had actually encouraged me to enjoy my vacation. If only Frannie could be so supportive.

"I don't want you to do this," she said again.

"I know, but I'm going to do it. Now I'd better get going. I have to return the rental car, then I'm meeting Alice."

"Ellen, no."

But I hung up before she could guilt me into changing my mind.

Which didn't mean the guilt didn't linger. My whole life, I'd never spent more than a couple of nights away from Frannie. Even at home, we were separated only by the few hundred feet between our condos. I'd never much questioned my closeness with my sister, who had been, in many ways, more like a mother to me. We each had our own businesses and our own homes. We had our own lives.

But Frannie's almost hysterical response to the news that I was extending my trip made me wonder how healthy that closeness had really been, for either of us.

I called Alice next and she agreed to meet me at the rental-car agency. I checked out of the hotel, then made the short drive to the airport and turned in my car.

When I stepped out into the parking lot once more, Alice was waiting, the bright orange-and-white moving truck humming like an overgrown cat as it idled at the curb. "Ready to hit the road?" she asked as she helped me stow my suitcase behind the driver's seat.

"I'm looking forward to it," I said as I hoisted myself into the high cab. "I've never traveled much."

"I'm an old hand at this cross-country stuff." She settled into the driver's seat and handed me a stack of maps and travel guides. "You can navigate," she said.

I looked through the pile of papers. Maybe now wasn't the time to tell her I wasn't very good at reading maps. "Where are we headed first?" I asked as she steered the truck onto the highway.

"Amish country. Pennsylvania." She glanced at me. "I hope you don't mind if we don't take the most direct route. I'm not in any big hurry and thought it would be fun to take in a few sights."

"Sure. I'm in no rush." Since I was my own boss, I didn't have to be back at work any particular day. "I've never been to Amish country. What's there?" Besides, obviously, the Amish.

"It's where Bobby—my first husband—and I spent our honeymoon." She laughed. "Not a lot of people's idea of romance, but we were young and broke and it was far enough from Ridgeway to feel exotic to us."

"How old were you?" I asked.

"Eighteen." She sighed. "Too young, that's for sure."

"When I was eighteen I started a full-time job at the florist's where I'd worked after school and during summers the previous two years." Coming into Hollywood High the last month of my sophomore year, I'd found it difficult to make friends. I felt as if I had nothing in common with the perpetually tanned 'cool' kids who surrounded me. They all had at least one parent at home, and often multiple step-parents and siblings. I lived with my older sister, who worked all the time. It was easier for me to get a job and claim I was too busy to participate in extracurricular activities than to deal with the rejection that comes along with being different in any way.

Food was the only thing that gave me any pleasure. By the time I graduated, I'd ballooned to 185 pounds. Even if I'd wanted to wear the stylish clothes favored by my peers, I couldn't have fit into them.

Hiding behind the counter at a florist shop seemed preferable to going off to college, where I'd have to face a whole new gamut of girls who would laugh behind my back or, worse, pity me, and boys who would never date me.

"Earth to Ellen."

I started out of my reverie. "Huh?"

"You wandered off there for a minute," Alice said. "Where to?"

I made a face. "Just remembering my eighteen-year-old self. Not a pretty sight."

Alice laughed. "You should have seen me. All bony elbows and knees and stick-straight hair. I wore a white eyelet peasant dress to my wedding. Bobby wore a baby-blue tuxedo. I still wince at my horrible fashion sense when I see the pictures."

"I bet you were a beautiful bride," I said. "All brides are."

"Yes, well, I suppose it could have been worse. We both fancied ourselves sort of hippies. We threatened to get married on the beach, barefoot, before my mother put a stop to it."

"Why did you pick Amish country for your honeymoon?"

"Like I said, we were into all this natural, back-to-the-land living. We dreamed about building our own cabin in the woods, growing our own food and living happily ever after with no artificial preservatives or corporate claptrap. The Amish seemed like good role models, and Pennsylvania was close enough we could drive there, and we could afford a cheap room."

I studied Alice's chic haircut and multiple pierced ears. "I'm trying to picture you as a granola girl," I said.

She laughed, that wonderful throaty laugh of hers. "I was! I was going to bake my own bread, sew my own clothes and raise chickens and goats and children."

It sounded like hell to me, but then I've never been overly domestic. "What was Bobby going to do while you were the domestic goddess?"

"Work for Markson's, what else? It's what half the boys who graduated from Ridgeway High School did in those days. But in the back of our heads we figured he'd eventually be able to quit his job and settle down with me on the homestead, selling handmade furniture or pottery or something like that."

I was fascinated by this glimpse of my friend that I'd never known. "So how did that work out for you?"

Her laugh was more of a snort this time. "I was a horrible baker, I couldn't sew a straight line to save my life, and I'd much rather sit on the porch and read novels all day than dig in the garden or clean up after chickens." She glanced at me. "The Amish make it look easy, but they've been trained since birth, plus they all have a houseful of children and relatives to help."

"How did you end up in California?"

"Bobby had a cousin who worked for Widder Enterprises in Ojai. It was a good job, making real money. We shed our hippie threads faster than you could say 'Neiman Marcus charge card' and became Silicon Valley yuppies." She laughed. "Instead of baking my own bread, I hired a housekeeper and a cook. Bobby traded in his work shirts for three-piece suits and bought a sports car. We were living high on the hog back then."

She put on her blinker and moved into the right lane and nodded at a billboard up ahead that advertised a local smokehouse. "Speaking of hog, why don't we get some barbecue for lunch. A pulled pork sandwich sounds so good right now."

I pretended not to notice the quick change of subject. Maybe Alice really was hungry. Or maybe she didn't want to talk about her first marriage anymore. I wasn't about to pry.

"Sure. Barbecue sounds good." Food was a safe enough topic of conversation. Neutral and not loaded with emotional minefields. Chocolate brownies or French fries are always so much easier to deal with than things like fears or hurts or our real motivations behind the choices we make.

★ ★ ★

When Alice had asked me to travel with her to Ojai, I'd immediately begun building a fantasy of two carefree pals seeking fun and adventure as they traveled cross-country. Female bonding and empowerment on the open road. We'd sing along with the radio, while away the hours remembering all the great times we'd had together as kids and stop at every tourist trap and souvenir stand on the way. It would be the kind of vacation celebrated in the movies, a time we would remember fondly in our old age.

By the time we pulled into Lancaster that afternoon I'd begun to deal with the reality that two middle-aged women in a moving truck were not exactly an updated version of Thelma and Louise. A giant orange-and-white truck doesn't have the same cool factor as a red convertible. Neither Alice nor I could carry a tune or remember the words to songs on the radio. You can only talk about the past so long before it begins to sound a little desperate. The souvenir stands and tourist traps had been replaced by McDonald's and Wal-Mart. And after eight hours of staring out the windshield I was positive no one would mistake me for Susan Sarandon.

Still, for a gal who hadn't traveled much, I was having fun. Amish country was exactly as I'd always pictured it—black horse-drawn buggies plodding along in the slow lane, women in bonnets and aprons selling fresh produce and colorful quilts from the front porches of neat white frame farmhouses and barefoot children in old-fashioned clothes playing in the fields.

Everything looked like a picture postcard, and many of the businesses continued the Amish theme. Farmer John Real Estate, Plain and Fancy Farm Restaurant, Countryside Apartments.

"It's more like a theme park than a town," I said as Alice maneuvered the truck across four spaces in the back lot of the Lancaster Econo Lodge.

"I think that's why I liked it so much when I was here on my honeymoon," she said. "It was Williamsburg without the boring guides."

We ate dinner at a farmhouse-themed restaurant. A strapping German waitress who had probably never bothered to count a calorie in her life brought out steaming bowls of mashed potatoes, beans, country ham and sausage, sauerkraut, creamed corn and a whole loaf of homemade bread. My mouth watered, but I resolutely allowed myself tiny helpings of the least-fattening choices.

I noticed Alice didn't eat much, either. "Don't hold back on my account," I told her.

"Oh, it's not you." She laid her fork across her half-full plate and pushed it away. "I still don't have my appetite back from the chemo."

"How long has it been?" I asked. For some reason—maybe her hair—I'd assumed Alice had completed her treatments months, maybe even a year or more, ago.

"About three months now." She sat up straighter. "But I'm doing great. And I'd be a fool to complain about losing the urge to overeat."

"Yeah." Twisted as it is, I could see the positives in her situation. When I was the most depressed about being fat, I used to fantasize about developing some mysterious but nonfatal illness that would cause the excess pounds just to melt away.

How many times have you heard someone—almost always a woman—say something like "Yeah, I puked up my guts for three days with the flu. But the good news is, I lost five pounds."

No telling what our waitress thought about all the food we left uneaten, but we left her a big tip and walked back to the motel. We'd rented a room with two double beds to save money.

Alice kicked off her shoes and crawled onto the bed closest

to the door. "When Bobby and I were here, we stayed at a bed-and-breakfast," she said. "The Farmhouse Inn or something. It really was a room in someone's farmhouse." She giggled. "We had to show them our marriage license to prove we really were married."

"Is the place still here?" I kicked off my own shoes and pulled my hair back into a ponytail.

"Who knows? I didn't see the name in the tourist brochures I ordered."

I lay down on the floor and began doing leg lifts.

"How can you do that on a full stomach?" Alice asked.

"Define full." I rolled over onto my other side.

"I thought you weren't supposed to exercise too close to bedtime." She aimed the remote at the television and switched it on, but kept the sound muted.

I stared up at the image of a serious female news anchor narrating video showing a burning house. "I usually try to exercise earlier in the day, but some days that doesn't happen." I rolled onto my back, arms overhead, enjoying the stretch. "Better late than never."

"I still can't believe you lost a hundred pounds. That's amazing."

"It was the hardest thing I ever did." I hugged my knees to my chest, stretching my lower back. "In fact, if I'd known just how hard it would be, I might not have ever started."

"Not even knowing how great the results would be?" She stretched out on her stomach and looked over the edge of the bed at me. "I mean it. You look great."

"Reasonably good with clothes on. Naked, my boobs are somewhere around my navel and my butt looks like a sharpei." I began doing sit-ups, counting in my head, trying not to grunt with each lift.

Alice watched me for a while, silent. I was up to seventy-five when she spoke again. "Still, it must have felt fantastic when you met your goal," she said.

I lay back, panting. When both my breathing and my heart rate had slowed a little, I said, "It did. But it was scary, too."

"Change is scary."

I hugged my arms across my chest. "I'd never been a normal size before—not since I was a little girl. I not only had to find a whole new wardrobe, I had to learn a different way of relating to people."

"You mean people treated you differently once you were thinner?"

"I mean I acted different with them. I never realized before I lost the weight how much I used my fat as a shield. Now when people look at me, I feel as if they are seeing the *real* me—the one I'd been hiding. It was terrifying."

Alice rolled over onto her back and stared at the ceiling. Neither of us said anything for a long while. The picture on the television switched to an ad for trucks. Brawny men in jeans and tight T-shirts raced big black trucks through mud puddles and over rocks.

"I really admire you," Alice said, her voice thick. "Maybe having you along on this trip, some of your courage will rub off on me."

"You don't need my courage." I sat up and looked at her. "You were never afraid of anything when we were girls."

"I'm afraid now."

"What are you afraid of?"

"Do you believe in karma?"

A chill washed over me and I rubbed my arms. "Like things we did in some other life coming back to haunt us?"

"I'm talking about things we did in *this* life coming back to haunt us." She sat up and pulled the bedspread around her, the quilted chintz billowing around her like a tacky hoop skirt.

I climbed up on the bed beside her. "I think," I said slowly, "sometimes things just happen and there's nothing we can do about them. Everybody makes mistakes. It's part of being human."

"But we can choose. And when we make the wrong choices, maybe we have to pay." She watched me out of the corner of her eye, the way you watch a wild animal you know you can't trust.

"I still don't think you could have done anything that bad." Even to me, the protest sounded weak. After all, a lot can happen in twenty years. The girl who'd been my friend possibly didn't even exist anymore.

Alice smoothed both hands down the folds of bedspread that fanned out from her waist. "When I was twenty-nine, I met a man. A friend of Bobby's. They played golf together sometimes, worked for the same company, though not in the same department. We met at some charity fundraiser or other. Bobby had begged off coming with me. I think he had to work. Anyway, I was there by myself and I met this man. Travis. The minute his eyes met mine and he smiled at me, it just took my breath away."

She pressed her palm flat to her chest and her cheeks turned pink, as if even the memory of that evening made her heart beat faster. "It was electric. That's such a romance-novel cliché, but it really was like sparks arcing between us."

"You fell in love?"

She frowned. "That's what I called it. I couldn't seem to stop myself." She held out her hands, palms up. "I don't know if it was hormones or boredom or having married so young or some flaw in my character, but I saw him every chance I could. Soon I couldn't bear to be away from him for even a few hours. I was reckless."

"And Bobby found out?" I asked.

She nodded. "I think I knew in the back of my head I'd get caught, but I didn't care. I think I *wanted* Bobby to find out. To force me to make a decision."

"What happened?" I asked.

"He gave me an ultimatum. He told me I had to choose. I suppose he was sure I'd pick him, but I'd convinced myself I needed Travis more than I needed anything else in my life. So I left."

"You left?" The words sounded so stark. So final.

She nodded. "I told him I'd sign whatever agreement he wanted and I left. Travis lost his job a few weeks after that. I'm sure Bobby had a hand in that. We moved to Chicago and two years later he left me for a woman he worked with."

She bowed her head, tears making dark splotches on the bedspread.

I reached out and touched her arm. "How awful for you."

She shook her head. "I remember thinking at the time that I'd gotten exactly what I deserved. As bitter as I felt at his betrayal, it was probably nothing compared to what Bobby must have gone through."

"Did you try to go back to Bobby? To ask forgiveness?"

"I couldn't." The word was a whisper. She took a deep, shaky breath and offered me a too-bright smile. "Anyway, you see what I mean about karma. I figured I'd paid my debt when Travis left. That things were even. Later, when I found out I had cancer, I wondered if I was being punished further."

"Alice, I don't believe God punishes people like that."

"No? But what if all that guilt I'd carried around all these years transformed into that tumor? Sort of a physical manifestation of the emotions that had been eating at me for years anyway."

"I don't believe that," I said again. "If that were true, there would be even more sick people than there already are."

"Maybe you're right. But it's worth thinking about." She looked at me, calmer now. Almost serene even, the lines around her eyes and mouth smoothed out, some of the pain gone from her eyes. "It's one reason I want to go back to California—to clear my conscience. No sense taking a chance on a recurrence of the tumor."

"I'm glad you're going back if you think it will help you feel better." I patted her arm again. "And I'm glad I'm coming with you."

"If nothing else, I figure this will be a fresh start," she said. "It's what I need."

I could use a fresh start, too, I thought as I watched her untangle herself from the blankets and walk to the bathroom. Sure, I'd told myself I was flying back to Virginia to impress my old friends and reconnect with the man of my dreams, but would anyone who was truly satisfied with her life place much importance on either of those things?

The truth was, I was a thirty-eight-year-old single woman who had lived all her life within shouting distance of her older sister. I had a job that sounded exciting but really wasn't, no truly close friends and a new body I didn't know what to do with.

I wanted a different life from the one I had, even though I didn't yet know how to define those dreams. But I had to start somewhere, and this seemed as good a place as any. I liked Alice's idea of asking forgiveness and healing old wounds, even if the thought of figuring out which of my sins needed forgiving—and which wounds I needed to heal— made me a little queasy.

5

When Frannie and I first moved to Hollywood, we rented a tiny Airstream trailer in a mobile-home park within sight of the famous Hollywood sign. Frannie went to beauty school during the day and worked nights as a switchboard operator at MGM.

I went to school, came home and baked brownies and lay across my bed, making halfhearted attempts to do my homework. Mostly what I did was daydream.

In my fantasies, I took glamorous trips around the world, often in the company of handsome men or with groups of friends—both things were noticeably absent from my life in those days.

Frannie was never part of those dream trips. How ironic that I waited another twenty-two years to actually go anywhere without her.

True, I wasn't in Morocco or Luxembourg, and there were no rich, dashing men in sight, but Alice and Amish country offered the same escape I'd craved all those years ago. I figured I was starting small. This year, Pennsylvania. Next year, Paris!

After breakfast the following morning Alice decided she wanted to try to find the place where she'd spent her honeymoon. "I think I remember the road it was on," she said. "I want to see if the house is still there."

We set out down a winding two-lane county road, slowing behind the occasional black Amish buggy. The scenery was straight out of a picture book—neat white farmhouses set back from rolling fields, draft horses grazing in pastures, laundry flapping on clotheslines in backyards.

"Briar Rose Lane." Alice read the wooden sign nailed to a fence corner. "I think this is it." She slowed and turned the big truck onto an even narrower road. We crept along while she studied the various houses we passed. "This is the one," she declared at last, stopping in front of a sprawling white house. "I remember the fence in front and that big oak tree with the swing."

"It looks like a private home," I said. As I spoke, a woman in a blue dress and white cap came out onto the porch and looked toward us.

"I think it is, now," Alice said. "It was then, too, but there was a little sign on a post out here that said they had rooms for overnight guests."

I looked at the woman on the porch again. "What do you want to do?" I asked. "If we keep sitting here, she's liable to call the cops. She might think we're casing the place."

"I'd kind of like to look inside." Alice glanced at me and shrugged. "Guess I'm feeling nostalgic."

I thought of my drive out to my childhood home in Ridgeway and wondered if Alice felt the same kind of pull. Except I'd had no desire to enter the house on Amaranth Avenue.

Instead of calling the police, the woman sent one of her children out to talk to us. The boy looked to be about nine. He was barefoot, dressed in too-short black pants and a white shirt with the sleeves rolled up to the elbows. His thick blond hair fell over his forehead and he stood on tiptoe to look into the cab of the truck. "Do you ladies need some help?" he asked.

"Hi." Alice smiled at him. "My name is Alice and this is

my friend Ellen. When I was younger, I stayed in this house on my honeymoon. I was in the neighborhood and wanted to see the place again."

The boy glanced back toward the house, his lower lip jutting out as he processed this information. Then he looked back at us. "Do you want to come in?" he asked.

"We'd love that. Thank you." Alice was out of the truck and standing beside the boy before I'd even unfastened my seat belt. I followed her and the boy up the long drive to the porch where the woman waited.

"These ladies want to see the house," the boy said.

The woman folded her hands across her stomach and studied us with a worried expression. "The house is not for sale," she said.

"Oh, I don't want to buy it." Alice offered up another of her hundred-watt smiles. "I'm on my way to California—I'm going to be living there. But twenty years ago I spent my honeymoon here. The people who owned the house then rented rooms and my husband and I stayed here."

Some of the stiffness went out of the woman. "Yes, I remember hearing the Stolzes sometimes rented rooms." She looked toward the end of the porch. "You would have stayed in this bedroom over here, is that right?"

"Yes. I remember the door onto the porch." Alice led the way to the white-painted door. The Amish woman opened it and ushered us in. "My oldest sons sleep here now, but you are welcome to look."

There was nothing remarkable about the room, except that it was much neater than I'd expected a teenage boy's room to be. A pair of maple twin beds shared space with a simple desk and an old-fashioned chest of drawers. Simple white curtains at the windows and patchwork quilts on the beds were the only decoration.

"When Bobby and I stayed here, there was a big white iron bed," Alice said. She stood in the middle of the room, a soft expression on her face. "It was spring, and we left the window open at night. I remember the smell of jasmine."

"The jasmine is still there," the Amish woman said. "And the white bed is in my daughters' room."

Alice nodded, as if satisfied to know these icons of her past still existed. "Thank you for letting me look," she said, and led the way back onto the porch.

"You were happy in your marriage?" the Amish woman asked, her tone puzzled, perhaps because she'd noted the lack of a wedding ring on Alice's finger and the absence of a husband.

"We were happy for a long time," Alice said. Her eyes still held a dreamy look, as if she was once more that child bride, ignorant of everything to come in her life. "Thank you," she said again, and descended the steps to the driveway.

I nodded to the Amish woman and her son, and took off after Alice. Neither of us said anything as she turned the truck around. When we were out of sight of the house, I said, "Is there anywhere else you'd like to visit? Anything that was special to you during your honeymoon?"

She shook her head. "No. That house was the only place." She glanced at me, and some of the sadness returned to her expression. "I just wanted to see, one more time, a place where I'd been really, truly happy."

Her words made me ache. "You can be happy again," I said. "Now that you've beat the cancer and you're going to Ojai to start over. You could meet someone and…"

She held up her hand to stop my babbling. "I'll never be happy in that way again—the kind of happiness that comes from being so innocent and untouched by tragedy of any kind. It's something only young people can know. And we're too ignorant then to know how precious it is."

I nodded, understanding what she was saying, but unsure if I'd ever known the emotions she was talking about. *Even children can be touched by tragedy,* I thought. *And yet, they're often happy in spite of it.*

Maybe that was the real test: to learn to be content in spite of our troubles. To find the good in the midst of all the bad.

The next morning we hit the road again, this time with me behind the wheel. Though I was a little nervous about piloting the big truck, I was also secretly thrilled. There's nothing like sitting above the rest of the traffic to make you feel a little superior and powerful.

"I always wondered what it would be like to be a long-haul trucker," Alice said as we sped west on Route 283. "Or one of those people who live in a motorhome, always traveling from place to place. In a way, it's very romantic and all, but I think I'd miss having a real home."

Funny word, *home.* Simple, yet charged with meaning. "I'm not sure I've ever had a real home," I said. "Not really."

"What do you mean? Of course you did. You lived in the same house for the first sixteen years of your life, and you've been in Bakersfield how many years now?"

"Nineteen. But neither of those were really homes. Not the way I think of them." I shrugged. "They were just places to live. A house. A condo."

She turned toward me, one leg tucked under her, the seat belt straining against her right shoulder. "So what's your definition of home?"

I thought a minute, trying to find words for the emotions that whirled through me. It wasn't something I'd spent a lot of time contemplating before now. Perhaps on purpose. "I think a home is someplace you can't wait to get back to. You feel so loved and accepted and, well, *at home* there. I don't know that I've ever had that."

"Not even when you were a little girl?" Alice's voice was gentle.

"Maybe then." My hands tightened around the steering wheel. "Maybe not. My parents weren't demonstrative, loving people. They were both sort of—*isolated*. To themselves. Even as a little girl I remember feeling like Frannie and I had to look out for ourselves."

"I remember how Frannie was always mothering you. Asking you if you'd done your homework, reminding you to wear a sweater—things a mother would do."

"Yes, that was Frannie." While other girls her age were pining for teen pop idols or TV stars, she was making sure I did my homework and forging our mother's signature on report cards and permission slips. I'd taken her solicitude for granted in those days. I glanced at Alice. "Did you think we were odd?"

She shrugged. "Not any odder than any other family. I mean, the Olsens lived across the street from me. Nine children, two parents and an ancient grandmother who had to be locked in her room to keep her from dancing around the front yard without her clothes on. Mr. and Mrs. Olsen were usually so frazzled they referred to the children indiscriminately as 'Hey you.' The older ones had to help the younger ones get dressed and get to school or no one would have ever made it."

"I remember Maida Olsen was in our class." I smiled at the memory of the freckle-faced girl with pigtails. "She and I were the only ones without our field trip money because our parents hadn't given it to us." This was obviously in Frannie's pre-forgery days. "The teacher felt sorry for us, I guess, so she let us go to the art room and do crafts all day while everyone else went to the science museum."

"Yeah, I was so jealous, too," Alice said. "I hated the science museum."

"And here I was, jealous that you got to go."

We laughed, then she turned the conversation back to

more serious matters. "So if you had a home, what would it be like?"

"When I was a little girl, I always thought a home was something I'd have when I grew up," I said.

"You're grown-up now, so what's stopping you?"

I waited until I'd passed a slow-moving minivan before I answered. "I think back then, I saw *grown-up* as meaning married with a husband and children. I mean, that's what people did—at least all the people I knew. They grew up, got jobs, got married and had children."

"Yeah." She sighed. "Hey, I gave it my best shot, but it didn't work out for me, either."

"I never pictured myself still single in my thirties." Saying the words made my throat ache. I glanced at her. "Guess I wasn't being very realistic. Do many people even have that husband-and-house-and-two-kids dream life these days?"

"Some do. And some are happy without that. If it's what you want, don't give up yet."

"Sure. You're right." My palms had started to sweat and I spread my fingers wide, trying to dry the dampness. "But it was a lot easier to be optimistic at twenty-eight than at thirty-eight. It doesn't help that I haven't had a real boyfriend in twenty years." Even the word *boyfriend* sounded absurd when applied to a man my age. Obviously the English language hadn't caught up with modern reality. There ought to be a word to describe someone who isn't yet a "significant other" but who has progressed beyond "date" and not quite to "lover."

"Nothing to say you can't start now," Alice said. "A woman who got rid of a hundred pounds ought to be able to brave the big, bad dating world."

"What do you know about it?" I looked at her again. "How long have you been divorced from your second husband?"

"Seven years. But that doesn't mean I've been alone and

celibate all that time. I've had boyfriends. Just none I wanted to marry."

"Because you still love Bobby?" I held my breath, waiting for the answer.

She looked startled. "What makes you say that?"

"Because…well, because you're going to all the trouble to move back to Ojai, where he is."

"I told you, this isn't about Bobby. I did love him once, but there's nothing there now. Just…indifference. This is about me. What I have to do."

I thought of our conversation the night before, about karma and retribution and forgiveness. Was redemption as simple as wanting to do better, or as impossible as trying to change the past?

Were there things in my past I'd change if I could? Certainly I'd wanted to weigh less. And sometimes I wondered if I should have fought harder to stay in Ridgeway instead of running to California with Frannie. But it's tricky dealing with the past. If I changed all the bad stuff, it seemed logical that would change the good times, too.

Probably just as well we couldn't go back and make things different. Better to keep moving forward, toward whatever dim vision of the future we can perceive. At least then we can hold on to the illusion that things are still under our control. This time, we would see disaster coming and head it off, the way a driver watches ahead and avoids a traffic pileup.

Which does nothing to account for all the accidents that happen every day. I gripped the steering wheel more tightly and refused to dwell on this thought. In thirty-eight years, surely I had learned enough to keep my life on the right road this time.

We stopped for lunch in Wheeling, West Virginia. I tried not to think what a steady diet of fast-food burgers and salads was going to do to my waistline. Maybe I'd suggest we find a grocery store and stock up on healthier stuff; we could eat better and save money, too.

Alice stretched and yawned as we walked back to the truck after we ate. "I don't know why I'm so tired," she said.

"You're probably worn-out from packing and getting ready to move." I pulled the truck keys from my purse. "I'll keep driving. You can rest."

"Are you sure you don't mind? We agreed to take turns."

"I'm good. I'm enjoying it, even."

The sun pouring through the windshield warmed the cab in spite of the air conditioner. Alice leaned her head against the passenger window and dozed, snoring softly. I turned the AC vents to blow full on me and studied the passing scenery, trying to stay awake.

Just outside of Cambridge, Ohio, I spotted a figure on the side of the road. A hitchhiker, head down, thumb out, walking along, back to the traffic as if he didn't really expect a ride.

As I passed I had the impression of a slight figure dressed in blue jeans and a T-shirt, a navy blue duffel slung over one shoulder, long hair whipped by the wind, dark eyes full of sadness in a pale face.

With a jolt, I realized the hitcher was a girl. A teenager, I guessed. I slammed on the brakes and steered the truck toward the shoulder.

Alice woke with a start. "What is it? Why are we stopping?"

"There's a girl back there who needs a ride," I said.

Alice glanced in the side mirror and saw the girl running toward us. She turned to me again. "Are you crazy? You don't pick up a total stranger."

"It's just a girl. She doesn't look that old. And she shouldn't be out here alone." I watched the girl jog toward us, the duffel bouncing against her side.

"That doesn't mean we have to give her a ride," Alice said.

"Better us than some man with trouble on his mind." She had almost reached us now. "Scoot over," I told Alice.

Still frowning, she unfastened her seat belt and moved over into the middle of the bench seat. The girl reached the truck and yanked open the passenger door.

Up close, she looked even younger. She had straight dark hair cut all one length, not a trace of makeup on her alabaster skin. She was wearing jeans and a jean jacket and tennis shoes. No fancy designer names that I could see from here. "Where are you headed?" I asked.

"Sweetwater, Kansas. I'm going to see my cousin."

My geography was a little hazy, but Alice had said we weren't in a hurry, right? A detour to Kansas shouldn't take much time. "Climb in," I said.

She hoisted herself into the cab and settled into the seat, the duffel at her feet. "This is Alice, and I'm Ellen," I said as I steered the truck back onto the highway.

"I'm Ruth." She fastened her seat belt. "I sure appreciate this." Her voice was soft, with the slightest lilt of a European-flavored accent.

"You should," Alice said. "What if two men had stopped? There are a lot of crazy people out there. You could have been hurt."

"Alice!" I gave her a warning look. We'd just picked up this girl and Alice was grilling her like a burglary suspect. I was half-afraid Ruth would jump out of the moving truck if we came down too hard on her.

"I wouldn't have gone with two men." Ruth's lower lip jutted out in a pout. She smoothed her hands down her thighs. Her nails were trimmed short, unpolished. "Thank you for stopping, though."

"What are you doing out here by yourself?" Alice asked, refusing to let up. "Where are your parents?"

"I told you, I'm going to see my cousin," Ruth repeated. "In Sweetwater." Her words were defiant, but I heard the undercurrent of fear in her voice.

The fear made me speak. "Ruth, are you all right?" I asked gently. "You're not in some kind of trouble, are you?"

"No." The word was a squeak. When I glanced her way I saw that her eyes were huge and dark in her pale, pale face.

Alice fell silent, though her gaze remained focused on the girl. I drove on, still gripping the steering wheel tightly, the tension in the air making it difficult to breathe. Whenever I glanced at Ruth and Alice, they were both staring out the front window, expressionless.

I'd begun to relax a little after the first hour when Alice spoke again. "If you're going to see your cousin, why not have your parents take you?" she asked.

Ruth shook her head and stared down at her lap. "They couldn't. They're too busy."

I looked at Ruth more closely. No jewelry. Not even earrings. No pierced ears. Everything about her was so plain. And her accent sounded familiar. I realized she sounded like the woman who had shown us the house where Alice had honeymooned. "Ruth," I said, speaking as gently as possible. "Are you Amish?"

She shook her head again, violently, her whole body tensed.

"It's okay if you are," I reassured her. "If you're running away, we can help you."

"That depends—" Alice's voice was tense "—on what you're running away from."

Ruth hung her head so that her hair fell forward, hiding her face. "Please don't make me go back," she whispered.

The desperation I heard brought a lump to my throat. "We won't make you go back," I said, giving Alice a hard look.

Alice started to say something else, but I cut her off. "It's almost suppertime," I said. "Let's stop and get something to eat and we can talk more."

I stopped at a roadside diner and Ruth disappeared into the ladies' room. I started to follow her, but Alice grabbed me and pulled me aside.

"What do you mean, telling her we won't make her go back?" Alice demanded. "She has a mother somewhere who must be out of her mind with worry. We should call the police."

"Maybe. Or maybe not." I shook off Alice's restraining hand. "I'm not going to hand her over to the police until I know more. Didn't you hear her? She sounded terrified."

"Maybe she's terrified of getting caught. What if she's committed some crime? We could be accessories if we help her."

"Do you seriously think she's some kind of criminal?" I wasn't an expert on the criminal element, but I was pretty sure most of them don't look like teenage Amish girls.

Alice folded her arms under her breasts. "There's something she's not telling us."

"She's scared. She doesn't know any more about us than we know about her."

"I still think we should turn her over to the police. Let them handle this."

"No." I met her gaze and held it. She looked angry but hurt, too. I felt a pinch of guilt. Alice had invited me on this trip. She was my friend. I should respect her wishes.

But the memory of Ruth's fear was stronger than my guilt. I could feel that fear in my gut. It had been a very long time since I'd been afraid that way, but I could still remember the chill of cold sweat on the back of my neck and the metallic taste in my mouth.

"Look," I pleaded, "there are some things that are worth running away from. I know. If we can help this girl, then I want to do it."

Alice narrowed her eyes at me and started to say something, but we were interrupted by Ruth's emergence from the bathroom. Alice turned away, but the stiffness went out of her shoulders. She led the way to a booth by the front window.

"Feeling better?" I asked Ruth as she settled into the seat beside me. She'd washed her face and combed her hair and didn't look as pale as she had in the truck.

She nodded. "Thank you," she said again. "For everything."

"My pleasure. What would you like to eat?" I took a menu from the stack behind the napkin dispenser and opened it. "I don't know about you, but I'm starved."

Actually, my stomach was in so many knots I wasn't sure I'd be able to force anything down, but I wanted to encourage Ruth. She looked a little on the thin side.

We ordered. I was trying to decide the best way to go about finding out more about Ruth's situation when a group of loud young men came in. Ruth shrank in the seat and ducked her head, hiding her face behind the fall of dark hair. I met Alice's gaze across the table. Even she couldn't deny now that the girl was afraid of something.

Ruth was so quiet and timid; I wondered how much nerve it had taken her to stand out on the side of the road with her thumb in the air.

When our food arrived, Ruth picked at her burger and fries; Alice and I did the same. Maybe I'd discovered a new diet plan: Lose Weight with Anxiety.

"If you're Amish, where did you get your clothes?" Alice asked after a while. "I didn't think you people wore blue jeans."

I wanted to slap her. Would she let up on the questioning already? The brashness I'd often admired in her was annoying now. She deflected the dagger looks I sent her as if she were wearing armor.

Ruth's eyes widened again and she looked around to see if anyone had overheard us. But no one seemed to be paying attention. Alice's gaze remained fixed on her, demanding an answer.

"They belong to a neighbor," Ruth said softly. "An English—non-Amish—neighbor."

"And does this 'neighbor' know you took her clothes?" Alice asked.

Ruth nodded, then shook her head. "I left a note, and some money I'd saved from a lamb I sold this fall."

"Did you think of asking your neighbor for help?" I asked.

"I couldn't. She lives right next door."

I nodded. Maybe everyone wouldn't understand that reasoning, but I could. I grew up in a house where my mother would cook dinner without salt before she'd walk across the alley and ask to borrow some from a neighbor. Frannie paid a petsitter to look after her dogs when she went out of town rather than asking a neighbor to look in on them. And even at my most desperate, I wouldn't have asked a neighbor to fix me up on a date. Without even realizing it, I guess we'd absorbed the message that you didn't let others know about anything that was lacking in your life.

Ruth pushed her plate away. "How far is it to Sweetwater?" she asked.

"You don't know?" Alice said.

She shook her head.

"I don't know, either," I said, and looked at Alice expectantly.

Alice sighed. "If we stay on I-70, we can be there tomorrow afternoon." She looked at Ruth again. "What's your cousin's name?"

"Mary Sutler." She glanced at me. "She's five years older than me. She married a man who isn't Amish. A mechanic from Dayton."

"So she left the Amish?" I asked.

Ruth nodded.

Another clue, perhaps, as to why Ruth wanted to see her cousin. How much easier would it have been when Frannie and I moved to California if we'd had a relative there to show us around, introduce us to people—be the family we still needed.

Alice picked up the check and stood. "Let's go," she said.

On the way out of the café, Alice took the keys from me. "I'll drive," she said.

I didn't argue, though I hoped she wouldn't head straight for the nearest police station.

Alice didn't drive to the police station. Instead, she headed out on I-70, west toward Kansas. We'd brought along a number of books on tape and I popped in Nora Roberts's latest. Ruth was enthralled, and I was grateful for something to fill the awkward silence between Alice and me.

When we pulled into the motel that evening, I managed to catch Alice alone after we'd registered. "I know you think this is crazy, but thanks for going along with it," I said. "Tomorrow we'll take Ruth to her cousin's and let them deal with her."

"What we should do is take her straight back to her mother." Alice's eyes burned with an intensity that made me want to take a step back, but I forced myself not to back down.

"Maybe her mother is part of the problem," I said.

She looked away. The harsh fluorescent lighting of the hotel hallway gave her skin a sallow tint, and the bones of her face stood out sharply, making her look thinner and older. For the first time since we'd reunited in Ridgeway she looked truly ill. "Are you okay?" I asked, and started to put my hand on her arm, but she pulled away.

"I'm fine," she said. "I'll go along with taking Ruth to Sweetwater, but don't expect me to be happy about it."

I stared after her as she stalked off to our room, a heavy

feeling in my stomach. It took everything in me not to run after her and tell her she was right—that we should take Ruth back to her home. Only the memory of Ruth's fear held me back. I hated having Alice upset with me, but I would hate betraying Ruth more.

The fleeting thought occurred that if I'd listened to Frannie and stayed home, I wouldn't be in this situation right now. I'd be living the same unexciting, uncontroversial life I'd lived for years. An easy life, but one that hadn't been enough for a while now. I'd set out on this trip wanting more, but hadn't counted on some of that "more" being unpleasant or difficult.

I straightened my shoulders and took a deep breath. If I wanted the good, I had to take the bad, too. Facing that truth made me feel stronger, and more hopeful that there was good up ahead to balance out the present rough patches.

In the room, Ruth stretched out on the bed she and I would share while Alice headed for the shower. I decided to call Frannie.

My sister answered on the second ring, her voice impatient. "Hello!"

"Hi, Frannie. Just thought I'd call and let you know how things are going so far."

"Ellen, where are you?"

"We're in Missouri. The country's beautiful."

"When are you coming home?"

"I should be home in a week or so."

"Aren't you tired of this by now? I can't think spending all day in the cab of a moving truck would be much fun. I can wire you the money to fly home."

"If I wanted to fly home, I have my own money," I said, trying to hide my annoyance. "I'm having a great time, seeing a lot of the country I've never seen before."

"I can't believe you're neglecting your flower shop for so long."

I ground my teeth and took a deep breath, determined not to argue with her. "I'm not neglecting it. Yolanda will take care of things. What have you been doing while I'm gone?"

"Working. What you should be doing."

"People take vacations, you know."

"You and I take a vacation together every year. That ought to be enough."

But what if it's not? I wondered. *What if I want more than a trip to the wine country with my sister?* "You work too hard," I said. "You should get out more. Maybe join a club. Or start dating again."

"I told you I'm not interested in any man to look after," she said.

"Maybe he could look after you." Frannie had been taking care of me my whole life. *She* deserved to be taken care of for a change.

"I don't need that," she said. "What I need is for you to come home. It feels strange here without you."

Coming from a lover or a spouse, such a declaration might have been touching. Hearing these words from my sister made me uneasy. "Frannie, you're forty-one years old," I said gently. "You ought to have other people in your life besides me. It's not healthy."

"Are you saying it's unhealthy to care about the only family I have? If more people looked after family, we'd have a lot fewer problems in this world." Her words were rushed, her voice high-pitched and anxious. I could picture her pacing her living room, phone clamped to her ear. "You of all people should realize how important that is."

"It's important," I agreed. "But it shouldn't be the only thing in your life."

"I have plenty in my life. Now when are you coming home?"

"When I'm ready and not before. I have to go now.

Goodbye." I hung up before she could protest further. I couldn't make Frannie happy—not when what she wanted and what I needed were so opposed.

"Who were you talking to?" Ruth asked.

"My sister." I turned to look at her. "She's not happy I'm taking this trip. She thinks I should have stayed home with her."

"Where does she live?"

"California. Bakersfield. It's where I live, too."

"What are you doing in Missouri?"

"I'm helping Alice move from Virginia to California. She and I went to school together and met again at our twentieth class reunion. She needed someone to help her and I was free so I figured, why not?"

"Then why is your sister upset? Wouldn't she want you to help a friend?"

"Good question." I leaned forward, chin in hand, elbows on knees. "I think Frannie is a person who doesn't like any kind of change. She's used to me being there, right next door to her, so now that I'm not there, she's unsettled."

I glanced back at Ruth. She had raised herself up on her elbows and was watching me. "Do you have any sisters?"

"No. Four brothers."

"Older or younger?"

She looked away. "Both."

Alice came out of the bathroom, toweling her hair. "Ruth, do you want to call your mother, just to let her know you're okay?" she asked. "You don't have to tell her where you are."

"That's a good idea." I gave Alice a grateful smile.

"My mother is dead."

We both stared at her. The words hung in the air, stark and cold.

"Dead?" Alice sank onto the bed. "When did she die?"

"A long time ago. When I was very little." Ruth sat up

and hugged her knees. "My father remarried another woman. She doesn't care what happens to me."

Alice and I exchanged glances again. Wicked stepmothers are a staple of fairy tales, but I didn't doubt they were a fact of real life, too, sometimes.

"What about your father, then?" Alice said. "He must be worried."

She shook her head. "He'd only try to talk me into coming home, and I won't do that. I have nothing to say to him."

A shiver danced up my spine. If my own father were alive, would I feel the same?

Ruth stood and walked to the window and looked out. "I saw a Wal-Mart across the highway. I need to go over there and get a few things."

"We'll go with you," I said. I felt responsible for Ruth now and was afraid if she got away from us, she might get into real trouble.

So the three of us drove to Wally World, a place as different from the simple Amish community as I could imagine.

Ruth, however, was apparently right at home here. She headed straight for the cosmetics department and plucked packets of foundation, blush, eye shadow and mascara off the racks. "Do you see a lipstick called winter rose?" she asked, scanning the pegs. "That's my favorite."

"I thought Amish didn't wear makeup," Alice said.

"They don't. But when my friends and I would sneak away from the house, we would put it on." She plucked a blister pack of lipstick from a peg and added it to her basket. "Let's look at the clothes."

Ruth carried an armload of jeans and shirts into the dressing room. Alice and I waited outside. "I hope we're not making a mistake," Alice said.

"She didn't hitch a ride on the highway just so someone could take her shopping," I said. "I believe her when she says she's running away from something."

Alice stuck out her lower lip. "She doesn't act very upset right now."

"People can fake being all right." Being *normal*. I'd done it for years.

"I don't trust her," Alice said.

"I know." I wasn't sure I entirely trusted Ruth, either. She wasn't what I'd expected from an Amish teen, but then I'd judged plenty of other people wrong before, and no doubt been judged by them. "We can't just turn her back out on the streets," I said. "And I won't hand her over to the police when I don't even know if she's done anything wrong. Let's get her to her cousin's and see what happens then."

Alice nodded, her expression grim.

Ruth emerged from the dressing room with a pair of jeans and two shirts. "I'll take these."

At the checkout she produced a thick wad of cash. Alice and I exchanged glances, but Alice waited until we were out the door before she said anything. "Where did you get that money?" she asked.

"I sold a lamb at auction last year," Ruth said. "I've been saving it ever since."

Back at the hotel, Ruth turned on the television and began flipping through the channels. Alice sat down on the bed near the girl.

"Ruth." Alice leaned toward her, her voice gentle, her features aged by concern. "Sometimes parents say or do things that they later regret. Whatever reason you're angry with your father, it's very likely that now that he's had time to think about it, he's regretful, and wants your forgiveness."

I could tell Ruth believed this about as much as I did. No matter how sorry Alice was over the mistakes in her own past, most people I knew lived without such qualms.

"You don't understand," Ruth said. "With the Amish, once a person turns her back on the group and leaves, she ceases to exist. So for my father, I no longer exist."

She said these words with a kind of relief I found all the more disturbing.

"That's impossible," Alice said. "Parents don't forget their children."

Ruth shrugged. "If the leaders of our church tell the people to forget, then they do their best to forget."

"I think that's horrible," Alice said.

Ruth frowned. "It seems that way to outsiders, but in our religion, the prospect of being shunned is a way to keep people from doing wrong."

"But it didn't stop you from running away," I said.

"No." She stretched her arms over her head and yawned. "I'm tired. I think I'll get ready for bed now."

I thought about what Ruth said later as I lay in the darkness beside her, listening to her even breathing. It was a terrible idea, that one's very existence to another could be wiped out by sheer force of will. Convenient if one had things she wished to leave behind—as apparently Ruth did.

Convenient, too, for the person exorcizing all memory and thought of someone they no longer wished to remember, though I had my doubts such a thing was even possible. Old memories are as indelible as ink, long-lasting as iron. Even when senility sets in and people forget the faces of loved ones, the oldest memories cling fast, the joy and grief within them preserved like frozen bodies, both beautiful and terrible.

When we woke the next morning it was raining—a heavy downpour soaked us as we raced from our hotel room to the restaurant. Our moods matched the gray weather; none of us said much over breakfast. When we were on the road again, Alice once more behind the wheel, she asked Ruth for her cousin's address in Sweetwater.

Ruth fidgeted in her seat. "I don't know the exact address. Just Sweetwater. It's not that big a town, is it?"

Alice's eyebrows rose. "Do you have a phone number?"

"No." Ruth stuck out her lower lip. "We didn't have a phone, so there was no reason for me to have her number. Besides, since she left the Amish, she's been shunned."

That whole ceasing-to-exist concept again. "When was the last time you talked to your cousin?" I asked.

"Two years ago."

Alice blew out her breath. "So she might not even be living in Sweetwater."

"That's where she said she was going to live," Ruth said. "Where her husband had a job." She turned to me. "She said I was welcome to visit her anytime."

"Do you know her husband's name?" Alice asked.

"Rob. Rob Sutler."

Alice sighed. "I guess we'll start with that, then."

Ruth stared out the windshield, not that there was much to see beyond the wipers turned on high and the heavy veil of rain that merged with the dark, wet highway. "When will we get to Sweetwater?" she asked after a while.

"This afternoon," Alice said. "Maybe later, if this weather doesn't let up."

The weather showed no sign of doing so. If anything, it became more fierce. Rain poured from the sky and ran in the road, obscuring everything but the watery blur of taillights from the cars ahead of us. Wind buffeted the truck. Alice hunched forward, her hands white-knuckled on the steering wheel as she fought to keep the truck on the pavement. Intermittent flashes of lightning showed a world that looked more river than road.

When a vicious blast of wind sent us skidding sideways, Ruth screamed and clutched at me. I grabbed the dashboard and sucked in my breath while Alice muttered a steady stream of profanity.

I closed my eyes and my whole body went rigid as the sound of the tires squealing on the pavement filled my ears. Ruth's fingers dug into my arm, but the pain scarcely registered. I waited for the impact of steel on steel, the thrust of my body against the seat belt, the crush of another vehicle into ours.

We came to a shuddering stop, and Ruth released her death-grip on my arm. I opened my eyes and saw we were parked on the side of the road. I looked at Alice. "We didn't crash."

"No." She raked one hand through her hair and drew a shaky breath. "I brought us out of the skid, but that was close."

"Too close." I put my hand to my chest, which ached from holding my breath so long.

"I thought we were going to die," Ruth said.

"No." Alice started the truck again. "Not yet. I'm not ready to die yet." She drove slowly to a sheltered underpass and stopped. "We're staying here until the storm lets up," she said, and switched on the hazard flashers.

"Good idea." I sat back in the seat and tried to relax.

"What do we do now?" Ruth asked.

"We wait." Alice reached behind the seat and pulled out a big tote bag. "Anyone want a snack?"

When in doubt, eat. It was a motto I'd lived by for most of my life, one whose allure I'd resisted for most of the past year. But after narrowly escaping death or disfigurement on the slick highway, junk food sounded like the perfect sedative. "What have we got?" I asked.

"Twizzlers, pretzels, Cheetos, beef jerky, Oreos and salted peanuts."

I'll take half a dozen of each. This is what my brain said. My mouth said, "Twizzlers and peanuts. And one Oreo." I was a wild woman.

"What are Twizzlers?" Ruth asked.

"Good question." Alice handed her one of the skinny red ropes. "Candy. Pure sugar. Probably some artificial dye. Guaranteed to have little children bouncing off the walls."

She bit off the end of another rope and chewed thoughtfully. "My theory is the sugar revs up my metabolism enough to offset the calorie intake."

"Dream on," I said, and took a bite of my own rope.

"Pretty good," Ruth said between chews. "A little artificial tasting."

"That's the point," Alice said. "Junk food shouldn't be real food. If it was the same as what you ate all the time, what would be the attraction?" She ripped open a bag of Cheetos. "Try these. Crunchy, cheesy, salty—and they turn your fingers orange. What could be more decadent?"

Ruth giggled and plunged her hand into the bag. "These are good," she said.

"Don't tell me you've never had any of this stuff before." Alice looked shocked.

Ruth nodded. "I've had the Oreos, at a friend's house, but mostly we ate food my stepmother made at home." She crammed another handful of Cheetos into her mouth.

"So what's it like being an Amish kid?" Alice asked. "Are there a lot of rules you have to follow?"

Ruth shrugged. "Don't all children have to follow rules? I don't think most of ours were that different. Pretty much everyone we knew was Amish, so it didn't matter much, especially when we were little."

"What about when you were a teenager?" I asked. The teen years were when I'd become most aware of my own differences from my peers.

"Then it's a little different." She tilted her head, considered the question while she chewed. She licked orange salt from around her mouth, then said, "When you're older, you have a little more freedom to come and go. And on trips to town, you notice things—all the people who don't dress the way you do, all the cars and the things for sale in shops. My friends and I would sneak around to the magazine racks in the stores and look at the clothes and hairstyles and read the stories about celebrities. It was like reading about people on another planet, but we knew they were right there all around us." She frowned. "That's when I think I really noticed all the rules. Especially all the things I could never do, not just because I was Amish, but because I was an Amish woman."

"Is that why you left?" Alice asked. "Because you didn't like living that way anymore?"

"Not just that. I mean, when we turn sixteen, we're allowed to experiment more, see what the world of the English is like."

"You mean, like, go to the mall?" Alice asked.

Ruth nodded. "It's called *rumspringa*. It means 'running around.' We can drink and party and listen to rock music or go to the mall—whatever we want. Some kids get really wild."

"Amish kids?" Alice asked. "Then what happens to these wild kids?"

"Most of them get it all out of their system and decide to go back to being Amish."

"But not you?"

Ruth shook her head. "I didn't do much. I mean, I wore makeup and listened to rock music and had a few drinks, but I didn't start using dope or having sex with a lot of different boys like some girls I knew."

"Then why did you leave?" I asked.

She looked at her hands in her lap. "Once girls join the church, they're expected to settle down. To marry and have children and be good Amish wives and mothers."

"And you didn't want to do that?" I asked.

"I didn't want to marry so young. And not the man my father picked out for me."

"He chose someone for you to marry?" Alice asked. "Like, arranged it without talking to you?"

"He talked to me," she said. "He told me I must marry

his friend Mr. Fisher. That he was a good man who needed a mother for his children."

"How many children?" I asked, both horrified and fascinated by the scenario she was describing.

"Six."

"Good grief. You're still a child yourself," Alice said. "How are you supposed to look after six others?"

Ruth frowned. "I'm sixteen. In our community, I'm an adult."

"How old is Mr. Fisher?" I asked.

"He is my father's age. Thirty-seven, I think."

I felt sick to my stomach at the idea of this child—and she was a child, no matter what she said—and a man twenty-one years older. "I don't blame you for not wanting to marry him," I said.

"The worst part is not even that my father wanted me to marry this old man," she said. "I was already a servant to my stepmother. Being a servant to Mr. Fisher and his six children would not be any worse."

"My God. Then what was the worst part?" Alice asked.

Ruth sighed. "The real reason my father wanted me to marry is that Mr. Fisher agreed to give him forty acres of pasture if I agreed to the wedding. My father wanted to trade me for a hayfield, as if I were a cow."

She began to cry then, silent sobs shaking her shoulders, big tears rolling down her cheeks and splashing onto the hands clasped in her lap. I put my arms around her and pulled her close. "You were right to leave," I murmured. "You deserve better than that."

"Are you sure your cousin will help you?" Alice asked.

Ruth sniffed. "I think so. She'll understand how I feel. Her father wanted her to marry a man from their church. He was her own age and not a bad man, but she didn't love him. She loved Rob Sutler. She was brave enough to follow her heart, even if it meant going against her whole family."

It sounded terribly romantic. And tragic.

"We'll get you to Sweetwater," Alice said. "We'll find your cousin and things will be better for you then. You can start over, have a new kind of life. A better one."

A different one. I wasn't sure about better. Some things would be better, certainly. But for every gain there was a loss. I'd started my own life over when I was no older than Ruth. Moving to California with my sister had been exciting and it made me feel very grown-up. I'd pictured long summer days on the beach, fun parties with beautiful people and everything flowers and sunshine.

The reality had been lonely afternoons at the trailer park while Frannie worked, summers watching soap operas on television and eating myself out of any hope of wearing a bikini. The only beautiful people I saw were on TV and the reality in my own mirror was so depressing I stopped looking after a while.

Frannie kept telling me we were better off than we'd ever been in Virginia, but at least there I'd had friends. I'd had Alice. In California I'd had only Frannie, and that wasn't enough—not then, and not now.

It was after four o'clock by the time we reached Sweetwater. The rain had dwindled to a heavy mist and the lights from the storefronts reflected off the wet streets like spilled watercolors. Alice parked the moving truck at the curb on Main Street. "We need to find a phone book and see if there's a listing for Rob Sutler," she said.

I looked up and down the street. "I don't see a phone booth. With almost everyone having cell phones these days, they're not too popular."

"Maybe one of these businesses has a phone book they'll let us flip through," she said.

I considered the options: office supply store, bakery, dry cleaners, florist… I grinned. "I'll try the florist." Before either one of them could object I was out of the truck, hurrying down the sidewalk.

A string of brass bells behind the door chimed as I entered the flower shop, and the familiar sweet-spicy smell of carnations and roses surrounded me. I felt hollow inside as I stroked the feathery tips of a potted fern and admired a shelf of African violets. While I didn't miss Frannie so very much, I did miss my florist's shop. It was always the one place where I felt complete and truly happy. Even when I was at my fattest I could lose myself in arranging flowers and tending plants.

"Good afternoon. How can I help you?"

I whirled and found myself face-to-face with a brown-eyed man. I know his eyes were brown because they were looking right into my eyes. I'd never realized eyes could hold so much warmth and laughter in a single glance.

Gradually I became aware of the rest of him—the smile lines fanning out from the corners of his eyes, medium brown hair with a touch of gray at the temples, a strong jaw and the weathered skin of someone who spent a lot of time out of doors.

"Can I help you?" he asked again, startling me out of my stupor.

My tongue felt thick, my brain mired in a fog. "Um, is this your shop?"

"Yes, I'm Martin." He pointed to the sign in the window. Franklin's Flower Wheel. "Martin Franklin."

"I'm Ellen. Ellen Lawrence." I offered my hand. "I own a florist's shop in California. In Bakersfield."

"Can't stay away from it, even on vacation, can you?" He took my hand and grinned. Both his touch and the grin made me feel weak, my stomach fluttering as if I'd swallowed moths.

We stood there staring at each other for a long moment.

I knew I should say something. Do something. But I was paralyzed. He must have thought I was an idiot.

"Would you like me to show you around?" he asked.

"I'd love that." I was finally able to pull myself away, and managed to look calm as he showed me the two walk-in coolers, the small section devoted to gifts and cards, and the larger workroom in the rear.

"This is really nice," I said when we were back at the front counter. "I love your workroom and your front window displays."

"I'll bet your place in California is larger," he said.

"Not really. I don't have a retail business like this. I do flowers for movie and television sets."

"Really? So if I'm watching a show and see a really nice arrangement, that could be one of yours?"

I nodded. "It could be." I shrugged. "Most people probably don't even notice."

"I would." His smile was so...so *warm*. Like a blanket wrapped around my shoulders. I wanted to snuggle into it.

Who was I kidding? I wanted to snuggle into *him*.

"We don't have anything like that in Sweetwater," he said. "Though I have been thinking of expanding. The space next door is going to be vacant next month and I've been considering adding more gift items. But it would mean hiring more help and I'm not sure I'm ready to do that."

"Yes," I agreed. "More employees mean more responsibility and expense." I casually glanced at his hand. No wedding ring. Not a sure indicator but promising. "Do you and your wife run this place alone now?"

"No wife. I have an older woman who helps me part-time, and a man who takes care of some of the deliveries, but mostly it's just me."

"I'd say you're doing very well."

I could have stood and talked to him all day, but the bells on the door rang again and Alice and Ruth came in.

"Did you find the number?" Alice asked.

The number! Flustered, I turned back to Martin. "Do you have a phone book I can look through?" I asked. "We're trying to locate a friend we think lives here."

"Sure." He reached behind the counter and handed me an inch-thick directory. "What's your friend's name?"

I couldn't remember. At this point I was doing well to remember my own name. I looked at Ruth.

"Rob Sutler," she said. "His wife is named Mary."

Martin shook his head. "Doesn't ring a bell, but then, there are a lot of people in town I don't know."

Alice came and looked over my shoulder. Using my finger to keep my place, I scanned the columns of names. Slater, Statton, Super...

"Here's a Robert Sutler," I said. "On Orchard Street. That could be it."

Alice grabbed a slip of paper and a pen from the counter and copied down the number.

"Would you like to use my phone?" Martin asked.

"Thanks, but we have a cell phone," Alice said. She dragged me to the door.

"Thank you," I called to Martin. "You have a lovely shop."

"Come back anytime."

Alice didn't let go of me until we were out on the sidewalk. "What was that all about?" she asked.

I smoothed my hair. "What was what all about?"

"The goo-goo eyes you and the flower guy were making at each other."

"We weren't making goo-goo eyes." My face felt hot, and my clothes were suddenly too tight.

"Yes, you were." She glanced back at the store, the beginnings of a smile making dimples on either side of her mouth. "He's kind of cute. Is he single?"

"Yes." Her glee irritated me. "What difference does it make? We talked about flowers."

"Well, that's a start."

"Don't be silly. I'm never going to see him again." I spoke the words with a pang of regret. Why couldn't I have met Martin in California, where we might have had a chance to get to know each other better?

"Can we call my cousin, please?" Ruth said.

"Do you want one of us to call, or do you want to do it?" Alice asked.

Ruth pressed her lips together in a thin line. "You do it," she said after a moment. "I'm too nervous."

Alice handed me the slip of paper with the phone number and I punched it into my cell phone. A woman answered on the third ring.

"Hi. I'm looking for Mary Sutler," I said.

"This is she."

"Mrs. Sutler, I have someone here who wants to talk to you." Then I handed the phone to Ruth.

She looked startled, then cautiously put the phone to her ear. "Mary? This is Ruth Beiler."

Alice touched my arm. "Let's give her a little privacy," she said.

We walked down the sidewalk, past the dry cleaners and the office supply store, and stopped in front of the coffee shop on the corner. "If you want, we could hang around here a couple days," Alice said. "Make sure Ruth gets settled."

"I think she'll be fine with her cousin."

"It would give you a chance to get to know your handsome florist better."

My heart fluttered, but I shook my head. "There's no point. I live a thousand miles away from here."

"No reason not to have fun for a couple of days. You said you wanted this trip to be an adventure, didn't you?"

I stared at her. "Why would I want to start something with a man that I couldn't stay around to finish?"

"There's a lot to be said for loving them and leaving them. You'd probably both enjoy it."

I shook my head. The words *I'm not that kind of girl* crossed my mind, but I didn't say them. Some other time, with someone else, I might very well want to be that kind of girl, but I couldn't see it with Martin. Not when one smile from him had me so flustered. Loving him and leaving him didn't seem possible.

What was I thinking? Loving him at all was impossible. I didn't even *know* the man. "I doubt if he's interested in me at all," I said. "He was just being friendly."

"Trust me. I've known a lot of men. When they look at a woman the way he was looking at you, they're interested."

I shook my head, too afraid of what might come out if I tried to talk.

Ruth came running up to us. "She said to come right out to her house. She said I can come live with them, no problem."

"That's great." I hugged her and we started back toward the truck. "This looks like a nice place to live," I said. "I hope you'll be happy here."

She nodded. "I'm feeling a little better about my future."

"That makes one of us anyway," Alice said.

I glanced at her. I guess Alice was worried about what awaited her in California.

Me, I told myself not to think about the future. It was too easy for my thoughts to drift into a hazy daydream of some perfect day to come that was always just out of reach. Reality was never as lovely or easy as my dreams and the letdown all that much harder to take for the build-up I'd given myself.

Better that I learn how to be happy right now. Right. As if I could wave my hand and make it so. I had a feeling that kind of contentment was one of those Zen things that was easier to accomplish when I thought happiness was a piece of chocolate cake or a top that hid my thighs.

7

We drove Ruth to the Sutlers'. Her cousin Mary turned out to be a petite twentysomething dressed in jeans and a T-shirt, a blond toddler balanced on her hip. As soon as Ruth climbed out of the truck, Mary enveloped the younger girl in a hug. "I'm glad you're here," she said. "Let's go inside and get you settled."

Alice and I trailed after her. The house was small and neat and decorated in country-cute. Mary poured iced tea and we all sat around the kitchen table looking at each other. "Tell me everything," Mary said.

Ruth told her story, including some details she hadn't shared with us, such as the fact that her stepmother had already sewed Ruth's wedding dress and a date had been set for the nuptials—the following Tuesday—hence Ruth's haste to get out of town.

"We'll have to call Uncle Samuel and let him know where you are," Mary said. "Just in case he's gone to the police."

"He wouldn't do that," Ruth said. "He wouldn't want to get outsiders involved."

"You're probably right, but we'd better call anyway."

Even this proved problematic, since Ruth's father didn't have a phone. In the end, it was decided to call the non-Amish neighbor—the one from whom Ruth had "borrowed" the jeans—and ask her to pass along the message.

Then Mary invited us to spend the night. After a meat loaf-and-mashed-potatoes supper, Alice and I ended up sharing a small guest bedroom decorated with a sunbonnet-girl quilt and blue-and-pink-plaid curtains. I wondered if this would be Ruth's room after we left. I hoped she'd get to decorate it with something teen cool.

"This reminds me of the slumber parties we had when we were kids," Alice said.

I smiled into the darkness. "I remember. One time we waited until everyone was asleep and sneaked down to your kitchen to make hot-fudge sundaes." Such innocent daring had seemed positively wicked to us back then.

"We had good times, didn't we?" Alice fell silent again and I imagined her smiling into the darkness.

Or maybe she wasn't smiling. "How come we never stayed over at your house?" she asked. "It was always my house."

"Your house was more fun. And you didn't have a sister. We'd have had to include Frannie in anything we did at my house."

"That would have been okay. I liked Frannie."

I squirmed, trying to get more comfortable on the hard mattress. "I liked Frannie, too, but it was nice to have a friend all to myself sometimes."

Her hand found mine under the covers and she gave it a squeeze. "I'm glad we met up again and you could come on this trip," she said.

"Me, too." A person couldn't have too many friends in her life, and I was beginning to think that old friends were the best ones of all. My friends in California were more acquaintances—women with whom I had lunch or went to the movies or the races. They were fun to be with, but our relationship was all on the surface. They knew I was from Virginia and little else. I would never have felt comfortable confiding anything deep to them.

Alice was different. She was the keeper of stories from my

past and secrets we had shared long ago. She knew a version of me that was less nicked up by life, the unripe, unsophisticated self that only a parent—or a childhood pal—could really love.

We woke the next morning to raised voices. I pulled the covers up to my chin and stared, wide-eyed, at the closed bedroom door. Alice sat up. "Sounds like Ruth and Mary."

The cousins weren't yelling at each other, though. Apparently, they were arguing with Ruth's father. Alice and I listened to the one-sided conversation in which Ruth, at first tearful, then defiant, refused to return home to marry her father's choice of groom. "I'd rather stay here with Mary and never see you again than be sold off that way like livestock."

Then Mary took up the cause, declaring Ruth was "too good and smart to spend the rest of her life slaving after some old man and his snot-nosed children."

The words grew more bitter from there, and ended with an unbearable silence.

Alice and I dressed and gathered our things, making as little noise as possible. When we emerged from the bedroom, we found the others gathered around the kitchen table. Except for Ruth's red eyes, everything appeared normal.

"Ruth is going to stay here," Mary said as she set a mug of coffee in front of me. "She can enroll in the local high school, and she'll be a big help to me around the house." She smiled at her younger cousin. "I thought this afternoon we'd go shopping for some new clothes for her."

"Thank you again for helping me," Ruth said. "I don't know what I'd have done if you hadn't stopped when you did." She stared down at her half-empty bowl of cereal. "I was really scared."

"Proves you're no dummy," Alice said gruffly. "We're glad we could help."

After breakfast, we said our goodbyes. I gave Ruth my address and asked her to write, then Alice and I piled back into the truck.

Instead of turning toward the highway, Alice circled back through town. "Where are you going?" I asked.

"I wanted to look around a little more."

We drove past a red stone courthouse set amid a grove of live oak trees. A small white library sat next door, across from a gray brick city hall and the police station. In short order we passed the post office, American Legion hall, elementary school, Baptist, Methodist and Catholic churches, and were back on the town square.

"I haven't lived in a small town since Frannie and I left Ridgeway," I said as I admired the Veteran's Memorial in front of the courthouse. "I'd forgotten how nice they could be." All the familiar small-town institutions were straight out of a Hollywood set designer's idea of middle-American warmth and friendliness. We were a long way from traffic jams and gang violence and urban decay.

Here was the life most of us—or at least *I*—considered ideal. Safe. Familiar. Welcoming.

"It would be nice for about three days," Alice said. "Then I'd start to miss the shopping mall, the gourmet grocer and the ability to run errands without half the people in town knowing what I was up to."

"I wouldn't mind," I said. "Always being anonymous can get old, too."

"Do you want to hang around a little longer?" she asked. "We could stop by and say hello to that good-looking florist again."

The mention of Martin sent a hot shimmy through my middle, but I sat up straighter and ignored it. "A man that good-looking in a town this size probably has every single women for fifty miles after him."

"Yeah, but he was interested in you." She turned down the street leading to the florist's.

"What are you doing?" I protested.

"At least go in and say goodbye," she said. She parked and switched off the engine. "Give him your phone number."

I stared at the little shop with its display of ferns and roses in the window. "Why should I do that?"

She looked at me as if I was an idiot. "So he can *call* you. Then you two can get to know each other."

I looked at her, trying not to show how desperate I was feeling. While I'd been full of confidence and hot-to-trot for Marc, I felt completely out of my league with Martin. Marc had been a fun, wild fantasy. Martin felt too *real*. Too important. I was terrified of screwing up.

Of being hurt.

"What would I say to him?" I asked.

"Tell him you really enjoyed talking to him yesterday, that you have to leave town right now, but you'd love it if he called you sometime." She nudged me toward the door. "Just do it."

I stared at the flower shop. Through the front window I could see Martin working behind the counter. I remembered the way I'd felt when he'd looked into my eyes yesterday, as if he'd looked past my physical body and seen the *real* me. And still he hadn't turned away.

I swallowed hard. "I can't do it," I said.

"Of course you can." She shoved me again, but at that moment, the door to the shop opened and Martin came out. Smiling, he walked over to my side of the truck. I stared at him, feeling sick.

"Roll down the window," Alice said.

I did. "Martin! Hello!" I said, as if I was surprised to see him.

"Is everything okay?" he asked. "I saw your truck sitting out here."

"Everything's fine." I couldn't wipe this stupid, sick smile off my face. God, he was gorgeous!

"We're on our way out of town," Alice said. "Ellen wanted to stop and say goodbye."

"You're leaving so soon?" His disappointment felt genuine.

I nodded. "We have to go, but…I really enjoyed talking with you yesterday."

"Me, too." He reached inside the truck and took my hands. My heart fluttered wildly. Why did excitement feel so similar to terror?

"Ellen wanted to give you her phone number, so you could call her." Alice pressed on, relentless.

"I'd love that." He let go of my hands and pulled a business card from his front pocket. He gave it to me, along with a pen. "Write it here," he said.

I scribbled my name and number and thrust it at him before I lost my nerve. He read it over carefully. "This is your home number?"

"My cell phone. I won't be home for a while."

"Call anytime," Alice said.

His eyes met mine again. Such a beautiful brown—like the richest potting soil. "I will." He fished another card from his pocket and pressed it into my hand. "And here's my number."

I folded my fingers over the rectangle of cardstock, the corners digging into my palms. I felt as if I'd slipped into an alternate dimension where time froze and I hung suspended in air. I sort of wanted to hang there forever, enjoying the admiration in his eyes, and the way my skin tingled. If one look from him could do this to me, what would happen if we touched?

The bells on the door jangled as a woman and two little

girls entered the shop and the spell between us was broken. Martin looked over his shoulder. "I'd better go," he said, but stayed right where he was.

"Yeah. We'd better go, too."

"I'll talk to you soon," he said. "I promise."

Promise. The word itself had me feeling light-headed. A promise was a vow. A guarantee. As if I was already important enough to him that a phone call was sacred.

He finally turned away and started toward the shop, but stopped in the doorway to wave at me.

I waved back, fighting the desire to giggle. Thirty-eight-year-old women shouldn't giggle, but I felt anything but mature when Martin was around.

"He's going to call me," I said, watching through the front window as he waited on the woman and her girls.

"That's a good start, then." Alice put the truck in gear and backed out into the street.

I put my hand on my chest, as if I could calm my fluttering heart. A start to what?

For once even my vivid imagination couldn't come up with a fantasy grand enough to match the possibilities captured in those few words.

I took the wheel when we stopped for gas in Kansas City. I was paying the bill when I spotted a rack full of postcards next to the cash register. An outsize load of guilt slammed into me at the sight of Dorothy in her blue gingham dress and ruby red slippers with the legend Welcome to the Land of Oz arching over her. Before I could think too much about what I was doing, I put a hand out to stop the clerk from totaling out my credit card. "Wait. I need some of these postcards."

"They're three for a dollar. How many you want?"

I hesitated, the colorful cards a blur. "Just give me one of each." If Frannie wanted postcards, I'd give her a whole scrapbook full.

When I shoved the plastic bag into the truck cab ahead of me a few minutes later, Alice looked at me as if I'd turned into a munchkin myself. "What could you possibly find to buy at a truck stop?" she asked.

While I buckled my seat belt, Alice dove into the bag and pulled out a handful of cards. "Planning on writing a lot of people?" she asked.

"They're not for me, they're for Frannie." I started the truck and checked my mirrors. When I'd spotted the display I'd realized I hadn't bought a single souvenir on this trip for my sister.

"She collects postcards?" Alice studied an illustration of a giant ear of corn.

"She doesn't really collect them. She puts them in scrapbooks." I pulled onto the highway and tromped down on the accelerator. The moving truck drove like a slug, taking forever to get up to speed. "She saves everything—postcards, newspaper clippings, ticket stubs—everything. She has books and books full of it all, going back to when we were kids."

Alice put away the postcards and stashed the bag behind the seat. "I tried scrapbooking once. I ended up with a box full of stickers, fancy paper, hole punches, glitter and glue. I kept it on a shelf in the hall closet until I faced up to the fact I wasn't the crafty kind and gave the whole lot away to Goodwill."

"Frannie tried to get me interested in scrapbooking with her, but I didn't care for it," I said. "I guess I'm just not the sentimental type."

"What about when you were a kid?" Alice asked. "Did you have any hobbies, like collecting stamps or troll dolls or anything like that?"

I shook my head and pulled out to pass a slow-moving VW bug. "I never liked having a lot of stuff around."

"Dust catchers, my mother always called them."

"Something like that." I was distracted by a bright reflection in the rearview mirror.

About that time, I heard a siren wail and recognized the flashing as the blue-and-white strobe of a highway patrol car coming up fast on my rear bumper.

"Shit! Are you speeding?" Alice leaned over to check the speedometer.

My heart hammered and my hands shook so badly I could hardly flip on my blinker. I hit the brake and guided the truck onto the shoulder, numb. *Stay calm,* I told myself. *You haven't done anything wrong.* Still shaking, I managed to roll down the window.

When the officer walked up to the truck, I had the impression of clean-cut good looks behind mirrored sunglasses. But he could have been Elvis himself for all the difference it made to me.

"Good afternoon, ma'am. May I see your driver's license and registration, please?"

"Th-they're in my purse," I stammered. I groped on the floorboard for my bag, then dug through it, light-headed and dizzy. Where was the damn license?

Finally, Alice reached in and handed me my wallet and the envelope from the glove compartment with the registration. "Calm down," she whispered. "It's just a speeding ticket."

I shoved the identification at the officer and stared straight ahead out the windshield, clutching the steering wheel as if it was a life preserver.

"Ms. Lawrence, do you know how fast you were going?"

I shook my head. "I guess I wasn't paying attention." A warm breeze gusted in as an 18-wheeler zoomed past. My whole body felt clammy with sweat and I had to keep reminding myself to relax.

"You were doing seventy-five in a fifty-five zone." The

officer scribbled something on his clipboard. "May I see some identification, ma'am?" he asked Alice.

"You can see anything you like, Officer." I gaped at her as she gave him a wide smile and handed over her license. Leave it to Alice to flirt at a time like this!

The officer remained stone-faced. "I'll be with you in just a moment," he said and left us.

I watched in the mirror as he walked back to his patrol car. The urge to turn the key and drive away was so strong I took my hands off the steering wheel and sat on them.

Alice was watching the cop, too, in the side mirror. "Isn't he a hottie?" she said. "There's just something about those tight pants and those boots…" She squirmed. "Talk about a fantasy come to life."

"Stop it," I snapped. "There's nothing sexy about this."

"Don't you think?" She grinned. "With those handcuffs and those dark glasses." She checked the mirror again. "And that gorgeous ass."

I shut my eyes. I didn't care about the cop's ass or his boots or anything but getting out of here as soon as possible. I'd never felt less sexy in my life. In fact, I felt like throwing up.

He came back to the truck and returned our licenses. "Where are you ladies headed?" he asked.

My throat was so dry I didn't know if I'd be able to answer, but I didn't have to. "We're going to Ojai, California," Alice said. "I'm moving there from Virginia. Ellen lives in Bakersfield and agreed to help me make the drive. We're taking our time, seeing the country." She all but fluttered her eyelashes, sending the message that she'd like to see more of him.

He was immune to her charms. "Are you carrying any drugs in the vehicle?" he asked.

"No!" I blurted. Did I look like someone who carried drugs? Me?

"Are you carrying any weapons in the vehicle?"

"No." I shook my head. I had no idea what Alice had packed in her moving boxes, but I hoped it wasn't weapons.

"Mind if I take a look?"

"No." All I really wanted was to be left alone, but I didn't dare say that.

A second patrol car pulled up behind the first. Apparently we struck the cop as so dangerous he'd already radioed for backup.

"If you ladies would wait back at the car with my colleague, he has a consent form for you to sign." The officer opened the driver's door, a perfect gentleman.

I scooted past him and hurried toward the other cop. Alice was slower, sauntering past him with an exaggerated sway.

I grabbed her arm and pulled her alongside me toward the other cop. "What are you doing?" I asked. "This isn't some silly game."

"Stop, you're hurting me." She pushed me away and rubbed her arm where I'd grabbed her. "Settle down," she said. "We don't have anything to worry about."

I was too shook up to actually read the form the other cop stuck under my nose. For all I knew I was confessing to being a terrorist.

The three of us stood there on the side of the highway and watched as the first cop crawled through the cab. I was sure he was digging through my purse. Belatedly I remembered the condom I'd stashed there in a moment of bravado before leaving Bakersfield. Maybe he'd think it belonged to Alice. She was certainly more likely to use it than I was at this point.

The sun beat down, so bright I had to squint, even though I was wearing sunglasses. Sweat pooled in the valley between my breasts and in the small of my back. I wondered what would happen if I passed out here on the side of the road.

Alice made small talk with the other cop, as if we were having cocktails at a backyard barbecue. She looked content to spend all day here, while I fought the urge to look at my watch.

How long did it take to search one damn truck cab? Especially one with nothing in it? Unless someone had decided that Kansas postcards were contraband.

When I was sure I was seconds away from either screaming or fainting, the first cop sauntered back to join us. "Everything looks okay." He had me sign the speeding ticket, then handed me my copy. "The instructions for mailing in your fine are on the back," he said. "You keep your speed down from now on."

"Yes, sir," I muttered, already headed for the truck.

Somehow I managed to fasten my seat belt, start the truck and merge onto the highway at a sedate speed. I took the first exit I saw and pulled into the driveway of a fast-food place and rested my forehead against the steering wheel.

"What is wrong with you?" Alice asked. "I never saw anyone get so worked up over a speeding ticket."

"I don't like cops," I said. "They make me nervous."

"They shouldn't make you nervous if you haven't done anything wrong."

"It's their attitude," I said. "They automatically assume everyone's a criminal. You heard him, asking all those questions about guns and drugs, searching the truck."

"Only because you acted as if you were guilty of *something*," she said. "Honestly, you broke out in a cold sweat the minute he walked up, and your hands were shaking so badly you could hardly open your wallet."

"I just don't like cops, okay? Everybody has phobias. The police are mine."

"Well, it's over with now. At least he didn't find this." She dug into her pocket and pulled out a short, fat cigarette.

I stared, my heart in my throat. "Is that what I think it is?"

She laughed. "It is if you think it's a joint."

"Alice! If he'd have found that we could have been arrested."

"For one joint? Nah, it's probably just a fine. And he didn't find it, so it's all good." She put the joint back in her pocket.

"What are you doing with that?" I asked.

"What do you think? I'm going to smoke it later."

"But why?"

"Why? Because it feels good." She leaned toward me. "Don't tell me you've never smoked pot."

I shook my head. "Frannie would have killed me."

"Who cares what Frannie thinks? You're thirty-eight years old."

I looked away from her, embarrassed, and at the same time angry with her for making me feel that way. "I never saw any reason to do drugs."

"Go through chemo and you might think differently," she said. "When I was puking up my guts around the clock, marijuana was the only thing that saved me."

"Oh." I looked at her, touched by the pain in her eyes. "I'd forgotten they use it for cancer patients."

"Yeah, well, this cancer patient intends to keep using it. There's too much misery in life. There's times when it helps to soften the edges a little."

I nodded, regretting that I'd judged her. "Yeah, well, if it helps you, why not?" I handed her the keys. "I think I'll run in and get something to drink. You want anything?"

"I could go for a Coke and some fries."

"Sure thing. Then you can drive for a while."

"Think if I speed that cute cop will stop us again?" I must have looked as horrified as I felt, because she laughed and punched my shoulder. "Just kidding."

I hoped this would be one of those things I could laugh about later. They say life's a joke, but right now I felt like the butt of it.

★ ★ ★

The afternoon stretched out before us as empty and fea-
tureless as the fallow fields that rolled past the car windows
like an endless loop of videotape. I let my eyes lose focus
until the world around me was a blur of dusty green, gold
and brown. It was a talent I'd perfected as a child on endless car trips to distant relatives. Hours would pass while my
thoughts hummed like static above the soft pop music on
the radio.

Embarrassment over my silly fear of the cop lingered like
the ache in my legs after too much time on the treadmill. I
was mortified that I was still such a martyr to my emotions.
It was a simple speeding ticket, for God's sake. And I'd nearly
had a panic attack.

"I...I'm sorry about what happened back there, with the
cop," I said, after an hour or more had passed without either
of us saying anything.

"Don't worry about it," Alice said. "People who've never
been in trouble with the law often have an overdeveloped
conscience. At least that's my theory."

"Alice!" I stared at her. "You've never been in trouble
with the law, have you?"

She gave me a sly wink. "I've never been caught, if that's
what you mean." She laughed at my incredulous expression.
"Relax. I'm not wanted or anything. I dated a guy for a while
who was into some shady dealings—a little drug running,
some work for the mob. He taught me the cops aren't nearly
as smart as they'd like you to think."

"Alice! Did you really? I mean...drugs? And the mob?"
This new image of her as a Mafia princess was both fascinating and repellant.

"It wasn't anything big-time or glamorous, believe me,"
she said. "I mean, I'll admit at the time I thought it was very
exciting." She glanced at me. "It wasn't too long after I split
with Travis. I went through a kind of self-destructive phase,

I guess. After a few months with Stan—that was the crook's name—I came to my senses."

"Thank goodness for that," I said. "You could have ended up in real trouble."

"But I didn't. Though I learned pretty quickly I wasn't cut out for a life of crime." She made a face. "I didn't even do anything wrong and I felt guilty. Anyway, that was years ago, so you don't have anything to worry about."

"I'm not worried," I said. "To tell the truth, I'm a little jealous."

She arched one eyebrow. "Jealous of my foolish relationship with a small-time hoodlum?"

"Not that," I said. "But I envy how much you've done with your life. I haven't done anything." In so many ways, I felt as if I'd been standing still since I was sixteen. I'd moved to California with Frannie and had sat there ever since, letting things happen to me, but never taking an active role in my own life. Even the flower shop happened by accident. I'd taken a part-time job, discovered a love of flowers, met someone from the movies who knew a set designer who needed flowers, and the next thing I knew, I had my own business.

Losing weight had been the most proactive thing I'd done in years. And I guess shedding those pounds was really the trigger that got me moving again—away from California and Frannie, out here on the highway, trying to figure out where I really wanted to end up. I knew I didn't want the same kind of life I'd had before, but I couldn't yet picture my life in the future.

"Don't be ridiculous," Alice said. "You have your own business, you own a house. Everything I own is in this moving truck. And I never had a job in my life that paid more than twelve dollars an hour."

"But you've done things," I protested. "You've traveled and lived different places, had relationships with men."

"What's stopping you from doing any of those things?"

Her question caught me off guard. For years, I'd used my weight as an excuse not to move out of my comfortable routine of work, food and evenings in front of the television. "I'm thirty-eight," I said weakly.

"As if that's old! You have a lot of years ahead of you. Even if you don't, all the more reason to get busy and live the life you want."

The idea was as fascinating and frightening as an exotic serpent. "I guess I never thought about it that way before."

"You're off to a good start," she said. "You lost all that weight. You came to the reunion, and now you're making this trip. That doesn't sound like a dangerously dull person to me."

I laughed, the nervous, giddy giggling of a person who's afraid of heights who finds herself standing too close to the edge. "I guess it doesn't."

"The next thing is to decide what to do next. Where do you want to travel? What kind of man do you want to meet?"

"I don't think I'm going to find a man just by deciding what kind I want," I said.

"It's the first step. Of course, all this is coming from a two-time divorcée whose longest relationship outside of marriage lasted eight months. So you should probably take everything I say with a grain of salt."

"I'll keep that in mind."

Alice arched her back, stretching, and glanced at the clock on the dashboard. "Check the map and see how far it is to the next town big enough to have a decent motel," she said. "I've about had enough of the highway for one day."

Salina was less than an hour away. Once there, we found a so-called "budget" motel and gratefully claimed a room. It had all the requirements: two beds that didn't sag in the middle and weren't too hard, frigid air-conditioning, enough clean towels that we could have two each and an in-room coffeemaker so that we didn't have to go out in public in the morning before we'd had a shot of caffeine.

Alice lay back on one bed, arms out at her sides. "God, it feels good to get out of that truck," she said. "I don't see how truckers do it."

"Me, either." I reclined on the other bed. "Who knew basically sitting all day could be so exhausting?"

"Thank God you agreed to come with me," she said. "I don't know if I'd have made it this far without you."

I rolled over onto my side so I could look at her and cradled a pillow beneath my head. "I'm glad you invited me," I said. "I really needed to get away from the shop and everything for a while. I don't think I realized how much until you asked me to make the trip."

"Glad I could help." She propped herself up on her elbows. "What should we do now? I don't think I could face going out again."

"We could order pizza."

"Sounds like a good deal. But it's a little early yet."

I checked the clock. It was only a little past five. "So what do you want to do?" I asked.

She rolled onto her side and dug in the pocket of her jeans. "I've still got this." She pulled out the joint. "Why don't we smoke it and get happy?"

8

"Alice!" I tried to sound horrified, but I wasn't really. I'd been sort of expecting this ever since she'd showed me the joint in the first place. But I still didn't quite know how to react.

She sat up. "Don't tell me you've never wanted to smoke a joint, either."

For half a second I thought about lying, but what was the point? "I've thought about it, but never had the opportunity," I said. "I tried cigarettes for a while because I heard they were a good appetite suppressant, but Frannie nagged at me so much about it I ended up quitting."

"Well, Frannie isn't here right now." She scooted to the edge of the bed and swung her legs to the floor. "And I promise not to tell a soul."

I glanced toward the door, as if I expected a cop to burst in at any moment. "Aren't you worried it's illegal?"

"Who's going to know?" She shrugged. "And who cares? It's just one joint. It's not like I'm shooting heroine or anything."

"I know." And I believed her. My hesitation was like an itchy sweater—familiar but increasingly uncomfortable. I was probably an endangered species—the only child of the sixties who had never smoked dope.

"Is it a moral objection that's holding you back, or are you just scared?" Alice asked.

"Why would I be scared?" I winced at the quaver in my voice.

"Lots of people are scared of new things." She leaned forward and grabbed the pack of matches out of the ashtray on the dresser. "My theory is that the more new experiences you try, the less you have to fear."

Everything she said made sense, yet a lifetime of avoiding any kind of change held me back. "All right," I admitted. "I *am* afraid. I'm afraid I'll make a fool of myself."

"We've all been fools at one time or another, thank God." She struck the match and held it to the end of the joint. The end glowed and a thin trickle of smoke curled up like a genie escaping from a magic lamp. "I'd hate to be the only person in the world who'd made mistakes."

I came and sat on the end of the bed next to her. She handed me the joint. I stared at it as if it were a lit firecracker. "What do I do?"

"It would be better for your first time if we had a bong, but we don't, so just inhale slowly and hold the smoke in as long as you can."

Feeling very self-conscious, I stuck the joint between my lips and inhaled—and immediately exploded in a coughing fit. My lungs burned and my eyes watered.

Alice took the joint from me. "Go slower next time." She demonstrated. "Like that," she squeaked. She held the smoke in her lungs for a moment, then released it in a fragrant cloud.

I did better on my second try. I handed the joint back to Alice and waited. "So what's supposed to happen?" I asked.

"Give it a minute. You'll start to feel mellow."

We smoked in silence for a while, passing the joint back and forth. At first I didn't think this was anything special and was disappointed. Then I noticed my mouth was dry. That was it?

"Look at the bedspread," Alice said. "Aren't the colors pretty?"

When we'd first entered the room, I'd noted that it was done in what I'd come to think of as typical motel decor, complete with odd-colored chintz bedspreads and matching drapes.

Except this bedspread didn't look odd-colored at all. The tones were deep, almost jewel-like. I ran my hand over the floral design. I could almost feel the flowers.

"It's nice, isn't it?" Alice lay back and took another deep drag on the joint, then handed it to me.

"It *is* nice." I smiled and admired the way the light glinted off the brass lamp base. "I feel...good." Better than I'd felt in a long time.

"It's good to let go of our inhibitions," Alice observed.

"But I like my inhibitions," I protested, then started giggling.

Alice giggled, too. "That's like saying you like wearing a girdle."

"I liked that wearing a girdle made me look better," I said.

"You don't need a girdle to look good now," Alice replied. "So maybe you don't need a lot of those inhibitions anymore."

I stared at her. "For a woman smoking dope, you make a lot of sense."

"That's not much of a compliment, considering you're high, too," she said.

"I am not." I discovered it's hard to sound indignant when you keep falling over and giggling.

"You are, and it's a good thing. I'd hate to be having this much fun all by myself."

"Are we having fun?" I asked, giggling again.

"You sound the way we did when we were kids and would try to stay up all night," she said. "We'd get the giggles and couldn't stop."

"Your mother would always come in and tell us to settle down and we'd laugh at her, too." I smiled. "I always liked your mom. Better than my own."

Alice patted my hand. "She liked you, too."

"I wanted to be your sister," I said. "And live at your house all the time."

"You should have done it. I'd have let you move in."

"I should have," I agreed. I took another toke and thought again of those giggly slumber parties we'd had. "This *does* feel something like those nights we stayed up really late," I said.

"One of the worst things about being an adult is we take ourselves too seriously," Alice said.

"Being an adult is serious business." I tried to frown and failed.

"Oh, yeah. It's damn serious. Sometimes I want to chuck the whole thing and go join a commune. Sit and smoke dope and contemplate my navel all day."

"That would get awfully boring," I said.

"Yeah, and the hippie chicks I remember probably all look like hags now anyway. Twenty years of not wearing a bra or shaving your legs or cutting your hair are bound to haunt you by the time you're forty."

I doubled over laughing again. "Maybe the hippie dudes don't care," I choked out.

"That's another thing." She pinched the end of the joint between her fingers and waved it at me. "Have you seen an old hippie man? Bald on top with a little gray ponytail and beard and a pot belly."

"Stop!" I screamed, holding my stomach. "I can't stand it!"

"I can see it now," Alice continued. "I'd show up at the

commune with my high heels and makeup and offer free makeovers for everyone."

"You could be queen of the commune," I said.

"More likely they'd kick me out." She sighed and fell back on the bed. "Guess I'd better stick to smoking the occasional joint and doing the grown-up thing the rest of the time." She smiled again. "It isn't so bad. Grown-ups get to have sex."

"Some of you do, anyway."

She turned her head to look at me. "Your turn will come, my dear. You just have to find the right man."

"Mythical Mr. Right. If he exists."

"What about that good-looking florist?" She grinned.

I nodded. "A possibility. Except he's in Kansas." And he hadn't called. I don't know what I was expecting. I'd been away from Sweetwater less than a day. Still, I couldn't help hoping my phone would ring and I would hear his voice on the other end of the line.

Another ridiculous fantasy, I guessed. "Do you think there's a Mr. Right in California?" I asked.

"Maybe a movie star," Alice said. "Robert Pattinson?"

"Too young," I said.

"Johnny Depp?"

I made a face. "Too scruffy."

"Brad Pitt?"

"Taken."

"Then who?"

"I don't want a movie star," I said. "I just want an ordinary guy."

"There's plenty of them out there, but I think you deserve someone extraordinary."

Unexpected tears pricked my eyes. "That's such a sweet thing to say."

She sat up again, her gaze still locked to mine. "You deserve the best. We all do."

"Do you think you'll find Mr. Right in California?" I asked.

She shook her head. "I'm not looking."

"Maybe you'll find him anyway. When you least expect it."

"You always were a romantic," she said.

"You were, too," I said. "After all, you married your high school sweetheart and wanted to live in the woods and make bread and babies."

"Yes, and look where that fantasy got me." She shook her head. "But it's not too late for you. I can live vicariously through you."

I giggled. "I hope you're not disappointed. My life hasn't been very exciting so far."

"That could change at any time." She leaned over and dug the phone book out of the drawer by the bed. "Let's order that pizza. What size should we get?"

"A large. I'm starved." Funny, saying that would have usually made me feel panicky. I'd fought so hard to overcome my addiction to food, I didn't want to backslide, but right now that didn't seem to matter.

"See, you're already going for the gusto. I'm proud of you."

"It's just pizza, Alice."

"It's a start. Today pizza, tomorrow the man of your dreams!"

She laughed, a wonderful, carefree sound that made my heart hurt. In spite of everything that had happened to her, the fact that Alice could still laugh like that made me believe anything was possible.

After we finished the pizza I fell into a doze, my stomach uncomfortably full and my mind still fogged from the marijuana.

I woke hours later, to a dark, unfamiliar room and the

tinny sound of *Boléro* grating at my nerves. I sat up and blinked, then realized the music was coming from my phone. I lunged for the nightstand and grabbed my purse and dug for the phone.

"Hello?" I was out of breath, clutching the phone to my ear and trying to orient myself in the darkness.

"Ellen, this is Martin Franklin. Did I call at a bad time?"

"Martin!" I sat up straighter, my heart in my throat. "No! No, this isn't a bad time at all." I smoothed my blouse—pure reflex, since obviously he couldn't see me.

"How was your drive today?" he asked. "Where are you now?"

"Salina, Kansas." I looked over at the other bed. Alice was an inert lump under the covers. I scooted back on my own bed and settled against the pillows, pulling the blankets around me. "The drive was okay. I got pulled over for speeding." Even at this distance I felt queasy, remembering.

"Tough," he said. "I'll admit I like to drive fast, too. Especially on the long, straight stretches of highway we have around here."

"I wouldn't have pegged you for a speed demon," I said.

"There are a lot of things about me that might surprise you." His tone was teasing, flirtatious.

I swallowed, wishing I could think of something witty to say. "What are you doing right now?" I asked.

"I'm working. I'm doing the arrangements for a funeral tomorrow."

"That's sad," I said.

"It is and it isn't," he said. "I didn't know this gentleman, but his family obviously think a great deal of him. I like to believe that the flowers I put together will help comfort them in their grief."

"That's a beautiful way to look at it. The only funeral flowers I've ever done were for characters on soap operas.

The only grief involved was what the set designer would give me if I didn't get them right."

He laughed—a warm chuckle that sent desire curling up through my middle like smoke. "I bet you always get them right." There was a burst of static. "Sorry." He came back on the line. "I had to shift the phone to my other ear. What do you think of lilies for funerals? Too cliché?"

I frowned, seriously considering the question. "Depends on the person the funeral was for. Was he a traditional, formal man? Then lilies are good. But if he's more colorful, less formal, the flowers should be less formal, too."

"Exactly what I told the family! So we're going with blue and red delphiniums and asters."

Flowers were such a natural topic of conversation. Non-threatening. I felt myself relax. "It sounds beautiful." I smiled.

"You're welcome to use the same idea the next time you do a television funeral." He laughed. "My life must sound pretty dull compared to all that Hollywood glamour."

I shrugged. "There's nothing glamorous at all about my life, really."

"No one's ever going to see my work on TV."

"No, but your work will mean more to the people who *do* see it." I hugged my knees to my chest. "I envy you," I said.

"Why is that?"

"You work with real people. The flowers you provide make a difference in their lives. They cheer them up when they're sick or mourning and help them celebrate all the landmark events. They *mean* something." For all their beauty, my fantasy creations for pretend situations didn't mean anything to anyone.

"I think that's one of the reasons I enjoy this work so much," he said. "I really like most of my customers."

"The movie people I work with can be fun," I said, "but

it's not the same as putting together an arrangement for a birthday party or a real wedding."

"Maybe you should think about adding a retail section," he said. "That way you could keep your movie business, but do other work that was more satisfying on a personal level."

"I never thought about it that way before." I shifted my position in the bed. "There are a lot of florists in Bakersfield. I'm not sure I could compete." I could almost hear Frannie's voice in my head, telling me to stay in my niche, to stick with what I knew. Taking risks was dangerous and could only lead to grief.

"That's one of the advantages of a small town," he said. "There's not a lot of competition here."

"I liked Sweetwater," I said. "What I saw of it." Mainly I liked *him*.

"I hope you'll come back to visit. I'd like to see you again."

"I'd like to see you, too." I'd like a lot of things—to have a real home and real friends with whom I could be close. The question was, did I have the courage to break away from the familiar to pursue all that? I didn't want to abandon Frannie, but I could see the attraction now of not always working so hard to please her.

"I don't want to hang up, but I have to finish up these arrangements," he said. "It's getting late."

"Call again anytime."

"I will. And you feel free to call me." I could hear the smile in his voice. "You're a very special lady," he said. "I knew it the minute you walked into my shop."

The praise made me feel like laughing—and like crying. I had never thought of myself as special. And for a lot of years—my fat years—I wouldn't have enjoyed being singled out as such.

But to be thought special by a man, one with whom I'd felt a connection from our first meeting, was a gift I'd treasure no matter what the future held. "Thank you for saying that," I said.

"I mean it. Good night, Ellen. I hope you have sweet dreams."

"Good night." My dreams would be sweet if they featured Martin.

I cradled the phone to my chest and stared off into the darkness, a goofy grin stretching the corners of my mouth. Was this what falling in love felt like—this giddy rush down a raging waterfall, bobbing and bouncing and not caring at all if you drowned, only reveling in the excitement of the ride?

All I knew about love was contained in novels and acted out in television and movies. My limited dating experience had involved a few fumbling lust-filled exchanges in the backseats of cars or bachelor apartments, all of which ended after a few weeks when one of us—usually the man—lost interest. Even during sex I'd felt no real closeness to the men—certainly not the connection I'd experienced with Martin.

Knowing this didn't give me a clue as to what I was going to *do* about him, however. He was firmly planted in a small town in Kansas and I was headed back to my life in Bakersfield. As wild as my imagination could be at times, even I was sensible enough to know that a person didn't leave behind an established business and the only family she had on the basis of a few brief conversations.

I sighed and leaned over and replaced the phone in my purse. Frannie would have a conniption if she knew the direction my thoughts had taken, so I resolved not to tell her. I needed to think this through without my sister telling me what to do.

The other bed creaked as Alice shifted and mumbled in her sleep. Alice would tell me to "go with the flow" and see what happened next. I slid farther under the covers, my head on the pillow, trying out the idea. I'd spent my life looking ahead, anticipating, dreaming. My dreams were a way to escape the present and head off any problems in the future. After all, if I'd already imagined the worst, I could avoid doing anything to make that bad reality come true. If those fears kept me from trying very many new things at least they helped me avoid a lot of hurt, too.

But what if I did—just this once—avoid thinking about the future altogether? Would it be so wrong to enjoy the moment? I didn't *have* to do anything right this minute but enjoy this feeling of being appreciated by a handsome man. I'd wait for the next phone call and see what developed. One conversation at a time.

I was still feeling good the next morning and volunteered to drive first. We were a few miles outside of Colby, Kansas, when I heard what sounded like a gunshot. The truck lurched to one side and I fought to keep it in the lane, heart pounding.

"Blowout," Alice said, steadying herself with one hand on the dash. "Just ease it over to the shoulder."

Once we were safely stopped, we both piled out to survey the damage. "Bad news," Alice said as we contemplated the shredded rubber that barely clung to the wheel rim.

"Can we change it?" I asked, meaning *can you change it?* because I've never changed a tire in my life. That's why I have AAA.

"Are *you* going to jack up a vehicle that size?" she asked. "I don't think so." She pulled out her cell phone. "The moving company has an emergency service. We'll let them take care of it."

After a cryptic conversation, Alice reported the moving company had promised to send someone "in about an hour."

We climbed back into the cab of the truck and Alice

fanned herself. "Put the key in and crank the air back on," she said. "It's like an oven out there."

I obliged and for a moment we basked in the full force of the air-conditioning. "I'll sure as hell be glad when we get out of Kansas," Alice said after a moment. "It's been one thing after another in this state."

I nodded. Except for Martin, Kansas had had more than its share of adventures. I stared out at the mostly empty highway, heat lakes shimmering on the pavement. "If Frannie were here, she'd be having a fit," I said. "She hates anything that doesn't go according to schedule."

Alice snorted. "How did she get this far in life and not figure out things almost never go according to plan?"

"I guess she's not very patient."

"I'm not so much patient as resigned," she said. She looked at me. "And I'm used to this kind of thing. I've never had great luck with cars. Or trucks." She chuckled. "Do you remember that green Ford Maverick I had?"

"The one you got right after your sixteenth birthday?" I had a vague memory of the car Alice acquired the month before I left town.

"That's the one. My older brother sold it to me for six hundred dollars—money I'd saved from my job as a car hop at the drive-in. God, I loved that car."

"Whatever happened to it?" I asked, more to keep the conversation going than anything else. I liked it when Alice remembered happier times.

"Larry Westover talked me into trading it for a Camaro his cousin had." She shook her head. "Biggest piece-of-shit car I ever owned. Damn thing left me stranded more times than I can count."

"You should have made the cousin buy it back," I said.

"Ah, but then I would have to admit I'd made a bad choice," she said. "What seventeen-year-old wants to do that?"

I laughed. "So you drove the lemon?"

She nodded. "Until I traded it for a used Chevy pickup. It was a good truck. That was right after Bobby and I got married. We thought the truck would be more practical for our back-to-the-land adventure, but after a year or two, I wanted something flashier, so I got a Dodge Dart." She smiled. "That's the story of my life—always looking for something better. Cars. Jobs. Men. They all look dull to me after a while."

"I'm just the opposite," I said. "At least when it comes to cars."

Alice turned toward me, one leg tucked under her. "What was your first car?"

"A 1987 Toyota Camry. I got it right after I graduated." I could still remember the new-car aroma of that Camry. It smelled like money and success to me. "I drove it ten years, until Frannie threatened to have it towed when I wasn't looking."

"What was your next car?"

"Another Camry." I laughed at her look of disbelief. "Hey, when I find something that works for me, I stick with it."

Alice threw her head back and howled. "God, we are a pair!"

We were still laughing when a tapping on the window startled us. I turned to see a black-haired man with a beard and a faded camouflage T-shirt. "You ladies need some help?" he asked.

I glanced in the rearview mirror and saw a battered LTD parked a few hundred yards behind us.

"No, thanks," Alice said. "Someone's on the way."

The man's smile dimmed a little before brightening again. "No need to wait for them when I'm right here."

"No, thank you." Alice's expression was stony. She reached over me to depress the lock but Black Beard was faster. He yanked open the driver's door and grabbed my arm.

I screamed and tried to pull away, but he dragged me to the ground. I fell hard on my knees in the gravel at the side of the highway.

"What do you think you're doing?" Alice shouted. She lunged for him and tried to rake the side of his face with her nails, but he batted her away as if she were a gnat.

"I'm taking this truck, lady," he said as he climbed into the driver's seat. "You can come with me or not. Your choice."

I struggled to my feet and stared into the cab of the truck, a sick feeling of helplessness churning my stomach. My purse with my cell phone inside was still in there with Alice and this wacko. "Get out of the truck, Alice!" I shouted. "Don't go with him."

Alice ignored me. "You idiot! We're stuck here in the first place because we had a tire blow out."

"Who are you calling an idiot?" he demanded.

"Only an *idiot* would try to steal a truck with a flat tire," she said.

"I figure I can go pretty far on the rim."

As if to prove his point, Black Beard put the truck in gear. It started rolling forward. I screamed and trotted alongside. "Alice, get out!" I shouted. "Let him have the damn truck!"

"Everything I own is in this truck!" she shouted back. "I'm not about to let some *idiot* take it from me." Moving faster than I would have thought possible, she reached behind the seat and grabbed the little cooler where we kept our snacks and drinks. She dumped the entire thing—ice, bottles and all—into Black Beard's lap. Then she reached down and took off one of her shoes and started beating him with it.

Black Beard roared and the truck lurched to a stop. I stared, openmouthed, as he bailed out of the driver's seat. Alice came after him, flailing away with her shoe—a pink kitten-heeled sandal I'd privately thought was impractical for travel.

That heel was making its mark now, literally. The would-be thief had a dozen round bruises on his face and arms, and blood ran from the corner or one eye. "Think...you can...take advantage...of a couple...of women...do you...*idiot?*" Each word was emphasized with another blow from the shoe.

Black Beard stopped trying to fight. He curled into a ball and lay in the gravel at the edge of the highway, his arms cradling his head. "Stop it, lady!" he begged. "Are you trying to kill me?"

"It's no better than you deserve!"

I had never seen Alice so angry. She continued to whale on the now-helpless man, until the shoe broke and half of it went flying off into the weeds.

Flashing lights appeared on the horizon and I steeled myself for another encounter with the police. Surely I could hold myself together a little better this time.

But the lights turned out to belong to a wrecker. The driver pulled in front of the truck and a burly older man with a long gray ponytail climbed out. He looked at Black Beard, who still lay curled on the ground. "What's this?" he asked.

"This is the piece of shit who tried to steal our truck." Alice aimed a halfhearted kick at the man on the ground, then turned to face the wrecker driver. "I hope you're here to fix our tire, because I am in no mood to deal with another man who's out to cause trouble."

The wrecker driver looked as if he was biting back a grin. "Yes, ma'am, I'm here to fix your tire. But even if I wasn't, I wouldn't give you any trouble." He looked at the man on the ground. "What do you want to do about him?"

"He can lie there and rot for all I care." With more dignity than I would have thought possible for a woman wearing only one shoe, she turned and limped away.

Alice and I waited in the cab of the wrecker while the

driver changed our tire. Alice stared straight ahead, not saying anything. Her cheeks were flushed and she was still breathing hard.

Movement in the rearview mirror caught my attention. "The idiot is getting up," I said. I watched as he heaved himself to his feet and began hobbling toward his car. "He's leaving."

"Let him go," she said, not even glancing in the mirror. "He'll think twice about messing with a 'helpless' woman again."

"I've never seen you so angry," I said. "I was a little afraid."

Her expression softened and she turned to me. "You didn't have anything to be afraid of," she said. "I would never hurt you."

"I was afraid you were going to kill him," I said.

She nodded. "I might have, if the shoe hadn't broken. Or that other guy hadn't shown up when he did."

"Alice! You don't mean that."

"I was that angry." She looked out the front window again. "Haven't you felt like that before? Just…enraged at everything that was wrong with your life?"

I shook my head. Anger was an unpleasant emotion I shied away from like a skater avoiding thin ice. I secretly feared that once unleashed, I might rage out of control…as Alice had done.

"I'm angry at the cancer, at getting old and at being alone. At the way my life has turned out." She sighed. "He was just the spark that set me off."

"I'm glad you didn't kill him." I shuddered. "You wouldn't want that on your conscience."

"Don't you think you could kill someone if you had to?"

I felt weak, my skin clammy. "No," I whispered.

"I could. To protect myself or someone I love, I could."

I shook my head. "No. Don't even think it." I struggled to get a grip on my emotions. All this talk of death, on top of the scare we'd just had, was too much. My knees hurt from where I'd fallen in the gravel and my heart hurt from the words my friend was saying.

"All set, ladies." The wrecker driver returned and handed Alice a clipboard. "Sign at the bottom and you're good to go." He glanced down the road. "I see your friend left."

"Good riddance." Alice returned the clipboard. "Thanks."

Together, we limped back to the truck and climbed in. "Okay if we make it another early night?" I said.

"Best idea I've heard all day." Alice leaned her head back and closed her eyes. "I need a drink."

"Me, too." A Valium and a boatload of chocolate would be welcome, too, but I'd take whatever I could to numb my emotions for a little while. I knew it would be a long time before the memory of Alice beating the man who lay helpless on the side of the road left me, or the cold sound of her voice talking about killing him stopped echoing in my ears.

9

The next morning I discovered our encounter with Black Beard had shaken Alice more than she'd let on. "Two women traveling alone are a target for every lowlife out there," she said. "We need to take steps to protect ourselves."

I looked up from folding my nightgown. "Steps?" This sounded ominous. "What kind of steps?"

"We should buy a gun." She nodded. "Two guns. One for each of us."

"A gun?" The idea knocked all the wind out of me. I sagged onto the bed. "I don't want anything to do with guns."

"Don't be such a ninny," she said. "Every woman should know how to handle a weapon."

"You were doing pretty well yesterday with nothing more than a kitten heel."

"Only because that guy was stupid. If he'd been after more than the truck, or if he'd had a knife or a gun himself, the two of us might not be sitting here right now."

The thought made me queasy. I hugged my arms across my stomach. "If you'd had a gun yesterday, you probably would have killed the guy. We could both be in jail right now."

"Maybe it wouldn't have gone that far."

In my mind, that was a big "maybe." "Don't you have to have a license to buy a gun?"

She looked smug. "Not in Kansas. We should buy a couple before we go any farther."

"How do you know these things?" I asked.

"Stan bought guns in Kansas." She dragged the open telephone directory closer to her. "I found a gun shop just a couple blocks from here. We should check them out."

"I am not buying a gun," I said.

"Fine. But I want one." She stood and picked up her purse. "Come on. It won't hurt you to learn a little about guns. You might even change your mind."

I doubted it. Guns frightened me and I wasn't afraid to admit it. Anything that could blow a person away with a twitch of the finger was something I wanted to stay far away from.

Alice had no such qualms. Twenty minutes later, she waltzed into the gun shop as if it were a fancy clothing boutique. I followed more slowly, warily eyeing the thick iron bars on the windows and the NRA stickers on the display counter. The glass cases and bright lighting were reminiscent of a jewelry store, but that's where the similarity ended.

A barrel-chested man with a shaved head and a Fu Manchu mustache greeted us with a booming voice. "How can I help you ladies?" he asked.

"I'd like to buy a handgun." Alice plopped her purse onto the counter. "Something easy to carry."

"I'd recommend an intermediate caliber semiautomatic." Mustache Man led us to another glass case. "This Beretta here is a nice ladies' pistol."

My attention drifted as they discussed the merits of various grip styles, finishes and calibers. I wandered over to a third case and studied a collection of brass knuckles, handcuffs and other things I couldn't identify.

"Can I help you, pretty lady?"

I looked up to see a tall man with a blond pompadour grinning at me. He had big white teeth and long sideburns.

If he'd been wearing a powder-blue suit he could have passed for a televangelist.

"Um, no thanks," I said, backing away. "I'm here with my friend." I turned toward Alice in time to see her and Mustache Man disappearing behind a closed door. I frowned.

"Don't worry about her." Blondie came up behind me. "Jake's taking her to the shooting range to try out the piece she picked out."

Right. And left me here with a man who kept leering at me as if he was the Big Bad Wolf and I was Little Red Riding Hood. "Do you like guns?" he asked.

"No." I backed away from him again, but he followed right along. "My friend just wanted one for, um, self-defense," I said.

"We have a lot of great choices for self-defense." He reached up on a shelf and pulled down what looked like a bottle of breath-freshener spray. Maybe this one gave you instant garlic breath for defense against vampires and people you didn't want to kiss.

"This pepper spray can stop an assailant in his tracks from ten feet away," Blondie said. His grin widened. "It works good on bears, too."

"Do you have a problem with bears here in Kansas?" I asked, retreating farther.

He threw back his head and roared with laughter. "Damn, I like a woman with a sense of humor. You're cute."

I'd been called a lot of things in my day, but I hadn't heard the word *cute* applied to me since fifth grade. "Thanks. I think I'll just wait for my friend in the truck."

I darted toward the door, but Blondie intercepted me. "Wait a minute. You haven't seen our other self-defense choices. We've got a nice line of stun guns over here."

He dragged me over to a display on the back wall and took down a wicked-looking black plastic baton. "This baby is small enough to fit in your purse and can send three hundred thousand volts through anybody who tries to mess with you."

"Sounds dangerous." I eyed the weapon.

"Oh, it won't kill anybody." He stuck the gun in my hand. "It'll just make 'em wish they were dead for a while." He roared again. Gun shop humor.

"I'm not interested." I tried to hand it back to him, but he put his hands behind his back. "Aww, come on," he said. "I'd think a cute gal like you would need protection. You probably have men hitting on you all day."

"Only when I visit gun shops."

"There you go again. You are just too funny!"

I glanced toward the door Alice had disappeared through. When was she going to return and rescue me from the Blond Bomber?

I was annoyed at myself for even thinking this. Why should I need someone else to rescue me from an annoying man? It had been bad enough standing by watching yesterday while Alice worked Black Beard over. At least then there really hadn't been anything I could do. Now I was merely acting helpless, when I knew I wasn't.

I turned to Blondie. "Look, I'm not interested."

"In the stun gun or in me?" He leered and leaned closer.

"Both." I laid the weapon on the counter and looked him in the eye. "Leave me alone."

"Aww, don't be like that, darlin'. I can be real nice once you get to know me. Maybe the two of us could go out later and I can prove it to you."

I shook my head. "I don't think so."

He took my hand in his. "Then think again. You and I could have a great time together, I just know it."

"Are you deaf?" I pulled my hand away and glared at him. "I said I wasn't interested."

"I just want the chance to change your mind." He reached for my hand again and something in me snapped.

When Alice and Mustache Man returned a few minutes later, Blondie was rolling around in the middle of the floor, groaning. "What happened to him?" Alice asked.

"He got fresh and I kneed him in the nuts." I hitched my purse higher on my shoulder. "Are you about ready to leave?"

"Sure. Just let me pay for this."

I waited by the door while Alice completed her transaction. Blondie still lay on the floor, hands between his legs. He'd stopped moaning, but he didn't look inclined to get up anytime soon. At last Alice joined me. "All set?" I asked.

"All set." She glanced back at Blondie. "I guess you don't need a weapon to defend yourself," she said.

"He was annoying me." I shoved away the guilt that tried to creep in. Yes, I'd hurt the man, but he'd deserved it.

"Good for you." Alice grinned at me. "You should get that angry more often."

"What makes you say that?" I climbed up in the cab of the truck and waited while she stowed her purse, the gun inside, on the floorboard next to me.

"Women don't get angry enough," she said. "We're taught to hold everything inside. We let people get away with mistreating us because we want to be thought of as 'nice.' Then one day, Boom! We explode."

I remembered her explosion yesterday and nodded. "All the more reason not to carry a weapon. I'd like to limit the damage."

"I don't intend to hurt anyone." Alice started the truck. "But I'm not going to let them hurt me, either."

"If only there was a weapon that could truly protect us from all hurts," I said. After all, the worst wounds I'd suffered hadn't been from physical blows. Words could cause more pain than fists, and as far as I knew, there was no foolproof protection against the things people could say to you.

The rest of Kansas passed by in a blur of fast-food restaurants, dusty small towns and cheap motels. The only highlights were my conversations with Martin. We'd been talking a couple of times every day. He'd call to ask if I thought he should use alstroemeria or dianthus in a bridal shower arrangement, or if I thought Mylar balloons at sixty cents each wholesale was a good price.

I chose alstroemeria, since it lasts longer, and said I thought that was a good price for the balloons.

We talked about more serious things, too, things that made me nervous, though I tried not to let my uneasiness show in my voice.

"I was married before," he said once, causing me to almost drop the phone. Not that this should have been such a surprise. He was forty-one—a lot of forty-one-year-old men had been married before—but just as I'd avoided dwelling on the future, I hadn't given any thought to his past.

"What was she like?" I asked. *Was she anything like me?*

"She was a good woman, but we weren't right for each other," he said. "We parted amicably."

I thought that said a lot for a man, that he got along even with his ex. "I've never been married," I said. Would he think I was some kind of freak for saying that?

"It can be hard to find the right person," he said.

I wanted to kiss him just for saying those words. All right, I wanted to kiss him anyway. I had since the moment we met. His acceptance was making me braver. "I used to be fat," I said. I held my breath, waiting for his answer.

I don't know what I expected—that he'd gasp in horror or be disgusted by the idea. "You're not fat now," he said.

"I was really fat," I said. "I weighed a hundred pounds more than I do now."

"That's amazing," he said. "Congratulations. It must have taken a lot of hard work to lose that weight."

"It was tough," I admitted.

"If you can do that, you can do anything."

"That's me." I laughed. "Superwoman. This mild-mannered persona costume is just a disguise."

"You have a sense of humor, too. I like that."

The same thing Blondie in the gun shop had used, but coming from Martin, it sounded much nicer. "You're good for my ego," I said. "I'm not used to all these compliments."

"Stick with me and I promise you'll get used to them."

The idea made me uneasy. Not that I didn't want to see him again, but I didn't trust my own feelings when it came to men. "How can you say that when we've never even had a real date?" I asked.

"I feel as if I've known you for years," he said. "And I want the chance to get to know you so much better."

I swallowed hard, fighting a fear I couldn't begin to explain. "You might not like me so much if you learned all my secrets," I said, trying for a teasing tone, though it was hard to talk around the tightness in my throat.

"None of us are perfect," he said. "I'll forgive your flaws if you forgive mine."

"You have flaws?" Probably nothing I'd count a real flaw. Martin seemed perfect, out of reach even.

After the fiasco with Marc, I'd imagined myself working my way up to serious dating in baby steps. Maybe coffee with someone I met online, then a blind date arranged by friends. The guys would be completely average. Nothing threatening.

Instead, I'd skipped way over average to superior. It felt exhilarating and magical.

And more than a little scary.

★ ★ ★

We left Kansas and entered eastern Colorado, but we were still a long way from California, a fact Frannie complained about whenever I called to check in.

"Are you angry with me about something?" she asked one morning two days after our encounter with Black Beard. "If you are, you should just say so instead of trying to punish me by staying away like this."

"I'm not trying to punish you," I said. "That's ridiculous."

Frannie refused to let go of the idea. "Are you upset because I objected to your going to the reunion in the first place?"

"You didn't stop me from going, so why should it matter?" Was I angry with Frannie? Maybe a little. Her desire to control every aspect of my life grated more than I cared to admit.

"I wish I *had* stopped you," she said. "Then you wouldn't be off on this crazy trip instead of home where you belong."

"Why do you say I belong there? It's not as if I have a husband or children waiting for me."

"You have me. I'm your family. Isn't that enough?"

No, it wasn't enough. It hadn't been enough for a long time. I'd tried to fill the void with food, but now even that crutch was gone. Still, I didn't know how to confess this to Frannie.

"Isn't that enough?" she repeated. Her voice shook, and I realized with a start that she sounded afraid. Frannie, who was always so sure of herself, so decisive and strong. What did she have to be afraid of? That something bad might happen to me?

Or that she might lose her hold on me?

"I'll always be your sister," I said. "Whether I'm right next door to you or all the way across the country doesn't change that."

"As long as you remember that." She sniffed. "You *will* be home soon, won't you?"

"Soon," I promised.

When I hung up the phone, Alice, who was driving today, gave me a sympathetic look. "Big sis misses you," she said.

"It's more than that." I shook my head. "I don't think I realized before how much Frannie needs me. I always thought of her as the strong one.

"She always made a point of telling me how much I needed *her,*" I said. "Reminding me of how she looked after me when we were little and after we came to California. But maybe it's been the other way around all along." The idea made me uncomfortable, like too-tight shoes.

"Maybe it started when you lost all that weight," Alice said. "I mean, that was something you did on your own, without her help. Maybe that was the first time she realized that she wasn't indispensable."

I shifted, trying to find a more comfortable position. "I don't think loving someone should have anything to do with whether you *need* them or not."

"For some people, maybe it does."

I didn't want Frannie to be one of those people. I had enough trouble dealing with my own neuroses without being burdened with my sister's.

I turned my attention back to the highway, immediately distracted by movement at the side of the road. "What's that?" I pointed ahead.

Alice hunched forward, squinting toward the brown blob on the shoulder. "I think it's a dog." She slammed on the brakes, sending me lurching into the dashboard, my seat belt biting into my shoulder. By the time I'd recovered, Alice was out of the car and running toward the dog.

When she was a few yards away, she crouched down, one hand extended. I watched the muddy brown animal amble toward her. Then it was in her arms and she was hurrying back to the truck.

"What are you doing?" I cried when she jerked the door open.

"It's just a puppy." She dumped the wet, wiggling bundle into my lap. "Some son of a bitch must have dumped it out here. If I knew who it was, I'd string him up by his balls. Leaving a baby out here to die on the side of the highway... some people don't deserve to live."

She threw the truck into gear and we shot out onto the highway. The pup yelped and dug his claws into my thighs as it struggled to hang on. "Alice, what are we going to do with it?" I pressed back against the seat, trying to avoid touching the dirty, smelly beast.

"I thought maybe you could keep it," she said. "Didn't you say you didn't have any pets?"

"I don't want any pets!"

"Oh, but you'll love having a dog. They're wonderful."

"Then why don't you take him?" I didn't see any need to add that she was the one who'd stopped and picked up the pup.

"The apartment I rented in Ojai doesn't allow pets. And you've got that nice, empty condo that would be perfect."

"I don't want a dog," I said again.

About that time I made the mistake of looking at our little hitchhiker again. In the midst of all that mud and matted hair, a pair of butterscotch brown eyes stared up at me, filled with limpid longing. I sensed a tug of recognition in those eyes, the pull of knowing that I'd felt what that dog was feeling now. It had been a while, but at one time that mixture of hope and fear had been as familiar to me as my own reflection in the bathroom mirror.

"We'd better go ahead and find someplace to stop for the night," Alice said. "We need to get her cleaned up and get some food into her."

"Her? You know it's a girl?" Frankly, I had a hard time identifying the creature in my lap as a dog.

"I checked. She's part cocker spaniel, I think. Maybe with a little poodle thrown in."

"Are you sure you didn't smoke another joint while I was in the restroom?" I asked. "Maybe that would explain these hallucinations you're having that this beast could be in any way related to a recognizable breed."

"You'll see when we get her cleaned up. You're going to fall in love with her."

No, I wasn't. As far as I was concerned, love was a voluntary emotion, one I had no intention of volunteering for a stray dog.

Alice named the dog Cocoa, because of the color of her fur. Why did I care what name she gave the dog? Despite her assumptions otherwise, I wasn't going to keep the pup.

After a stop for puppy food and supplies, we checked into a Super 8 outside of Burlington, Colorado, and Alice used most of a bottle of balsam conditioning shampoo to wash the mud and stench out of the pup.

When she was done, I studied the results. "Are you sure you didn't pick up an overgrown rat?" I asked, eyeing the thin, shivering figure huddled in the motel room sink.

"You'll hurt her feelings!" She cupped her hands over the animal's drooping, dripping ears. "You wait and see. She's going to be beautiful."

She shut the door to the bathroom in my face. I lay down on the floor and began doing sit-ups. I was up to sixty-three when the door opened and Alice emerged carrying a honey-brown ball of fluff, a pink bow at her throat.

"Here we are," Alice announced. "Isn't she precious?" She deposited the animal in my lap. I stared in wonder at what looked more like a child's stuffed toy than a real dog. Two solemn eyes stared back up at me. All the resolve I'd been marshaling for the last hour dissolved and I burst into tears.

"Ellen, what is it? What's wrong?" Alice knelt beside me, one arm around my shoulder, the other cradling the dog. "Please tell me so I can help."

I shook my head, feeling ridiculous for the umpteenth time that day. "She's so beautiful," I sobbed. "How c-could someone e-ever throw away something so s-s-sweet."

"Oh, honey, I know." Alice hugged me tighter. "There are some real bastards in this world, aren't there?"

We sniffed and sobbed together for a few minutes, until a high-pitched yip from Cocoa reminded us that she'd been neglected enough, thank you very much.

We spent the rest of the afternoon into the evening watching Cocoa devour most of a can of gourmet puppy food, then playing endless games of fetch with a soft ball Alice had bought along with the food.

When Cocoa finally curled up next to Alice on her bed, I was as exhausted as the pup looked. I fell asleep almost immediately, praying for a less eventful day to come.

"Ellen. Ellen honey, wake up."

I heard sobbing, then realized the awful, wrenching cries were coming from my own constricted throat. I struggled to break free of the paralyzing stupor of sleep, my throat sore from crying, my eyes burning with tears.

"It's okay, Ellen. I'm right here. You're okay." Alice's voice was soothing, her arms around me reassuring. Maternal. I managed to sit up, still gulping back sobs, shaken by an awful sadness whose cause I couldn't name.

Alice switched on the light between our beds and I blinked in the sudden brightness. Cocoa sat between us at the end of the bed, her eyes wide and frightened.

"It's okay, Cocoa," I said, leaning over to scratch behind her ears. "I was just being silly."

"I don't think there was anything silly about it," Alice said. She pulled the dog into her lap and smoothed her hand down its back. "It sounded like a horrible nightmare. Do you want to talk about it?"

At her words the mental door I'd slammed shut opened and the memory of the dream rushed in. I swallowed hard against a fresh wave of tears and shook my head.

"It might help," Alice said gently. "You know anything you tell me will never go any further."

I stared at Cocoa, her soft fur haloed by the lamplight. My stomach churned with an old fear. Would telling Alice make me less afraid? "I don't know if I can tell you," I whispered. "I've never told anyone."

Her hand squeezed mine and held on. "Then maybe it's time you did."

10

Some memories are like heirlooms, tucked carefully away and taken out to be admired only on special occasions. Others are hidden in dark corners, never to be considered, like bloody clothes locked in a trunk in some distant corner of the attic.

And then one day, perhaps while moving, you find the trunk and the clothes and the awfulness of a particular moment overwhelms you. You want to stuff everything back into the trunk and never look at it again.

But maybe Alice was right. Maybe the thing to do was to air out the clothes and throw them away.

"I dreamed I was a little girl again," I said. "I was about eleven, I guess. Brian Garrity's dog had puppies."

"I remember the Garritys' dog," Alice said. "A golden retriever, right?"

I nodded. "The neighbor's mutt dug under the fence and mated with her, so the puppies were mutts. Brian said I could have one. I was so excited—I wanted one so badly." A new wave of tears overflowed. I didn't bother to wipe them away.

"Your dad..." Alice's voice trailed away. She cleared her throat and tried again. "Was he mad when you brought the dog home?"

I nodded. "But I promised to look after it. To make sure it didn't give him any trouble."

Her hand squeezed tighter. "What happened?"

"I named her Goldie. We had her three days."

I squeezed my arms across my chest, rocking back and forth against the pain. Alice waited, her hand stroking Cocoa's soft fur over and over again. The pup closed her eyes and went to sleep.

I took another deep breath, determined to get through this. "On the fourth day, she peed in his house slippers. I begged him not to be mad at her. I promised to use my allowance to buy him a new pair of slippers, but he wouldn't listen."

The words came in a rush now, awful and so real, like the dream I had just had. I was eleven again, on my knees before my father, my face buried in the soft fur of the pup's neck.

My father loomed over us, his face all hard lines and gray shadows. He tore the dog from me and dragged us both into the backyard. I could hear Frannie yelling, was dimly aware of my mother standing in the doorway, holding Frannie back.

I screamed and crawled toward my father and the dog. He never once looked at me. The gun went off and I choked on my sobs, blacking out and falling on my face in the dirt.

It was Frannie who brought me to, Frannie who took me inside and washed my face, who gave me half of one of mother's tranquilizers and sat by my bed, holding my hand until I fell asleep.

Later, Frannie showed me the grave she had dug, in a secluded corner of our side yard where our parents never went. She'd planted flowers all around it, and told me she'd said a prayer, so she was sure Goldie was in heaven.

Then, eyes burning with a passion I'd never seen in her before, she told me she was just as sure that one day our father would go to hell for what he'd done.

Even now it bothered me how much comfort I'd found in those words.

"I knew your father wasn't a nice man," Alice said after I'd told her everything, "but I never knew how awful he was. It's a wonder you survived to be so normal."

I would have laughed if I had had any emotion left in me. "How normal is it when you're afraid to get too attached to anything?" I said. "Frannie and I learned to hide our affection for anything. It didn't matter if it was a toy or a dress or a person. He'd find a way to take them from us. When Frannie was seventeen, Walt Peebles invited her to the senior prom. She saved the money she made working at Weisman's and bought the most beautiful dress to wear. Then she hid it under her mattress so Father wouldn't find it."

"And did he find it?"

I nodded. "Then he stood over her and made her cut it up with a pair of sewing scissors. She was devastated." The Frannie in those days had been a different girl, dark and despairing. "She told Walt she couldn't go with him to the prom, but she didn't tell him why. I think he guessed some of it, though. He showed up the night of the prom with a new dress he bought for her, and insisted on taking her." I smiled at the memory. "I thought it was the most romantic thing a man had ever done."

"He was a nice boy, and I think he grew up to be a good man. Too bad Frannie didn't stay to see how it would have all turned out."

"It was probably better that we left."

"I guess I can understand wanting to get away from the bad memories." Alice glanced at me. "I always had a feeling something wasn't quite right at your house. I was half-afraid of your father myself. Not that he ever said two words to me—there was just something about him."

"Yes, there was something about him." A kind of menace scarcely hidden by a calm exterior.

"Did he...did he beat you? Or anything else?"

I shook my head. "He never laid a hand on us. He didn't have to." I sighed. "Awful as a beating would have been, I think I could have gotten over that easier than the other punishments." I plucked at the bedspread, determined now that I had started to empty everything out. "If one of us spilled milk, we had to scrub the whole house on our hands and knees. Or if he didn't like something we said, or the way we looked at him, he'd lock us in the tool shed overnight." I shivered, remembering. "It was so cold out there sometimes, and there wasn't a thing to wrap up in. Frannie sneaked some blankets out there once and hid them, but he found them and burned them."

"What did your mother do while all this was going on?"

"Nothing. Nothing at all." Mother never said a word in our defense. When my father flew into one of his rages, she'd retreat to the bedroom, often locking the door behind her. I suspected she drank. I had memories of whole weeks when she never got out of bed. "Her way of coping was to pretend we didn't exist. Sometimes I blamed her even more than I blamed my father. A mother should be there for her children, you know?"

Alice's quickly indrawn breath made a short, sharp sound. She gripped my wrist and squeezed. "I'm sorry. I wish I could have done something."

"You were my friend. That was something. I could spend the night at your house and pretend my life was like anybody else's."

"You're okay now, right?" She studied my face as if searching for some sign of craziness.

I nodded. "I guess. I mean, it's part of who I am. I think it's probably why I struggled with overeating for so many years."

"It was because of what happened when you were a child?"

I nodded. "Being fat was a way of insulating myself from that kind of hurt again. It gave me an excuse not to get close to people."

"And now that you aren't fat anymore?"

I took another deep breath. "It's scary sometimes. I feel vulnerable. But I'm doing okay so far." I rubbed Cocoa behind the ears. "This trip is a good start."

Alice stifled a yawn. "Sorry." She squinted at the clock, which showed 2:33 a.m. "I haven't been up at this hour since my wild partying days."

"I should have known you were a party girl."

She gave me a sleepy grin. "I guess I still am, when the mood strikes." She stretched her arms over her head and arched her back. "But I need my beauty sleep."

"You can go back to bed. I'm fine now." I slid under the covers, careful not to disturb the dog. "Thanks for listening."

"Hey, anytime." She switched off the lamp and crawled into her own bed. "Sweet dreams," she murmured.

"You, too." All my dreams should be sweet ones, I thought. I'd had enough nightmares to last a lifetime.

I woke early the next morning with Cocoa curled against my stomach, her soft, warm body like a poultice on the hurt place in my heart. I stroked her silken fur and she yawned and turned belly up, revealing pink, freckled skin.

Alice was still sleeping, so I slipped into sweats, clipped the leash we'd bought yesterday on Cocoa's new collar and took her out for a walk.

The sky was the color of pewter, streaked with salmon. In the cool stillness even the drab motel parking lot seemed fresh and serene. A few early risers were packing their cars to leave.

I had an overwhelming urge to talk to Frannie. It was early in California, barely 6:00 a.m., but Frannie was an early riser, and surely she wouldn't mind if I woke her.

While Cocoa entertained herself sniffing around the Dumpster, I pulled out my cell phone and punched in Frannie's number.

She answered on the third ring, not sounding at all tired. "Hey," I said. "I hope I didn't wake you."

"No, I'm up. Where are you?"

"Burlington, Colorado," I said.

"What's that like?"

"Not much to see," I answered. "We'll be in the mountains later today. I should be able to find some great postcards for you there."

"I can't believe you've been traveling all this time and you're only to Colorado."

"We're taking our time," I said. "Making a vacation of it." I hurried to block any more lectures about how I needed to be in California. "Guess what I got?"

"Nothing contagious, I hope," she said drily.

"No, silly. I got a dog."

Silence on the other end of the line. I guessed she was shocked. "You don't even like dogs," she said after a while.

"I never said I didn't like dogs. I just never wanted one before."

"You won't have anything to do with my dogs."

I rolled my eyes. Frannie's standard poodles, Midge and Pidge, were devoted to her and her alone. "Your dogs don't want anything to do with *me*," I said.

"They would if you'd give them a chance."

Another old argument not worth repeating. "Don't you want to hear about my new dog?"

"What kind is it?"

"It's a cocker spaniel—poodle mix." I had no idea if this

was true or not, but until someone proved different, I'd take Alice's word for it. "We named her Cocoa."

"We?"

"Well, Alice named her. We found her on the side of the road. Someone had abandoned her. Can you believe that?"

"I can't believe you collected some stray off the side of the road. She probably has fleas and no telling what else."

"She does not have fleas. We gave her a bath and as soon as we get home I'll take her to the vet for her shots." I took a deep breath, trying to calm down. "She's beautiful. I know you'll love her."

"I still can't believe you, of all people, would get a dog."

"I've always loved dogs," I said. "I was just afraid to let myself fall for another one, after what happened with Goldie."

More silence on the line.

"You remember Goldie, don't you?" I prompted.

"I don't want to talk about that. Ever." Her voice was hard. Cold.

"Maybe we *should* talk about some of the things that happened when we were little," I said gently. "The bad things. It might help."

"You can't change the past. I see no point in revisiting it."

"But sometimes you can change how you look at the past, or how you let it affect you," I argued. "Last night I told Alice about Goldie. Just telling her the story made it not hurt as much. It drove home the fact that what happened wasn't my fault." I swallowed fresh tears at the memory. Before last night, I don't think I'd ever let myself believe—*really* believe—that the bad things my father had done hadn't been at least partly my fault.

"You had no business talking to Alice about that!" Frannie's rage took me by surprise.

"I had a dream…about Goldie," I stammered. "Alice woke up and asked me what was wrong. That's all."

"What else have you told her?" Frannie demanded.

"Nothing," I said. "Nothing important." I'd told her quite a lot actually about our father. I'd told her about Frannie's prom dress, which I knew would upset my sister even more if she found out.

"We agreed a long time ago that we wouldn't talk about certain things…to *anyone*."

"You *told* me I couldn't talk to anyone and I agreed." Even when I'd seen a therapist for my problems with food, I'd never told her everything about my father and the things he'd done. "But I don't think that's best anymore. I think there are things I *need* to talk about." How much better off would I be now if I hadn't kept silent all these years?

"You had no right," Frannie said.

"I didn't do it to hurt you," I said. "And Alice is my friend. She won't tell anyone else. I didn't tell her everything," I said. There were some things I couldn't bring myself to say. Things I wasn't sure I could ever let out in the open.

"Make sure you don't," Frannie said, sounding somewhat mollified.

"It will be fine," I reassured her. "I just wanted to call and tell you about Cocoa."

"I'll make an appointment with my vet and my groomer for you," she said. "They'll take good care of her. And you'll need to have her spayed as soon as possible."

Part of me resented her making these decisions for me, but I knew this was Frannie's way of making peace. She couldn't express her feelings with words, so she showed them by "taking care" of me. "We'll talk about it when I get home," I said. "Thanks."

I tucked the phone away and Cocoa and I did another turn around the edges of the lot. There was more activity now—

people going in and out of the office, big rigs warming up, extra traffic on the highway out front.

When we got back to the room, Alice walked out to meet me with a cup of coffee. "How are you feeling this morning?" she asked.

"Better." I looked down at Cocoa, who was sniffing the corner of a planter, her tail sweeping back and forth like a metronome. "The dog was a good idea. I'm glad you talked me into keeping her."

"No problem. I'm good at solving everyone's problems but my own."

The bitterness in her voice surprised me. "Is something wrong?" I asked.

She shook her head. "Just woke up on the wrong side of the bed. I'll be fine once I've had breakfast and we're on the road again."

I sometimes forgot that the whole purpose of this trip was to move Alice to a new home. "I bet you're anxious to get to California and be settled," I said.

"Not really." She drained her cup and tossed it into a trash can. "But I suppose I have to get there eventually, so we might as well get going."

I drove most of the day. Alice slumped against the passenger window, quieter than usual. I didn't know what to do, so I kept quiet. The way I see it, everyone's entitled to a bad mood now and then. Eventually it would pass and Alice would be back to her lively self.

When we pulled into Grand Junction, Colorado, that evening, she said, "I can't face sitting around a hotel room one more evening. Let's go out somewhere."

"What about Cocoa?" I looked at the pup, who had proved to be a good traveler. She'd spent the day alternately napping on the bench seat between us and sitting up gazing intently out the windshield.

"We'll put her in the bathroom with a blanket and a

bowl of food and she'll be fine. She'll probably go right to sleep."

Which is what I felt like doing after the rough night I'd had previously. But I wanted to help Alice the way she'd helped me. If going out would cheer her up, then I was all for it.

We set out on foot from the motel, down what looked to be the main drag of the town. "Where are we going?" I asked as we crossed the street.

"We're out West, right?"

"Right."

"Then let's find some cowboys." She nodded toward a neon sign a half block away. Next to a well-lit, oversize cowboy boot were the words *The Silver Spur.*

Despite the bright lights outside, The Silver Spur was a dim paneled room with a mirror-backed bar along one wall and pool tables at the rear. Country music from the jukebox competed with the laughter from the pool players. Everyone I saw was dressed alike, regardless of their sex—colorful shirts, jeans, boots and cowboy hats.

I felt as out of place as a dandelion in a wedding bouquet. As we walked in, at least a dozen Stetson-covered heads swiveled in our direction. I watched, amazed, as Alice turned up the wattage on her smile, exaggerated the sway of her hips and developed a drawl I'd never heard before. "Howdy, fellas," she said. "Anybody care to buy a couple of new gals in town a drink?"

The shuffle of booted feet on the hardwood floor was so loud I shrank back, half-afraid they were all going to run over us on their way out the door. I don't know why I was worried, though. Within seconds we were seated at a large round table, with a pitcher of beer and a quartet of admirers. None of them were movie-star handsome, but they made up for any physical shortcomings with an avid appreciation that was enough to make me more light-headed than a whole pitcher of beer.

I couldn't get over the transformation in Alice. The woman who had sat silently in the truck all day was now positively effervescent. She laughed and flirted, eyes sparkling and cheeks flushed in a way that made her seem ten years younger.

The four men ranged in age from late twenties to closing in on fifty. They had the weathered skin and calloused hands of men who spend a lot of time outdoors, though for all I knew they coached football or ran landscaping businesses rather than working on ranches. Not that that mattered to me. They were clean and nice-looking and decidedly masculine.

One in particular, a rangy, dark-haired man named Tom, paid particular attention to Alice. He had a wide smile and a hint of gray at his temples and a charming manner that made him easy to be around. Alice turned toward him and kept her eyes locked to his, reaching out every so often to touch his arm or his hand.

After a while, two others gave up and drifted away, while the fourth man turned his attention to me. His name was Gary, and he was the oldest of the group, with kind blue eyes and a large white hat I suspected covered a balding head. He talked about his job as a county road supervisor and asked me about the floral business. From there we moved on to the weather and baseball. The conversation flowed smoothly, but it was clear neither one of us was strongly attracted to the other. I got the sense Gary was playing wingman—keeping me occupied while Alice and Tom got to know each other better.

And they were definitely getting to know each other. By nine o'clock they'd progressed from occasional hand touches to clinging to each other on the bar's tiny dance floor. When the song ended, they exchanged a long, passionate kiss that had me looking away in embarrassment.

When they returned to the table, I stood. "It's getting late. I think I'd better call it a night," I said.

"So soon?" Gary said, without much enthusiasm.

I smiled at him. "Thanks for the drinks. It's been great talking to you."

"You don't have to run off now," Tom said. He was holding Alice's hand as if to keep her from fleeing, as well.

"I need to use the little girl's room," Alice announced. She slipped out of Tom's grasp and grabbed my arm. "You come with me."

When we were alone behind the doors of the ladies' room, Alice released me. "Will you be okay walking back to the motel by yourself?" she asked.

"I guess so." I frowned at her. "What are you going to do?"

She studied her reflection in the mirror, then pulled out a lipstick and began carefully applying it. "Tom and I are going to get a room, so you can have ours to yourself tonight."

I stared at her. "You can't be serious. I mean…you just met the man. You don't know anything about him."

"I know I think he's sexy, and he makes me feel sexy." She glanced at me. "I told him about the mastectomy. He says he doesn't care."

I think I was as shocked that she'd told a stranger about her cancer as I was that she'd have sex with a man she barely knew. "Are you sure?" I asked.

She nodded and fluffed her hair with her fingers. "Gary really likes you, you know. He probably wouldn't say no if you invited him back to our room."

"I couldn't do that!" The idea made me feel shaky.

"Why not?" She turned to face me, hands on her hips. "It's just sex. It doesn't always have to mean something."

"Maybe to me it does."

The look she gave me made me feel small. "Maybe that's

why you're alone. I don't feel like being alone tonight." She pushed past me out of the ladies' room.

I slumped against the sink, fighting a sense of...I don't know...betrayal? It wasn't as if Alice owed me anything. She was a grown woman, free to do whatever she wanted. She wasn't even kicking me out of our room.

Was I making too big a thing of this? After all, this was the twenty-first century. Women could be as free with their sexuality as men. If I asked Gary back to my room, would that make me a more fulfilled, liberated woman?

I shook my head. No. I wasn't like Alice. I'd spent so many years longing for real intimacy with a man, unable to break out of my shell enough to find it. Now that that protective shield I'd built was cracking, I wasn't willing to settle for less than my dreams of real love.

Maybe that made me foolish; I didn't care.

I washed my hands, brushed my hair, then squared my shoulders and left the ladies' room.

I was surprised to find Gary waiting outside the door. "Can I walk you back to your motel?" he asked.

"Oh. I...well, I'm really pretty tired," I stammered.

"I know. It's okay. But you shouldn't walk by yourself this time of night."

His concern touched me. "Thanks. I...I'd appreciate that."

We didn't say anything on the walk back. True to his word, he left me at the door to my room with a tip of his hat. I couldn't help but wonder if we'd met under different circumstances if things would have ended differently.

Inside the room, Cocoa greeted me with gratifying enthusiasm. She ran in circles around the room, leaping on the beds and skidding to a halt in front of me, her entire body wagging. I dropped to the carpet and rubbed her belly. After a moment, she grew still and fell into a half doze. I smiled, a contentment I recognized as love filling me.

Love for a furry puppy. Not much by some standards, but I considered it a good start.

I thought about Alice and what she might be doing right now. What *I* could be doing if I'd invited Gary in. That led to thoughts of Martin. I checked the clock. It was after ten in Kansas. Late, but I hoped not too late.

He answered on the fourth ring. "I hope I didn't wake you," I said.

"No, I was watching the news." The voices behind him silenced. He must have shut off the TV. "Is everything okay there?" he asked.

"Fine. Why do you ask?"

"You sound a little sad."

I was amazed he'd picked up on that. "Yeah, well..." I combed my fingers through Cocoa's hair. "I'm a little down, I guess."

"Want to talk about it?"

"Not really." I wasn't ready yet to tell Martin about my father or my screwed-up childhood. I didn't trust him to see that side of me just yet; I settled for a simpler truth. "I just wanted to hear your voice."

"I'm happy to oblige. Where are you?"

"Grand Junction, Colorado. I'm at the hotel. With a dog Alice and I picked up on the side of the road."

"That's kind of you. Where's Alice?"

"We went to a bar and she picked up some cowboy and went home with him. Or somewhere."

"Ah."

"What does that mean? Ah?"

"Are you ticked off that she abandoned you or jealous that she's with someone and you're not?"

The directness of the question caught me off guard. "I'm not jealous," I said. "I'm not interested in sex with a stranger."

"I didn't mean it that way," he said. "I never thought you

were the kind of girl who would give her affections easily. And I mean that as a compliment."

"Sometimes I wish I did find it easier to be comfortable with people," I confessed.

"You're comfortable with me, aren't you?"

"Yes." As comfortable as I was with anyone, but there was still so much of me holding back. "Tell me what you did today," I said. "What arrangements you put together." Talking about flowers was safe and familiar, not too personal.

"A dozen pink roses for a new mom and a potted fern for a man who fell off a roof and broke his leg."

"Did you get the white roses you ordered for the wedding this weekend?" I asked.

"Yes. Thanks for giving me that source. The bride thinks I'm a miracle worker now."

He was working minor miracles with me, making me feel so much better about life and myself. "You'll have to send me pictures of some of your arrangements. I bet they're beautiful."

"I'll do that. When do you think you'll be in California?"

"I don't know. A few days. I'll probably stay with Alice a little while to help her get settled. I'm worried about her."

"What do you mean?"

"She seems...depressed. Tired. Not well."

"Traveling can be tiring, and she's probably anxious to get to California and her new home."

"I suppose." I felt there was something more going on, something related to her first husband and the forgiveness she'd said she was seeking. But I couldn't tell Martin that without betraying Alice's confidence. "I'd better let you go. It's late."

"You'll feel better when you're home again, too," he said.

"I hope so." But I was less sure. After the freedom of

the open road, I wondered if my little condo wouldn't feel stifling—if my whole life wouldn't feel too confining now that I'd stretched the boundaries of my world, met new people and tried new things.

11

I woke early the next morning to the rattle of Alice's key in the lock. I rolled over and stared at her through bleary eyes. "You okay?" I mumbled.

"Of course I'm okay. I'm great. Go back to sleep."

So I did, only to open my eyes an hour later, wide-awake. Alice was a lump in the other bed, the faint rise and fall of the covers assuring me she was alive. I dressed quietly and took Cocoa out for her morning walk.

As I passed the rows of pickup trucks and cars nudged up to the curb in front of the rooms, I wondered if one of them belonged to Tom. Or maybe he'd already left. Maybe that was why Alice had returned to our room so early.

When I got back to the room, Alice was in the shower. I fed Cocoa, then began to pack.

Alice emerged from the bathroom wrapped in a towel, another coiled, turbanlike, around her hair. "I'll be ready in just a minute," she said.

"No hurry." I had a million questions I wanted to ask her, but felt I didn't really have a right to the answers. So I pressed my lips tightly together and hoped she'd volunteer some details about her evening with Tom. Something to help me understand how she'd been able to be so intimate with a man who was a stranger. Was it experience or sophistication or some other quality I lacked that had made last night possible for her?

Instead, I made small talk, something I don't think I'm particularly good at. "Why is it after only a single night in a hotel room, I end up with my stuff scattered all over?" I asked as I collected a pair of socks from a chair.

"Maybe you're marking your territory." Alice tossed aside the towel and began to dress, her back to me.

"You mean like a dog?" I shook my head. "Why would I do that?"

"Not like a dog. More like, I don't know—maybe those explorers who planted a flag and declared this land belonged to their king. You're staking a claim." She turned and watched me stuff a pair of sweatpants into my suitcase.

"What's that?" she asked.

"What's what?"

"That." She came over and pointed into my suitcase. "It looks like a stuffed animal."

My face burned and I quickly flipped the leg of the sweatpants across the top of the suitcase. "Oh, it's nothing."

"It's not nothing. It's a lamb." She reached over and plucked the somewhat dingy stuffed toy from the middle of the suitcase. She studied the lamb, then fixed her gaze on me. "I know there's a story here."

I snatched the lamb from her and clutched it to my chest, my fingers digging into the familiar knotted wool covering. "It's a lamb I had as a baby," I said.

"I can see that. But why do you have it now?"

I searched for some glib remark to explain why a grown woman would have an infant's stuffed toy in her suitcase, but found none. I opened my hands and looked down at the lamb. One felt eye looked up at me. "My father gave it to me," I said.

Alice was silent for a moment. When I raised my head I saw she was watching me, her eyes glittering with unshed tears. "I don't understand why you'd want to keep it," she said softly.

I shrugged and carefully nestled the lamb among my clothes. "He gave it to me when I was a baby. I've always had it." When I was growing up, I kept it hidden in our bedroom dresser so he wouldn't find it and destroy it, the way he had destroyed so much that meant anything to me. "I guess...I guess I keep it to remind me that he did care about me. Once upon a time." My own childhood fairy tale. The one without the happy ending.

Alice put her arm around me and neither of us said anything for a long time. Then she returned to the bathroom to put on her makeup. I closed the suitcase and zipped it, shutting the door once more on memories of my father and my own peculiar way of holding on to him.

We were loading the cab of the truck to leave when Tom came out of the motel office and crossed in front of us on the way to his truck. He never even looked up, though Alice stared through the windshield at him, a hopeful expression on her face. All my misgivings about everything that had happened the night before came rushing back, but I could think of nothing to say and Alice volunteered nothing.

The silence between us grew more strained with each passing mile. Alice was driving, and I stared out the window, searching for words to break the ice, my stomach a twisted lump in my middle.

Finally she slammed her hand against the steering wheel and said, "There's nothing wrong with taking pleasure where you find it."

I stared at her, stunned and relieved by her outburst. "I never said there was."

"But you were thinking it. You'd never pick up a man in a bar and take him back to a hotel, would you?"

"No. But then I don't have the kind of confidence you do. I haven't had a lot of experience with men."

"Ha! You think I spent the night with Tom because I'm confident?"

I frowned. "Didn't you?"

She shook her head, then stared out the windshield for a long moment, biting her lip. She blew out a breath and straightened her arms, pressing back against the seat. "Have you dated much?" she asked.

"Not much." I shifted. I could count on one hand the number of actual dates I'd had in my life. I told myself it was because no one wanted to date a fat girl, but then again, I'd never given anyone a chance, my attitude as much as my bulk keeping other people at a distance. I sighed. "Hardly at all, actually."

"Well, I dated a lot. After Travis left I told myself I didn't need him, that there were plenty of men out there who were better-looking or had more money, and who would really appreciate me." She glanced at me. "But I think what I was really trying to do was prove to myself that a man could still want me."

"Of course they wanted you," I said. "You're pretty and fun to be with. You were always popular in school."

"Yeah, well, the older you get, the less that counts for anything. I didn't want to get married again, but I didn't want to be alone, either, so I always had a boyfriend." She shrugged. "It was part of my life, like having a job and a car and a good hairdresser. A man was another accessory."

"It sounds...a little impersonal." Depressing even.

"I don't mean it that way. I did care about every one of the men I dated." She ran her hands along the steering wheel. "But I never wanted to depend on them, you know?"

I nodded. "People can be undependable."

"Exactly. And my last boyfriend proved that point ten times over."

The bitterness in her voice made my stomach tighten in sympathy. "What did he do?" I asked.

"When I was diagnosed with cancer, he was as shocked as I was, but he swore he'd stand by me." Her knuckles whitened on the steering wheel. "But after the mastectomy, while I was still in the hospital, he told me he couldn't handle it." She took a ragged breath and swallowed. "He couldn't handle having a lover who wasn't a...a whole woman."

Tears stung my eyes and I leaned toward her, but the still way she held herself warned me away. "That must have hurt a lot," I said quietly.

"It did. But it made me mad, too. I said fuck him. I'll show him. There are better men than him out there."

Understanding opened a door in my brain. "Was Tom one of those better men?"

"I like to think so." Her eyes met mine, a plea for understanding in them. "Sometimes I just need...I need that confirmation that I'm still a woman, even if I am a skinny one with no breasts."

How much courage had it taken her to be with any man again after that kind of rejection? And here I sat, too afraid for too many years to so much as flirt with a man. "Oh, Alice...I never thought... I'm sorry."

"Forget about it. I just wanted you to know there are a lot of reasons two people might decide to go to bed together—and some of them don't have anything to do with sex."

"I guess I'm really naive about these things." I sighed, realizing once again just how sheltered I'd been. There was so much I didn't know about, so much I wanted to know about, but I was torn between wanting to retreat to my safe cocoon—my condo and Frannie and my familiar job and acquaintances—and wanting to stay on the road forever, constantly experiencing new places and people. I couldn't yet see my way to a middle ground.

Alice grinned at me. "I think two stunning, single babes like us deserve a break from the open road," she said.

"What did you have in mind?"

"I hear St. George, Utah, has a terrific outlet mall. How about we take a little detour for some retail therapy?"

"I think that's the best idea I've heard in days." I laughed. "I may not have much experience with men, but I am an expert shopper."

Zion Factory Stores was a suburban paradise of designer closeouts, name-brand seconds and this year's bargains that held the tantalizing promise of a "deal." We left Cocoa at an adjacent motel and set out to make our contribution to the local economy.

"We should check out Bass and Factory Brand for shoes," I said, studying the directory. "Tuesday Morning is a good place to look for household stuff and this time of year Ralph Lauren will have end-of-season mark-downs on women's clothing."

Alice stared at me as we set off across the central plaza toward the Ralph Lauren store. "You weren't kidding when you said you were an expert at this."

I shrugged and failed at an attempt to look modest. "When I was fat, I was determined not to look frumpy. I learned which designers had clothes in my size and bought the best pieces I could afford. And of course, my choice in shoes and purses wasn't limited, so I always had fabulous accessories."

"When you lost all that weight, you must have been like a kid in a candy store."

I nodded. "I had to limit myself at first, I was so afraid I might replace one obsession with another." I pulled open the door to Ralph Lauren and we stepped inside. I paused to take a deep breath. The wonderful smell of new cotton and polyester and leather filled my senses. There's no other aroma quite like it.

"You look great," Alice said. "Maybe you could help me pick out some things that would flatter me. I've been wearing the same styles for so long I'm not even sure what would look good."

"I can definitely help you there. Come on." I took her arm and led her toward a rack of dresses. "Let's pick out some things to try on."

For the next four hours we literally "shopped till we dropped." We tried on shoes, dresses, pants, blouses and jackets. We tied scarves and modeled purses. We paraded in evening gowns and draped ourselves in costume jewelry. And we laughed and laughed.

"I wish I had you to shop with all the time," I said as we sank into chairs in the food court, our purchases piled around us. "It's never this much fun by myself."

"Doesn't Frannie go with you?" Alice shoved a tall paper cup of diet soda toward me and took a long sip from her own drink.

"Frannie has no interest in clothes," I said. "She wears a black beautician's smock over black slacks and a black sweater at work and when she gets home in the evenings, she changes into sweats. I've tried to get her to let me dress her up, but she refuses. She thinks black is slimming and chic. I think it makes her look like she's in mourning all the time."

"Doesn't she ever go out?" Alice asked. "With friends or on a date?"

"No." I shook my head. "She's even more of a recluse than I was." It hurt to think of Frannie, alone and hiding from the world. I'd come a long way toward healing the hurt in my own heart. If only I could find a way to heal hers, as well.

"When I'm settled in Ojai, you'll have to come see me," Alice said. "I won't let you be a recluse anymore."

"It's a deal." I looked at the shopping bags scattered at my feet. "What are we going to do with all our fabulous new clothes?"

"I have an idea." She pulled out a sequined minidress that had been a steal on the clearance rack and held it in front of her. "Don't you think this would look great in Las Vegas?"

"Las Vegas? Are you serious?"

"Why not? We're free, single and over twenty-one. Let's live it up."

The idea made my heart race. I had a sudden image of myself in a fabulous gown, winning at roulette, surrounded by handsome men in tuxedos, a glass of champagne in my hand. Why *not* live it up? "Let's do it!"

She raised her cup of soda in a toast and I joined her. "To Las Vegas," I said.

"To Vegas," she echoed, then added, "Sin city, here we come!"

The morning after our shopping expedition, I woke up excited about our trip. Alice and I needed a fun break from the road and Vegas seemed perfect.

But when I returned from taking Cocoa for her morning walk, I was surprised to find Alice still in bed. "Get up, sleepyhead," I said. "Vegas is waiting." I pulled open the drapes, flooding the room with harsh sunlight.

Alice moaned and rolled over, her hand covering her eyes. "I can't go today," she mumbled into the sheets.

"What is it? What's wrong?" I hurried to the bedside. Cocoa jumped up beside Alice and whined.

"I'm sick," Alice moaned.

"What kind of sick? Is it the flu? Do you need to see a doctor?" I fluttered my hands, feeling helpless. I wasn't good at dealing with sick people. Frannie and I were almost never ill.

"I think I just ate something that didn't agree with me." She rolled onto her back again and looked up at me. Her skin was ashy, almost translucent, the blue veins visible beneath the surface. Her eyes were sunken, dark circles beneath them.

I bit my lip, unsure whether to fuss or leave her alone. "Are you in pain?" I asked. "Should we call a doctor?"

"No, I'll be fine. I just need to rest. Get my strength back." She closed her eyes again. "I just need to rest," she said again. "I'll be fine, really."

I looked at her a long moment, undecided. "If you needed to see a doctor, you'd tell me, right?" I asked.

"I'd tell you." She pulled up the covers. "I'll be fine by tomorrow, I'm sure. Go do something fun."

Reluctant to leave her, yet even more reluctant to spend the day in a darkened hotel room, waiting for Alice to throw up or pass out or worse, I collected my purse and Cocoa's leash. "You have my cell number if you need me," I said.

She made a noise I took for consent. I snapped the leash to Cocoa's collar and we fled the room.

I didn't know what opportunities for fun were available in St. George. I could return to the outlet mall, but with Cocoa in tow I wouldn't be able to do much shopping. I saw a sign for Historic Downtown and decided to check it out, though it meant driving the moving truck, not exactly a convenient method of transportation.

Thankfully I was able to find parking in a lot two blocks off the main street, and Cocoa and I set out walking. We amused ourselves window-shopping the boutiques and antiques shops in the restored downtown area.

The sign on a café caught my eye and I had to stop. The Two Sisters was set back from the street a little, with a wrought-iron fence enclosing a patio area with tables for outdoor dining. I studied the menu that was posted on a marquee by the gate.

"We don't allow dogs inside, but you're welcome to sit out here on the patio." A pretty teenage girl looked up from laying out silverware on one of the tables.

It was barely past eleven, but I was hungry, so I opened the gate and led Cocoa to a table in a corner. "What can I get you to drink?" the waitress asked.

"Iced tea would be nice," I said.

"I'll be right back with a menu."

As the waitress was entering the restaurant, a striking older woman, her gray hair in a neat chignon, stepped out. "Are you the bride?" she asked.

I looked around, but no one else had arrived. "The bride?" I asked.

The woman shook her head. "I take it you're not. We do catering, too, and I'm expecting a bride this morning to go over the menu for her reception." She checked her watch. "She's already ten minutes late."

"No, I'm not her." I resisted the urge to apologize, though the woman had the kind of schoolteacher demeanor that always made me feel I was guilty of *something*.

"I wondered about the dog, but I did do one wedding where the matron of honor was a golden retriever and the best man was a German shepherd," she said. "I had to make special dinners for both of them."

"I did flowers once for a wedding where the bride and groom were Lhasa apsos," I said. "I'm a florist near L.A."

"Oh, L.A." She shook her head. "Doesn't surprise me a bit."

The gate squeaked and I turned to see another woman coming up the walk. She was older than I was, but younger than the gray-haired woman. Turned out she wasn't the bride, either.

"Did you remember to call Mr. Anderson about the problem with the drains?" the older woman demanded. "And I hope you didn't let him put you off until next week. He needs to see to it today."

"I spoke to him and he's going to take care of it," the

younger woman said placidly. She straightened a vase of
flowers on one of the tables, a half smile on her lips.

"Did you get those forms we needed from the tax office?"
The older woman followed the younger one to another table.
"And did you talk to Anthony about working the Wuensche
family reunion next weekend?"

"It's all taken care of. Don't worry."

They both went inside as the waitress emerged with my
glass of tea, a bowl of water and a menu. "I thought your
dog might like a drink, too," she said, setting the bowl in
front of Cocoa, who wagged her tail and began lapping at
the water.

"I take it those are the two sisters," I said, nodding toward
the entrance to the restaurant.

"Yes. That's Karen and Kelly."

"Have they had this place long?"

"Twenty years, can you believe it?" The waitress grinned.
"I could never be in business with my sister. She's too
bossy."

"Older sisters tend to be that way," I said.

She left me to study the menu and I thought about sisters.
At one time, Frannie had tried to talk me into going to
beauty school and joining her at her salon. I'd hated the idea
of doing hair and nails for a living and had told her so.

I wondered now if I should have stood up to Frannie more
often. It had been easier to go along with most of her ideas,
but I wasn't sure I'd done either of us any favors by being so
acquiescent.

The sisters came out of the restaurant again. The older
was carrying a pitcher of ice water, the younger a stack of
trays, which they carried to a serving station in the opposite
corner. "I think you should wear the blue pantsuit to the
Chamber dinner," the older sister was saying.

"That's your favorite, isn't it?" the younger sister replied.
"Maybe I will wear it."

I winced at words that sounded too familiar to me. Was this how Frannie and I appeared to outsiders? Silently I rooted for the younger sister to tell her older sibling to back off, that she was capable of choosing her own clothes.

The waitress emerged again. "Mom, we're almost out of Asiago cheese," she said.

The younger sister smiled at the girl. "There's a delivery this afternoon, but thanks for letting me know."

I could see the resemblance between the teenager and the younger sister now. They both had honey-blond hair and dimples when they smiled.

The waitress was still smiling when she approached my table. "Have you decided what you'd like?"

"I'll have the Greek sandwich," I said, handing her the menu.

"Great. It'll be right out."

When she was gone, I returned my attention to the women, who were bickering over the arrangement of tables. The gate squeaked again and a good-looking man entered. He was dressed in jeans and a pale pink shirt that stretched across broad shoulders, a touch of gray at his temples. He walked over and kissed the younger woman on the cheek. "Hello, beautiful," he said. "Wanna buy me lunch?"

The younger sister's eyes sparkled. "Play your cards right and you can have dessert, too."

The gate announced yet another arrival. A dark-haired young woman and a harried-looking older one bustled in. "I'm so sorry we're late," the older woman said. "We had a fitting at the bridal shop and it took forever."

"That's quite all right. Why don't you come inside." The older sister led them away. The younger sister and her husband followed, their arms around each other. He stopped in the doorway to greet the waitress, who hurried over with my sandwich.

I smiled to myself, remembering the cozy domestic scene.

Maybe I was wrong about the younger sister. Maybe she didn't feel the need to argue with her older sibling because she was aware of all her blessings, and didn't begrudge her sister the illusion of control.

After all, it was just an illusion. No one else can really control your life unless you let them.

12

Though she still looked pale, the next morning Alice said she was feeling well enough to head for Vegas. We arrived that afternoon and I felt like Alice in Wonderland. Anyplace where the predominant decorating theme is rhinestones and neon and nobody thinks twice about seeing Elvis walk by is not the real world.

"It's Disney for grown-ups," Alice said as I followed her through the lobby of the Venetian Hotel, where we'd splurged and booked a room. Cocoa was tucked into an oversize tote bag slung over my shoulder. I could feel her shifting around in there, but she was being quiet. For all I knew, this fancy place allowed dogs, but I wasn't taking any chances.

The Venetian Hotel was more opulent and definitely cleaner than the real Venice had ever been. From the elaborately frescoed ceiling to the canal winding through the adjacent shopping center and the musicians strolling through the lobby, I felt as if I'd stumbled into an over-the-top Italian restaurant. Just looking at the plastered columns made me hungry for cannoli.

Of course, there was more to the hotel than frescoes and canals. Even at registration I could hear the bells and whistles of the casino, which a brochure boasted was 120 thousand square feet, with twenty-five hundred slot machines.

"What should we do first?" I asked when we were settled

in our room. Cocoa had curled up at the end of my bed and promptly gone to sleep, unimpressed by the grandeur of her surroundings.

Alice grinned. "I feel like a drink. Something fancy, with an umbrella and fruit in it."

Ten minutes later, mai tais in hand, we stood in the lobby again, looking around.

"Travis and I were married here, did I tell you?" Alice said. "Not in this hotel, of course, but in Vegas."

"No." I wondered what had prompted her to mention this now.

"We wanted a quickie wedding and Vegas seemed the right place."

"A lot different from your Amish honeymoon," I said, staring up at the elaborate fresco overhead.

She nodded. "Vegas was loud and flashy and exciting. We drank and gambled and generally had a good time, but I think what we were really trying to do was run away from our own guilt."

She glanced at me. "I thought I'd succeeded for a while, but it never really left, and it tainted our relationship."

"Because you felt bad about leaving Bobby?"

She nodded. "I loved Travis, but it wasn't enough. Who would have thought guilt would be more powerful than love?"

Right. Who would? I took a big drink. "Let's not think about that now," I said. "We're here to have fun."

"Yes, we are." She was smiling again, even if the expression was a little forced. "Let's check out the slot machines."

For the next two hours we flitted from one machine to the next, trying our luck. I favored the ones that were more like video games, with bonus rounds and lots of action to keep things interesting even when I wasn't winning much.

Alice was a more serious gambler, lingering at traditional

one-line machines, feeding them quarters and yanking down the handle with robotic precision.

After a while the allure of the machines faded and we headed for the ticket office to try to score seats to a show that night. We quickly learned we'd waited too late, so we settled for tickets for the next night.

We went upstairs to check on Cocoa and sneaked her out a side door to an alley for a potty break. When she was settled once more, I turned to Alice. "What now?" I asked.

"Dinner. One thing about Vegas—you can eat cheap."

We ended up at a crowded buffet. Alice's choice, not mine, but I didn't bother arguing. When I was overweight, buffets were heaven. Everyone expects you to pile your plate full at a buffet, so I never felt self-conscious about the amount I ate. Just remembering those days was enough to help me keep my portions small now.

Alice didn't take much advantage of the bounty, either. No wonder she was so skinny. I hadn't seen her eat a complete meal yet.

We found a table next to a family with two children—a boy and a girl I guessed were around eight and six. The whole family was dressed in shorts and T-shirts, with wheat-blond hair and blue eyes. They could have stepped right out of a brochure that advertised Vegas as the perfect family vacation destination.

I was about to say this to Alice when I noticed her staring at the family, a troubled expression on her face. "What's wrong?" I asked. "Do you know them?"

She shook her head and turned her attention back to her plate, but I noticed her gaze kept straying to the table whenever she thought I wasn't looking.

I ate my sugar-free gelatin and tried not to take Alice's sudden glumness personally. This wasn't exactly the glamorous, high-rolling trip to Vegas I'd fantasized about. Where were the champagne, the gambling winnings and handsome men in tuxedos?

I was probably just tired. I was about to suggest we turn in early when Alice shoved her plate aside and stood. "Let's get out of here. We're in Vegas, dammit. We should see the sights!"

After the air-conditioned chill of the hotel, the Vegas night felt soft and warm around us. The liquid colors of blue, gold, orange and green neon spilled onto the street and sidewalk and crowds jostled for position like spectators at a Mardi Gras parade.

"Where is everyone going?" I asked as we were pushed along with the throng.

"Let's find out," Alice said.

We found ourselves in front of the Treasure Island Hotel and Casino, pressed against what appeared to be a huge lagoon. "Look!" Alice pointed toward a full-size ship sailing toward us. "Pirates!"

For the next quarter hour we watched, mesmerized, as pirates battled a group of seductive sirens. With music, swordplay and acrobatics, the show had something for everyone.

From Treasure Island, we followed the crowd to the Mirage, where a volcano erupted in a spectacular display of color, light and noise. Definitely the thing to wake me up.

"I'm glad you suggested we get out of the hotel," I told Alice. "I wouldn't have wanted to miss all this."

"Hmm." She looked up and down the street, distracted.

"Let's walk down this way," she said, and headed off at a fast clip.

I rushed to keep up with her. We headed north up the Strip, away from the newer resorts toward old downtown Vegas. Alice walked quickly, cutting through the crowd, never pausing to look left or right. "Where are we going?" I asked, a little breathless.

"There's someplace I want to see."

The crowd was thinner at this end of the Strip. We passed fewer families and obvious tourists and more less-prosperous-looking individuals. I noticed more dark corners and shady alleys and began to feel nervous. "Maybe we should turn around," I said. "I don't feel safe down here."

"Don't worry." She patted her purse. "I have my gun."

I didn't find this as reassuring as she probably intended. I clutched my own purse tightly to my side and kept an eye out for anyone who seemed suspicious. Unfortunately I'd spooked myself enough that everyone looked suspicious, from a waiter taking a smoke break in an alley to a man in a dark suit who was hailing a cab.

Alice slowed as we neared the starlit exterior of the Riviera. She stared up at the sparkling facade. "This is where Travis and I spent our honeymoon," she said.

I shouldn't have been surprised. I was beginning to realize that an important part of this whole journey for Alice was revisiting significant places from her past.

We stepped into the lobby. Less opulent than some of the newer super-resorts, the Riviera had a retro feel. It was easy to imagine sixties movie stars and high rollers emerging from the elevators or congregating in the bar.

I glanced at Alice. She was looking around, but I had a feeling she wasn't seeing the Riviera today, but rather the hotel of her younger days. "Has it changed much?" I asked.

"Some." She ran her hand along the back of a sofa. "I'd never been to Vegas before then, so everything was impossibly glamorous. Not to mention all I wanted to do when we were here was get Travis upstairs and take our clothes off."

"He was that hot, huh?"

"Almost *too* hot." She walked over to a display of photos of past famous guests and studied it. "I think part of our problem was that the whole relationship was based on sex. We couldn't get enough of each other in the beginning. When that stage passed…" Her voice trailed off and her expression grew distant again.

She turned away from the photos and started across the lobby again. "I need another drink," she said. "Let's go to the bar."

"Not here." I grabbed her arm and held on. "Let's go back to the Venetian." She'd been drinking all afternoon, taking advantage of the free cocktails the waitresses brought to gamblers. Though she was still steady on her feet, if the liquor really hit her I wanted her close to the room.

"I don't want to walk all the way down the Strip just to get a damn drink," she said, trying to break free of my grip.

I wouldn't let go. "We can take a taxi. Then we won't have as far to go *after* we drink."

She saw the sense in this and nodded. "Okay."

We hailed a taxi and climbed in, and ten minutes later were back in the lobby bar at the Venetian. I ordered a Diet Coke, while Alice asked for a dirty martini.

She drained the first drink with alarming speed and ordered another. I wanted to tell her to take it easy, but was reluctant to start a fight.

When the waitress brought the second drink, Alice took a big swallow. "It's not that I like them so much," she said when she noticed me staring at her. "It's just so much fun to order." She giggled a little. That's when I knew for sure she was drunk.

"After this drink, why don't we go back up to the room and relax," I said as I followed Alice to a table in a dim corner of the bar. I really was exhausted and figured she was, too.

"Why would you want to do that?" she said, her tone belligerent. "This is Vegas. Party city. No one goes to bed early here."

"I guess I'm just not much of a party person," I said. "All the noise and lights and…and the artificialness…are getting to me."

"Don't be silly. The night is young." She took a sip of her drink, then her face crumpled. "The night is young, but I'm not anymore."

Then she started to cry.

I stared at her, unsure what to do. I leaned toward her, my voice low. "Alice, honey, please don't cry." I took her hands in mine and squeezed them. I hated to see her in such distress. "What's wrong?" I asked. "Maybe I can help."

She shook her head. "No one can help me. I screwed up my life and it's too late now." A new wave of sobs overtook her. "I never should have left Bobby."

"Oh, honey." I squeezed her hands again. "Does he know you're still in love with him? Maybe if you told him—"

"No! I told you I don't care about him anymore."

I drew back. "I remember you said that. And that you were going back to California to ask his forgiveness. Maybe once you've done that you can let this go."

"Not *his* forgiveness." She shook her head and dabbed at her eyes with a cocktail napkin, smearing her mascara.

"Then whose?" I asked, puzzled.

She choked back another sob. "I need to ask my *children* to forgive me." She buried her face in her hands and rocked back and forth in her chair. "I don't see how they ever can."

I stared at her, my stomach heaving. "Children?" Alice had never mentioned children before now. "I...I didn't know."

"I don't have the right to call them my children. I gave that up when I walked out on them to go with Travis." She shook her head, fresh tears welling in her eyes. "Can you believe a mother could be so cold? I abandoned my babies to chase after some man."

I stared at her and tried hard to regain my equilibrium. "How old were they?" I whispered.

"Tina—Bettina—was eight. Clark was six." She sniffed. "I haven't spoken to them in almost ten years."

"Why not? Why didn't you call?" I took a deep breath, fighting a surge of anger.

"I was too ashamed. I know they hate me. I don't blame them. I hate myself." She buried her head in her arms on the table and cried.

I stared at her, torn between sympathy and disgust. How could Alice do such a thing?

Then I thought of things I'd done that were wrong, mistakes I'd made and words I'd said that I wished I could take back. I reached over and patted Alice's shoulder. "It's okay," I said.

"It's not okay."

"No, what you did wasn't okay, but it's done. You can't change it now. All you can do is go back and tell them how sorry you are and work on building a relationship with them. It's not too late for that."

She raised her head and stared at me, hope grappling with despair in her eyes. "How do you know that?"

"I don't. Not really. But I know you're a good person at heart. You could be a good friend to your children."

"How can you say that after I've told you what I've done?"

"We've all done bad things," I said. "The hardest part isn't asking others to forgive us. It's learning to forgive ourselves."

I got Alice up to bed, where she all but passed out, then I took Cocoa out again. I watched the little dog sniff around the trash cans in the alley. My earlier exhaustion had fled, leaving me too wired to sit still, but I didn't want to return to the lights and noise of the casino.

I took out my cell phone and tried to call Martin, but was only able to reach his voice mail. I hung up without leaving a message. What would I say? *I'm lonely and depressed and I need you to cheer me up?* I didn't want him to know I was that needy.

I looked at the dog. "Want to go for a walk, Cocoa?" I asked.

She wagged her tail wildly at the familiar word and we set out in search of fresh air and some kind of peace, both rare commodities on the crowded streets of Sin City.

We walked down the sidewalk and I looked for some likely retreat. The neon-lit hotels were too bright and gaudy, the casinos too noisy. Everywhere I turned I saw people who were smiling too brightly and laughing too much, trying too hard to have a good time.

When I came upon a small white church, I ducked inside. Apparently churches, like everything else in this town, never closed. If anyone said anything about the dog, we could leave, but until then I wanted the chance to sit in relative quiet and think.

The sanctuary was tiny, with a half-dozen wooden pews and a simple blue carpet. Arrangements of white gladiolas flanked a white pulpit and a simple gold cross hung on the wall behind this. I stared at the cross and prayed for calm to slow my racing heart.

"I'm sorry, I didn't see you come in. Are you wanting the deluxe package or the Saturday-night special?"

I started and turned to see Elvis walking toward me. This Elvis had the expected white sequined jumpsuit and thick black pompadour hairdo, but his face was weathered and wrinkled, and he studied me from behind thick-lensed glasses. Grandpa Elvis.

"Excuse me, what did you say?" I asked.

"Did you want the deluxe wedding package? It comes with a video and a floral bouquet you can keep." He looked around the otherwise empty room. "Will the groom be arriving shortly?"

"Groom? Oh no, I didn't come here to get married!" I

laughed, amused that for the second time in a week I'd been mistaken for a would-be bride. I stood to leave.

"No, you don't have to go." He waved me back down and took a seat beside me. "It's a slow night." He smiled at Cocoa and reached out to scratch behind her ears. "So if you didn't come in here to get married, why did you come in here?"

I pressed my lips together, debating answering. Why should this stranger care about me or what was happening in my life?

But then, I'd had more practice at trusting strangers this trip—Ruth and Martin, and even Alice who, though she'd been a dear friend to me at one time, was in many ways a stranger, as I'd discovered tonight. "I just wanted somewhere quiet. To think," I said.

He nodded and looked up at the cross. "This is a good place for that. The world out there can get a little hectic."

"Are you really a preacher?" I asked.

"Got a license on the wall back there that says I am." He grinned again, a friendly, open smile as down-home as a grandpa should be. "Next you're going to ask me what's with the Elvis getup."

I nodded. "How does a preacher end up in Vegas as an Elvis impersonator?"

"How does anybody end up anywhere? I came here in 1974 to get a divorce and ended up staying. This place grows on you."

"I don't think it would grow on me."

"It's not for everybody, I guess. So where is home, young lady?"

Again, I hesitated. But his grandfatherly concern—coupled with his ridiculous costume—broke through my normal reticence. "I live in California. Bakersfield. I'm not sure it's home, though." I smoothed my hands down my thighs. "I think I'm still trying to find the place where I fit."

"Now see, you're looking at it all wrong." He angled his

body more toward me. "You're looking for the space where you fit in like you're a puzzle piece and only one certain slot will do. What you need to do is make a space for yourself. Understand the difference?"

"I…I'm not sure."

"You find where you want to be, then you make it fit you, see?"

"That's what you did?"

He nodded. "That's what I did." He looked around the chapel once more. "This life ain't for everybody, but it suits me. You got to find what suits you. That might mean trying on a few places first."

He made it sound easy, like buying a dress. "I'm good at shopping around," I said.

"Then you won't have any problem." He patted my knee and stood. "Anything else I can do for you?"

"No. Thank you." I stood and Cocoa and I followed him toward the exit. "Good night."

"Good night. You come back when you find that groom. I'll fix you up real nice."

I smiled as I walked back to the hotel. Grandpa Elvis made life sound a lot less daunting, as if happiness was just a matter of tailoring the circumstances and situation to fit, the way you'd alter a suit.

And maybe he wasn't so far off at that. I'd been looking for the place that was perfect for me, but I wasn't perfect, so why should I expect a place to be? Maybe the idea was to find a place whose imperfections fit my own, and work on improving both at the same time.

"Are you okay?" I asked Alice as we stood in yet another buffet line for breakfast the next morning.

"Yeah. Just a little hungover." Her smile was sheepish. "I promise you I don't do that sort of thing often."

"No harm done." Our eyes met. "It's going to be okay," I said.

"I hope so."

We decided to get out and see some of the sights of Las Vegas, so after settling Cocoa in the room and hanging the do-not-disturb sign on the door we once again joined the throngs on the sidewalks. The sun beat down like a giant tanning lamp and the heat was a physical weight pressing against us, but it didn't seem to affect attendance at the fountains at Bellagio.

We stood and watched along with everyone else, taking respite in various boutiques, coffee shops and casinos along the Strip.

We passed the wedding chapel I'd visited the night before, and I told Alice about Grandpa Elvis.

"I think an Elvis wedding would be fun," she said. "It's probably a good sign if a marriage starts off with a sense of humor."

I hadn't thought about it like that before. "I guess I always thought a wedding should be a solemn, sacred affair," I said.

"Maybe. Then again, it's all the stuff that comes after you say 'I do' that determines how solemn or sacred it is. The wedding is just the party to get things started."

I nodded. "I've always wanted a big, fancy wedding like the ones they show in bridal magazines." The idea of being a fairy princess for a day appealed to me. But that was just a dream, and real life so seldom measured up to dreams. "I guess all I really want is to settle down with a good man. Everything else is just trimmings."

"Then see? Elvis would be perfect. Especially a Grandpa Elvis. He sounds sweet."

"He was sweet." We paused at a crosswalk and waited for the light to change. I pulled my shirt away from my chest, hoping for a breeze to dry the sweat. "He told me that instead of looking for a place where I fit in, I should find a place I liked and make it fit me."

"Sounds like Grandpa is pretty smart." She surprised me with a wink. "Besides, I think fitting in is overrated. It's the noncomformists in the world who stand out. And they probably have more fun than the rest of us."

The light changed and we crossed the street and passed in front of a brightly painted storefront. *Vegas Tattoo,* proclaimed the sign in bright pink neon.

"Did you know I have a tattoo?" Alice asked.

"No, you never mentioned that." Not that I was shocked. Alice had always struck me as the type who'd try anything once. "What is it?"

"A hummingbird and some flowers."

"And where is it?"

"On my right breast. Or where my right breast used to be. After I'd stared at the scar from my mastectomy for a year or so, I decided to put something beautiful there."

"So you decided not to have reconstruction?"

"I just couldn't face another surgery, and keeping the scar was sort of my badge of honor. My reminder of everything I'd been through, and that I was still here, still fighting."

"Why a hummingbird?"

"Because they're beautiful and look fragile, but they're about the toughest creatures in nature."

I smiled at her. "Like you."

"At least the tough part."

"The rest, too. You are beautiful, and to some people you probably look fragile."

"But not to you?"

"I know better." We reached the Venetian and followed the crowd inside. "I think it was really gutsy of you to decorate your scar that way."

"We all have scars," she said. "I just didn't want to hide mine anymore." She reached out and gave my hand a quick squeeze. "I'm glad you know the truth about me and my kids, and I'm glad you understand. I was afraid you'd hate me if I told you."

"I don't hate you." I didn't really understand, either. How could a mother abandon her children that way?

Then a sharp pain of realization pinched at me as I thought of the way Frannie and I had left our mother after our father died. She'd seemed distant and uncaring at the time, but maybe that was only a way of walling off the hurt. Why hadn't I thought of her that way before? Was it because Frannie had told me over and over that Mother didn't need us?

Or because it was easier to believe that than to deal with my guilt?

I believed Alice was truly sorry for what she'd done, and that she'd suffered for it. "I'm glad you told me the truth. That took a lot of courage, too." More than I'd ever had.

"It feels like a weight has been lifted, knowing you know." She grinned at me. "We should celebrate."

"No more mai tais or dirty martinis," I said.

She laughed. "Not that kind of celebration. Tonight let's put on our fancy new dresses and treat ourselves to a really nice dinner. We'll see the show, then try some real gambling."

"Real gambling?"

"Not those Mickey Mouse slot machines. Let's hit the table games—blackjack, craps and roulette. We'll flirt with all the handsome men and pretend we're high rollers."

My Vegas fantasy come to life. "Let's do it."

Martin called that afternoon while I was waiting for my turn in the shower. "I saw your number on my caller ID last night," he said. "What's up?"

"Nothing much. We're in Vegas." I shoved Cocoa over and lay back on the bed, the phone cradled to my ear.

"Won any money yet?"

"No. I'm a terrible gambler."

"So am I. Too conservative, I guess."

I bit back a laugh. The man didn't know conservative. He should meet Frannie, a woman who kept all her retirement money in a regular savings account because she didn't trust the stock market. "Where were you when I called?" I asked, then immediately regretted the question. What business was it of mine?

"I had to deliver flowers for a funeral that was held this morning."

"You do a lot of funerals," I said.

"Weddings and funerals. The big events in most people's lives."

I thought again how different *our* lives were. Martin was so involved in his community, there for every milestone—at least in the form of the flowers he provided. In my condo in Bakersfield, where the sun shone most of the time and the weather was always perfect, I lived in a fantasy world, scripted drama and artificial occasions replacing real human events. I'd loved it because it was safe and predictable, but I realized now it was also a world where I never really had to *feel* anything—good or bad.

"I was thinking about something you said before," I said. "When you suggested I open a retail business to go along with my movie work. I think I'd like that."

"You'd be good at it," he said. "You're very empathetic."

"How could you know that just from talking to me on the phone?"

"I heard what you and Alice did for Ruth. And you've told me how concerned you are for Alice. And you took in that stray dog."

"Alice took in the dog. I just happened to be in the truck, too."

"A minor detail. The thing is, you're a warm and

compassionate person. It's one of the things I like most about you."

I wanted to ask him to list what else he liked about me but thought that would be too self-serving. "Thanks," I said. "I really like you, too."

"I'm glad to hear you say it. I hope we're going to be friends for a long time."

The words made me feel funny in the pit of my stomach. I sat up and took a deep breath. The bathroom door opened and Alice came out, rubbing her hair with a towel. "I have to go now," I said. "It's my turn in the shower."

"The idea of us being friends shouldn't make you nervous," he said.

"Of course not!" I stood and began pacing. "That sounds great. I really do have to go."

"Goodbye, then. Have fun tonight."

"Bye."

I closed the phone and laid it on the bedside table.

"Was that Martin?" Alice asked.

I nodded. My face felt hot and I covered my cheeks with my hands, trying to cool them.

"What did he say to get you so flustered?" Alice asked. She took a comb from the dresser and ran it through her spiky hair.

Pretty much everything Martin said left me flustered, trying to make sense of a tangle of feelings. "He said he wants us to be friends."

"I thought you were already friends."

I wet my lips. "But I think he really meant more than friends."

She smiled at me in the mirror. "That's a good thing, isn't it?"

I nodded again, feeling foolish and helpless and more than a little silly. "I think…" I hesitated, then tried again. "I think Martin is a little like Frannie's prom dress."

Alice laid down the comb. "Come again?"

I twisted my hands. "I'm not explaining this well at all. What I mean is that, well, you know how I told you Frannie hid her prom dress so our dad wouldn't take it away?"

She nodded.

"I think…I think I still do that sometimes. When I really, really want something I try not to let it show. In case something happens to take it away."

A soft look of sympathy filled her eyes. "And you really want Martin."

"I think so. Yes."

She turned and put her hand on my arm. "Then don't give in to your fear," she said. "You'll be okay."

I took a deep breath. "Yeah." I wanted to believe that. I wanted to believe that I would be okay—that the future would be a happy one, even better than any fantasy I could create. I wanted to believe, but I hadn't had much practice yet.

Alice and I put on our slinky sequined dresses and highest heels, coiffed our hair and used every trick in our cosmetics bags. Afterward, we stood side by side and studied our reflection in the bathroom mirror. "Are we a couple of hot babes or what?" Alice asked.

"We'll have to fight the men off," I said, half believing it as I stared at the glamorous, skinny version of myself I'd only imagined before now. Despite all the weight I'd lost and all the new clothes, most of the time when I looked in the mirror I still saw a plainer, plumper version of me that I now realized was firmly in the past.

We had dinner at the Lutece, overlooking the Grand Canal in the Venetian. Sitting at the white-draped table, surrounded by the other diners dressed in their finest, I could immerse myself in my fantasy of wealthy woman about town.

We flirted shamelessly with the waiter, who flattered us by flirting back.

After dinner, we took a cab to Treasure Island for Mystère and marveled at the acrobats and clowns. A pair of handsome older men bought us drinks, but we declined their invitation to spend the evening with them. "This is a girls' night out," Alice said, grabbing my hand and pulling me into the casino.

Over the next couple of hours, I learned I was horrible at blackjack. The rules of craps confused me and I was intimidated by the überserious poker players.

But I found my calling at the roulette wheel. A game where the chief elements you had to remember were even, odd, red or black was just my speed. I enjoyed a heady dose of beginner's luck as well, winning again and again. Soon I had a pile of chips in front of me and an appreciative crowd around me, including a number of handsome men, some of whom even wore tuxedos.

I leaned forward and placed a stack of chips on the first range of numbers and waited for the dealer to spin the wheel.

I glanced up to smile at Alice and a tall man moved into my field of vision. He was so familiar I was sure at first I was dreaming. He looked right at me, his expression bland, and I almost doubled over in pain. I had to grab on to the edge of the table and started shaking uncontrollably.

13

"Ellen? Ellen, are you okay?" I was dimly aware of Alice calling me.

"Move back. Give her some air." Alice clutched my shoulders and shook me gently. "Ellen, what is it? What's wrong?"

"I'm okay." I stared at the spot where the man had been, but he was gone. Had I imagined the whole encounter? Was my conscience playing tricks on me?

Someone brought a glass of ice water and I drank half of it in one gulp. "I...I'm tired," I said, pushing the glass away. "I think I'd better go back up to the room." I turned to go, leaving my chips on the table, but Alice remembered to collect them. She swept the pile into her purse, then put her arm around me and led me toward the elevator.

By the time we got up to the room, I was feeling more stable and very foolish. "I'm sorry," I said, and sank onto the edge of my bed. "I don't know what came over me."

Cocoa came over and shoved her nose under my hand and whimpered. I absently rubbed her ears.

"What happened?" Alice shoved her purse into the room safe and locked it, then came and sat across from me on the other bed. "One minute you were fine, then the next you looked like you were going to pass out."

"It's silly." I stared at the floor.

"Try me."

I took a deep breath. If she could trust me with the secret she'd revealed last night, I could tell her this. "I swear I saw a man who looked just like my father. As if his ghost was right there in front of me."

"A doppelgänger," Alice said.

"A what?"

"A doppelgänger. It means double in German. Someone who looks just like someone else."

"I thought my mind was playing tricks on me."

"It's happened to me before, too."

"It has?"

She nodded. "I've seen men who reminded me of both my ex-husbands. It's unnerving to say the least."

"No kidding." I still felt queasy with the aftereffects of the encounter. "I know he's dead, but there he was—it was too creepy."

"I guess it's like they say—the past always comes back to haunt us."

The idea angered me. "Why should it have to?"

"Retribution? Redemption? Karma?" She shook her head. "All I know is I've been trying to put my past behind me for years and I never could. I'm hoping things will be better for me now that I've decided to own up to my mistakes and face the consequences, but I can't be sure."

"We can't make amends for every mistake we've made in life," I protested. "That's impossible."

"You're probably right. But it's impossible to forget them, either."

"I just want to forget about my father," I said. "I don't want him—or his doppelgänger—sneaking up on me when I least expect it."

"Maybe you need to do something to bury him again."

I shuddered. "How would I do that?" Frannie had accused

me of digging up the past when I'd gone back to Ridgeway, but I don't think she had this in mind.

"I don't know." Alice lay back on the bed, her feet still on the floor. "Don't mind me. It's probably just a weird coincidence and it doesn't mean anything. Or maybe it's your Puritan conscience getting back at you for winning at roulette."

"You think I have a Puritan conscience?"

"I didn't say there was anything wrong with that, but I'm guessing living it up in Vegas is not exactly your style."

"I'm doing a lot of things on this trip I've never done before," I said. "That's sort of the point."

I had left home unsure of what I wanted from life now that I'd met my goal of losing weight. I only knew I hadn't found it yet—not in Virginia or Kansas or Las Vegas. Maybe Alice was right—I couldn't move forward because the past continued to drag at me, an anchor pulling me down.

"Good for you." Alice sat up again and looked at me. "Maybe it's all part of making your own place in the world, like Grandpa Elvis talked about."

"What would seeing my dad have to do with that?" I asked.

She shrugged. "You're sort of leaving your old life behind, right?"

I nodded.

"Then maybe your dad just stopped by to say goodbye."

I called Frannie the next morning, needing to hear her voice. "Where are you?" she asked, then before I could even answer: "When are you coming home?"

"I'm in Las Vegas. I should be home in a few days."

"What are you doing in Las Vegas?"

Planning an Elvis-themed wedding. "I'm doing what people usually do in Las Vegas. Gambling. Seeing some shows."

"It's a waste of money." She sniffed.

"I won more than four hundred dollars playing roulette last night."

She had no answer for that. "I went over and cleaned your place yesterday," she said. "There was dust everywhere and everything in the refrigerator was bad. I threw it all out."

I winced at the idea of Frannie tossing out my rotten eggs and spoiled milk. "You didn't have to do that," I said. "I would have taken care of that when I got back."

"I changed your diapers when you were a baby. That was a lot worse than dealing with spoiled food."

I made a face. Frannie brought up the diaper thing as a way of putting me in my place—a not-so-subtle reminder that there was nothing about me she didn't know. "You were three years old when I was born," I said. "You couldn't have done much diaper changing."

"I was five by the time you were toilet trained. Believe me, I changed my share."

I rolled my eyes. "I didn't call to argue over my diapers," I said.

"Then why did you call? To brag about your gambling winnings?"

She was peeved, though whether at me or at life in general I couldn't tell. "I called because I wanted to talk to my sister. I've missed you."

A long silence, then, "I've missed you, too."

"I had an odd thing happen to me last night," I said. "While I was playing roulette, I looked up and saw a man who looked just like Daddy."

"You never did hold your liquor well."

"I wasn't drinking. I just looked up and there he was. It was such a shock I almost fainted."

"Maybe you should see a doctor when you get home. When was the last time you had a complete checkup?"

"I'm not sick. Or crazy." At least I didn't think I was. "Alice says it was a doppelgänger—Dad's double."

"That's ridiculous." Then she changed the subject again. "I've been working on a new scrapbook. It's all about my most famous clients. I'm going to put it on display at the shop when I'm finished."

I refused to let her avoid this topic anymore. "Do you ever think about him much? About Daddy?"

"No. Never." The words were clipped. Final.

"I think about him all the time," I admitted. "Even when I don't want to." Lately I'd been thinking about him more than ever. Wondering if things could have ever been different between us. Could I have done something, said something—

"Don't," Frannie said. "No good will come of it."

I pushed on, refusing to drop the subject, no matter how painful it was. "When I was in Ridgeway, I thought I should go by the cemetery, visit his and Mama's graves. But I couldn't make myself do it."

"They're gone. You don't owe them anything."

"Don't I? Frannie, they were our parents, even if they weren't very good ones. I always wonder if we couldn't have done something different—"

"No. We did the only thing we could. It's over now. I don't want to talk about it, ever again."

Always before, I had let her silence me, but I couldn't stifle my feelings any longer. "Maybe we *should* talk, Frannie," I said. "Maybe part of the problem is that we've kept silent for too many years."

"It would be a waste of words."

"I told Alice some of what happened."

"You didn't! How dare you!" I recoiled from the fury in her voice.

"I didn't tell her everything," I said. "Just some of it. I think it helped, getting it out in the open. Like airing a wound."

"Those are *my* secrets, too." Her voice shook with rage.

"You didn't have the right to share them with someone who's little more than a stranger."

"Alice is my friend," I said. "And what I told her was about me."

"It's about me, too. It can't help but be. You and I lived all that together. You can't separate your part from my part."

This was the problem with our relationship in a nutshell. I loved my sister dearly, but her feelings for me went beyond that kind of love. She couldn't separate my life from her own. She wanted to own not only the day-to-day events, but my feelings and emotions and reactions, as well. And we'd been twined together for so many years, I wasn't sure how I could ever untangle myself. "Alice won't say anything," I tried to reassure her. "You can trust her."

"I don't trust anyone."

Which was perfectly true. Frannie didn't even trust me. Not really. Which was probably another reason she was so disturbed by my long absence. "I'll talk to you again in a few days," I said.

"Hurry home," she pleaded. "I've been thinking we should plan a really nice trip somewhere this year. Maybe Mexico, or even Europe."

This was her peace offering. If I was so eager to travel, she would go with me, so that she could look after me, as she'd always done.

And so she could keep an eye on me.

"What do you think about taking a trip out to see the Grand Canyon?" Alice asked the next morning as we loaded the truck and prepared to leave Las Vegas behind.

I studied her over the tops of my sunglasses. "I think it's time we headed for Ojai. You've put it off long enough."

"Wouldn't you like to see the Grand Canyon first?" She busied herself arranging the cooler behind the seat and avoided looking at me.

"It's going to be okay with your kids," I said. I had no way of knowing this for certain, but it was the most comforting thing I could think of to say. "Maybe not right away, but eventually."

"I wish I could be sure."

"Putting it off longer won't make it any easier," I said gently.

"You're right." She swung up into the driver's seat and reached for her seat belt. "I guess we'd better get going."

The next five hours seemed like the longest of the trip. Alice fidgeted constantly, changing the radio station, adjusting the air-conditioner controls and shifting in her seat. She drummed her fingers on the steering wheel and hummed under her breath.

Her nervousness was contagious. My stomach fluttered and my skin felt clammy. I wanted things to work out well for her. I wanted her to reunite with her children and find the happiness and healing she needed.

Frannie would have told me I read too many novels— that nothing ever worked out that way in real life. But why shouldn't happy endings be as real as tragic ones? Maybe it's just that good times don't get the press bad events do.

Much as I wanted good things for Alice, I couldn't think of anything I could do to help her. I settled for praying, though my emotions were so raw the best I could come up with was *please*.

We pulled into Ojai that afternoon and found the apartment Alice had rented. "It's got two bedrooms," she said as we climbed the stairs to take a look. "Will you stay with me a few days longer?"

"What about Cocoa?" I looked at the little dog in my arms. Funny how she felt so much a part of my life after such a short time.

"What about her?"

"You said the apartment doesn't allow dogs."

"She's little—no one will see her. And if they do, I'll explain you'll be here only a couple of days."

That was one big difference between Alice and me. I'd spent so much of my life adhering strictly to every rule, while Alice looked at rules more as guidelines, to be followed when it was convenient to do so and overlooked when it suited her.

"I'll stay a couple of days," I said. "To help you get settled." I wasn't all that anxious to return to Frannie and my routine life, not when so much felt so unsettled between me and my sister and within myself.

After the furniture was unloaded and we'd returned the truck, we took a taxi back to the apartment. I followed Alice into the kitchen, where she opened a box and began unwrapping dishes. "Do you want me here when you call your children?" I asked. I knew it had to be on her mind, though she hadn't said a word about it. I wanted to let her know I was there to help if she needed me.

"I can't call yet. I don't have my phone hooked up yet." She unwrapped a plate and avoided looking at me.

"You have a cell phone."

She nodded, then set aside the plate and faced me. "I'm scared."

I moved closer and took her hand in mine. "I know you are. Just call. I think it will hurt worse if you don't."

She nodded and retrieved her purse from the living room. "Do you want me to leave?" I asked.

"No, stay."

Her hands shook so much she had to try three times before she could punch in the number. I waited, eyes fixed on her, scarcely breathing, silently counting the electronic rings. One...two...three...four...

"Hello!" Alice's voice was strained, artificially cheerful. "Is this Bettina?"

She clamped the phone tighter to her ear, so that I was

only able to hear one side of the conversation. I turned my back, feeling like an intruder, yet aching for a happy ending to all Alice's years of pain.

"This is Alice MacCray...your mother... I...I know it's been a long time since we talked, and I wanted you to know how sorry I am about that... Yes. I understand that. But I'm in Ojai now. I wondered if I could see you... Yes, but if I could just..."

There was a long silence, then I heard the phone clatter on the counter. Alice stood, slumped, head down, so still she might have been a mannequin.

My heart twisted, and I wanted to put my arms around her, but I was frozen in place by fear and uncertainty. "What did she say?" I asked.

"She said she didn't want to see me. That...that she didn't have a mother." A dry sob ripped from her throat, and her knees buckled.

I rushed forward to catch her and half dragged her to the living room onto the sofa. "She's hurt and angry right now," I said. "That's only natural. But now that she knows you're here, that will change."

"How can you say that?" Alice sobbed. "Why should she change her mind about me?"

I searched desperately for some word of comfort. Why *should* Alice's daughter change her mind? Why did I believe she would?

"You remember the stuffed lamb?" I said after a moment. "The one my father gave me, that I carry in my suitcase?"

Alice didn't look up or answer, but I kept talking. "In spite of all he did, I wanted so much to love him." A lump rose in my throat at the memory of how much I had longed for even the smallest gesture of affection from my father. "Your children want that, too," I continued. "They can't help it. If you'll keep trying, I know you'll get through to them."

"You can't know that." She buried her face in her hands.

"I'm going to die knowing my children hate me. And I don't blame them. I deserve their hatred."

"Don't say that," I protested. "It isn't true. Everyone deserves forgiveness."

Alice raised her head and stared at me, her eyes burning. "You don't know what you're talking about. You never did anything in your life that needed forgiving. Not the way I do. You'd never abandon your own children."

I laced my fingers together, so she wouldn't see how badly my fingers were shaking. "You're wrong," I said. "I may never have abandoned children, but I've done bad things." I swallowed hard. "Horrible things."

"Name one."

I stared at her, heart racing, unshed tears burning my eyes, a lifetime of denial a vise around my chest.

"You can't think of anything, can you?" She turned away. "You don't know anything about the awful things people can do to each other."

Oh, but she was wrong. I took a deep breath, the truth crowding my throat until it was a physical pain that had to be relieved. "I've done bad things," I repeated.

She didn't raise her head. "I don't believe it."

"Believe it." I wet my parched lips, and closed my eyes against the images that loomed up from my memory. A picture of Frannie, standing before the kitchen stove in the house on Amaranth Avenue, a small glass vial in her hand… Frannie smiling to herself as she stirred the pot of stew on the stove…. Me standing by the door, waiting for my father to come home…knowing what was happening but refusing to believe it…watching the scene unfold and doing nothing to stop it.

"I did the most horrible thing you can imagine," I said.

Alice shook her head. "No. You couldn't have."

"Yes." I took another deep breath, struggling for air, then let the words out with a rush, each one like a physical blow.

"I killed my father."

14

I closed my eyes, terrified of the consequences now that I'd said the words out loud. Alice sat with her head buried in her hands, not looking at me.

"Did you hear me?" I said, my voice stronger now. "I killed my father." As horrible as the words were, each time I said them I felt something loosen inside me.

Alice lifted her head and stared at me. "You're not serious," she said.

"Frannie killed him, actually." I straightened my shoulders, as if shrugging off that terrible burden. "But I knew and I kept quiet. That makes me just as guilty." A guilt I'd tried to deny for far too long.

"But..." Alice shook her head. "How?"

"Poison. Something she got from the pharmacy where she worked." I sighed. "She put it in some stew she heated for his supper one night. She told me what she was going to do and I didn't try to stop her."

"And it killed him?"

I nodded, cold calm stealing over me. Even after all these years, the memory of that night was crystal clear. Standing in the hallway, peering around the doorway, watching my dad eat the stew... Numbing horror filling me as he grew pale and clutched at his chest...the sound of my mother's screams turning into the wail of the ambulance...the pain of Frannie's fingers digging into my arm as she dragged me to our room…the smell of onions on her breath as she put her face close to mine.

"Tell no one," she whispered fiercely. "Not a word. Ever. Do you understand?" She squeezed harder, her fingernails cutting into my skin.

I nodded, more terrified of her wrath than of the consequences of silence.

"Good." She straightened and smoothed my hair, the weight of her hand heavy on the top of my head. "Just remember, he can't hurt you anymore."

Oh, how wrong she'd been.

But now, talking to Alice, a different numbness settled over me—a weariness and profound relief. *This is how criminals on the run must feel,* I thought. *When they finally surrender and are taken in.* My voice was flat and calm as I continued my story. "All the men in his family died young of heart attacks. Everyone assumed that that was what had killed him. Ridgeway was a small town then, and the police force didn't have much experience with murder."

"Did your mother know?"

I shook my head. "I don't think so." No one knew but me and Frannie, and we've kept the secret all these years.

"That's why you left town right after the funeral?" Alice asked.

I nodded. "Frannie was scared. She wanted to get as far from Ridgeway as possible before anyone got suspicious."

Alice looked at me, her eyes soft with compassion. "He was a horrible man. He made your life hell."

"That doesn't mean he deserved to die. Or that we had the right to sentence him to death." Or to sentence ourselves to living with the knowledge of what we'd done.

"What a terrible secret to keep all these years."

It was terrible, and I had paid a heavy price for my guilt, afraid to get too close to anyone who might learn the truth, hiding behind a shield of fat and trusting no one. Only when I'd lost the weight and moved out of the familiar confines of the small world I'd built in Bakersfield could I confront what I'd done all those years ago.

"I promise I won't tell anyone," Alice said.

I nodded. "Frannie and I never talk about it. It's a relief to have it out in the open, really."

"Will you tell her you told me?"

I hesitated. "I don't know." Would it make any difference? If Frannie knew our secret wasn't so secret anymore, would it shake her out of her denial? Would it help her see all that was wrong with the way we'd been hiding ourselves from the world? "But I don't know if I can go back to her—not to live. I...I don't want a life like that anymore, always hiding, always holding back." I could see now how pathetic we'd both been, cutting ourselves off from everyone and everything, nursing our guilt. I couldn't go back to that.

Alice put her arm around me. "Oh God, we're a pair, aren't we?"

I nodded. "The question is, a pair of what?"

She took a deep, watery breath. "A pair of women who've made mistakes." She looked at me. "Big ones. And we've suffered for our crimes."

I nodded again.

"Will you tell Frannie you told me about your father?" Alice asked again.

"I just don't know. All these years, we've never talked about it at all. Not a single word. It's as if we've been pretending it never happened. That the first sixteen and nineteen years of our lives never happened."

Alice sighed. "If only we could go back in time and do things differently."

"I wish I knew for sure that given the chance I would act differently," I said. "That's maybe the worst part—I don't know that I would. I was afraid of my father and part of me hated him. In a lot of ways my life was easier once he was gone."

"If I had another chance, I wouldn't leave Bobby," she said. "No man was worth what I gave up."

"You can still have a relationship with your children," I said. "Not the one that could have been, but a relationship. It's not too late."

"Maybe it is." She sighed. "I'll try again, I promise, but not today. Maybe in a few days. I thought I was prepared, but when I heard the hate in her voice..." She shook her head. "God, it hurt. It hurt worse than anything in my life."

We held each other and cried for a while. "It'll be all right," I whispered over and over. A stupid, foolish promise, but the only one I knew to make. If I said the words often enough, maybe I could make them true, like an incantation to ward off evil, to erase the bad things we'd both already done.

Martin called that afternoon, but when I saw his number on the screen I let the call roll over to voice mail. I couldn't face him right now, not with my confession to Alice still ringing in my ears. I wasn't ready to reveal that much of myself to Martin, yet to talk about inconsequential things with him right now would feel like a lie. I needed more time to sort out my feelings—about myself and about Martin.

Alice and I didn't talk any more about that afternoon, though we were both more kind and considerate of each other in the days that passed. Alice bought a used car and I moved into the tiny spare bedroom of the apartment. I ran the flower shop long distance, as I'd been doing for weeks now, and I didn't call Frannie or answer her calls to me. I didn't want to talk to her again until I had my feelings sorted out in my mind.

At the end of my first week in Ojai, Alice asked me if I would drive down to Santa Barbara and pick up a part for the dishwasher. "The landlord says he can fix it right away if we pick up the part," she said. "Otherwise, we have to wait a week for them to ship it. You can use my car. I'd go, but I've got a job interview that afternoon."

"Sure. No problem."

The next morning, I wished Alice luck with her interview and headed to Santa Barbara. I picked up the part at the supply house, then treated myself to lunch and some shopping. Traffic was heavy and it was late afternoon before I made it back to find the house silent and deserted.

Cocoa greeted me at the door, beside herself with joy to see me and unwilling to leave my side as I unloaded the car and went into the kitchen to make tea. "Have you been by yourself all day?" I asked, rubbing behind the pup's soft ears. "Maybe Alice had errands to run, or they asked her to start right away."

But when six o'clock rolled around and I still hadn't heard from Alice, I began to worry. Surely she could have called and left me a message. Then again, I was only her houseguest. Maybe she didn't feel she needed to explain her whereabouts to me.

"I hope she's not at some bar drinking," I told Cocoa as I gathered her into my lap. "She hasn't said anything, but I know she's depressed about the situation with her children. Who wouldn't be?"

A chill went through me as I thought of what a terribly depressed person might do. One who thought she had nothing to live for...

I shoved Cocoa aside and began to pace. What should I do? I could call hospitals, looking for her. I could call the police, but I doubted they'd do anything about a grown woman who had failed to show up in time for dinner. Besides, though I knew the local police had no inkling of the crime I'd committed in my youth, I didn't want anything to do with the law.

In the end, I went next door and knocked. An older woman with oversize glasses answered. "Hello?" she asked cautiously.

"Hi. My name is Ellen and I'm staying next door with my friend, Alice. Have you seen her today?"

"An ambulance came in the middle of the afternoon and took her away," the woman said.

"No!" I steadied myself against the door frame and tried to breathe normally, which was impossible. "Where did they take her? What was wrong with her?"

"I don't know any of that. I think she was still alive, though. They had one of those oxygen masks clamped over her face."

"Th-thank you." I staggered back into the house and searched for a phone book. Of course there wasn't one, because Alice still hadn't had a phone installed.

I grabbed up my cell phone and dialed directory assistance. "I'm in Ojai and I need to find the closest hospital," I gasped.

"You need to call 9-1-1," the operator said.

"No, I'm not the one who needs the hospital. I mean, my friend was taken away in an ambulance and I need to find out where they've taken her."

"Do you know the name of the ambulance company?"

"No. Could you just give me the numbers of all the hospitals in the area?"

The list was short and I found Alice with my first call. "Yes, she was admitted this afternoon," they said. "Are you a relative?"

"No, just a friend. Thank you."

I left Cocoa chewing on a piece of rawhide and set out for Ojai Valley Community Hospital. After a few wrong turns, I found it and raced into the lobby. "Can you tell me where I can find Alice MacCray? She's a patient here."

The efficient woman behind the desk consulted her computer. "Third floor. Room 316."

I didn't bother to ask if Alice was allowed visitors. If she was on a psych ward, maybe not. I had the vague idea that was where they consigned attempted suicides. But maybe I could sneak in for a few minutes to see her...

As it was, I was able to walk right into Alice's room. All my courage left me at the door. The woman in the bed looked so small and frail, her skin only a shade darker than the sheets that were tucked around her, tubes leading from her nose and her arm.

I must have made some noise, because she turned toward me. "Ellen?" she whispered.

I came to stand at her bedside. "What's going on?" I asked.

She waved her untethered hand vaguely in the air. "Cancer. I had a bad spell and got scared. Had to call the ambulance."

"Oh, Alice. I had no idea it had come back."

"More like it never really left."

I took her hand and held it gently. "I'm glad you're here where they can look after you. You beat this before. You can do it again."

She looked at me sadly. "It's in the lungs now. Doesn't look good."

I didn't know what to say, so I continued to hold her hand, stroking it softly. "Should I call your children and tell them?" I asked after a while.

"Why? They don't want to hear from me."

I squeezed her hand. "No matter what, you're their mother. They deserve the chance to make peace with you...."

"Before it's too late." She finished the sentence and closed her eyes. "I'll call them. I don't want them hearing this from a stranger." She smiled. "Or at least not from a stranger who isn't related to them."

This was the Alice I knew, still joking. Tears clogged my throat and I swallowed hard. "I'll let you get some rest now," I said. "Is there anything you need from the house?"

"No, I'm fine. I had a bag packed that I brought with me." Her eyes met mine again. "I had a feeling something like this might happen."

I thought back to all the times on the road when she said she wasn't feeling well. Was it the cancer making her sicker?

I promised to come back the next morning and drove back to Alice's apartment. Once there, I held Cocoa close and cried. The little dog licked my face and whined, which only made me cry more.

All that night, I tossed and turned, thinking about Alice, and my own life. If I knew I was going to die soon, what would I do differently? Would I find the courage to accept my past or change my future? Would dreams that had seemed impossible now be within my reach with that change in perspective?

Would I know what I needed to do, instead of struggling with paralyzing doubt?

The third day after Alice entered the hospital, Frannie called me and I answered. I knew it was long past time for us to talk. "You've got to come home, Ellen. I don't know what the hell to do."

The panic in her voice rattled me, and I gripped the phone tightly, as if trying to hold Frannie herself steady. "What is it?" I asked. "What's wrong?"

"I got a call just now, from the cemetery people. They want to dig up Mama and Daddy."

I steadied myself against the counter, reeling from the impact of the words. "Perpetual Rest Memorial Park called you?"

"That's what I said. They want to dig up Mama's and

Daddy's graves. They need to move them because of some highway expansion."

"The state's building a bypass around town," I said, recalling the construction I'd seen while I was there. "Then I guess we have to let them move them." It wasn't as if either of us ever went back and visited. "I can't see that it makes any difference."

"But what if they d–decide, as long as they're dug up, to do an au…an autopsy or something?" Frannie's voice shook so badly she could scarcely get the words out.

"I don't think they can do an autopsy on a body that's been buried twenty-two years," I said. "And why would they want to?"

"Somebody new could be at the police department, going through old cases, getting suspicious."

"You've been watching too many detective shows on television," I said. Frannie had always been prone to mild paranoia, but this new anxiety worried me. "Just give your permission to move the graves and that will be the end of it."

Except it wouldn't, really. How could either of us entirely shake the guilt over what we'd done?

"Come home and you can tell them," Frannie said.

"I can't come home right now," I said. "Alice is in the hospital. Her cancer's back."

"If she's in the hospital there's nothing you can do for her there. I need you *here*."

"I'll call the cemetery from here."

"No. You have to come home." She sounded hysterical.

I took a deep breath. I resisted the temptation to give in and tried to calm her, but I couldn't back down now. I had to push on with the decision I'd made. "I'm not coming home again," I said. "Not to stay. I can't."

"What do you mean you're not coming home?"

"Just that. I can't live there with you anymore. I need to

get out on my own and make a new life. One that doesn't revolve around guilt and secrets."

Her sharply indrawn breath left a ringing silence in my ears. I waited, giving her time to process this news. After a while I wondered if she'd hung up the phone. "Frannie? Are you still there?"

"What are you going to do?" she asked, her voice brittle. "Now that you've started sharing all our secrets with Alice, are you going to tell everything? Do you think that will absolve you from all guilt? Or do you just want to see me punished?"

"I think we've both been punished enough," I said. "But we can't keep pretending what we did never happened. We have to acknowledge that what we did was wrong."

"It wasn't wrong!" The words hit me like a slap. "He deserved to die."

"You poisoned him, Frannie," I said. "And I let you. That was wrong."

"I did it to protect *you*." She spoke through tears. Frannie, who never cried. "Don't you even appreciate that?" It frightened me a little that I wasn't more moved, as if I really had become immune to her manipulation.

"You made sure I did," I said. "I've spent my whole life feeling as if I owe you. But now I can see that living with the guilt has hurt me worse than he ever could have."

"You're wrong! When he died we were set free. We were able to make a new life."

"A different life. Not a better one."

"How can you say that?"

How could she be so blind? "Look at us!" I demanded. "You're practically a recluse and I've wasted too many years, too afraid to have the family I've always wanted."

"*I'm* your family."

"But it's not enough. Not anymore." I swallowed the tears

that finally threatened. "I want a chance to meet a man and have children and…and to have a *real* life."

Her wet sobs and choking breaths filled my ear. "What are you going to do?" she asked. "Are you going to the police?"

I'd wrestled with this question for days and arrived at the only answer I thought I could live with. "I don't see what good that would do now," I said. "It won't bring our father back, and it won't give either of us back all the years we've wasted."

"Then what are you going to do?" she asked again.

I took a deep breath. Here was the hardest part, the part that would take all the courage and strength I could muster— maybe more than I actually had. "I'm going to start over. I'm going to stop being afraid of other people, of other relation-ships. And I'm going to try to help other people not screw up the way you and I did."

"All I ever wanted was for you to be safe and happy, and now you hate me."

I sighed, drained by the battle I'd been fighting. "I don't hate you, Frannie. I just think it would be better if we tried to live our own lives. Both of us."

"You won't admit it, but you need me. You always have. I can see it, even if you can't." Some of her old forcefulness was back, but she failed to sway me.

"Goodbye, Frannie. I'll talk to you soon."

"I'll be here. I've always been here for you. One of these days you'll appreciate it."

I hung up the phone and slumped into a chair. My insides felt heavy. I'd known confronting Frannie would be difficult. I'd expected to feel guilty, even sad. But I hadn't counted on this despair and, yes, *anger* that weighed me down.

The Frannie I'd talked to now was a stranger to me. She refused to admit she had done anything wrong. She couldn't see how twisted her perspective was and how it had hurt us both.

Cocoa whined and climbed into my lap. I scratched behind her ears. The sadness I felt was beyond tears. For all I'd gained from my new resolve to make changes in my life, I felt as if I'd lost my sister.

Maybe forever.

When I went to visit Alice that afternoon, I was surprised to hear voices coming from her room. I assumed she was with her doctor, but when I peeked in I saw a man and woman about my age and two teenagers. I tried to duck out before anyone had seen me, but Alice called my name. "Ellen. It's okay. Come on in."

I reluctantly entered the room. Alice was sitting up in bed, looking less pale than she had when she'd first been hospitalized. Her hair was combed and she was wearing lipstick. "This is my friend Ellen," she said. "Ellen, this is Bobby MacCray and his wife, Margie."

Bobby was a solid man with graying hair and blue eyes pulled down at the corners by sadness. He nodded to me, his expression rigid. The look of a man determined not to cry.

Margie twisted her hands together and looked as if she would rather be undergoing a root canal than standing in this hospital room. Her lips were compressed to a thin line and every few seconds her gaze darted to her husband, as if she was prepared to flee after him if he decided to bolt.

"And this is Bettina and Clark." Alice smiled at the two teens, who stood between the bed and the window. Clark, the younger of the two but also the taller, slouched against the window frame, hands shoved in his pockets, watching Alice with a troubled expression.

Tina stood closest to the bed, her arms folded beneath her breasts, eyes downcast. She never looked at Alice, but I had the feeling that, of all of us in the room, she was most aware of her every movement, her every breath.

I noticed Alice didn't introduce the children as her son or daughter. Perhaps they had all agreed not to use those loaded words. Not yet. The fact that they were all here now spoke to the gravity of the situation, and the charity dire circumstances can call forth.

"It's nice to meet you all," I said. "I didn't mean to interrupt. I'll just wait outside." I was already backing toward the door, and ducked out before anyone could stop me.

I found a chair at the end of the corridor, where I could watch Alice's door but not be readily seen. Then I waited. I strained my ears, listening for raised voices. For sobs. For any clue as to how the scene in that little room was playing out.

Maybe fifteen minutes later, the family emerged. Bobby had his hand on Clark's shoulder, and Margie had her arm around Tina. They walked, heads down, to the elevator, none of them saying a word.

When I was sure they had left, I stood and walked slowly back to Alice's room. I was surprised to find her out of bed, standing at the window. She looked over her shoulder when I entered. "I still can't believe they really came to see me," she said, her smile stretching the skin across the fine bones of her face. I had heard of people glowing with happiness—brides and new mothers—but this was the first time I'd actually seen it. Alice's face was illuminated by a light from within. A happiness that was like a heat radiating out from her.

"They're great-looking children," I said. "Bettina looks just like you."

"Do you think so?" Her face crumpled a little and she pulled a wad of tissue from the pocket of her robe. "I'm sorry. I'm just so emotional with everything that's been happening."

"Don't apologize," I said. "You should never have to

apologize for your feelings. Of course you're emotional." I pulled a tissue from the box by the bed. "I'm getting choked up myself just thinking about it."

She sat on the edge of the bed and I pulled a chair closer. "Tell me all about it," I said.

"I called again last night," she said. "After you left." She flashed a half smile. "It took me all this time just to work up the nerve. I asked to speak to Bobby. When he came on the line, I told him everything."

"Everything?"

She nodded. "I told him about the cancer first, then I told him the rest—about Travis and moving back to Ridgeway, and how sorry I was for everything I'd done. I accepted full blame. Then I told him that the only thing I wanted was the chance to apologize to my children face-to-face." She sniffed and tried to stem a fresh tide of tears. "I told him I didn't want to go to my grave with them thinking I never cared about them."

I mopped at my eyes and swallowed past the knot in my throat. "What did he say?"

"He said he would talk to them, and that he would bring them to see me. And he said…he said he forgave me."

"Oh, Alice." I leaned over and squeezed her hand. This was the best gift anyone could have given her.

She nodded and sniffed. When she'd composed herself, she said, "About an hour ago, he called and asked if they could come over right away. Of course I said yes." She pressed her palms to her cheeks. "I was so nervous one of my heart monitors went off. A nurse came rushing in and fussed at me for getting too worked up, but when I told her what was happening she helped me get fixed up to see them. And she said she'd pray for me."

"That's great." I blinked back fresh tears. "When they arrived, were you surprised to see Margie with him?"

"I didn't know what to think." Her eyes met mine, bright

with tears, excited as a child's. "I didn't really even look at her at first. I was too busy staring at Bobby. He looks...he looks so much like his father."

"And Tina and Clark—what did you think of them?"

"I couldn't think. It was so strange. Foolish as it sounds, I couldn't help picturing them as these little children I'd left so many years ago. But here they were, practically grown." She stared down at her hands, knotted in her lap. "I was so afraid they'd hate me," she whispered.

"They don't hate you," I said. "I'm sure of it."

"I hope they don't." She raised her head again and stared past my shoulder. "They didn't say much really, except Clark did say he was sorry I was sick."

"It will take a while. They'll have to get to know you all over again. But they'll be glad they did." Whatever happened now, they would know Alice had loved them. The empty place her leaving had left inside them could now be patched over and partially filled.

"How are you doing otherwise?" I asked.

She sighed. "As well as can be expected. Isn't that a meaningless assessment?"

"Are they going to start treatment soon?" I asked. "More chemo? Or surgery?"

She shook her head. "It's too late for that." She looked around the room, blinking rapidly. "Someone from hospice is coming to talk to me tomorrow. They apparently have a very nice facility here in Ojai. Like a private home, where family can come visit." She smiled through cascading tears. "Isn't that great? Now I actually have family who can visit. Bobby promised they would. He was always a man who kept promises."

I bit my lip, determined not to break down in front of her. I'd had no idea Alice was that sick. She looked so...so like Alice. Older. Thinner. Sadder. But weren't we all? "I'm sorry," I whispered.

Her eyes met mine, full of sympathy. "It's all right. I've had some time to get used to the idea. When I first started getting sick again, I had a feeling this time would be different. It's one reason I decided to move back here and try to repair at least some of the damage I'd done." She smiled. "I won't have a lot of time with them, but I'll have some. That's more than I had a right to ask."

You're wrong, I wanted to say. *You deserve better. We all do.*

Alice crawled back under the covers, tucking them carefully around her thin frame. "Now that we know what my future looks like, what about yours?" she asked.

"I talked to Frannie this afternoon," I said. "I told her I won't be returning to Bakersfield to live."

Alice's eyes widened. "How did she take that?"

"She wasn't happy. She couldn't understand why I'd want a different life from the one we've had."

"She'll be okay. Frannie's a strong woman."

I wasn't so sure my sister was strong in the right way, but I didn't argue the point. "I hope she'll be okay. It's up to her now if she is or not."

"What about your flower shop?"

"I'll sell it to Yolanda. She's said for years she'd like to have her own place."

She nodded. "Then what?"

"I don't know." I shrugged. "I haven't gotten that far."

She smiled. "You know what I think?"

I returned the smile. "No, but I'm sure you'll tell me."

"I think you should take Grandpa Elvis's advice. Find a place you think you'd like and make a space there where you'll fit."

I nodded. "Good advice."

"You're a lucky person, you know."

"I know." I didn't have cancer. I wasn't in jail for murder. I'd had a lot of luck in my life and, until now, had taken it all for granted.

"Not too many people get a chance to really start over and get things right," Alice said. "I can't wait to learn how it all turns out."

My gaze met hers, questioning. Did she mean she intended to stick around to find out?

She winked at me. "Don't worry. Wherever I end up, I'll be checking up on you. I've been nosy my whole life—I can't see cancer or anything else stopping that."

I smiled in spite of my sadness. "I can't wait to see how it all turns out, either." For Alice and Frannie and most of all for myself.

Epilogue

A string of brass bells behind the door chimed as I entered the flower shop, and the familiar sweet-spicy smell of carnations and roses surrounded me. I closed my eyes and inhaled deeply, taking comfort and courage from that rich perfume. It smelled like home. Exactly where I belonged.

"Hello, may I help— Ellen!"

Martin rushed from behind the counter, then drew up short a few steps away from me. "You haven't been returning my calls," he said.

I nodded. "I know. A...a lot has happened. I wanted to try to explain."

He nodded, still cautious, arms folded across his chest.

"Alice is in a hospice in California. Her cancer has come back."

All the stiffness went out of him, and he held out his arms to me. "Ellen, I'm so sorry."

I stepped into his embrace, and it was like coming home. To a *real* home, full of love and warmth and all the things I'd longed for all my life. I struggled to compose myself. "There's more, but I can't talk about it now." I would tell him everything later. He deserved to know the truth, but first, I wanted to enjoy this closeness. This *acceptance*.

I stepped back a little, though he still didn't completely

release me. "I notice the space next door is empty now," I said.

"Yes." He looked toward the empty storefront. "I guess it's too small of a space to be practical for most businesses. The tax service that was in there outgrew the place and no one else has been interested."

"When I was here before, you were talking about expanding," I said.

"Well sure, I'd like to." He shrugged. "Can't quite talk myself into taking the financial risk, though."

I nodded and tried to look everywhere but at him. But I found his brown eyes mesmerizing and my gaze was continually drawn back to him. "Have you thought about taking on a partner?" I asked.

He took his time answering, a curious light in his eyes as he looked me up and down. I forced myself to stand still, to pretend to be unaffected by his scrutiny, though in truth it was all I could do not to fidget and fan myself like an overwrought teenager.

"Do you have someone in mind?" he asked at last.

I took a deep breath, trying to remember the speech I'd rehearsed on the way over here. "I sold my business in California," I said. "I'm thinking of relocating."

"And Sweetwater, Kansas, is on your list?"

"Right now, it's the only place on my list."

He grinned. "Then maybe we should talk." He checked his watch. "Where are you staying?"

"At the La Quinta out on the interstate."

"I close up at six. Why don't we have dinner tonight and talk."

I let loose the smile I'd been holding back. "I'd like that very much."

We were doing the movie thing again, standing there grinning at each other. I decided to give in to the lighter-than-air feeling that surrounded and filled me. I breathed in the floral perfume of the shop and noted the fine lines that fanned out from the corners of Martin's eyes, and the way the blue of his shirt set off the rich chocolate of his eyes. I listened to the muffled traffic on the street outside and admired the brilliant red of a blooming hibiscus and the deep green of the Boston fern by the register. I inventoried every sense and filed away every image like a photograph.

This was a memory I wanted to keep forever, of the moment when I'd started over. All those things I wished I'd done, all the things I wished I'd said—here was my chance to act and speak, suffer the consequences and receive the rewards. All I had to do was get started and see how far I could go.

★ ★ ★ ★ ★

THE
BIRDMAN'S
DAUGHTER

For Daddy

Prologue

There are joys which long to be ours. God sends ten thou-
sand truths, which come about us like birds seeking inlet; but
we are shut up to them, and so they bring us nothing, but
sit and sing awhile upon the roof, and then fly away.
      —*Henry Ward Beecher*

For a man who'd spent his childhood on the arid plains of
west Texas, the jungle was a place of magic. Martin Engel
had hardly slept the night before, anxious to be on the trail
again, completing his quest. He'd roused his companion on
this trip, Allen Welch, from bed at 3:00 a.m. "We've got to
be there before dawn," he'd reminded Welch. "We're going
to have good luck today. I can feel it."

Martin's intuition was seldom wrong. Some people complained that he'd had more than his share of good luck in his
pursuits, but Martin preferred to depend on hard work and
experience. Over the years he'd taught himself everything
there was to know about his quarry.

Still, there was something mystical about the hunt, a point
in every search where he found himself locked in, putting
himself on a different plane, trying to *think* like the ones he
sought.

Martin was a birder. Not a backyard hobbyist or vacation
afficionado. He was an acknowledged champion, a "big lister"

who had seen more different kinds of birds than only a handful of people in the world.

Seven thousand, nine hundred and forty-eight. Today he was trying for seven thousand, nine hundred and fifty. On this trip he planned to clean up Brazil. When he got on the plane to head home to Texas, he would have seen every bird that existed in this country's jungles and plains. The promise of such an accomplishment made him tremble with excitement.

He and Welch were at the trailhead by three-thirty. Welch slugged coffee from a thermos and stumbled over roots in the path, while Martin charged forward, eyes scanning the canopy overhead, binoculars ready. Even at this early hour, the air was thick and fetid around him, the ground beneath his feet spongy with decay. His ears filled with the whirring of insects. Insects meant birds.

He reviewed his quarry in his mind. The Pale-faced Antbird, *Skutchia borbae,* with its dark rufous head and black eye patch; the Hoffman's Woodcreeper, *Dendrocolaptes hoffmannsi,* with its straight blackish bill and the brown to rufous-chestnut upperparts; and the Brown-chested Barbet, *Capito brunneipectus,* with its distinctive chunky silhouette. They had haunted him for months now, taunting him with the blank lines beside their names on his list, lines where he would record the date, time and location of his sighting of them.

He'd seen the Pale-faced Antbird his first day out this trip. He and Welch had scarcely stepped onto the jungle path when it flashed by them, lured by the sounds of a Pale-faced Antbird call Martin had played on the tape deck strapped to his pack. The other two had been more wary. He'd hunted three days for them, scarcely noticing the sweat drenching his clothes or the hunger pangs in his belly or the cotton in his mouth.

Only two more names and he would have cleaned up Brazil. Only fifty more birds and he would have his eight thousand, within reach of the record as the most accomplished birder in the world. And he'd done it all on his own, while working and raising a family. No fancy paid guides to point out the birds for him. He'd taught himself to recognize them and tramped out to hunt on his own.

People talked about the ecstasy of drugs or spiritual quests. For him that feeling came when he spotted a new bird to add to his list. The flash of wing, a hint of color, the silhouette of a distinct form against the sky was like a glimpse of the divine. He, Martin Engel, unremarkable middle son in a large family of accomplished athletes and academics, had been singled out for this privilege. With each new sighting, his heart raced, his palms grew clammy and his breath came in gasps. When he was certain of his quarry, he'd been known to shout and pump his fists. A new bird added to his list was the equivalent of a grand slam in the World Series. He'd done what few in the world had ever accomplished.

Sometimes guilt pricked at him—guilt over spending so much time away from his family. But more often than not, he didn't think about them. When he was out there, hunting, it was all about the birds and the numbers.

He'd awakened this morning with the sense that this would be the day he'd see the other two birds he needed. But as the morning dragged on, his certainty faded. The trees were filled with Variegated Antpittas, Fuscous and Boat-billed Flycatchers and White-throated Hummingbirds—all birds he'd seen before. As if to taunt him, a second Pale-faced Antbird darted across the path in front of them. But no sign of the Woodcreeper or the Barbet.

"We should stop and rest," Welch said, coming up behind Martin when he stopped to train his binoculars on a bird overhead. A Glittering-bellied Emerald, its iridescent blue and green feathers shimmering in a beam of sunlight.

"Just a little farther," Martin said, letting the binoculars hang loose around his neck again. "We're close."

"It's like a steam room out here." Welch wiped at his neck with a crumpled bandanna.

"Is it?" Martin hadn't noticed.

He'd known this feeling before, this sense that the bird he sought was nearby. He only had to look at the right location at the right moment and it would be his.

And that was how it was again. He turned his head slightly, prepared to argue with Welch, and he saw the flash of color in the trees. He froze and brought his binoculars up to his eye, his spirits soaring as he zeroed in on the distinctive straight black bill. "That's it!" he shouted, adrenaline surging through him. "I told you it was here."

But the last words came out muddled, and the next thing he knew, he was sinking to his knees in the thick forest muck, the world whirling around him, until he was staring up at a wavery patch of sky framed by leafy branches. Welch was saying something to him, something he couldn't hear. All he could think as he slipped into blackness was *Only one more bird to go....*

1

*Life is good only when it is magical and
musical... You must hear the bird's song without
attempting to render it into nouns and verbs.*
—*Ralph Waldo Emerson, "Works and Days"*

When Karen MacBride first saw her father in the hospital,
she was struck by how much this man who had spent his life
pursuing birds had come to resemble one. His head, round
and covered with wispy gray hair, reminded her of the head
of a baby bird. His thin arms beneath the hospital sheet
folded up against his body like wings. Years spent outdoors
had weathered his face until his nose jutted out like a beak,
his eyes sunken in hollows, watching her with the cautious
interest of a crow as she approached his bed.

"Hi, Dad." She offered a smile and lightly touched his
arm. "I've come home to take care of you for a while." After
sixteen years away from Texas, she'd flown from her home
in Denver this morning to help with her father for a few
weeks.

That she'd agreed to do so surprised her. Martin Engel was
not a man who either offered or inspired devotion from his
family. He had been the remote authority figure of Karen's
childhood, the distracted voice on the other end of the line
during infrequent phone calls during her adult years, the

polite, preoccupied host during scattered visits home. For as long as she could remember, conversations with her father had had a disjointed quality, as if all the time he was talking to her, he was thinking of the call of the Egyptian Goose, or a reputed sighting of a rare Hutton's Shearwater.

Which, of course, he was. So what kind of communication could she expect from him now that he couldn't talk at all? Maybe she'd agreed to return to Texas in order to find out.

He nodded to show he understood her now, and made a guttural noise in his throat, like the complaining of a jay.

"The doctors say there's a chance he will talk again." Karen's mother, Sara, spoke from her post at the end of the bed. "A speech therapist will come once a week to work with him, and the occupational therapist twice a week. Plus there's an aide every weekday to help with bathing and things like that."

Karen swallowed hard, resisting the urge to turn and run, all the way back to Colorado. A voice in her head whispered, *It's not too late to get out of this, you know.*

She ignored the voice and nodded, smile still firmly fixed in place. "The caseworker gave me the schedule. And Del said he got the house in order."

"He built a ramp for the wheelchair and put handrails in the shower and things." Sara folded her arms over her stomach, still looking grim. "Thank God you agreed to come down and stay with him. Three days with him here has been enough to wear me out."

"Mom!" Karen nodded to her dad.

"I know he can hear me." Sara swatted at her former husband's leg. "I'm sure it hasn't been any more pleasant for him than it has been for me." Sara and Martin Engel had divorced some twenty years before, but they still lived in the same town and maintained a polite, if distant, relationship.

A large male nurse's aide filled the doorway of the room.

"Mr. Engel, I'm here to help you get dressed so you can go home."

"Karen and I will go get a cup of coffee." Sara took her daughter by the arm and pulled her down the hallway.

"You looked white as a ghost back there," Sara said as they headed toward the cafeteria. "You aren't going to get all weak and weepy on me, are you?"

Karen took a deep breath and shook her head. "No." It had been a shock, seeing Dad like that. But she was okay now. She could do this.

"Good. Because he's not worth shedding any tears over."

Karen said nothing. She knew for a fact her mother had cried buckets of tears over Martin at one time. "What happened, exactly?" she said. "I understand he's had a stroke, but how?"

"He was in Brazil, hunting the Pale-faced Antbird, the Hoffman's Woodcreeper and the Brown-chested Barbet." Sara rattled off the names of the exotic birds without hesitation. Living with a man devoted to birding required learning to speak the language in order to have much communication from him at all. She glanced over the top of her bifocals at her daughter. "If he found those three, he'd have 'cleaned up' Brazil, so of course he was adamant it be done as soon as possible."

"He only needed three birds to have seen every bird in Brazil?" Karen marveled at this. "How many is that?"

"Seven thousand, nine hundred and something?" Sara shook her head. "I'm not sure. It changes all the time anyway. But I do know he's getting close to eight thousand. When he passed seven thousand, seven hundred and fifty, he became positively fanatical about topping eight thousand before he got too old to travel."

Ever since Karen could remember, her father's life—and thus the life of his family—had revolved around adding birds to the list. By the time she was six, Karen could name over a hundred different types of birds. She rattled off genus species names the way other children talked about favorite cartoon characters. Instead of commercial jingles, birdcalls stuck in her head, and played over and over again. To this day, when she heard an Olive-sided Flycatcher, she could remember the spring morning when she'd first identified it on her own, and been lavished with praise by her too-often-distracted father.

"He'd just spotted the Woodcreeper when he keeled over right there in the jungle." Sara continued her story. "Allen Welch was with him, and he's the one who called me. He apologized, but said he had no idea who else to contact."

Karen shook her head, amazed. "How did you ever get him home?"

"The insurance paid for an air ambulance. All those years with Mobil Oil were worth something after all." Martin had spent his entire career as a petroleum engineer with Mobil Oil Company. He always told people he kept the job for the benefits. They assumed he meant health insurance and a pension, but his family knew the chief benefit for him was the opportunity to travel all over the world, adding birds to his list.

They reached the cafeteria. "I'll get the coffee, you sit," Sara said, and headed for the coffee machine.

Karen sank into a molded plastic chair and checked her watch. Eleven in the morning here in Texas. Only ten in Colorado. Tom and Matt would be at a job site by now and Casey was in math class—she hoped.

"Here you go." Her mother set a cardboard cup in front of her and settled into the chair across the table. "How are Tom and the boys?"

"They're fine. This is always a busy time of year for us, of course, but Matt's been a terrific help, and we've hired some new workers." Tom and Karen owned Blue Spruce Landscaping. This past year, their oldest son, Matt, had begun working for them full-time. "Did I tell you Matt's signed up for classes at Red Rocks Community College this fall? He wants to study landscaping."

"And he'll be great at it, I'm sure." She sipped her coffee. "What about Casey? What's he up to these days?"

Karen's stomach tightened as she thought of her youngest son. "Oh, you know Casey. Charming and sweet and completely unmotivated." She made a face. "He's failing two classes this semester. I'm beginning to wonder if I'll ever get him out of high school."

"He takes after his uncle Del." Sara's smile was fond, but her words made Karen shudder.

"The world doesn't need two Dels," she said. Her younger brother was a handsome, glib, womanizing con man. When he wasn't sponging off her parents, he was making a play for some woman—usually one young enough to be his daughter. "Are he and Sheila still together?" Sheila was Del's third wife, the one who'd put up with him the longest.

"No, they've split up." Sara shrugged. "No surprise there. She never let the boy have any peace. Talk about a shrew."

"I'd be a shrew, too, if my husband couldn't keep his pants zipped or his bank account from being overdrawn."

"Now, your brother has a good heart. People—especially women—always take advantage of him."

No, Del had a black heart, and he was an expert at taking advantage of others. But Karen knew it was no use arguing with her mother. "If Del's so good, maybe *he* should be the one looking after Dad," she said.

Her mother frowned at her. "You know your father and Del don't get along. Besides, for all his good qualities, Del isn't the most responsible man in the world."

Any other time, Karen might have laughed. Saying her

brother wasn't responsible was like saying the Rocky Mountains were steep.

She checked her watch again. Eleven-twenty. At home she'd be making the last calls on her morning's to-do list.

Here, there was no to-do list, just this sense of too much to handle. Too many hours where she didn't know what lay ahead. Too many things she had no control over. "Do you think he's ready yet?" she asked.

Her mother stood. "He probably is. I'll help you get him in the car. Del said he'd meet you at the house to help get him inside, but after that, you're on your own."

"Right." After all, she was Karen, the oldest daughter. The dependable one.

The one with *sucker* written right across her forehead.

Of course Del was nowhere in sight when Karen pulled her father's Jeep Cherokee up to the new wheelchair ramp in front of his house. She got out of the car and took a few steps toward the mobile home parked just across the fence, but Del's truck wasn't under the carport and there was no sign that anyone was home.

Anger gnawing a hole in her gut, she went around to the back of the Jeep and took out the wheelchair her mother had rented from the hospital pharmacy. After five minutes of struggling in the already oppressive May heat, she figured out how to set it up, and wheeled it around to the passenger side of the vehicle.

"Okay, Dad, you're going to have to help me with this," she said, watching his eyes to make sure he understood.

He nodded and grunted again, and made a move toward the chair.

"Wait, let me unbuckle your seat belt. Okay, put your hand on my shoulder. Wait, I'm not ready…well, all right. Here. Wait—"

Martin half fell and was half dragged into the chair. Sweat

trickled down Karen's back and pooled at the base of her spine. She studied the wheelchair ramp her brother had built out of plywood. As usual, he'd done a half-ass job. The thing was built like a skateboard ramp, much too steep.

In the end, she had to drag the chair up the ramp backward, grappling for purchase on the slick plywood surface, cursing her brother under her breath the whole way. At the top, she sagged against the front door and dug in her purse for the key. A bird sang from the top of the pine tree beside the house.

She felt a tug on her shirt and looked over to find her father staring intently at the tree. "Northern Cardinal," she identified the bird.

He nodded, satisfied, apparently, that she hadn't forgotten everything he'd taught her.

Inside, the air-conditioning hit them with a welcome blast of cold. Karen pushed the wheelchair through the living room, past the nubby plaid sofa that had sat in the same spot against the wall for the past thirty years, and the big-screen TV that was a much newer addition. She started to turn toward her father's bedroom, but he tugged at her again, and indicated he wanted to go in the opposite direction.

"Do you want to go to your study?" she asked, dismayed.

He nodded.

"Maybe you should rest first. Or the two of us could visit some. I could make lunch...."

He shook his head, and made a stabbing motion with his right hand toward the study.

She reluctantly turned the chair toward the back bedroom that none of them had been allowed to enter without permission when she was a child.

The room was paneled in dark wood, most of the floor space taken up by a scarred wooden desk topped by a sleek black computer tower and flat-screen monitor. Karen shoved the leather desk chair aside and wheeled her father's chair into the kneehole. Before he'd come to a halt, he'd reached out with his right hand and hit the button to turn the computer on.

She backed away, taking the opportunity to study the room. Except for the newer computer, things hadn't changed much since her last visit, almost a year ago. A yellowing map filled one wall, colored pins marking the countries where her father had traveled and listed birds. Behind the desk, floor-to-ceiling shelves were filled with her father's collection of birding reference books, checklists and the notebooks in which he recorded the sightings made on each expedition.

The wall to the left of the desk was almost completely filled with a large picture window that afforded a view of the pond at the back of his property. From his seat at the desk, Martin could look up and see the Cattle Egrets, Black-necked Stilts, Least Terns and other birds that came to drink.

On the wall opposite the desk he had framed his awards. Pride of place was given to a citation from the *Guinness Book of World Records,* in 1998, when they recognized him as the first person to see at least one species of each of the world's one hundred and fifty-nine bird families in a single year. Around it were ranged lesser honors from the various birding societies to which he belonged.

She looked at her father again. He was bent over the computer, his right hand gripping the mouse like an eagle's talon wrapped around a stone. "I'll fix us some lunch, okay?"

He said nothing, gaze riveted to the screen.

While Karen was making a sandwich in the kitchen, the back door opened to admit her brother. "Hey, sis," he said, wrapping his arms around her in a hug.

She gave in to the hug for two seconds, welcoming her brother's strength, and the idea that she could lean on him if she needed to. But of course, that was merely an illusion.

She shrugged out of his grasp and continued slathering mayonnaise on a slice of bread. "You were supposed to be here to help get Dad in the house."

"I didn't know you were going to show up so soon. I ran out to get a few groceries." He pulled a six-pack of beer from the bag and broke off a can.

"You thought beer was appropriate for a man who just got out of the hospital?"

"I know I sure as hell would want one." He sat down and stretched his legs out in front of him. "Make me one of them sandwiches, will you?"

"Make your own." She dropped the knife in the mayonnaise jar, picked up the glass of nutritional supplement that was her father's meal and went to the study.

When she returned to the kitchen, Del was still there. He was eating a sandwich, drinking a second beer. The jar of mayonnaise and loaf of bread still sat, open, on the counter. "I'm not your maid," she snapped. "Clean up after yourself."

"I see Colorado hasn't improved your disposition any." He nodded toward the study. "How's the old man?"

"Okay, considering. He can't talk yet, and he can't use his left side much at all, but his right side is okay."

"So how long are you staying?"

"A few weeks. Maybe a couple of months." She wiped crumbs from the counter and twisted the bread wrapper shut, her hands moving of their own accord. Efficient. Busy. "Just until he can look after himself again."

"You think he'll be able to do that?"

His skepticism rankled. "Of course he will. There will be therapists working with him almost every day."

"Better you than me." He crushed the beer can in his palm. "Spending that much time with him would drive me batty inside of a week."

She turned, her back pressed to the counter, and fixed her

brother with a stern look. "You're going to have to do your part, Del. I can't do this all by myself."

"What about all those therapists?" He stood. "I'll send Mary Elisabeth over. She likes everybody."

"Who's Mary Elisabeth?"

"This girl I'm seeing."

That figured. The divorce papers for wife number three weren't even signed and he had a new female following after him. "How old is Mary Elisabeth?"

"Old enough." He grinned. "Younger than you. Prettier, too."

He left, and she sank into a chair. She'd hoped that at forty-one years old, she'd know better than to let her brother needle her that way. And that at thirty-nine, he'd be mature enough not to go out of his way to push her buttons.

But of course, anyone who thought that would be wrong. Less than an hour in the house she'd grown up in and she'd slipped into the old roles so easily—dutiful daughter, aggravated older sister.

She heard a hammering sound and realized it was her father, summoning her. She jumped up and went to him. He'd managed to type a message on the screen

I'm ready for bed.

She wheeled him to his bedroom. Some time ago he'd replaced the king-size bed he'd shared with her mother with a double, using the extra space to install a spotting scope on a stand, aimed at the trees outside the window. Nearby sat a tape recorder and a stack of birdcall tapes, along with half a dozen field guides.

She reached to unbutton his shirt and he pushed her away, his right arm surprisingly strong. She frowned at him. "Let me help you, Dad. It's the reason I came all this way. I *want* to help you."

Their eyes met, his watery and pale, with only a hint of

their former keenness. Her breath caught as the realization hit her that he was an old man. Aged. Infirm. Words she had never, ever associated with her strong, proud father. The idea unnerved her.

He looked away from her, shoulders slumped, and let her wrestle him out of his clothes and into pajamas. He got into bed and let her arrange his legs under the covers and tuck him in. Then he turned his back on her. She was dismissed.

She went into the living room and lay down on the sofa. The clock on the shelf across the room showed 1:35. She felt like a prisoner on the first day of a long sentence.

A sentence she'd volunteered for, she reminded herself. Though God knew why. Maybe she'd indulged a fantasy of father–daughter bonding, of a dad so grateful for his daughter's assistance that he'd finally open up to her. Or that he'd forget about birds for a while and nurture a relationship with her.

She might as well have wished for wings and the ability to fly.

2

You must have the bird in your heart before you can find it in the bush.
—*John Burroughs,* Birds and Bees, Sharp Eyes and Other Papers

When Karen woke the next morning, she stared up at the familiar-yet-not-quite-right ceiling, then rolled over, reaching for Tom. But of course, he wasn't here. She sat up and looked around the bedroom she'd occupied as a girl. A line of neon-haired Troll dolls leered back at her from the bookshelves beside the window.

The clock showed 7:25. She lay on her back, sleep still pulling at her. She told herself she should get up and check on her father. The occupational therapist was coming this morning and the nurse's aide was due after lunch. Today would set the tone for the rest of her days here, so she needed to get off on the right foot. Still she lingered under the comfort of the covers.

When she did finally force herself into a sitting position, she reached for the phone. Tom would be up by now, getting breakfast for himself and the boys.

"Hello?" He answered on the third ring.

"Hi, honey. Good morning."

"Good morning. How's it going?"

"Okay, so far. Dad's not as helpless as I thought. He can't talk, but he can type with his right hand on the computer, and he tries to help me move him in and out of his chair, though sometimes that's more trouble than if he sat still. The therapist is coming today to start working with him, so I'm hoping for good progress."

"That's good. Don't try to do too much by yourself, though. Get some help."

"I saw Del yesterday. I told him he'd have to help me and he volunteered his girlfriend-du-jour."

Tom laughed and she heard the scrape of a spatula against a pan. He was probably making eggs. "How's it going there?" she asked.

"Hectic, as usual. We're starting that big job out at Adventist Hospital today, and we've still got ten houses left to do in that new development out near the airport."

Guilt squeezed her at the thought of all the paperwork those jobs would entail in the coming weeks. She was the one who kept the office running smoothly, not to mention their household. "Maybe you should hire some temporary help in the office," she said. "Just until I get back."

"Maybe. But I don't trust a stranger the way I trust you. Besides, you'll be back soon."

Not soon enough to suit her. In nearly twenty-three years of marriage, they'd never been apart more than a night or two. The thought of weeks without him, away from her familiar routine, made her want to crawl back in bed and pull up the covers until this was all over. "How are the boys?"

"Matt's doing great. He's running a crew for me on those subdivision jobs."

"And Casey?" She held her breath, waiting for news of her problem youngest child.

"I got a call from the school counselor last night. He's going to fail his freshman year of high school unless he can pull off a miracle on his final exams. And he's decided he doesn't want to work for me this summer."

There was no mistaking the edge in Tom's voice. He took this kind of thing personally, though she doubted Casey meant it that way. "What does he want to do?"

"Apparently nothing."

"Let me talk to him."

She heard him call for Casey, and then her youngest son was on the phone, as cheerful as if he'd been awake for hours, instead of only a few minutes. "Hey, Mom, how are you? I thought about you last night. Justin and I went to see this really cool band. They write all their own songs and stuff. You would have really liked them."

It would have been easier to come down hard on Casey if he were surly and uncommunicative, but he had always been a sunny child. She reminded herself it was her job as a mother to try to balance out some of that sunniness with reality. "Dad tells me the school counselor called him last night."

"It's all such a crock," he said. "All they do is teach these tests. The teachers don't care if we learn anything useful or not. Why should I even bother?"

"You should bother because a high school diploma is a requirement for even the most entry-level jobs these days, and Mom and Dad aren't going to be around to support you forever."

"You don't have to worry about me, Mom. I'll be okay."

Okay doing what? she wanted to ask, but didn't dare. The last time she'd hazarded this question, he'd shared his elaborate plan to become a championship surfer in Hawaii—despite the fact that he'd never been on a surfboard before.

"What are you going to do this summer?" she asked instead. He had only one more week of school before vacation.

"I thought maybe I'd just, you know, hang out."

He was fast becoming an expert at *hanging out.* "Your dad could really use your help. Without me there he's having to do more of the office work."

"Matt's helping him. A friend of mine has a job life-guarding at the city pool. He thinks he can get me on there. That would be a cool job."

Any job was better than no job, she supposed. "All right, if you get the job, I'll talk to your dad."

"When are you coming home?"

The plaintive tone in his voice cut deep. "I don't know. In a few weeks. By the end of the summer, for sure." Her original plan for a short visit seemed unrealistic now that she'd seen her father and realized the extent of his disability.

"How's Grandpa?"

"He's okay. The stroke paralyzed his left side, though with therapy, he should be able to get back to almost normal." She hoped.

"That's good. Tell him I said hi. Dad wants to talk to you again."

Tom got back on the line. "He says he's going to get a job lifeguarding at the city pool," she said. "Maybe it would be a good thing for him to work for someone else for a summer."

"Yeah, then he'd find out how good he's got it now." He shifted the phone and called goodbye to the boys as they left for school and work, then returned to their conversation. "What did you tell Casey when he asked how long you'd be gone?"

"I told him I'll be home by the end of the summer, at the latest." She didn't know if she'd last that long, but she'd made a commitment and couldn't back out now.

"I don't know how we're going to do without you here for that long. I was thinking it would only be a few weeks."

She took a deep breath, fighting against the tension that tightened around her chest like a steel band. "I know I said that, but now that I'm here, I can see that was unrealistic. He's going to need more time to get back on his feet."

"Then your mother and brother should pitch in to help. They live right there and neither one of them has a family."

"They won't help. Del hardly spent five minutes here yesterday."

"What about a nursing home? Or a rehab facility? His insurance would probably even pay for part of it." Tom was in problem-solving mode now. For him, everything had a simple answer. But there was nothing simple about her relationship with her father.

"It would kill him to be in a place like that. To have strangers taking care of him. You know how he is about his privacy. His dignity."

"I know he's never gone out of his way to do anything for you. And we need you here." The no-nonsense tone she admired when Tom dealt with vendors and difficult customers wasn't as welcome when it was aimed at her.

"I know you do," she said, struggling to keep her temper. She'd been away from home scarcely twenty-four hours and he was already complaining. She'd wanted sympathy from him. Support. Not a lecture. "Right now, Dad needs me more."

"What are you going to do if your father doesn't recover enough to look after himself again?" Tom asked.

"I don't know." Having him come live with them in Denver was out of the question. The doctor had already told her his lungs couldn't handle the altitude. She sighed. "If Dad doesn't improve by the end of the summer, we'll probably have to put him in a nursing home. But give me this summer to try to help him, please."

"I'm sorry." His voice softened. "I don't mean to pressure

you. I just… It's hard to think about dealing with the business and the boys without you. Casey's not the only one in this house who didn't realize how good he's got it."

She laughed, as much from relief as mirth. "You keep thinking like that. And see when you can get away to come see me."

"I'll do that."

They said their goodbyes, then she dressed and made her bed, and went to get her father ready for his first therapy appointment.

What she hadn't been able to say to Tom was that she needed to stay here right now as much for herself as for her father. She needed to see if being forced together like this, they could somehow find the closeness that had always eluded them before.

That afternoon, Casey lay on his bed and tossed a mini-basketball at the hoop on the back of the bedroom door. If he aimed it just right, the ball would soar through the hoop, bounce off the door and sail back to him, so that he could retrieve it and start over without changing positions.

Matt was in the shower in the bathroom next to the bedroom they shared. Casey could hear the water pounding against the tile wall, and smell the herbal shampoo Matt liked. He was getting ready to go on a date with his girlfriend, Audra. Were they going to have sex? Casey knew they'd done it because he'd caught Matt hiding a box of condoms in the back of his desk drawer, where he thought Mom wouldn't find them. Casey had given him a hard time about it. "You're nineteen, for Christ's sake," he'd said, while his older brother's face turned the color of a ripe tomato. "You shouldn't have to hide something like that."

Matt had shoved the box back in the drawer. "Right. Mom would have a cow if she knew."

"Mom's always having cows. She'll get over it."

He smiled and tossed the ball again, remembering the exchange. The trick to handling Mom was to smile and nod and let her go on for a while, then give her a hug or a kiss and continue as you always had. She was really pretty easy to handle once you knew the secret.

She'd sounded all worried and sad on the phone this morning. Maybe she was upset about Grandpa. That would be pretty rough, seeing your dad in the hospital, all helpless and old. That had probably freaked her out. Mom pretended to be all tough sometimes, but she was still a girl.

He caught the basketball on the rebound and launched it again. What would it be like to have a stroke? Mom had said Grandpa couldn't use his left side. Casey lay back and stiffened his left arm and leg, pretending they were useless. He imagined trying to walk, dragging his paralyzed leg behind him. If you tried to eat, would you get food all over yourself?

He relaxed and let his mind drift to other topics. Mom had said she'd talk to Dad about the lifeguard job. That was cool. He knew he was a disappointment to his dad, who wanted him to be more like Matt. Matt was the perfect son. He was going to college and would take over the business someday. Cool, if that's what he wanted, but couldn't they see Casey didn't want anything like that?

Trouble was, he wasn't sure what he wanted. Still, he was only sixteen. He had plenty of time to figure it out. Whatever he ended up doing, it wasn't going to require going to school for years and years. Maybe he'd be a musician or an artist. Or he'd invent something fantastic that would make him tons of money.

Maybe he'd be a writer. He'd like that. For as long as he could remember he'd kept notebooks full of his writing—stories, poems, even songs.

Matt came out of the bathroom and threw a wet towel at him. "I need to borrow your hair gel," he said.

"For a dollar."

"What?" Matt glared at him.

"You can borrow my hair gel for a dollar."

"You're crazy." Matt turned away.

Casey didn't argue. The problem with Matt was that he carried the honest, upstanding young man thing too far. If it had been Casey, he would have used his brother's gel without asking and chances were, Matt never even would have noticed.

"Here, loser." Matt turned back and tossed a dollar bill toward the bed.

Casey reached out and caught it, smiling to himself. He knew big bro would pay up. He probably hadn't even thought long about not doing it.

Mentally, he added the dollar to the stash in his backpack. He had almost two hundred dollars now. Not bad for a guy without a job. He made money other ways, like writing love notes to girls for their boyfriends, or blackmailing the jocks who smoked out behind the gym. Dangerous work, but so far he'd managed to charm his way out of harm.

It was a gift, this ability to smile and talk his way out of tricky situations. A man with a gift like that could go far, no doubt.

"So are you going to work with us this summer?" Matt studied Casey in the dresser mirror as he rubbed gel through his hair.

"No, I'm going to get a job as a lifeguard at the city pool."

"You can't make a career out of being a lifeguard."

"Why not, if I want to?"

"For one thing, what'll you do in the winter, when the pool closes?"

"Maybe I'll move to Florida, or California, where the pools never close."

"You are such a loser." Matt pulled a shirt over his head, sneered at his brother one last time, then left.

Casey sighed and lay back on the bed again. Why did people think if you weren't just like them, you had to be wrong?

He thought about Mom again. Had she sounded so sad on the phone because she was worried about him? He'd tried to tell her she had nothing to worry about, but she probably couldn't help it. Worrying was a mom thing, like the way she told them, every time they left the house, "Be careful."

"No, tonight I think I'll be reckless," he always answered. She pretended not to think that was funny, but her eyes told him she was laughing on the inside.

He missed her. She'd sounded like she missed them, too. He sat up, put the dollar in his pocket, and decided he'd take a walk downtown, to see what was going on.

While Martin worked with the occupational therapist, an energetic young woman named Lola, Karen took inventory of the refrigerator and pantry and made a shopping list. When the nurse's aide came this afternoon, Karen could slip out to buy groceries and refill Dad's medications.

She was disposing of half a dozen petrified packages of frozen food in the outside trash can when a red minivan pulled into the driveway. As she waited with her hand on the garbage can lid, a plump blonde in pink capris and a pink-and-white-striped sleeveless shirt slid from the driver's seat. The blonde propped her sunglasses on top of her head and waved.

Karen broke into a run, laughing as she embraced Tammy Collins Wainwright. "Look at you, girl!" Tammy drew back and looked Karen up and down. "I guess living up there in the mountains and working at that landscape business is keeping you young and trim."

"Denver isn't really in the mountains, but I guess it does

agree with me. And what about you? You look great." Except
for a few lines on her forehead and around her eyes, Tammy
hadn't changed much since their days behind the wheel in
driver's ed class at Tipton Senior High School. The two girls
had been pretty much inseparable after meeting in that class.
They'd worked behind the counter together at the Dinky
Dairy, and had double-dated whenever possible.

Tammy had been the matron of honor in Karen's wedding,
having already married her high school sweetheart, Brady
Wainwright. While Karen had moved to Austin and later
Colorado, Tammy had stayed in town to raise four children;
her youngest, April, was ten.

Tammy's smile faded. "I'm so sorry about your dad," she
said. "It must be just awful for you."

Karen nodded, not quite sure how to respond. It was much
more terrible for her father, after all. And it wasn't as if he'd
died.

Or was Tammy referring to the fact that Karen had left
everything she knew and loved to come take care of a man
she wasn't even sure liked her?

"I brought a cake." Tammy reached into the van and
pulled out a yellow-and-white Tupperware Cake Taker. "I
remember how Mr. Martin had a real sweet tooth."

"And his daughter inherited it." Karen took the cake
carrier from Tammy and walked beside her toward the house.
"Did you make this yourself?" She couldn't remember the
last time she'd made a cake.

"Me and Betty Crocker." Tammy threw her head back
and let out peals of laughter.

Lola met them at the door, her "bag of tricks," as she called
her therapy equipment, in hand. "He did very well for his
first day," she said. "He's worn-out, though. I imagine he'll
sleep for a couple of hours or so. Just let him be and feed him
when he wakes up. And I'll see you Thursday."

Karen thanked her, then led the way through the house to

the screened back porch. This side of the house was shady, and two ceiling fans overhead stirred the slightly cool air. "Do you mind if we sit out here and visit?" she asked. "That way we won't disturb Dad."

"That would be great." Tammy settled in one of the cushioned patio chairs. "I wouldn't say no to a glass of iced tea."

"Coming right up. And I thought maybe we'd try this cake with it."

"I shouldn't, but I will."

Karen returned a few minutes later with two glasses of iced tea and two plates with generous slices of the lemon cake. "I already stole a bite," she said as she sat in the chair across from her friend. "It's delicious."

"Thank you." Tammy took a bite and moaned. "Ooooh, that *is* good, isn't it?"

"So tell me what you've been up to," Karen said. "How are Brady and the kids?"

"They're doing great. April is going into fifth grade in the fall. Brady's still racing. Our twenty-third wedding anniversary is next month and we're going to San Antonio for the weekend."

"That's great. Congratulations."

"I'm pretty excited. I can't remember the last time we went anywhere without the kids. Which is why I shouldn't be eating this cake." She pushed her empty plate away. "I want to still be able to fit into the new clothes I bought for the trip."

"Sounds like fun."

"Your twenty-third is coming up soon, isn't it?"

Karen nodded. "This fall. I can't believe it's been that long." It seemed like only yesterday she'd been working as a receptionist at the new hospital and Tom had been hired to do the landscaping work. He caused quite a stir among all the young women when he took off his shirt to plant a row of shrubs along the front drive. They'd all wasted countless hours admiring his bronzed muscles and tight blue jeans. When he'd asked Karen to go out with him, she'd been the envy of her coworkers.

"We're thinking about renewing our vows for our twenty-fifth. You and Tom should think about that. You never had a big wedding. This would be your chance."

Karen and Tom had eloped. They'd gone to Vegas for the weekend and been married at a chapel there. It had been very sweet and romantic, though at times she regretted not having the big church wedding with the long white dress, et cetera. She pressed the back of her fork into the last of the cake crumbs. "Did I ever tell you the real reason we eloped?" she asked.

Tammy's eyes widened. "Were you pregnant?"

She laughed. "No. It was because I was afraid my father wouldn't show up for the wedding and I wanted to save myself that humiliation."

"Oh, honey!" Tammy leaned over and squeezed Karen's hand. "Of course he would have shown up for your wedding."

She shook her head. "He wasn't there for my high school graduation. He was in the Galapagos, bird-watching. When Matt was born, he was in Alaska, and when I had Casey, he was in Guatemala."

"But surely your wedding…"

"I didn't want to risk it."

Tammy sat back and assumed an upbeat tone once more. "Well, it doesn't matter how you got married. The point is, it took. Not many couples can say that these days."

She nodded. The fact that she and Tom had stayed together all these years was pretty amazing, considering they'd known each other all of three months when they decided to tie the knot. She had been only eighteen, trying to decide what to do with her future. She'd liked Tom well enough, but when he'd told her he planned to move to Austin at the end of the summer—over two hundred miles away from Tipton—she'd decided to throw in her lot with him.

She'd latched onto him as her ticket out of town, but stuck with him because he'd showed her a kind of love she'd never known before. Now he was the rock who supported her.

"So how is the birdman?" Tammy asked, using the name the townspeople had given Karen's father long ago.

"Cantankerous as ever." Karen sipped her iced tea, then cradled the glass between her palms, letting the cold seep into her skin. "That's good, I guess. He's a fighter. He'll fight his way back from this, too."

"They did an article on him in the paper last year. Said he was one of the top ten bird-watchers in the whole world."

Her mother had sent her a copy of the article. "He's getting close to eight thousand birds on his list now."

"Goodness. I can't imagine seeing that many different birds."

"It's taken a long time." More to the point, listing birds had taken *all* his time, to the exclusion of almost everything else.

The doorbell sounded and both women jumped up. "That's probably the nurse's aide," Karen said. "The county is sending one every day to help with bathing and things like that."

"That's good. That'll help you." Tammy sighed and stood. "I'd better go. Jamie has a Little League game tonight, and April has piano practice. Somewhere in there I've got to figure out what to fix for supper."

"Thanks for the cake. And thanks for stopping by. It was good to see you."

They hugged, then walked arm-in-arm to the door. "If you need anything, you just holler," Tammy said. "And when you can get someone else to sit with Mr. Martin for a while, you come out and have dinner with us. Brady and the kids would love to see you."

"I'll do that." Karen let Tammy out and the aide in, then returned to her grocery list. Maybe staying here wasn't going to be such a hard thing, after all. She did have friends here, and this was a chance for her to get to know her father better, while he was forced to sit still.

It was a second chance for them, and how many people got second chances these days?

3

Casey had never ridden a Greyhound bus before, but it was pretty much the way he'd imagined: tall-backed, plastic-covered seats filled with people who all looked a little down on their luck. They wore old clothes and carried shopping bags stuffed with packages and groceries and more old clothes. They were brown and black and white, mostly young, but some old. The woman in front of him had three little brown-haired, brown-eyed boys who kept turning around in their seats to look at him. Their mother would scold them in Spanish and they would face forward again, only to look back in a few minutes, unable to keep from staring at the white kid all alone on the bus.

At first he'd only intended to see how much it would cost to get from Denver to Tipton, Texas. But when he saw it was only a hundred and thirty dollars and there was a bus leaving in thirty minutes, he'd decided to buy the ticket and go. Mom had sounded so sad and worried on the phone. She was down there all alone with her sick father and nobody to help her, really. He could cheer her up and help, too.

The main thing about traveling on a bus was that it was boring. He spent a lot of time listening to CDs on his portable player and staring out the window. Not that there was much to see—the bus stayed on the interstate, mainly, cruising past fields and billboards and the occasional junkyard or strip of cheap houses. He made faces at the little boys in front of him, until their mother turned around and said something to him in Spanish. He didn't understand it, but from her tone it sounded as if she was cussing him out or something.

After that, he slept for a while. When he woke up, it was dark, and the bus was stopped at a station. "Where are we?" he asked the man in the seat behind him.

"Salina, Kansas," he said. "Dinner break."

At the mention of dinner, Casey's stomach rumbled. The driver wasn't anywhere in sight, so he figured that meant they were stopped for a while. He pulled himself up out of his seat and ambled down the aisle, in search of a diner or McDonald's or someplace to get something to eat.

The bus station was next to a Taco Bell. Casey bought three burritos and a large Coke and ate at a little table outside. He thought he recognized a couple of other people from his bus, but they didn't say anything. They all looked tired or worried. He decided people who traveled by bus weren't doing it because they wanted adventure or a vacation, but because it was the cheapest way to get to where they needed to be.

When he got back on the bus, the seat he'd been sitting in was occupied by a thin guy with a shaved head. He had red-rimmed brown eyes that moved constantly. He looked at Casey, then away, then back again. Casey tried to ignore him, and searched for another seat, but the bus was full.

So he gingerly lowered himself into the seat next to the young man. "Hey," he said by way of greeting.

The guy didn't say anything. He just stared. He was skinny—so skinny his bones stuck out at his wrists and elbows and knees, like knobs on a tree limb. His plaid shirt and khaki pants still had creases in them from where they'd been folded in the package, and he wore tennis shoes without laces, the kind skateboarders used to wear five or six years ago.

The bus jerked forward and Casey folded his arms across his chest and slumped in his seat. It was going to be harder to sleep without the window to lean against, but he guessed he could manage it. Sleeping made the time pass faster, and he had the whole rest of the night and another day before they reached Tipton.

"What's your name?"

His seatmate's question startled him from a sound sleep. He opened his eyes and blinked in the darkness. The only light was the faint green glow from the dashboard far ahead, and the headlights of passing cars. He looked at the man next to him. "My name's Casey. What's yours?"

"My name's Denton. Denton Carver."

"Casey MacBride." Casey offered his hand and the man took it. His grip was hard, his palm heavily calloused. For someone so skinny, he was really strong.

"Where you goin'?" Denton asked.

"To Tipton, Texas. My mom's there, looking after my Grandpa, who's sick."

"That's too bad." Denton didn't look all that sorry, though.

"Where are you going?" Casey asked.

"Not sure yet. Thought I'd get off in Houston and look around. I used to know some people there."

"So you're just, like, taking a vacation?" Maybe he'd been wrong about the people on the bus.

"You might say that." Denton grinned, showing yellow teeth. "I just got out of prison."

Casey went still. He told himself not to freak out or

anything. He kept his expression casual. "I guess you're glad to be out, huh?"

Denton laughed, a loud bark that caused people around them to stir and look back. "I'm glad to be shed of that place, all right," he said.

Casey wondered what he'd been in prison for, but knew enough not to ask. He settled back in the seat and crossed his arms again. "Good luck in Houston," he said.

He closed his eyes, figuring Denton would get the message, but apparently once the skinny man had decided to talk, he wasn't interested in stopping. "I used to have a girlfriend in Houston. Her name was Thomasina. Kind of a weird name for a girl, but she was named after her daddy, Thomas. She was a big, tall girl, and she could hit like a man. She worked at this little store her daddy owned and once these two dudes tried to rob the place. She punched one guy in the nose and hit the other one upside the head with a can of green beans. He tried to run and she just wound up and threw that can at him. Knocked him out cold."

Casey stopped pretending to sleep and laughed. "I wish I could have seen that."

"Thomasina was something." Denton shook his head. "Maybe I'll look her up while I'm in Houston."

"You should do that. I bet she'd be glad to see you."

Denton was still shaking his head, back and forth, like a swimmer who had water in both ears. "I guess you got somebody coming to meet you at the station when you get to wherever it was in Texas you said you was going," he said.

"Uh, yeah. Sure. My mom will come get me." He hadn't exactly thought that far ahead. He hadn't told anyone he was going to do this—not his mom, or his dad, either. Maybe at the next stop, he'd look for a phone and call home, just so his dad wouldn't worry. Then when he got to Tipton, he'd call Grandpa's house and let Mom know he'd arrived.

"Ain't nobody coming to meet me." Denton pressed his

forehead against the window and stared out into the darkness. "I done my time and the state turned me loose. They gave me one new suit of clothes and a bus ticket to wherever I wanted to go, and that's it."

"That's tough." Casey didn't know what to say. He wondered if he could pretend to go to sleep again.

Denton raised his head and looked at him again. "You got any money, kid?"

The hair rose up on the back of Casey's neck and his heart pounded. Denton didn't have a gun in his hand or anything, but the way he said those words, you just knew he'd said them before when he *did* have a weapon.

"I got a little," he mumbled. He had a little over thirty dollars in his billfold in his backpack. Enough to buy meals the rest of the trip, he guessed.

"I saw you eating dinner when we stopped back there, so I figured you had money. You ought to give me some money so I can buy some dinner. You ought to help out a fellow traveler."

Casey wondered if Denton was telling the truth. Would the state turn somebody loose with no money in his pocket? That seemed like a sure way for someone to end up back in jail really quick. Maybe Denton was just trying to scam him.

"When we stop again, I'll get some food and we can share it," he said. He fought back a grin, proud of the way he'd handled the issue. But then, he'd always been good at thinking on his feet. It was another talent he knew would come in handy throughout his life.

Denton grunted, apparently satisfied with this answer. He rested his head against the window and closed his eyes and was soon snoring.

Casey slept, too. The rocking motion of the bus and the darkness, punctuated by the whine of passing cars and the low rumble of the bus's diesel engine, lulled him into a deep slumber. He dreamed he was wandering through the streets of Tipton, searching for his grandfather's house, unable to find it.

When Karen returned from the grocery store, the aide, an older black woman named Millie Dominic, met her at the door. "Mr. Martin is carrying on something fierce, but I can't figure out what he wants," she said.

Karen dropped the bags of groceries on the kitchen table and ran to her father's bedroom. He was sitting up on the side of the bed, one foot thrust into a scuffed leather slipper, the other bare. When he saw her, he let out a loud cry and jabbed his finger toward the chair. "I asked him if he felt up to going outside for a walk and he *roared* at me," Mrs. Dominic said.

"I think he wants to go back to his office." She looked at her father as she spoke. At her words, he relaxed and nodded.

"What's he gonna do in there?" Mrs. Dominic asked as she helped Karen transfer Martin to the wheelchair.

"He can work on his computer. He types with his right hand, so he can communicate." She lifted his left foot onto the footrest and strapped it in place. "I guess that's less frustrating for him."

Once at his desk, he waved away Karen's offer of a drink, but she brought him a Coke anyway, with a straw to make it easier to sip. He was alarmingly thin, and the doctor said she should try to get as many calories into him as possible.

She thanked Mrs. Dominic and sent her on her way, then began putting away groceries. At home right now she'd be answering phones for their business while trying to decide what to cook for supper. If Casey was around, he'd suggest they have pizza. He would have gladly eaten pizza seven days a week.

How were Tom and the boys managing without her?

Was paperwork stacking up on her desk at the office, while laundry multiplied at home? *We need you here.* Tom's words sounded over and over in her head, like an annoying commercial jingle that refused to leave, no matter how hard she tried to banish it. He'd sounded so…accusing. As if she'd deliberately deserted them in favor of a man who had earlier all but abandoned her.

No matter what Tom might think, she'd never desert her family. They were everything to her. But she couldn't turn her back on her dad, either. He was still her father, and he needed her. Maybe the only time in his life he'd needed anyone. She might never have a chance like this again.

She decided to make corn chowder, in the hopes that her father could eat some. Though he'd never been a man who paid much attention to what he ate, content to dine on ham sandwiches for four nights in a row without complaint, she thought the diet of protein drinks must be getting awfully monotonous.

After living so long with three boisterous, talkative men, the silence in the house was getting to her. She started to switch on the television, then at the last minute turned and headed for the study. Her father couldn't form words, but as long as he could type, they could have a conversation. It was past time the two of them talked.

"Hey, Dad," she said as she entered the room.

When he didn't look up, she walked over and stood beside him. "What are you doing?"

He glanced up at her, then leaned back slightly so she could get a better view of the monitor screen. He'd been studying a spreadsheet, listing birds by common and scientific names, locations where he had seen them, columns indicating if he had tape-recorded songs for them. Birds he had never seen were indicated in boldface. There weren't many boldfaced names on the list.

"Mom said you had just seen a Hoffman's Woodcreeper when you had your stroke," Karen said.

He moved the mouse back and forth, in jerky motions, until the cursor came to rest on the entry for the Wood-creeper. It was no longer boldfaced, and he had dutifully recorded the time and date of the sighting.

"That's great, Dad. You've done a phenomenal job."

He shook his head, apparently not happy with her praise. She wasn't surprised. As long as she could remember, he hadn't been satisfied. When he was home, he was always planning the next expedition, making list after list of birds he had not yet seen, counting and recounting the birds he *had* seen, and frowning at whatever number he had reached so far.

In addition to the life list of all the birds he'd ever seen, he also kept a yard list of birds seen at his home, a county list, state list, as well as various regional and country lists. This accumulation of numbers and ordering of names seemed to be almost as important to him as the birds themselves. Maybe more so.

He closed the spreadsheet and opened a new file. Using the index finger of his right hand, he slowly typed in a number: 8000.

Karen nodded. "The number of birds you've been trying for."

He typed again: 7,949.

She studied the number, wondering at its meaning. "The number you've reached on your list?"

He nodded, and punched the keyboard again. Another number appeared on the screen: 1.

She shook her head. "I don't understand. What's the one for?"

He grunted, and typed again: Brazil.

"One more bird you haven't seen in Brazil." Her eyes met his, and the anger and pain she saw there made her stomach hurt. Her father was so upset over a single species of bird that had escaped him in Brazil. Had he ever cared so much about another person? About *her*?

She patted his shoulder. "I'm sorry you didn't get to clean up Brazil while you were there. But the doctor says you should be able to regain a lot of function on your left side, and you can learn to talk again. Going back to Brazil and finding that bird can be your motivation." Never mind staying around to see his grandchildren grow up, or to enjoy his own children in his old age. Some people were inspired by goals like that; for her father, the only thing that mattered was birds.

The next morning, very early, the phone rang, jolting Karen from sleep. She groped blindly for the receiver, her hand closing around it as her other hand reached for the light. "Hello?"

"Have you heard from Casey?" Tom asked, without bothering to say hello.

The urgency in his voice jerked her wide-awake. She sat on the side of the bed and clutched the receiver with both hands, heart pounding. "No. Why? What's going on?"

"He went out walking before supper last night and hasn't come home."

Fear, like a freezing wind, stole her breath. She stared at the phone, as if she were staring down the barrel of a gun. "What do you mean, he hasn't come home?"

"Just what I said. At first I thought he was at a friend's house, or was staying late at the mall, but I've called everyone he knows and driven all over town looking for him and no one knows anything."

News stories of missing children flashed through her mind, the headlines stark and chilling: *Abducted. Missing. Gone.*

"Karen, are you still there? Have you heard from Casey?"

Tom's words jolted her to life again. She forced herself to breathe deeply. Now was no time to fall apart. "No, I haven't heard anything." She looked at the clock. 6:00 a.m. Five in Denver. Tom must have been up all night. "Was he upset when he left? Did you have a fight about something?"

"No. We hadn't talked at all since morning, when I'd agreed to let him apply for the lifeguarding job. He seemed happy about that."

"What does Matt say?"

"He says Casey seemed fine. I don't know what to think."

Tom's voice was ragged with exhaustion. She imagined him, unshaven, running his fingers through his hair the way he did when he was upset. Of course he had handled this for hours by himself. "Maybe you'd better call the police."

"I already did. They promised to keep an eye open, though they're treating it like a runaway situation."

"Why would Casey run away?" Granted, he didn't like school, but he'd always been happy at home. Things that would get other kids down didn't seem to touch him. More than once, she had envied her youngest son his easygoing demeanor. "Maybe he has a friend we don't know about, and he's staying with them."

"Maybe. His backpack is gone, and Matt thinks he took some money with him, but his clothes are still here."

"He's probably with a friend." He had to be. Surely he wouldn't be one of those kids you read about in the news—children abducted by strangers. She resolutely shoved the thought away.

"If he was going to stay with a friend, he should have called us."

"He should have. But you know Casey. He doesn't think about things like that." When he was little, she could always find him in the house by following a trail of his belongings to the room he occupied. She used to berate him for being so inconsiderate, but he'd look at her with genuine confusion. "I wasn't doing it to be inconsiderate," he'd say. "I was just thinking about other things."

That was Casey, head in the clouds all the time, dreaming big dreams no one else could comprehend. Lost in thought, had he stepped off a curb and been hit by a car? "Did you... did you check hospitals?" she asked, her breath catching on the words. "Maybe he's been hurt and can't call."

"I'll do that as soon as I get off the phone with you. I'm sorry to worry you, but I was hoping you'd heard from him. He talks to you about things more than he does me."

And if I was home, maybe this wouldn't have happened. The unvoiced accusation hung between them.

"Please, let me know if you hear anything."

"I will." He sighed. "I'd better go."

After he hung up, she cradled the receiver to her chest, fighting tears. Casey might be sixteen years old, but he would always be her baby; the sweet, contrary boy, the child she worried about the most.

Tom was right—Casey did confide in her more. If she'd been home, he might have talked to her about whatever was bothering him. And if she'd been there, she could have run interference between him and his father. Though Tom denied it, she was still convinced he'd said something to upset their youngest son. Casey was sensitive, and Tom had a way of saying hurtful things without even meaning to.

Every part of her wanted to get on a plane and fly straight to Denver. Surely she, his mother, would be able to find him when others had failed.

But the sensible part of her knew that wasn't true. And if she went back to Denver, who would look after her father? She couldn't count on Del for anything, and her mother was too self-centered and argumentative to last for long. Within half an hour, Mom and Dad would be fighting, and only sheer luck would keep her dad from having another stroke.

They could all use a little luck now. She closed her eyes and sent up a silent prayer for Casey's protection. *Please let him be all right. Please let us find him soon.*

She was still sitting on the side of the bed, eyes closed, when she heard the bell ringing. She'd given it to her father yesterday, so he could summon her without resorting to banging on the furniture. The ringing meant he was awake, and impatient for something. She sighed, stood and reached for her robe. Somehow, she'd get through this day. Whether she did it without snapping someone's head off or raiding the liquor cabinet remained to be seen.

Casey woke with a start when the bus pulled into the station in Texarkana, Texas. The sign identifying the stop glowed dull red in the hazy gray dawn. Casey squinted at it, rubbing his eyes. He yawned and stretched his arms over his head, then realized the seat beside him was empty. Skinny Denton must have slipped past him and gone into the station to use the men's room or something.

He retrieved his backpack from the overhead bin and went in search of breakfast. He'd buy enough to share with Denton, and maybe some snacks for later on down the road.

He hit the men's room first, and washed his face and combed his hair. He stroked a finger over the faint mustache showing over his upper lip, and ran his palm along his jaw, hoping to feel some sign of whiskers there.

He hadn't packed a toothbrush, so he swished his mouth out with water, then headed for the station cafeteria. He looked for Denton, but didn't see him. Maybe he was already back on the bus.

In the cafeteria, he filled his tray with two breakfast sandwiches, two muffins and two cartons of milk. At the cash register, he added two cellophane sleeves of peanuts, for later.

"That'll be $12.67," the woman at the cash register said.

He reached in the outside pocket of the backpack for his wallet, shoving his hand all around inside when he didn't feel it right away. "Must have put my wallet inside the pack last night," he mumbled, and slung the pack off his shoulder to search the main compartment.

A good minute of searching proved fruitless. Feeling sick to his stomach, Casey looked at the woman. "I think somebody stole my wallet."

She frowned at him, and looked pointedly at the food on his tray. "You gotta pay for this," she said.

He looked down at the food, too sick and angry to eat it now, anyway. "I'm sorry. I can't." He shoved the tray away from him and fled the diner, running all the way back to the bus.

As he'd expected, Denton wasn't there. He looked around at the other passengers, half hoping to see Denton in another seat. But there was no sign of the con. "Anybody seen the guy who was sitting here? Real skinny dude, plaid shirt?"

A few people looked at him. Even fewer shook their heads, then went back to reading or napping or whatever they'd been doing.

"Bastard stole my wallet!" Casey said, louder now. Denton had probably taken the wallet and slipped out while Casey slept. "Somebody must have seen him."

No one looked at him now. Casey punched the back of the seat, hard. His hand stung almost as much as his eyes. He blinked back tears of frustration and sagged into his seat as the bus lurched forward. Chin on his chest, he stared out the window. He'd been such an idiot! He should have kept his wallet with him, and kept his mouth shut about having any money. He never should have talked to Denton in the first place.

Maybe Matt was right. Maybe he was a big loser.

A young woman had flown with Martin on the air ambulance that had transported him to Texas from Brazil. She was a nurse, he supposed, and her name was Karen, too. Her name was printed on a badge she wore on her crisp blue uniform, a uniform the color of a jay's wing.

He'd been strapped into a stretcher before they brought him onto the little plane. He'd fought against the restraints, hated being confined. He wanted to sit up, but he couldn't find the words to tell this Karen. When he'd tried to raise himself, he could only flounder weakly.

She'd rushed to calm him, her voice soothing, her eyes full of such tenderness he'd started to weep. She'd patted his hand and brushed the hair back from his face until he fell into a drugged sleep.

His Karen did not look at him that way. Her eyes held suspicion. Caution.

It seemed to him his daughter had been born holding back. She'd been almost two weeks late in arriving into the world. The doctors had been discussing inducing labor when Sara's contractions finally began in earnest.

Later, after she'd been cleaned up and swathed in a diaper and gown and knit hat and booties, a nurse had thrust her into his arms. He'd looked at her, terrified. She seemed so impossibly small and fragile. She'd opened her eyes and stared up at him with a grave expression, as if even then she didn't trust him to look after her.

Sara had taken over after that—feeding and fussing and diapering, shooing him out of the way.

He'd done what his own father had done, what most of the other fathers he knew did back then. He'd stayed out of the way. He'd gone to work and turned his paychecks over to Sara.

He'd come home from business trips and in his absence the two children (Delwood had been born by this time) and his wife had formed a cozy family unit in which he was the outsider.

He remembered once volunteering to dress Karen, then

about three, while Sara fussed over Del. Within five minutes, his daughter was in tears and he looked on, dismayed, with no idea what to do.

"Not that dress. She hates that dress." Sara rushed into the room, Del tucked under one arm, and snatched the offending garment from Martin's hand. "And she can't wear those shoes. They're too small. Go on." She shooed him from the room. "I'll take care of this. Wait for us outside."

The outdoors became his retreat. Those were early days, when he still thought of birding as a hobby. He knew he was good at it. Already his list numbered over a thousand birds. But as he spent more and more time searching for difficult-to-find species, and as he began to gain recognition from fellow birders, the idea of being one of the elite big listers became more and more alluring.

Here was his talent. His niche. The one place where he wasn't dismissed as incompetent or unnecessary. He wasn't blind to the knowledge that the records and rewards had come at a price. He was aware of how dearly he'd paid whenever his daughter looked at him and he saw the doubt in her eyes.

But it was easier to go out again and search for a rare species of bird than to overcome those doubts after all these years. Easier and, for him at least, the outcome was more certain.

Casey smoothed back his hair, straightened his shoulders, then pushed open the door of the lunchroom at the Houston bus station. A few customers waited in line at the cash register, but the lunch counter was empty save for the burly man who stood behind it.

"Excuse me, sir?" Casey remembered to speak up and look the man in the eye. Dad always said people trusted you more if you looked them in the eye.

"Yeah?" The man didn't look very happy to see Casey

but then, he was probably one of those people who weren't happy in general.

"I was wondering if I could wash dishes or sweep up or something, in exchange for a meal." Casey thought the approach was right—not too cocky, but not too downtrodden, either.

The man's expression didn't change. "If you want a meal, you'll have to pay for it."

"That's how it usually works, isn't it? Only thing is, my money was stolen." He took a few steps closer, gaze still steady on the man behind the counter. "I had my wallet in my backpack and this ex-con who was sitting next to me on the bus lifted it while I was sleeping."

The man shook his head. "You should have known better than to put your wallet somewheres where he could get his hands on it."

"Yeah, I should have. Guess I learned my lesson about that one." He shrugged. "So here I am, one dumb kid, not quite as dumb as when I started out on this trip."

The man seemed to think that was funny. He chuckled. "Where you headed?"

"To Tipton." He took a chance and slid onto a stool in front of the man. "I'm going down to help my mom look after my grandpa. He had a stroke."

"That's too bad. How old a man is he?"

He calculated in his head. "He's seventy. But he's never been sick before, so this took everybody by surprise."

"Where you from?"

"Denver. It's a long bus ride from here, that's for sure."

"Yeah." The man looked at him for a long moment. Casey waited, hardly daring to breathe. Finally, the man nodded. "I reckon I could fix you a burger. While I'm cooking it, you can sweep the floor."

Casey hopped up. "Thanks!"

"Yeah, yeah." The man waved him away. "Broom's over there."

Casey found the broom and began sweeping around the front counter and the tables beyond. As he worked, he hummed to himself. He didn't feel like a loser anymore. He felt like someone who'd found a way to look after himself. He wasn't even that mad at Denton. Maybe the state really had cut him loose without a cent. The guy probably did need that money more than Casey did. After all, Casey had talents. A man with talent would always get by.

4

When one thinks of a bird, one fancies a soft, swift, aimless, joyous thing, full of nervous energy and arrowy motions—a song with wings.
—*T. W. Higginson,* The Life of Birds

Karen didn't know if her father woke up in a rotten mood, or if her own anxiety over Casey made her impatient with him, but for whatever reason, getting Martin up and dressed was a battle. He rejected the first two shirts she chose for him before grudgingly relenting to the third, then refused to allow her to wheel him to the breakfast table, insisting on going to his study instead.

Anger burned like acid in her throat as she watched him switch on the computer, his gaze fixed on the screen as he waited for it to boot up. He apparently hadn't noticed how upset she was, or if he had, he didn't care enough to ask what was wrong. A person didn't need the power of speech to show someone he cared.

"You don't care about anyone but yourself, do you?" she snapped. "Yourself and birds you can add to your list."

He looked up and blinked, confusion in his eyes.

"Don't pretend you don't know what I'm talking about." She moved closer and bent over to look him in the eye. "You would rather sit in front of that computer all day, playing with your charts and numbers, than have a conversation with your own daughter."

He frowned, then tapped something out on the keyboard. She looked at the screen.

Can't talk.

"You can type, though. We can communicate that way. And you could listen, if you wanted to."

Still frowning, he typed again.

What do you want to talk about?

"We could talk about anything. The topic doesn't matter. We could talk about..." She looked around the room, searching for some likely topic, then decided on the one that had been utmost in her mind all morning. "We could talk about your grandsons."

Casey and Matthew.

"I'm glad to see you still remember their names."

How are they?

"Matthew is fine. Helping Tom with the business. He's planning on going to college part-time next semester."

What about Casey?

"Casey..." She looked away, unnerved by the knot of tears clogging her throat. "Casey..." She tried again, but could only shake her head.

What?

She cleared her throat and took a deep breath. "Tom called this morning. Casey's...disappeared. I mean, we don't know where he is right now."

Martin's right eyebrow rose and he leaned toward her, his expression demanding to know more.

"I don't know." She held out her hands, a gesture of helplessness. Exactly how she felt. "Tom says he didn't come home last night. He's not with his friends...."

Her father stabbed at the keyboard again.

He's run away?

"Maybe. I don't know. It's so unlike him." Casey wasn't one of those moody, belligerent teenagers who made life so difficult for some of her friends. He was always easygoing, uncomplaining—happy, even.

He's upset because you're here.

"No, he isn't. He was fine when I talked to him yesterday morning." Why did he automatically assume this was her fault? "He's probably staying with a friend and forgot to mention it to Tom." She refused to believe Casey had deliberately run away—or worse, that someone had harmed him.

Police?

"Tom says he notified them. I'm sure they'll locate him soon." She hugged her arms across her chest. "Are you ready for breakfast?"

Coffee.

"I could use some coffee, too." She went around to the back of his wheelchair and started to roll him toward the kitchen, but he put his right hand out to stop her.

I'll eat here.

She frowned at him, but he matched the expression and shook his head, then turned his attention once more to the computer screen.

She turned toward the kitchen to make coffee. So much for thinking he might want to stay with her, to keep her company in her distress, or to share his own concern over his grandson. Her father dealt with this trouble as he had with every crisis in his life, by retreating to his charts and birdcalls, to the logic and order of tables and numbers.

And Karen had nowhere to retreat, nothing that offered escape from worry and frustration.

Martin had once spent the better part of two days sitting in a blind on the edge of a Scottish lake, waiting for the

arrival of a pair of rare King Eider ducks which had report-
edly been recently spotted in the area. His patience had been
rewarded near dusk on the second day. The sight of the stocky
black-and-white male and his dark brown mate gliding over
the shrubby willows at the edge of the lake to land on the
wet pewter surface had erased the aching from his cramped
limbs and made the long wait of little consequence.

He had not been born with that kind of patience, but he
had learned it as a necessary skill for success as a serious birder.
And he had found the same stoicism practical in everyday
life.

He knew his daughter thought him cold and callous. He
didn't have the energy to explain to her that he saw no point
in becoming overly emotional and fretting. Wringing his
hands or storming about wouldn't help her locate her boy.

He was sorry to hear Casey was missing. Though he hadn't
seen the boy in a few years, he remembered his youngest
grandson as a thoughtful, intelligent boy who'd shown an
interest in birds and the ability to sit still for long periods of
time, contemplating the world around him. Martin thought
he had the potential to be a big lister, if he applied himself.

He moved the mouse to click on the desktop icon to open
his e-mail account. The stroke had temporarily incapacitated
him, but that didn't mean he couldn't stay abreast of news in
the birding world. Besides, focusing on birds was calming.
There was order and logic in the neatly aligned spreadsheets
of birds he had seen and birds he had yet to see, deep satisfaction in the number of sightings on each continent, in
each country, and within each genus. Reading through these
familiar lists would be a welcome distraction from worries
about one boy who was currently unaccounted for.

But first, the e-mail.

ABA recognizes Cackling Goose.

His interest sharpened when he spotted this header, and he
clicked on the message. He'd been waiting for this one after

hearing rumors for the past six months. Birds that were previously considered subspecies were sometimes awarded full
species status, thus adding to the total of species in existence.
His hand shook as he scrolled through the press release a
birding acquaintance had pasted into the e-mail. The Canada
Goose, *Branta canadensis,* had been split into large and small
species, the smaller birds now being designated *B. Hutchinsii,*
Cackling Goose.

Quickly, he shrank the e-mail file and opened his spreadsheet for North American birds. Triumph surged through
him as he verified that he had seen both versions of geese
at various times and locations. This allowed him to add the
new bird to his life list.

He leaned toward the keyboard, straining to control his
movements, to type in the new name beneath the original
species. Working one-handed was laborious; several times he
had to erase what he'd written and start over.

By the time he sat back and studied the new entry, sweat
beaded his forehead and he was breathing heavily. His gaze
dropped to the new total at the bottom of the spreadsheet.
Seven thousand, nine hundred and fifty.

He might reach eight thousand yet, even if his health
forced him to give up traveling. New species were added
every year. In the last year he'd added almost a dozen to his
count. Long-dead big listers continued to add to their records
through this process. Still, accumulating sightings this way
was not the same as seeing new birds for himself.

He scrolled through the list, each name bringing to mind
a successful hunt. He'd sighted the King Eider on a miserable cold day when the fog had settled around their party of
both serious and casual birders like a shroud. The others in
the group retired to a pub to banish the chill with pints of
beer and glasses of malt whiskey. But he'd insisted on staying
outside, willing the bird to come to him.

It had arrived like an apparition out of the mist, the

ink-black body sharp against the gray fog, the orange shield above its bill brilliant against the bright blue crest. Martin held his breath, immobile, transfixed by this glimpse of the divine. Was it so far-fetched to think that a creature with wings was one step lower than the angels?

The King Eider was the fourth new species he'd added to his list that day. Number 3,047. In those days, he'd seen four thousand birds as a lofty goal to attain. Only later, when he'd passed four thousand and was closing in on five thousand, did he begin to think of reaching for more. Of trying to do what almost no one before him had done.

When he'd joined the others in the pub, they had groaned at the news of the sighting, and cursed his luck even as they bought him drinks. No one questioned that he had actually seen the bird. Though worldwide, the birding community was a small one, where honesty and integrity counted for everything. Martin's reputation was unassailable. Others often said no one worked harder or was more dedicated than Martin Engel.

The respect of his colleagues was almost as important to him as the numbers on his list. When he was a child, he had sometimes felt invisible in the midst of his older and younger siblings. Their names were routinely in the local paper as winners of athletic competitions and academic honors. Trophies and award certificates lined shelves in the family room. Only Martin had no plaque or statue with his name on it. The family photo album was devoid of Martin's accomplishments, for there were none. His parents, busy with their other talented children, had left Martin to himself. Sitting in the bleachers at the innumerable football, baseball and soccer practices of his siblings, he had discovered birds, and what grew to be an avocation, an obsession—a calling.

He glanced at the framed awards that filled one wall of his office. His parents were no longer alive to see these honors. He seldom saw his siblings, and even his children took little notice of his accomplishments most days. It didn't matter as long as his fellow birders applauded him, and as long as he himself could look at this tangible evidence of all he'd achieved and feel satisfaction filling him, warm and penetrating as the African sun.

When he was gone, the records he'd set would live on. His grandsons could find his name in books and on Web sites, and they'd know that he'd been more than an odd little man who traveled a great deal and didn't have much to say. They'd see that he'd made his mark on the world, and maybe they would find a way to make their mark, as well.

Fortified by coffee and toast, Karen called her mother to give her the news about Casey. *I'm not in right now.* Sara's voice on the answering machine was soft and high-pitched, like a young girl's. *I hope it's because I'm out having a marvelous time. Leave a message and I'll get back to you as soon as I'm able.* That was Sara, determined in retirement to make up for what she had once referred to as "the dull and dutiful years" as wife and mother.

"Mom, I've got some bad news. It's about Casey. He… he's missing. He may have run away or something. Call me." She hung up the phone and stared at the receiver, agitation building. Not knowing what was happening was eating her up inside. She wanted to be there with Tom, talking to the police, questioning Casey's friends. Instead she was stuck here. Helpless.

She snatched up the receiver and punched in Tom's cell number. He answered on the second ring. "Hello?" His voice was gruff, anxious.

"It's me. I was wondering if you'd heard anything new."

"Someone reported a boy who looked like Casey hanging around the bus station yesterday afternoon. The police are trying to determine if he got on a bus, and where it was headed."

She sagged against the counter, and hugged one arm tightly across her middle, as if to hold in the nauseating fear that clawed at her. "Where would he go? And why?"

Tom sighed. "That's what the police keep asking me and I don't know what to tell them. All I can think is that he got some wild idea and acted on it. Maybe he's going to Hawaii to be a surfer or to California to be a movie star. The kid always has his head in the clouds."

"He means well. And he's still young." Yes, Casey was irresponsible and immature. But what was wrong with letting him enjoy his dreams while he still could?

"He's sixteen years old. It's time he grew up."

She refrained from rolling her eyes. This was a familiar litany of Tom's. Now was not the time to get into that discussion. "Call me if you hear anything else, okay?"

"I will."

She had scarcely hung up the phone when her mother's bright blue Mustang convertible pulled into the driveway. Sara breezed up the steps and into the house without knocking. "Good morning, darling," she said, depositing an air kiss to the left of Karen's cheek. "How are you this morning?"

She stepped back, and one look at her daughter had her shaking her head. "Is it that bad already? I was hoping—"

"Mom, did you get my message?"

"What message?"

"My phone message. I just called you."

"I haven't been home. I was having breakfast with Midge Parker. She tried to talk me into going to play tennis with her and Peggy Goldthwait, but I told her I had better see how things were getting on with you. Is your father being a tyrant?"

"No. I'm not upset about him. It's Casey. He's missing."

"Missing?" Sara's perfectly plucked eyebrows arched higher.

"He didn't come home last night. The police think he

might have run away. Someone saw him—or at least a boy who looked like him—at the bus station."

Sara put her arm around her daughter and steered her toward the sofa. "I'm sure you're terrified, but everything will be all right. Casey is a smart kid. He knows how to look after himself."

"He's only sixteen. He looks like a man, but he's still a boy." Karen leaned against her mom, grateful for the strong arm around her. "And he's so…impulsive."

Sara smiled. "I remember when you ran away once."

Karen's mouth dropped open and she stared at her mother. "I never ran away."

"Oh, yes, you did." Sara nodded. "You were nine years old and you told me you were going to find your *real* family."

The memory returned with a jolt. "I packed my Barbie suitcase," Karen said. She recalled the contents—two Barbie dolls, a flower identification book, her toothbrush, a change of underwear, four dollars and ninety-three cents in change, a Chapstick and a map of Texas she'd swiped from the glove compartment of her mother's car.

"You got as far as the Piggly Wiggly parking lot and Barbara Anne Jones from church saw you and talked you into letting her give you a ride home."

By the time Mrs. Jones found her, Karen had spent half her money on a package of Oreos and a pint of milk. She'd reasoned she'd be more likely to recognize her real family on a full stomach. "You gave me a spanking and made me clean out the hall closet as punishment."

"I told you this was the family you were stuck with, so you'd better get used to the idea."

But she never had. Not really. All her life she'd felt out of step with the rest of them. She wasn't interested in birds, like her father, or a daredevil like her brother. She couldn't talk to anyone about anything the way her mother did.

As a child, she would look in the mirror every night as

she brushed her teeth and imagine that somewhere, there was a family with a father who doted on his little girl, and a mother who knew all the girl's friends and everything that happened at the girl's school. Instead of spending all her spare time playing bridge and volunteering at the Y, the mother took the girl shopping for cute clothes, and the father helped her with her homework every evening. And the little girl had no siblings, so she was the center of her parents' attention.

"It'll be all right," Sara said again, and patted Karen's shoulder. "When he gets hungry, he'll come home. Sixteen-year-old boys can't go very long without eating."

She almost smiled. While her mother's complacency often annoyed her, she took comfort in it now. If Sara wasn't panicking, things couldn't be that bad.

"I need sugar," Karen said, standing. "I've got some cake Tammy Wainwright made. Would you like some?"

"You bet. And a big cup of coffee." Sara rose, also, and started to follow Karen to the kitchen, but the staccato beep of a car horn made them both look around.

"Who is that in your driveway?" Sara asked.

Karen shook her head. The battered green truck didn't look familiar. As the women watched, the passenger door opened and a familiar lanky figure slid to the ground. He waved to the driver, then shouldered a backpack and started toward the steps.

Karen blinked, half-afraid her eyes had deceived her.

Sara had no such fears. She looked at Karen and grinned. "Good Lord, is that Casey?"

5

A bird doesn't sing because he is happy; he sings because he has a song.
—*Anonymous*

Casey expected his mother would be surprised to see him, maybe a little annoyed that he hadn't bothered to call first. He didn't know what to think when she burst into tears.

"Thank God you're all right," she sobbed, running to him and pulling him close.

"Well yeah, of course I'm fine." Hungry and a little tired, but okay. He tried to pull away from her a little. Not that he thought he was too big for his mom to hug him, but she was getting his shirt all wet.

She stared at his face, as if to verify that it really was him. "What are you doing here?"

"I thought maybe you needed some help looking after Grandpa." He spoke with more bravado than he felt. As the miles rolled out beneath the bus wheels, the wisdom of his impulsive decision to take off for Texas had grown more questionable. His dad, for one, was sure to get bent out of shape about it. What if Mom got upset with him, too?

"Casey Neil MacBride, what do you mean scaring us all to death like that?" His grandmother stood on the top front step, hands on her hips. She looked exactly the way she had when he was little and she'd scolded him for swiping cookies from the cookie jar or tracking mud on her carpet. "Your folks have been worried sick. Your father has the police out looking for you."

"The police?" *Shit!* "Why did he do that? I mean, I know I should have called—I thought about it, but by that time I was almost here." Besides, by then Denton Carver had stolen all his money, so he didn't have change for a pay phone. And since his folks had refused to get him his own cell, there was nothing he could do. "I figured when I got here, I could explain everything."

Mom sniffed, and dabbed at her eyes with a wadded-up tissue. "You'd better start explaining."

"Yes, I'm interested in hearing this one," Grandma added.

He stuffed his hands in his pockets and hunched his shoulders. He wasn't always so good at explaining why he did stuff—not in ways that made sense to his parents. It was like, when you got to be an adult, you quit doing anything just because it felt right.

"Did you and your dad fight about something?" Mom asked.

He shrugged. Dad was always on his case about something. "He wasn't too happy after he heard from the counselor, but you know how he is."

"Then whatever possessed you to come all this way?"

He could hear the exasperation in her voice. How long did he have before real anger set in? "I guess after I talked to you the other morning, I thought you sounded so sad. And then I thought about how I'd feel if I was down here by myself and all. And it wasn't like I had anything big going on at home, so I thought, why not surprise you by coming down here?"

She still wore a pinched expression, like she was trying to

keep from crying again—or yelling at him. "You still have a week left of school. I think that's fairly *big*."

"Aw, I was failing anyway." He kicked at the dirt. "Why stick around to make it official?"

She shook her head, but put her arm around him and led him toward the house. At least she hadn't started crying again. He couldn't handle more tears.

"I'm going to go now," Grandma said. "I'll talk to you later."

"Thanks, Mom."

They went into the house. It was like stepping into some kind of time warp. He hadn't been here in, what, three years? Yet everything looked exactly the same. Amazing.

"Are you hungry?" Mom asked. "Did you have anything to eat on the way?"

"I had a burger and fries for lunch." More like a late breakfast, really. He hadn't had the nerve to ask for any more handouts after that. He rubbed his stomach. "I am kind of hungry."

"I'll fix you something to eat. But first, we'd better call your father."

He made a face. "Do we have to?" Dad would freakin' lose it when he heard what Casey had done. The old man never cut him any slack the way Mom did.

"Of course we have to. He's been up all night, worrying about you." She took him by the shoulders and turned him to face her. "You do understand how wrong it was of you to take off like that, not telling anybody?"

He nodded. "Yeah. I'm sorry."

"We didn't have any idea what had happened to you—whether you'd run away, or been abducted by a stranger, or hurt in an accident."

"I said I was sorry. I didn't do it to freak you out. I went down to the bus station to see how much the fare from Denver to Tipton would be, and when I saw there was a bus leaving right away, I thought, why not?" He hung his head. "I thought it'd be a cool surprise for you."

"Oh, honey." She put her hand to his cheek, the anger gone from her expression. "I am glad to see you. But until you have children of your own, you won't understand what an awful, awful feeling it is to know that your son is missing, and no one seems to know where he is."

He hugged her, tight. He hated thinking he'd hurt her. "I know. I screwed up again. But I'm here now. And I really am going to help you." He pulled back. "How's Grandpa?"

"Don't change the subject." She picked up the receiver, but stopped when a series of thumping, dragging noises from the hallway caught their attention.

Casey tried not to stare at the figure in the wheelchair. Grandpa Engel had always been such an imposing man. Not big, but tall and sort of *looming*. Now he looked as if he'd been shrunken and dried into this smaller, withered version of himself. His thick brown hair was now gray streaked with white, and Casey could see his pink scalp showing through in places. Only his eyes were as black and fierce as ever. Casey stood up straighter and raised his voice a little. "Hi, Grandpa. It's good to see you up and about."

The old man scowled at him, then looked at his mom and pointed at Casey.

"He got on the bus to come see us, but forgot to tell his father, or anyone else, where he was going."

"Humph!" Or at least, that's what it sounded like his grandfather grunted. Mom had said he couldn't really talk, but he didn't seem to have too much trouble getting his point across. He held up a coffee cup and waved it at Casey's mom.

"I'll make a fresh pot as soon as I've spoken with Tom."

Grandpa didn't seem happy with that news, but with his face sort of tugged downward on one side—Casey guessed from the stroke—it was probably hard for him to look really happy about anything. "You want me to wheel your chair somewhere for you to wait for your coffee while Mom's on the phone, Grandpa?" he asked.

His mom put her hand on his shoulder. "You stay right here, young man. You need to talk to your father."

He gave her a pleading look. "Can't I eat first? I defend myself better on a full stomach."

She gave him her you're-not-going-to-pull-one-over-on-me-this-time look and picked up the phone.

Casey slumped against the counter and stared at the floor. He supposed the situation wasn't completely bad. At least when Dad yelled at him this time, he'd be a thousand miles away.

Karen's hands shook as she punched in Tom's phone number, her initial rush of relief at seeing Casey safe and alive giving way to frustration and anger—all underlaid by the tenderness her vulnerable younger son never failed to engender in her. When he'd told her he'd been worried because she sounded sad, and that he'd come to help her, it had been all she could do not to break down into tears again and hold him close. But she couldn't let his no-doubt sincere good intentions negate the very real fright he'd given them all. He'd have to be punished, as soon as she and Tom decided what was appropriate.

Tom answered the phone right away, as if he'd been anticipating its ring. "Honey, it's me," she said. "Casey is here. He's all right."

"He's there? In Texas?"

She glanced at her son, who was slumped against the kitchen counter, arms folded over his chest, head bowed, as if bracing for a blow. "Yes, he showed up a few minutes ago. Someone in town gave him a ride out here from the bus station."

"He took the bus to Texas? What the hell made him do that?"

She sighed. If she knew the answer to questions like that, raising her children would be a lot easier. "You know Casey. It seemed like a good idea at the time, I guess."

"Let me talk to him."

She held out the phone. "Your father wants to talk to you."

He took the receiver, automatically straightening his shoulders before he spoke. "Hey, Dad."

Whatever Tom said made him wince. Karen's own forehead wrinkled in sympathy. She didn't blame Tom for being angry, but he sometimes let his anger get the better of him with the boys. He said hurtful things without thinking about their impact.

"Yeah, I know I should have told somebody," Casey said. "Yeah, I know this means I won't finish the school year. I thought Mom needed somebody to help her. She's here all by herself looking after Grandpa."

Karen's heart contracted again. How could she stay angry with him when he was so concerned about her? His father hadn't been this sympathetic to her position.

"Well, yeah. But Grandpa likes me. It'll be good for him to have me here."

Another long pause while he listened to Tom, the agitation in his expression increasing.

"Just because I don't do everything the way you'd do it doesn't make me stupid." Casey's voice rose, quaking at the end, sounding to a mother's ear as if he was dangerously close to tears.

She put her arm around him. "Give me the phone." She took the receiver from his hand. "You go wash up. And take Grandpa with you."

When Casey and her dad were gone, she put the receiver to her ear. "There's no sense yelling at him now," she said.

"He's here. He's said he's sorry. We have to decide what to do next."

"Saying he's sorry doesn't mean anything if he's going to keep pulling stupid stunts like this." Tom's anger was barely contained. "My God, he could have been killed on the way down there and we'd never know it."

"But he wasn't. He's okay. And I think he's really sorry."

"What about school? This guarantees he'll flunk his year."

"He seems to think he was going to do that anyway."

"Not if he buckled down and got an A on his finals."

"Then maybe we can talk to the school, make arrangements for him to take his finals later. Tell them it was a family emergency. That's not really a lie."

Tom ignored the suggestion. "If he thinks I'm going to let him take that lifeguarding job now, he can forget it. I've a mind to ground him until he's thirty."

"I think we should let him stay here. At least until I come home." The idea had just come to her. Tom's reaction made her reluctant to send Casey back to him. Maybe some distance would make the relationship between father and son less volatile. She couldn't imagine how tense things would be between the two of them without her there to act as a buffer. And it would be good to have him here.

"What's he going to do there? At least here I can put him to work. Maybe have the local police talk to him about what can happen to runaways. Scare some sense into him."

"That's not a bad idea, but it can wait until we're both home. Right now I really could use his help. And maybe a different environment will give him a new perspective."

"He needs more than a new perspective. He's sixteen years old. It's time he showed more responsibility."

"I don't think yelling at him is going to make him grow up any faster."

"Coddling him certainly isn't doing the trick."

She gritted her teeth. "Just because I choose to deal with his behavior rationally, instead of shouting at him, doesn't mean I'm coddling him."

"You're right. I am irrational. If you'd been through what I've been through the last twenty-four hours, you'd be irrational, too."

She pictured him, slumped against the wall, raking one hand through his hair. Maybe if she'd been worrying about Casey for the last twenty-four hours instead of the last six, she'd be more upset, too. "It'll be easier on you if you don't have him to deal with this summer," she said. "And I'll feel less guilty if I'm helping with at least one son."

"Yeah. You're right." He was silent a moment, and when he spoke again, his voice was gentler. "I'm glad he's okay."

"Me, too. Do me a favor and first chance you get, pack up some of his clothes and send them down here. It doesn't look like he brought much with him."

"That figures." He sighed.

"You must be exhausted," she said. "Try to make it an early day, so you can get some sleep."

"Not a chance, not with all the work I have to do. Plus I've got a stack of invoices six inches high that need to be dealt with."

No doubt an exaggeration, but she didn't feel like calling him on it. After all, she'd left everything in perfect order three days ago. Things wouldn't be that far behind—yet. "Call a temp agency and hire some clerical help. You can't do everything."

"I guess you're right." He gave a hoarse laugh. "See, I need you here to figure these things out."

This admission made her relax a little. "I'll be home as soon as I can. Dad's doing really well, so I'm hopeful it won't be too long. Now get some rest."

She hung up, then went looking for Casey and her dad.

She found them in the study, her father showing Casey his spreadsheets, Casey pretending to be interested.

Or maybe the interest was genuine. "Hey, Mom, did you know Grandpa has seen penguins in South America? And something called an Arctic Tern near the north pole?"

"Your grandfather has seen birds on every continent on earth." She showed him the certificate from Guinness. "He's set records which may never be broken."

Casey admired the certificate. "That's cool." He looked at his mother. "What's for lunch? I'm starving."

She laughed. Now they were back in familiar territory. "Let's go in the kitchen and see. Dad, you come, too."

For once, her father didn't argue. He allowed Casey to push him to the kitchen and even accepted a glass of the despised nutritional supplement, after Casey drank some and pronounced it, "Not as bad as I thought it would be. It might even be good if you put some ice cream in it, Mom."

Dad nodded and she laughed. "Now, why didn't I think of that?"

"See, it is a good thing I showed up, huh, Mom?"

"I guess it is." She had to admit, she didn't feel so alone now. She could count on her youngest son to be there to support her when no one else would.

The nurse's aide had just left the next afternoon when Del paid a visit. With him was a young, beautiful girl dressed in low-cut jeans and a tight T-shirt. She had a ring in her navel and another in her left eyebrow, and she made Karen think of the women in magazine ads for designer jeans or exotic perfume—the ones who always looked as if they had either just gone to bed with a man, or were about to.

"Karen, this is Mary Elisabeth."

Mary Elisabeth offered a hand with a ring on each finger. "It's good to meet you. I think it's really great of you to come down here and look after your daddy this way." She had a

Texas drawl that would melt butter, and a handshake as firm as any man's.

Was it possible Del had been singing his sister's praises? She looked over at him. He had his head in the refrigerator, probably searching for another beer. She turned to Mary Elisabeth again. The Catholic schoolgirl name seemed incongruous on the young woman before her. "Thanks."

"If you ever need any help, or just want to take a break or something, give me a call," she said. "I get along great with older folks."

"You do?" Karen looked at Del again. She'd been sure he was blowing smoke when he'd offered Mary Elisabeth's services. "Why is that, do you think?"

"Oh, I'm a good listener, and I don't get impatient with them like some people. I used to work at a nursing home, so I've seen pretty much everything related to gettin' old that there is to see."

"Where do you work now?" Karen pulled out a chair at the kitchen table and offered it to the younger woman, then sat across from her.

"I work for the city water department. It's not as interesting as the nursing home, but it pays better. But sometimes I think I'd like to go back to school to be a nurse."

"Interesting." How had this seemingly bright, ambitious young woman ever ended up with Del? She was about to ask as much when Casey emerged from the back bedroom, where he'd been taking a nap.

He cut his eyes to Mary Elisabeth and they widened a little, then he looked at Del. "Hey, Uncle Del." He went over to his uncle and gave him a hug.

"Casey, you brat." Del returned the hug, grinning. "What the hell are you doing here?"

"I came down to help Mom. Hey look, I'm as tall as you now." He held his hand over Del's head, showing the tops of their heads were even.

"So what? I can still whip your ass." Del faked a punch.

Casey dodged away, laughing.

"Del, honey, aren't you going to introduce me to your good-looking young friend?" Mary Elisabeth turned a dazzling smile on Casey, who instantly blushed to the tips of his ears.

"This is my nephew, Casey. He's sixteen. Way too young for you."

"Some people think you're too old for me." She winked at Casey, who laughed again.

"I thought maybe Mary Elisabeth could meet Dad, see how they get along," Del said.

"He's napping right now," Karen said. "He usually takes a nap about this time every day."

"That's all right. I'll see him some other time," Mary Elisabeth said. "I have to get to work now. But it was nice to meet you." She smiled at each of them in turn, gave Del a peck on the cheek and sailed out the door.

They were all silent a moment, as if she'd taken some of the air out of the room with her departure.

"Uncle Del, she's *hot,*" Casey pronounced.

Del laughed. "Stick with me, boy. I can teach you a thing or two about how to handle women."

"You'll do no such thing." Karen stood and went to the sink, where she busied herself washing up the breakfast dishes. The thought of her playboy brother teaching her son anything sent shivers up her spine. "She seems very nice. Very bright. How did she ever end up with you?"

"Obviously, she has excellent taste."

Karen snorted.

"That was really cool of her to offer to help you with Grandpa," Casey said.

"Yes, it was very nice." But why would a total stranger offer to do something so nice? She turned to Del. "She's not some gold digger out to talk Dad out of his money, is she?"

"You watch too many soap operas." He tossed his now-empty beer can into the garbage. "Mary Elisabeth is just a nice person who likes to help other people. There are still folks like that left in this world, you know?"

"Yeah, I met one of them on my way down here," Casey said. "He ran this restaurant near the bus station and he let me have a burger and fries in exchange for sweeping up for him."

"You didn't have any money with you?" Karen stared at her son.

He shoved his hands in his pockets and looked around the kitchen. "Well, I had some when I started out, but I sort of lost it."

"You lost it?" She sagged against the counter. Tom was right. The boy was completely irresponsible.

"It was stolen, actually." Casey shrugged.

"Stolen?" She stared at him.

"Yeah, well, this ex-con sat next to me, see, and I couldn't move because there weren't any more empty seats and—"

She put her hand over her eyes and waved away the rest of his explanation. "I don't think I want to hear any more."

Casey came over and put his arm around her. "It's okay, Mom. Everything worked out."

"That's right, sis," Del said. "You worry too much."

The rest of the world might be crazy, but she was the one with a problem, because she worried too much. "It's the worriers in this world who get things done," she said. "People who bother to think about problems figure out how to solve them. Not to mention, we're the ones who look after all you 'free' spirits."

"Maybe so, but I know who's having more fun, don't you, Casey?" Del winked at his nephew.

Casey laughed. "Maybe it's a chick thing." He hugged

Karen again. "Stick with us and we'll teach you to lighten up. And you never know. Some of your responsibility might rub off on us."

She sighed. "I hear pigs might fly, too."

Casey laughed again, and she managed a smile. Life was absurd sometimes. And this particular corner of Tipton, Texas, had always been the touchstone for most of the absurdities visited upon her. She'd be glad when she could get back to her ordinary life, where she was mostly in control and usually knew in advance how things would turn out. Unlike Casey, Karen wasn't a big fan of surprises.

We're never single-minded, unperplexed, like
migratory birds.
—*Rainer Maria Rilke,* The Duino Elegies

In his dreams each night, Martin strode through the jungles of the Amazon, or across the plains of the midwest, or along the shores of tropical beaches. Everywhere birds came to him, darting and wheeling about, the flutter of their wings and the lilt of their songs the soundtrack for his slumber. Ruby-throated Hummingbirds hovered before him like feathered jewels, and Black-necked Stilts stitched lines of tracks in the sand at his feet. He watched them with a lightness in his heart, as if at any moment he, too, might sprout wings and learn to soar with their grace.

He would wake buoyed by this excitement and anticipation, brought back to earth with a thud by the limitations of his body. The determination that had once enabled him to scale the peaks of the Andes or trek for days across waterless deserts, or endure all manner of hardships in the pursuit of birds for his list now could not will so much as a finger on his left hand to move or words to form on his tongue.

He silently railed at the injustice of being imprisoned by the frailty of his own flesh. His frustration exploded from him with the least provocation. He banged his wheelchair into walls and furniture, not caring what he destroyed. He swept the lunch tray from his desk, dishes shattering, when a slice of ham wasn't chopped fine enough to keep from choking him. He balked at being shaved or having his hair cut until the aide calmly pointed out that only a fool argued with a woman who held a razor to his throat.

And always there was Karen, watching him with such intensity, alternately cajoling and critical. "Dad, you have to eat more." "Dad, you aren't trying." "Dad, come away from that computer. You need your rest."

How did she know what he needed? She hardly knew him. She thought his pursuit of birds all over the world was a waste of time. Oh, she never said as much, but the shuttered expression she assumed whenever the topic of birding came up told him everything he needed to know. She didn't understand that peace could come in focusing on a part of nature so different from himself. She didn't know that beyond the pleasure of accumulating numbers and amassing records, there were the birds themselves, so diverse and diverting. They offered beauty without judgment. They demanded nothing from him.

Karen had been back in Texas about two weeks and was beginning to settle into a routine when Del showed up on her doorstep with a dog. "Look what I got for you, sis," he said, grinning like a schoolboy who's just handed his teacher an apple with a worm in it.

She eyed the dog warily. The oversize yellow mutt had floppy ears, legs that looked too long for its body and feet the size of Mason jar lids. It grinned up at her, tongue lolling, reminding her of Pluto from the Disney cartoons of her childhood. "What did you bring me?" she asked warily.

"I brought you a dog. Isn't she great?" He patted the dog's side. The animal responded by flopping over onto her back, tail whipping wildly back and forth, all four feet flailing in the air. A flea crawled across the dirty white fur on the dog's stomach.

Karen took a step back. "I don't want a dog," she said. "I especially don't want an overgrown, flea-bitten mutt."

"Aw now, don't be like that." Del shoved past her into the house. The dog followed, toenails clicking on the hardwood floor.

"No!" Karen rushed after them. "Get that beast out of here. I don't want it."

"You need a dog, sis." Del helped himself to a Coke from the refrigerator. The dog followed, eyes fixed on him adoringly. "She'll keep you company."

"I don't need company. And I don't need anything else to look after."

"Living with a dog will teach you to lighten up." As if on cue, the mutt rolled on her back again, and looked at Karen, as if waiting for some sign of approval.

Del bent and rubbed the dog's belly. "How serious can you be around this?" he asked.

She was seriously considering slapping her brother, to try to knock some sense into him. Or at least force him to listen to her. "No, Del. I mean it. Get that beast out of here."

"Hey, where'd you get the dog?" Casey ambled into the kitchen and grinned at the mutt, still on her back in the middle of the floor. He dropped to his knees beside her and began rubbing her belly. "She's a real sweetie, isn't she? Is she yours, Uncle Del?"

"I got her for your mom."

"Really?" Casey's smile grew even wider and he looked back at Karen. "She's great!"

Karen hugged her arms across her chest and frowned down at Casey and the dog, who were now rolling around together on the floor. When the boys were six and nine, they had launched a campaign for the family to adopt a dog. Tom had been willing to go along with the idea, but Karen had put her foot down, pointing out that if she'd wanted something else to look after, she'd have had another child. The boys and Tom had been wise enough not to press the point.

"No. No dog," she repeated.

Casey's smile crumpled. Crouched on the floor beside the animal, he looked closer to the little boy she remembered than the man he was fast becoming. The image tugged at her heart. "But, Mom, why not?"

"Dogs are dirty. They're noisy. They shed. They're destructive. And they need a lot of attention and time I don't have."

"I'll give it attention." Casey sat back on his heels. "Besides, how do you know all that stuff if you've never had a dog?"

"I've known other people who had dogs. A dog is just one more thing for me to look after, and I already have too much to do around here." Between nursing her father and taking care of the house she was stressed to the max already. Not to mention, adding a dog would be one more change in a summer that had brought too many changes to her life already.

"I'll look after her. I promise." Casey threw his arms around the dog and hugged her close. "She won't be that much trouble."

Karen had the feeling things were fast slipping out of her control. She shook her head again. "No."

Casey pretended not to hear her. "Hey, we could maybe train her to help Grandpa. You know, one of those assistance dogs."

The dog seemed intent now on licking the skin off Casey's face. Karen had her doubts this mutt could be trained for anything. "No, I don't want it." She turned to Del. "Get it out of here."

He took a long sip of Coke, then set the can on the counter. "Guess I'll just have to shoot it, then," he said.

CINDI MYERS

"Shoot it?" The outrageousness of the statement left her stammering. "Why...why would you do that?"

"If I take her to the animal shelter, they'll just put her down, plus they'll ask for a 'donation' to do it. A big dog like this is hard to find a home for. A bullet's cheaper."

"Mom, no!" Casey still clung to the dog. The animal herself turned to Karen, eyes the color of chocolate M&M's filled with sadness. Karen couldn't stand it. Why was everyone making her out to be the villain, when it was Del who'd gotten them into this mess?

She turned to her brother. "Do you even have a conscience? How could you try to foist this dog—that I don't want—off on me, and then threaten to kill her if I don't take her?"

His expression was guileless. "I thought you and Casey, and Dad, too, for that matter, would *enjoy* having a dog around. I saw it as a nice thing to do for you. You're the one trying to make it something bad."

He had had this talent all his life, the knack for twisting words to throw the blame back on someone else. The talent had enabled him to talk his way out of failing grades, traffic tickets, job layoffs and relationship troubles more times than Karen could count. She hated it, but at the same time, she couldn't help but marvel.

Casey rose and stood at her side. "I think Uncle Del had a good idea, bringing us this dog," he said. "This has been kind of a lousy summer for us so far, what with Grandpa being sick and all. A dog like this could give us something to laugh at."

God knew she could use a few laughs. Only she didn't see how a big dirty mutt was going to provide them. She looked down at the dog, who was on her back again, both paws over her nose as if she was hiding her face. It was a ridiculous pose, and Karen felt herself weakening. She still didn't want the animal. She hated being manipulated this way. But she wasn't hardhearted enough to sentence the pup to death, or to risk alienating her son further, at a time when she needed at least one member of her family on her side. She blew out a breath. "All right. She can stay for a little while. But if she causes any trouble, out she goes."

"That's super, Mom." Casey's hug squeezed all the air from her lungs. "I promise I'll help look after her. Come on, girl." He motioned to the dog. "Let's go outside and look around. And we have to think of a good name for you."

The dog trotted after him, tail waving. When Del and Karen were alone again, he turned to her. "I need to talk to Dad. Is he awake?"

"He's on the front porch." Martin liked to sit out there in the afternoons, alternately napping and scanning the area for birds. "Why do you want to see him?" As far as she could remember, Del hadn't spent a single minute alone with his father since Martin's stroke.

Del arched one eyebrow. "I have to have a reason?"

"No." Though she had no doubt he was up to something. She led him to the porch, half hoping Martin would be asleep. But he looked up as they approached.

"Hey, Dad. How you doing?" Del loomed over his father, his broad shoulders and air of radiant health in sharp contrast to his shriveled, pale sire. Still, Del was the one who looked awkward, head bent, hands clasped in front of him, posture slightly slumped, like a boy awaiting reprimand.

He glanced at Karen. "I need to talk to Dad *alone*," he said.

Translation: *I'm going to ask for something, or propose some scheme that you won't approve of.* She debated staying where she was, ready to defend her father against Del's manipulations.

Martin made a shooing motion with his hand, and grunted, waving her away. Hurt, but determined not to show it, she turned on her heel and fled to the kitchen. Why did she even bother resisting? Del always got his way.

The thought made her feel childish, and she struggled to regain an adult perspective. Del had a right to talk to his father in private. The stroke had left her father physically weak, but mentally he was as strong as ever. It was none of her business what Del did with his life. If she let him manipulate her, it was her own fault for giving in.

The thought rankled. Who wouldn't be annoyed at being manipulated? Why should she take the blame for Del's bad behavior? Maybe that was part of the problem between them—she was too willing to let him get away with being "just Del," too ready to think her own attitude was the one that needed adjusting.

She sagged against the counter, heart pounding. What would happen if she stopped letting the men in her life get away with unacceptable behavior? The idea was tantalizing, and more than a little frightening. Did she really have what it took to be more demanding and less accepting?

"So, you're looking pretty good," Del said when he and Martin were alone.

Martin frowned at the lie, and watched his son, enjoying his discomfort. Del stood awkwardly in front of the wheelchair, as if he was contemplating hugging his father or perhaps shaking his hand.

Martin had no delusions that Del had stopped by out of some concern for Martin's health. The boy never made any pretense of closeness unless he wanted something—to park his trailer on part of the land Martin owned, his father's signature on loan papers for his business, to borrow a car or a tool or money.

Theirs was a relationship of give and take. Martin gave; Del took. They both understood this and were comfortable in their roles.

Del dragged a heavy Adirondack chair over in front of his father and sat, hands on his knees, back straight. "Karen says you still can't talk much."

He couldn't talk at all, which might be an advantage in this instance. He shook his head no.

"Well, I guess you don't need to wear yourself out talking. You can just nod your head and we'll communicate fine." Del's shoulders relaxed a little, as if he liked this idea. "I wanted to ask you a favor," he said.

Martin nodded. Did he know the boy, or what?

"You know Sheila and I split up?"

He nodded again. Del's third wife had surprised him by staying around as long as she had. On Martin's visits home between birding expeditions, he couldn't fail to hear the fireworks from next door: the shouting, tears and slamming doors. Sheila could swear like a sailor, and had once fired a shotgun over Del's head as he and his girlfriend of the moment raced from the trailer one evening when Sheila had arrived home unexpectedly. Martin himself had paid to bail her out of jail that time, and advised her that a load of rock salt and a lower aim might do more good next time.

She had been the best of the Mrs. Del Engels, regularly bringing over casseroles and leftovers, keeping the bird feeders filled when he was out of town, collecting the mail and even mowing the grass Del let grow long. When she hadn't shown up to help since his stroke, Martin had figured Sheila had finally had enough of Del's flirtations and affairs and packed it in. He couldn't blame her, though he would have liked the chance to tell her goodbye.

"Anyway, she's hired some big-shot lawyer and is trying to get pretty much everything I own."

Half of little or nothing hardly seems worth fighting for, Martin thought, doing a mental inventory; the trailer house wasn't worth much, the oil change business was mortgaged to the hilt and, as far as he knew, Del had never had any savings to speak of.

"I told her I couldn't afford to pay what she wanted. She had the nerve to suggest I sell the truck and the motorcycle to get the money."

Martin chuckled. Heaven forbid Del part with his expensive toys.

"You okay?" Del half rose out of his chair and looked around, possibly for help. "You're not choking or anything, are you? Do I need to get Karen?"

He shook his head and waved the boy back into his seat, then motioned for him to continue.

Del sat, still eyeing him warily. "Anyway, I hired a lawyer who says he can work this so I don't end up in the poorhouse, except he wants five thousand dollars up front. I just don't have that kind of money."

Unless you sell the truck or the motorcycle.

"So anyway, I was wondering if you could lend me the money. I can pay you back a little at a time, if the business has a good quarter."

The business never had a good quarter, and Del had never paid back more than a hundred dollars of the thousands he'd borrowed over the years. Martin nodded.

"So you'll lend me the money? Great." Del stood, beaming. He glanced toward the door to the house again. "Uh, can you sign a check?"

Martin nodded again. He could sign a check. And then he wouldn't see much of his son until the next time Del was in trouble. It wasn't a very satisfactory pattern for a relationship, but at least it was predictable.

Del left, presumably to get the checkbook, and returned a few minutes later with Karen trailing after him. "Dad, what are you doing, agreeing to give him that kind of money?" she said.

Del sat again, opened the checkbook on his knee and filled in the blanks. "This is none of your business, sis."

Karen turned to Martin. "It's true? You're just going to hand over five thousand dollars?"

Martin nodded. It was his money. If he wanted to piss it away on his shiftless son, that was his business. He took the pen Del offered and bent to inscribe his signature on the check.

Karen folded her arms across her chest and frowned at them. "I can't believe you're taking advantage of a helpless old man," she said, as if Martin weren't sitting right there.

Martin glared at her, but she didn't notice. She was too busy facing down her brother.

Del let the anger roll off him like steam off wet pavement. He tore the check out of the book, folded it in half and tucked it into his shirt pocket. "Dad's in his right mind, so he isn't helpless. And if he wants to do me a favor, why shouldn't he? I'm his only son."

"You should be ashamed of yourself."

"Shame's a wasted emotion. It doesn't fix anything, change anything or stop anything. I don't see any point in bothering with it." He turned back to Martin. "Thanks, Dad. You take it easy now." He crossed the porch and exited down the steps, whistling as he went.

Karen turned to her father, hurt in her eyes. "How could you? Why do you let him take advantage of you like that? He never does anything for you. He just uses you."

Martin gave because it was easy for him to do so. The money or material goods Del needed didn't mean much to him. He could give them without a second thought. Sign the check, make the loan, hand over the goods and his obligation was met and his relationship with Del returned to normal.

With Karen, things were always more involved. She had always been the difficult child. The needy one. She wanted complicated things—words and emotions. And whatever he surrendered wasn't enough. Time hadn't changed that.

And who was she to accuse her brother of using him? She'd scarcely visited all these years and now that he was helpless, she'd dropped everything and swooped in to run his life. He'd been around long enough to know such sacrifices didn't come without a price. She wanted payment from him in a currency he didn't have in him to pay.

He turned away from her, steering his chair toward the door to his house. All this arguing had tired him. He needed to spend time at his computer. Later, he'd sleep, and be comforted by dreams in which he knew no limitations.

The following Thursday, Karen gave in to Tammy's pleas to have lunch. At eleven-thirty, she found herself seated at Tammy's kitchen table, a glass of iced tea in her hand, a pleasant lethargy enveloping her as she watched her friend bustle about the room. Karen had almost forgotten what it was like to have someone else wait on her, and to not spend every waking moment listening for some signal of distress from her father's room. Or lately, sounds that the dog, whom Casey had named Sadie, was getting into trouble or needed to go out. So far, the dog hadn't made any messes on the carpet—if you didn't count the hair she shed everywhere or the occasional fleas that showed up despite the bath and flea dip Karen had given her. But knowing that she *might* make a mess only added to Karen's stress.

And she could admit, if only to herself, that she'd lost far too much sleep stewing over the five-thousand-dollar *loan* Martin had given Del. While he'd been in talking with their father, she'd told herself she was going to call Del on his impossible behavior, that she wasn't going to let him charm her or browbeat her into meeting his demands.

But in the end, he'd worn her down, defeating her with the argument that while Martin's body might be damaged, his mind was working just fine. If he wanted to give his son money, it wasn't any of her business.

Maybe he was right, but she'd lost more than a few hours wondering what she could have done differently.

"I'm so glad we could get together like this," Tammy said as she chopped celery for chicken salad.

"Thank you for talking me into it." Karen sipped tea, the flavor of fresh mint sweet on her tongue. "It feels so good to get out of the house for a while."

"Now that Casey is here to help you with his grandpa, you should get away more often."

"I never realized what a big help he could be." Karen smiled as she thought of the one really bright spot in the past few weeks. She hadn't spent this much time with Casey since he was a preschooler. Now she had a chance to see a side of him she'd only guessed at before.

"A lot of the time he's more patient with Dad than I am," she said. "And he's better at the messy jobs, like managing bedpans and stuff. And Dad cooperates better for him." Sometimes she wondered if her father wasn't being obstinate on purpose, as if he blamed her for his infirmity, or the indignity of his condition.

"Mo-om, have you seen my new swimsuit?" Tammy's oldest daughter, Sheree, hurried into the room. At seventeen, she was all long legs and straight blond hair.

"In the top drawer, left-hand side of your dresser." Tammy added mayonnaise to the chopped chicken and celery and stirred vigorously. "Maybe Casey will be a nurse," she said when the women were alone again.

"Maybe." Karen looked into her half-empty tea glass, as if the answer lay somewhere in the jumble of ice cubes. "He doesn't know what he wants to do."

"Give him time. He's young." She reached into the cabinet overhead and took down two plates.

"Honey, did you pick up those shirts from the cleaners?"

Brady stuck his head around the kitchen door. "Oh, hi, Karen. How's your dad?"

"He's a little better. Slow going."

"That's good. And tell Del I said hello." He turned to Tammy again. "My shirts?"

"On the hook on the back of your closet door." She spooned chicken onto slices of bread.

"The videos need returning," Brady said. "I don't have time to do it."

"I'll take care of it this afternoon." She sliced the sandwiches in two and arranged them on the plates. "How is that brother of yours these days?" she asked Karen.

"Aggravating as ever. You'll never guess what he did the other day."

"What?"

"He brought over a dog. This half-grown yellow mutt. Said he got it as a present just for me. As if I needed something else to look after."

Tammy smiled. "What did you do?"

"What could I do? Casey fell in love with the dog the minute he laid eyes on it and Del threatened to shoot it if I didn't take it in." She shook her head. "So now we have a dog. Casey named her Sadie."

"Mo-om! I need ten bucks for the pool." B.J., fifteen, swept into the kitchen, pausing at the refrigerator to help himself to a can of soda.

"In my purse," Tammy said. She set the plate of sandwiches on the table. "Don't forget to wear sunblock. It's in the medicine cabinet."

"I'm tan enough I don't need it." He began eating the rest of the chicken salad directly out of the bowl. "Is there any more of this?"

"No. Don't eat too much if you plan to go swimming."

"I won't." He set the empty bowl in the sink and dropped in his fork. "See you later."

Tammy watched him go, a faint smile on her face. "When he turned fourteen, it was as if someone threw a switch. He's always hungry. And every time I turn around, his pants are too short." She turned to Karen. "Please tell me it gets better."

"Not for a while, I'm afraid." Karen shook her head. "I'd be happy now if the most I had to worry about was keeping Casey fed. If only he weren't so...so aimless."

"He's a smart kid. He'll figure it out."

"That's what I try to tell Tom, but he thinks Casey should be like him. He had his whole life mapped out by the time he was sixteen."

Sheree hurried past them. "Bye, Mom."

"You be home by six," Tammy called after her. "Call if you need a ride."

"I will."

B.J. and Brady left shortly after that, each receiving instructions and parting hugs from Tammy. Karen took it all in with mixed amusement and awe. Tammy was a general, in clear charge of her territory and her troops. As far back as Karen could remember, this was what her friend had always wanted.

"Did you ever want to do anything else with your life?" Karen asked.

Tammy froze with her sandwich halfway to her mouth. "What do you mean?"

"I mean, did you ever want to be more than a wife and mother? Not that that's bad. You're obviously really good at it. But did you ever wonder if you made the right choices?"

Tammy blinked. "What else would I do?"

"I don't know. I—" They were interrupted by the oven timer dinging.

"I'd better get that." Tammy jumped up from the table. "I promised the Boy Scouts I'd make four loaves of banana bread for the bake sale Saturday," she explained as she opened the oven and peered in at the loaf pans. The banana and walnut odor made Karen's mouth water.

"You could open your own bakery or catering company," Karen said.

Tammy laughed. "And run it in all my spare time?" She shut off the oven and slid the loaves out, one at a time.

"I guess you're right. Who has spare time these days?"

"If I'm not taxiing the kids here and there, I'm cooking or cleaning this place," Tammy said. "Weekends are full of more sports activities and racing."

"I can't believe Brady's still doing that." When they were teenagers, Brady had fixed up an old car and raced it in competitions all over the area. Tammy and Karen had spent many a Friday night or Saturday huddled on sun-scorched bleachers, watching cars race at insane speeds around an oval track.

"Gosh yes. He's in a seniors league now. Lots of guys our age. He's spent three years fixing up his car. You'll have to come see it sometime." She grinned. "Remember the fun we used to have at the track?"

"I remember getting my nose blistered on sunny Saturdays, and flirting with the mechanics in the pit." Karen laughed at the memory. She'd been an awkward teenager desperate to appear sophisticated and older. This translated into a pair of soot-black sunglasses and four-inch platforms that endangered her ankles every time she picked her way across the gravel parking lot to the track. She'd no doubt looked ridiculous, but at the time she was convinced she gave the impression that she was a woman of the world.

"Brady's racing next weekend. You should come with us."

"It would be fun to see the races again. But Casey would probably want to come with me."

"Tell him it's a nostalgia thing—that you're going to relive your childhood. He'll be too mortified to even think of joining you."

"I'll do it." She laughed. "My mother always said the best revenge of parenthood was being able to embarrass your children."

"She's right. Sometimes it's the only revenge." Tammy picked up her sandwich and shook her head. "They have so many ways of getting to us, without even realizing it."

Karen nodded. There was no one who could hurt you like your child, and no one who could bring you as much joy. It was the paradox of parenting, something you never thought about when you were the child.

If pain and joy were barometers of love, then her love for her sons knew no bounds. And her frustration with her father was almost as limitless. Having Casey here brought home the contrast. Sometimes she felt balanced between the two, trying frantically to make life run smoothly for them both.

Unfortunately, neither man appreciated her concern. Why should they, when she never gave them a chance to live without it?

And then there was Tom—the other man who was important to her. She was stuck with trying to placate him long distance, an impossible task. "You've known Brady a long time, haven't you?" she asked.

Tammy smiled. "Since third grade. The first day we met, he threw a spitball at me. I knocked him down on the playground later and sat on him." She laughed. "It was true love."

"So, does he ever say things that surprise you? Things you had no idea he was thinking?"

Tammy tilted her head, considering the question as she chewed. "Not really." She shrugged. "I don't think Brady's a very complicated person. He likes his job. He likes racing and fishing. He loves me and the kids. If something's bugging him, he broods about it a few days and then moves on. We're a lot alike that way. Why? Has Tom surprised you?"

Karen nodded. "I thought he'd understand why I had to come look after my dad. Instead, he's practically pouting because he has to look after Matt and the business by himself for a summer."

"He misses you," Tammy said. "That's sweet."

"He doesn't sound very sweet on the phone. It's like he wants me to *abandon* my father and come home."

"He's probably just feeling a little panicky about looking after everything without you to help. He'll get over it. I'd do the same thing in your shoes. Your dad needs you right now."

Except Tammy would never be in Karen's shoes. Her father lived two blocks away. She saw her parents every Sunday afternoon and countless times during the week.

"I'm trying to talk him into coming down for a visit," Karen said. "Maybe if he sees how helpless Dad is, he'll be more understanding."

"I'm sure he will be. And I know you've missed him."

She *had* missed Tom—especially at night, when she lay alone in her childhood room. But she didn't know what to expect from him these days, or what he wanted from her. They'd been married all these years and there were days when she felt she hardly knew him. They'd been so *busy*—raising the boys, running a business, managing a home—maybe they'd missed out on something important to their relationship, some exercise or habit or activity that would serve as insurance for the years ahead when it was just the two of them again. She wanted to think they could be close in the years to come. Closer than she felt to him right now. What would it take to get to that kind of closeness? Or was that another fantasy, like her dreams of bonding with her dad?

In some ways, her father, for all his sullen silences and uncooperative moments, was easier to deal with than Tom.

Having been away from home so many years, she no longer had a fixed role in his life, so there were fewer expectations to live up to.

She sipped iced tea and ate the last of her sandwich. She'd expected to learn a lot about her father while she was here; she hadn't counted on learning so much about herself. For instance, she drew an inordinate amount of satisfaction from the knowledge that whenever she and her father disagreed about something, she was sure to have the final say in the matter. She told herself this was a petty, mean attitude, but there it was. She wasn't always a sweet, nice person. Maturity had taught her to take comfort from that. There was peace in accepting one's faults.

Accepting others' faults was more difficult, as she was learning with her father, and Del, and Tom and even Casey. She hadn't had any luck changing their behavior, but silently accepting it felt wrong, too. What would it take to find her voice and tell them exactly what she thought?

More importantly, how much would the truth cost? Was it a price she was willing to pay?

Pay attention.

"I am, Grandpa." Casey refrained from rolling his eyes. After all, the old guy couldn't help it if he had to type everything instead of talking.

But his grandfather wasn't the most exciting person to be around even when he wasn't sick. Not to mention that having a *conversation* with him was like being back in school. But it wouldn't kill Casey to humor him. He leaned over the old man's shoulder and studied the spreadsheet on the screen. "You were saying something about the way birds are classified. Families and stuff. I remember that from biology class."

His grandfather stabbed at the keyboard once more, his one-fingered typing surprisingly fast.

Class = aves

Phylum = chordata

Subphylum = vertebrata

Orders = passeriformes (passerines) and non-passer-ines

He looked at Casey to make sure he understood.

"So every bird in the world is either a passerine or a non-passerine?" Casey asked.

The old man nodded.

23 Orders, 142 Families, 2057 Genera, 9,702 Species

Casey nodded. "I got that. And you've seen close to eight thousand of them."

First you learn the orders, then the families, and so on.

Casey frowned. "But why? I could just learn the names of the birds themselves. Why wouldn't that be enough?"

The old man glared at him, his eyebrows coming together, jutting over his beak of a nose. He looked like a caricature of an angry bald eagle. His hand shook as he typed.

There is a correct way to do this. You must learn the orders first.

"If you're going to get all cranky, I'll leave and go watch TV or something." Casey took a step back. He got enough grief about stuff like this from his mom and dad. He didn't have to take it from somebody he was trying to help, even if it was his grandfather.

Sadie sat up when Casey moved, and looked at him expectantly. The dog was the best thing about his summer so far. She followed him everywhere and had plopped down next to Grandpa's desk as if she'd been living here all her life.

The old man continued to scowl at him, then his shoulders sagged a little. He nodded and beckoned Casey to him once more.

All right. We'll learn names first. But the orders are interesting. When you know the names, you'll want to know the orders, too.

"Fair enough." Casey sat on the corner of the desk and watched as his grandfather highlighted the cells of the spreadsheet. *Ailuroedus buccoides,* White-eared Catbird. *Ailuroedus melanotis,* Spotted Catbird. *Ailuroedus crassirostris,* Green Catbird.

The old man stared at the funny Latin names like it was some hot porn site or something. He was so enthralled, he'd probably forgotten Casey was even there. Which was okay with Casey. He leaned down and scratched Sadie behind the ears and studied the man at the computer, thinking how odd it was that this was his mom's dad. They didn't look much alike; Mom took after Grandma in the looks department, which he guessed was good. Grandma still looked all right for an older lady. Even before he had the stroke, Grandpa hadn't been all that handsome. He kept himself neat and clean, but he didn't care about stuff like clothes or hairstyles.

But Mom did *act* like her father sometimes. When she was at the landscaping office, working on something on the computer, she had the same kind of intensity Grandpa had now. And she showed her emotions on her face the way Grandpa did. One look in her eyes and you knew she was happy or angry or upset. She never had to say a word.

Uncle Del looked a little more like his dad, at least around the chin and nose. But Casey couldn't imagine someone more different from Grandpa than his mother's brother. Del was real outgoing and friendly. Mom said he was a con artist, so maybe the friendliness wasn't always real, but he sure wasn't the type to spend days alone in the jungle looking for some rare bird the way Grandpa did. And if Uncle Del was mad or glad about something, he'd tell you right to your face.

When Casey looked at his mom and her brother that way, he had to wonder how they ever ended up with the same parents. Then again, he and Matt were plenty different. Matt was the smart, responsible one—just like Dad. Casey thought of himself as the more creative type. An artist, except that he didn't paint or play an instrument or anything like that. Dad couldn't understand him at all, so they clashed all the time.

Mom was easier to get along with, but even she wished he were different sometimes. More ordinary, he guessed. Easier.

Easier for her, that is. He couldn't imagine anything harder than trying to fit into a mold that wasn't right for you.

Grandpa tugged at his sleeve and cocked his head. Casey listened and heard a melodic, gurgling song. Three slow notes, *gluk, gluk, glee!* "I don't recognize it," he said.

Grandpa motioned toward the window, and gave Casey a gentle shove toward it. He shuffled to the glass and looked out. The call came again. *Gluk, gluk, glee!* This time, he saw the chunky, soot-colored bird with the shiny brown hood. "Brown-headed Cowbird," he announced.

Grandpa nodded, his mouth curved into a crooked grin. He turned to the computer and clicked on a new file. Casey's List was the heading at the top of the page.

"I guess I should add it now, huh?" Casey leaned around the old man and typed in the name of the bird and the time, date and location where he'd seen it. Grandpa added the Latin *Molothrus ater.*

Casey nodded, and admired the new entry. So far the list Grandpa had made for him had only about a dozen birds on it. He'd done it mainly to humor the old man. But he had to admit, it was kind of fun, seeing a bird and noting all the information about it. He didn't know anybody else his age who could identify half a dozen birds, much less more than ten.

Grandpa smiled, and patted his hand. Casey returned the look. At least some people in his life were easy to please.

7

I value my garden more for being full of blackbirds than of cherries, and very frankly, give them fruit for their songs.
—*Joseph Addison, the* Spectator

One of Karen's earliest memories was of standing beside her brother's crib, making faces and laughing with delight when he smiled at her. Even as a baby, he had charmed everyone who met him. He had grown into a sunny child and a willing accomplice in her elaborate games of make-believe.

When had that changed? Had adolescence formed this gulf between them, or had the divide come earlier, when she realized that Del's easygoing nature made him more popular than she would ever be? When he charmed teachers into overlooking neglected home-work assignments while she served detention for turning in a paper a day late, had that made her see him in a different light? When he borrowed money and failed to repay it, dismissing her attempts to collect with a lopsided smile and a lazy shrug, had that been the final straw?

She caught glimpses of the sweet boy she'd loved even now. On Saturday, he and Mary Elisabeth came to the house with a stringer of catfish and a paper sack of tomatoes, still warm from the vine. "Dinner's on us," he announced, holding up the fish.

"All right!" Casey shut off the television and joined them in the kitchen, Sadie close on his heels. To Karen's surprise, Casey had kept his promise to look after the beast, and Sadie slept each night on the floor beside his bed.

"Del said his daddy loves catfish," Mary Elisabeth said. "And the tomatoes are from my neighbor's garden." She began opening cabinet doors. "I'll cook, if you'll show me where everything is."

"Oh, you don't have to do that." Karen hurried to intercept the young woman as she hefted a cast-iron frying pan from the drawer beneath the stove.

"Let her cook, sis." Del steered her toward a chair at the kitchen table and set a long-necked bottle of beer in front of her. "Take a load off."

"You got anything in there for me?" Casey bent and poked around in the blue-and-white plastic cooler Del had deposited by his chair.

"Nothing for you, sport."

Karen studied the bottle in front of her. Sweat beaded on the brown glass and chips of ice clung to the label. She'd been up half the night with her father, who'd developed a worrisome cough, and weariness hung on her like a lead shirt. She couldn't remember when she'd seen anything more enticing and refreshing than that beer.

She raised the bottle to her lips and took a long drink, a sigh escaping her as the icy, slightly bitter liquid rushed down her throat. Del laughed and sat in the chair across from her. "I'd say it's been too long since you let your hair down."

She started to point out that people with responsibilities and some sense of duty didn't have time to *let their hair down,* but the words stuck in her throat. Maybe he had a point. Life couldn't be one big party, as he seemed to try to make it, but neither did it have to be a constant grind, as hers too often was.

Casey slid into the chair between them. "Where'd you catch the fish?"

"Mayfield Lake."

Karen arched one eyebrow as he named a body of water owned by one of the wealthiest families in town. "Isn't that on private property?"

He grinned. "Not if you know the back way in."

His expression was such an exaggeration of fake innocence, she couldn't help but laugh. "And of course, you know the way."

He glanced toward Mary Elisabeth, who was stirring cornmeal and spices in a bowl, humming to herself. Then he leaned toward Karen, his voice lowered. "I went around with the youngest Mayfield girl for a while. She knew all the places on their land where nobody would bother us."

She took another quick swallow of beer to distract herself from thinking about just what her brother and Miss Mayfield had been up to that they didn't want to be bothered. "You haven't asked about Daddy," she said.

The lines around his eyes tightened and he bent to retrieve another beer from the cooler. "I was going to. How is he?"

"He had a rough night. A bad cough kept him awake."

"He's better this morning," Casey offered. "I think something just went down the wrong way. He still doesn't swallow good sometimes."

Karen glanced toward the string of fish, wet and silver in the sink. "I don't know if fish is such a good idea."

"We'll mush it up for him. It'll be okay." Del popped the top off the bottle. "Where is he now?"

"He's asleep. I'll send Casey to wake him up in a little bit."

"Don't bother him. He probably needs his sleep."

Something in the overly casual way he said the words

made her look at him more closely. "You act like you don't want to talk to him."

"It's not like we can have a conversation." He stared across the kitchen, the muscles along his jaw tense. "Even before he had the stroke we didn't have a lot to say to each other."

"No, he was never much of a conversationalist." She wondered, sometimes, if all those years of sitting silent, watching birds, had taken away the habit of talking.

"I know what you're thinking." Del pointed the lip of the bottle toward her. "You think since I live next door to him, I ought to be over here all the time, checking up on him and playing the dutiful son and all. Well, he didn't want none of that and neither did I. Except for our genes, the two of us don't have anything in common." He set the empty bottle down with a thump.

The bitterness in his voice surprised her. She'd been so focused on her own problems with her father, she hadn't thought much about Del's relationship with him.

Her eyes met Casey's, and he quickly looked away. Had Del's words reminded him of his own uneven relationship with Tom? Her husband rarely hid his frustration that Casey didn't share his interest in the landscaping business or in working on projects around the house. Casey never said anything, but he must have felt his father's disappointment keenly.

It didn't help matters, though, when neither of them would consider the other's point of view—not unlike Del and Martin. "It's not true that you have nothing in common," she said. "You're both stubborn."

"Oh yeah?" He cocked one eyebrow. "I'd say it runs in the family."

"Del, you need to skin these catfish so I can cook them." Mary Elisabeth confronted him, hands on her hips. She'd tied a dish towel around her waist as a makeshift apron. The towel hung down longer than her shorts, so the effect was of a striped cotton miniskirt.

"Aw, sugar, I'll do it in a minute, don't worry." He reached out and pulled her close, one hand cupping her bottom like he was testing the firmness of a melon.

"I'll do it." Casey jumped up and pushed back his chair.

"You skinned catfish before, boy?" Del asked. "It's not like cleaning one of those Colorado trout, you know."

"I know." He rummaged in the drawer under the phone and came up with a thick-handled knife. He retrieved an enamel dishpan from under the sink, then picked up the stringer of fish. Sadie stood at attention, ears cocked, nose twitching. "You want fillets or whole?" Casey asked.

"Fillets," Mary Elisabeth said. "They're big fish."

When he and Sadie were gone, back door slamming behind him, Del turned to Karen again. "He doing okay?"

"Casey? Why wouldn't he be okay?"

He shrugged. "Seems kind of funny, him showing up here all of a sudden. I mean, what kind of summer is he gonna have, playing nursemaid to a sick old man?"

"He said he wanted to stay with me." She bristled. Did Del think she'd set out to ruin her son's summer?

"Yeah, well, maybe he's a nicer guy than I am." He opened another bottle. "Wouldn't be hard to do, according to you."

"At least he's trying to help."

"And I'm not." He lifted the beer in a mock toast. "Just doing my best to live up to your low opinion of me."

Where had he mastered the art of throwing all blame squarely back on her? He infuriated her, but there was enough truth in his words to choke off her angry reply.

And she didn't want to argue with him right now. She wanted to sit here and let the alcohol buzz smooth out all the rough edges of her emotions. They could have one afternoon together that didn't end in a fight, couldn't they? Maybe it was a fantasy, but if anyone deserved a break from harsh reality right now, it was her. Why not pretend, for a little while, that everything was as fine and happy as she used to fantasize it could be.

Casey had just cut the head off the largest fish when the back door opened and Mary Elisabeth stepped out. "Hey there," she called, and headed toward the picnic table where he was working. She'd taken off the dish towel apron and held an oversize pair of pliers out in front of her like a bridal bouquet. "I thought maybe these would help," she said, stopping beside him.

"Yeah, thanks." He took the pliers, trying to remember what he was supposed to do with them.

"The easiest way is to use the pliers to pull the skin back, and sort of turn it inside out." She smiled, and tucked her hair behind one ear. She had about five earrings in each ear, a row of sparkling stones curving up from the lobe.

"Right. I remember now." He gripped the leathery fish skin with the pliers and tugged it back, aware of the muscles in his arms bulging with the effort. He'd taken off his shirt to keep from getting it dirty, and because it was hot out. He hoped she didn't think he looked like a pale, skinny kid.

"Hey, you're pretty strong." When she wrapped her hand around his bicep and squeezed, he almost dropped the pliers, but managed to hang on to them and the slippery fish.

"Thanks," he choked out, and tossed the now-naked fish into the dishpan. Sadie sat next to the table, eyes focused hopefully on the pan.

"How's the pup working out?" Mary Elisabeth raked her long nails through Sadie's hair. The dog half closed her eyes and swept the dirt with her tail. "Del said your mom wasn't too happy about him bringing her over."

"Aw, she's pretty much over that now. Sadie's a great dog."

She smiled at him again, and it was as if someone had turned the sun's heat up a notch all of a sudden. He could feel sweat running down the small of his back. He started on the next fish and she moved closer. She wasn't wearing a bra and her nipples showed through the thin material of the tank top. He had to force his gaze back on the fish, or risk cutting his thumb off. "Not bad for a Yankee boy," she said as he stripped the second fish.

"I'm not a Yankee." *Or a boy,* he wanted to add, but of course to her he was. How old was she, anyway? Probably twenty-five or so, at least.

"My daddy always said anybody who lived north of Amarillo was a Yankee to him." She laughed and climbed up onto the table and sat facing him, her feet on the bench. The muddy scent of catfish mingled with the sweet flower smell of her perfume.

He didn't know what to think of her. Was she flirting with him, or was she just one of those women who flirted with everybody? He tossed a third fish into the dishpan. Probably the latter. It wasn't like she'd be interested in him or anything.

"So how did you meet my my uncle Del?" he asked.

"He came into the water department to pay an overdue bill. While I was processing the paperwork, he started telling these really corny jokes. Like, what weighs five thousand pounds and wears glass slippers?"

"Um, I don't know."

"Cinderelephant! Or, what's large and gray and goes around and around in circles? An elephant stuck in a revolving door."

"And you thought this was funny?"

She laughed. "They were so silly. And he had such a funny look on his face when he told them. He had us all in stitches. There's nothing a woman likes better than a man who can make her laugh."

He filed this away for future reference, though he wasn't sure how many women would be wowed by elephant jokes. "So that's what the big attraction is between you two—the fact that he makes you laugh?"

"Del is a man who doesn't let others' expectations interfere with his happiness. He's carefree, and I admire that."

He tossed a fish into the dishpan and picked up the knife again. "Mom says he's irresponsible." She said that about Casey, too, and she had the same sour look on her face when she said it. But Mary Elisabeth didn't make it sound like such a bad thing.

She sighed. "Yeah, sometimes he is. But you have to take the bad with the good with people, you know?"

A loud trilling sounded nearby, accompanied by the flutter of wings. They looked up, and Casey spotted the flash of red and black on the end of a branch of the pine tree overhead. "Cardinal," he said.

"Does everybody in your family watch birds?"

He turned back to the fish he was filleting. "Not really. But Grandpa is teaching me some things."

She looked toward the house, her expression sad. "It must be hard for him, not being able to talk or move very easy."

"Yeah, I imagine it's no fun."

"I mean, it must be worse for someone like him. He's spent his whole life watching creatures that can fly." She looked up again, her head thrown back, neck arched, emphasizing the smooth hollow of her throat. "Birds must be about the freest things in the world, and there he is stuck in a crippled-up body."

The tenderness of her words surprised him. Why would she care about his grandfather, a man she didn't even know? And why would someone who could be so poetic about birds be hanging out with his uncle Del? He couldn't figure this chick out.

He tossed the last fillet in the dishpan. "They're done."

"You did a great job." She hopped off the table and picked up the dishpan. "Thanks." She walked back to the house, hips swaying. He watched her go, feelings stirring up in him like sand on a creek bottom.

Sixteen was about the most miserable age to be, he decided. He was too young to do anything about his out-and-out lust for his uncle's girlfriend, and too old to pretend such feelings didn't exist. He was too young to be truly on his own, and too old to be happy spending the summer with his sick old grandfather and his mom, who acted as if she'd forgotten how to smile. Going back to Denver wasn't an option; he'd feel guilty for deserting his mom, and once there he'd end up fighting with his dad anyway.

He was screwed no matter what he did. He'd spent a lot of time looking for a way to make things better, but he couldn't get around that one truth: right now, it sucked to be him.

They sat down to dinner just before sunset. The table was heaped with bowls and platters and baskets of food—cole-slaw, sliced tomatoes, fried potatoes and hush puppies. Mary Elisabeth had knocked herself out making a feast, and hardly broken a sweat doing it.

Karen watched the young woman with the dispassion of an anthropologist. Mary Elisabeth really was too good to be true. She'd insisted on sitting next to Martin and helping him, "So we can get to know each other better." He could maneuver a fork fairly well with his right hand, but once the food was in his mouth, it didn't always stay. And he tended to choke, so small pieces and a reminder to chew thoroughly were important.

"You're doing real good, Mr. Engel," Mary Elisabeth said cheerfully, deftly wiping the corners of his mouth with a damp dish towel. When Karen talked to him like this, he glared at her, as if he realized just how patronizing she was being. But with Mary Elisabeth, he looked almost happy.

Even seventy-year-old curmudgeons weren't immune to the appeal of a sexy young girl.

So what was she doing with Del? And why should Karen care? Frankly, her brother deserved to have someone take advantage of him, the way he'd taken advantage of so many others.

"Casey tells me you've been teaching him about birds," Mary Elisabeth said as she laid another piece of fish on Martin's plate and cut it into tiny pieces. "I ought to have you teach me some. I only know the common ones around here, like cardinals and blue jays."

Her breasts in the thin tank top jiggled as she sliced into the fish. Karen wondered if her father appreciated the show. Probably. After all, he was male and breathing.

The girl would be easy to dislike, if nothing else because she was Del's floozy of the moment. But Mary Elisabeth was too genuine and just plain nice not to feel friendly toward. And the fact that she took so much time with Martin—more time than his own son—had landed her a permanent soft spot in Karen's heart.

"You want another hush puppy? Here's one that's not too greasy." She offered up the morsel of fried corn bread and Martin opened his mouth like a baby bird.

He chewed and chewed, mouth contorted. Karen looked away. It really wasn't a pretty sight.

"Guh. Guh!"

"Did you hear that?" Mary Elisabeth dropped her fork and beamed at them. "He said 'good.'"

"Didn't sound like anything to me." Del speared a slice of tomato and added it to his plate.

"No, he said 'good.' I know he did." She looked at Karen. "You heard it, didn't you?"

"I heard something." She studied her father. "Can you say it again?" she asked.

He worked his mouth, but nothing came out. His eyes sparked with frustration, and he shook his head.

Mary Elisabeth patted his arm. "That's okay. We know you said it. It's a start. It means the parts of your brain in charge of talking are starting to wake up."

Karen was skeptical of this unscientific explanation, but her father seemed placated by it. He picked up his fork and focused on eating again.

Del turned to Casey. "What's new with you, sport?" he asked.

"I got an e-mail from Matt this afternoon," Casey said. "He said to tell everybody hello."

"Oh? What's he up to?" Karen asked. The only time she heard from Matt these days was when *she* called *him*. It hurt to think he'd contacted his brother and not her.

"Dad's made him foreman on some job at a hospital or something. He and Audra had a big fight and broke up, but I'm guessing they'll get back together. They always do."

"He didn't say anything about any trouble with Audra when I talked to him two days ago." She stabbed at a piece of fish. "What happened?"

Casey shrugged. "I dunno. I guess they split about a week or so ago, so it was old news."

Old news to everyone but her. She tried to hide her hurt behind motherly concern. "I hope he's not too upset," Karen said. "He's awfully young to be getting serious about anyone."

"He's older than you were when you married Dad," Casey pointed out.

She flushed. "Girls are different. They mature faster. Not to mention *I* was too young, too. I just got lucky with your father." She'd been happy with Tom, but she couldn't help wondering what her life would have been like if she hadn't met him when she did. Would she have stayed in Tipton, married a local man and had a different kind of life? A life more like Tammy's? Or would she have found some other way to leave home, and distanced herself even further from her family?

"I think it's romantic when two people find each other when they're young and then spend the rest of their lives together," Mary Elisabeth said. "But I'm glad I didn't settle down too early."

"I hope you don't have any ideas about settling down now." Del opened a fresh beer. "Because I've spent way too much time tied down. I'm ready to cut loose."

Mary Elisabeth smiled, a Mona Lisa smirk. "No, I've still got a lot of things I want to do. I'd like to travel some, and see more of the world."

"I took you to Corpus Christi just last month." Del winked at the rest of them to let them in on the joke. "Ain't that enough traveling for you?"

"Not by half, big guy." She swatted his hand. "You'd better be nice to me and maybe when I decide to start my travels, I'll take you with me."

"I'm glad you haven't left just yet." Casey swabbed a potato through a pool of ketchup. "I bet Matt and Dad wish they were here right now, eating all this great food." He grinned at Del. "You sure lucked out, finding a girlfriend who could cook so good."

"Aren't you sweet." Mary Elisabeth reached over to take a swig from Del's beer, her own long since empty.

"Guh! Guh!" Her father's fork clattered against his plate and he glared at them, as if defying them to deny that he had, indeed, spoken.

"It *is* good." Karen reached across the table and took his hand in hers. He gripped her fingers tightly, his skin cool and papery. The gesture brought tears to her eyes, and she rapidly blinked them away. "You're making progress," she said. "You're going to get better."

How much better would things get between them,

though? He responded more to Mary Elisabeth, a woman he'd just met, than he ever had to her. Was she wasting her time trying to look after him, while her oldest son and her husband went on with their lives without her? How long could she stay away before they began to think they didn't need her at all?

What would she do with herself if the day ever came when she really wasn't needed? When she had only herself to answer to?

8

I am no bird; and no net ensnares me; I am a free human
being with an independent will…
—*Charlotte Brontë,* Jane Eyre

Walking through the gates at Mitchell Speedway the following Saturday was like stumbling across some relic in an attic trunk and being reminded of a part of life long since forgotten. Karen hadn't thought of this place in twenty-five years, yet it had once been one of the social centers of her universe. How many Friday and Saturday nights in spring and summer had she spent avoiding splinters on the wooden bleachers, or lined up along the chain-link fence breathing the sweet smell of high-octane fuel and lusting after the drivers who, more often than not, were more in love with carburetors and fuel cells than they ever would be with any woman?

She followed Tammy and her children to the stands, the warped boards rattling underfoot as they climbed toward the middle, where they'd have the best view of the track and the least risk of choking on dust and fumes. They filed into a row, Tammy's younger children, Jamie and April, climbing up one step to sit behind the women.

While Tammy distributed stadium chairs, binoculars and cold drinks, Karen looked out over the paved oval. "My

God, this place hasn't changed at all," she said, staring at the Whitmore Tires sign that had graced the back wall of the track when she was a girl.

"They put in a new grandstand three years ago," Tammy said as she worked on redoing April's ponytail. "Stand still, baby."

Karen squinted at the white-painted grandstand across the way. "It looks the same to me."

"Well, you know there's a lot of tradition associated with racing. People like to uphold that."

In her high school days, it had been tradition for the drivers to carry hip flasks, from which they offered sips of whiskey to the girls who hung around after closing. Karen had drunk from her share of those flasks, and taken more than one wild ride around the track lit only by moonlight, her escort a not-entirely-sober racer, the car fishtailing around curves, engine smoking down the straightaway as the driver sought to impress her.

She shuddered at the memory. Had she ever really been that young and clueless? That reckless?

"Do you want some Fritos?" Tammy offered the open bag of chips. "There's dip, too."

She shook her head. "What time do the races start?"

"Seven o'clock. I always like to get here a little early in case Brady or the guys need anything."

"Can we go down to the pits now?" Jamie said.

They made their way down from the stands toward the pit area. The scent of oil and fuel stung Karen's nose and the throb of engines vibrated through her chest. They picked their way around stacks of tires and groups of men who huddled around cars. The men stood in groups of four and five, their heads and shoulders disappearing beneath the open hoods like lion tamers swallowed up by their charges. They passed several familiar faces—some whose names she remembered, others she couldn't recall. They all seemed to remember her, however. "Hey, Karen, how's it going?"

"Good to see you, Karen."

As if they'd last laid eyes on her yesterday instead of twenty or more years ago.

Brady was bent over under the hood of his car, fiddling with a wrench. He straightened when they approached. "I brought you a cold drink," Tammy said, handing him a Coke she'd snugged into a Koozie with the name of the local auto parts dealer emblazoned on the front. She looked past him, into the engine compartment. "Did you get the problem with the clutch fixed?"

"Yeah, finally. She's hooked up now." He grinned over at Karen. "There's this old boy, Darren Scott, he and I have been trading first place in the standings all spring. I'm determined to beat him tonight."

"There he is over there," April volunteered.

She turned and saw a man with graying brown hair and a goatee, standing beside a black-and-white car with the number nine painted on its side. "Cocky sonovabitch," Brady said good-naturedly.

"April, don't forget you promised Sandra Wayne you'd watch little Seth for her," Tammy reminded her daughter.

"I hadn't forgotten." April scuffed the dirt with the toe of her tennis shoe. "I was just waiting to say goodbye to Daddy."

"You go on now, pumpkin." Brady leaned over and gave the girl a kiss. Karen felt a stab of longing as she watched them. Her father had never made such a casual gesture of affection.

"You should eat something," Tammy said to Brady. She smoothed the back of his flame-retardant suit. "You want me to bring you a corn dog or something after the race?"

"Nah, I'm okay. I'll probably go out with some of the guys for a few beers."

"All right, then." Tammy stood on tiptoe to kiss him on the lips. "Have a good race. We'll be cheering for you."

They made their way back to the bleachers. "It's amazing that Brady's still racing after all this time," Karen said.

"He did quit for a while, when the kids were little and we just flat didn't have the money. But he took it up again a few years back." She glanced at Karen. "He says it keeps him young. I'm happy it keeps him out of trouble."

"What do you mean? Brady never struck me as the type to get into trouble." Even in school, Brady had been one of the straightest arrows they knew. Except for racing cars, he never did anything illegal, immoral or inconsistent.

"Well, there was this little secretary at work who was sniffing around him, but I got wind of it and put a stop to it." The determination in Tammy's voice and the hard line of her jaw made Karen look twice at her friend. Tammy always seemed so easygoing. Then again, it made sense that she'd be fierce when it came to protecting her family, and by extension, her marriage.

"You don't worry about all the groupies who hang out at the tracks?" Karen asked, remembering her own youthful indiscretions.

Tammy shook her head. "With me and all the kids here, he wouldn't have a chance to look at another woman. Besides, when he's here, all he's thinking about is his car. That thing is his baby."

"You're not jealous?" Her tone was light, teasing, but she was serious.

Tammy shook her head. "Nah. I'm the one he goes to bed with every night. I'm not worried about anything else."

They found their seats and settled in to watch the first race. "Brady's in the second qualifying heat tonight," Tammy said.

Karen nodded, the racing lingo coming back to her. Groups of racers competed in the qualifying heat for post position in the main race, or feature. Brady raced stock cars, which started life as American-made street cars but were so highly modified now as to be unrecognizable as descendants of the family sedan.

The first heat was over almost before Karen knew it. Then it was Brady's turn. His bright red-and-white Chevrolet was easy to spot in the crowd, and he led the pack most of the way, crossing the finish line inches ahead of the next racer. "Oh, he'll be happy about that," Tammy said, grinning.

The qualifying heats out of the way, the track was prepped for the feature race. Karen amused herself watching the crowd. It was an eclectic audience, dominated by groups of men in cowboy hats or ball caps, jeans and T-shirts. There were a good number of families mixed in, the women carrying toddlers or babies on one hip, children playing tag and hide-and-seek beneath the glow of mercury vapor lights.

The teenagers segregated themselves in knots of five or six, the boys mostly separate from the girls, each group watching the other with a show of studied indifference.

She spotted one girl, probably sixteen or seventeen, her heavy makeup and teased hair a clue that she was trying to look older. She was standing with a pair of slightly older men—drivers or mechanics, judging by the shirts they wore that were plastered with the names of auto parts suppliers. The girl was smoking a cigarette. She laughed and threw her head back to blow the smoke out of her nose, while the men looked on admiringly.

Karen caught her breath, remembering herself at that age. For a brief period she, too, had taken up smoking, and carefully choreographed every gesture involved with the habit. Hold the cigarette like this. Tilt her head like that. This was how the cool people looked, how they acted. If she could get the moves right, she could be one of them. Someone better than herself.

Someone different than she'd turned out to be. Back then, she'd dreamed of having exciting adventures, passionate romances, visiting exotic places. She'd have laughed at the idea of settling for a staid life as a housewife and mother.

Was that what she'd done—settled for something less than her dreams? Had she taken the easy road, instead of the one she'd really wanted?

"Hey, Karen, you okay? What are you staring at?" Tammy's hand on her shoulder pulled her back to the present.

She shook her head. "Nothing. I'm fine."

"Are you sure? You've gone all white." Tammy shoved a Coke into Karen's hand. "You've been living in the mountains too long. You're not used to the heat." She turned to her son. "Jamie, wet a rag in that ice chest and wring it out for me."

"No, I'm fine." Karen tried unsuccessfully to fend off the wet towel, which Tammy draped around her neck.

"That'll help cool you off," Tammy said.

"Thanks." The damp chill did feel good in the lingering heat.

"I'll bet it's nice and cool in Denver right now," Tammy said, settling back in her seat once more.

"It does cool off a lot at night." Karen and Tom liked to take a drink onto their back deck after sunset, and sit in the growing darkness, talking. Mostly about work or the boys.

Rarely about things that mattered. The memory sent a pain through her chest, a sharp longing that stole her breath. What had she missed, by not making an effort to dig deeper?

To be more honest about her feelings and opinions, instead of always trying to smooth over any rough patches and dis-agreements.

"I'll bet you miss that." Tammy pulled a round cardboard fan from her bag and fluttered it back and forth under her chin. "I'd hate to live somewhere where it was cold in the winter, but summer does tend to drag on forever around here."

"Mama, I want a fan, too," Jamie whined.

"Here you go, honey." Tammy handed over her fan, which Karen saw now was imprinted with the name of a local funeral parlor.

Karen remembered all the hours she'd spent placating Matt and Casey this way. Small children were so needy at times. It grew tiring, but now that they were more independent, a deep nostalgia for those times lingered in her. The boys had counted on her then, and she'd always been there for them.

Now that they were more independent and all but grown, she felt an emptiness, and a selfish longing for the old days when she'd been the center of their universe.

"They're getting ready to start." Tammy elbowed Karen and directed her attention to the track. As the green flag dropped, the cars surged forward in a cloud of exhaust. Karen found herself watching Tammy, instead of the cars on the track. She could judge the action by the expression on her friend's face. When Brady's car skidded through a turn, Tammy gasped and bit her knuckle, her shoulders sagging with relief as he righted the car in the straightaway. When a crash ahead of him forced him to brake and lurch the car to the right, she gave a muffled shriek and rose up from her seat, plopping down again when he was clear of danger.

As the cars neared the final lap, she bounced in her seat, hands pumping. "Come on, baby. Come on, baby. Come on," she muttered, faster and faster as the cars raced on.

When the checkered flag dropped and the results board showed Brady had come in second, Tammy squeezed her hands together and released a sigh. "Second is good," she said. "But Brady would be a lot happier with first."

"Mama, I'm hungry," Jamie said.

"Have some chips and dip. And there's some beef jerky

in there, too." Tammy dispensed snacks, having easily transformed from cheering for her man to catering to her children.
She was so calm and efficient.

A sense of familiarity overwhelmed Karen as she watched
her friend. She recognized the urgency underlying the capable
movements and precision organization. You had to hurry to
stay on top of everyone's needs, your brain spinning at a
frantic pace to keep up. Even the outward calm was part of
the act. You could never look anything less than absolutely
capable. After all, if you fell apart, think how many people
you'd take down with you. People who depended on you.

Karen had been there. She'd done that and she'd gotten
the T-shirt and the souvenir crown that identified her as
the queen manager/mother/organizer/volunteer/et cetera,
et cetera....

The problem was, all this activity didn't leave any chance
to slow down or retreat from the constant busyness of life.
Sometimes she suspected that was the whole point. Being
perfect in all her roles as wife, mom and business partner
left little time to question her own needs, or to see her own
flaws.

The idea made her feel queasy.

"Brady likes to stay after the race to go over everything on
the car and talk to the other drivers," Tammy said. "There're
three more features on the program, but we won't necessarily
stay to see them all, if that's okay with you."

"That's fine. We'll leave whenever you're ready." Not
knowing the drivers or having followed their careers, the
races were interesting, but not compelling.

"I've got to get a roast ready for the Crock-Pot when we
get home, so we can take it over to Mama and Daddy's after
church tomorrow," Tammy said as she repacked the cooler
and gathered up trash.

"Do you have dinner with them every Sunday?" Karen
asked.

"Just about. Mama and I take turns cooking, so it works out."

"You don't get tired of that? I mean, do you ever think about doing something different? Just for a change."

"Not really. Besides, my folks would be so disappointed if we didn't show. There'll be plenty of time for doing things differently when they're gone."

Tammy's words echoed in Karen's head as she followed her friend out of the stands and across the grounds toward the parking lot. At what age did you cross over from feeling as if there was always *plenty of time* to the sense that the hours and days were rushing away from you, like water through your fingers? Certainly some sense of urgency had brought her here to look after her father. She'd come expecting to learn more about him, to maybe even figure out what made him the way he was.

She hadn't counted on having to face so much of herself in the hours when she wasn't caring for him. It unnerved her to think she didn't always like the things she was finding out.

The day after her visit to the races, Karen called Tom. She needed to hear his voice, and to try to put into words the things she'd felt sitting there in the bleachers the night before. "Do you think I'm a martyr?" she asked once they got past the initial hellos.

"Do I think you're what?"

"Do you think I'm one of those women who are always rushing around doing things for other people and never looking after themselves? The kind of woman who always eats the heels of the bread because no one else in the family will, or who doesn't buy new shoes for herself because her kid wants new sneakers."

"I thought that was all part of being a mom," he said. "What brought this on?"

"I don't know. I went to the races with Tammy Wainwright last night. I was watching her with her husband and kids and I saw myself—so busy looking after other people, I couldn't look after myself."

"I don't have a clue what you're talking about. But I can tell you I wish you were up here right now, looking after some of this paperwork. I'm drowning in it."

Was that her most important role in his life—personal secretary? "Isn't the temp working out?"

"She only works three days a week, and I spend as much time showing her what to do as I do on my own work."

Was that supposed to make her feel guilty for going out with her friend? "I'll be back before you know it. Dad's doing really well. He's started to say a few words. And Casey's been a big help to me."

"He could be a big help here, too, if he wanted to."

She could feel the tension between her temples, as if someone had fastened a band around her head and just twisted it tighter. She didn't know what to say to Tom. She couldn't say what he seemed to want to hear—that she would drop everything and run to help him. "We'll both be home as soon as we're able." Longing came back, sharp as a razor. "Maybe you can find some time to come down for a visit. Just for a weekend. I'd like that."

"Yeah. I'll try." He took a deep breath, switching gears. "So how were the races?"

"Good. Brady came in second."

"I can't believe he's still racing."

"Tammy says it keeps him out of trouble."

He laughed. "He should go into business for himself. He'll be too busy to get into trouble."

"How's Matt?"

"Great. I made him foreman on the Adventist Hospital job and he's doing terrific. I'm really proud of him."

"Casey said something about him breaking up with Audra."

"Oh, I think they split up for a few days, but he said something about going to the movies with her the other night, so I guess they're back together."

"You didn't ask?"

"It's none of my business."

Men! As far as she was concerned, everything that affected her son was her business, at least as long as he lived at home. Part of being a parent was caring about what happened to your children.

"Can I talk to him?" Maybe she could get him to tell her what had happened with Audra.

"He's not here right now. I'll tell him you called."

And he wouldn't call back. He was too busy—too much in his own world these days, which didn't have much room for his mom.

"Listen, I've got to go now," Tom said. "I'm meeting a client to go over a bid for a project."

"Think about getting away for a visit. You could use a break and it would be great to see you."

"I'll think about it."

He sounded sincere enough, but without facial cues it was difficult to tell if he was trying to placate her or he truly intended to fly down. Not for the first time, she wondered if being here with her father was worth the strain on her marriage. Why was she here, really? If it was just to nurse her dad back to health, she could hire someone to do that.

No, she'd come down here to try to build a relationship with her father, before it was too late. She wanted to learn about him—but also to learn about herself. She didn't want to go through life like someone else's servant, or a robot who was afraid to stop moving. Here was her chance to slow down, to reacquaint herself with the part of herself with whom she'd lost touch.

* * *

Karen was putting away laundry the following Wednesday when she found an old photo album in the hall closet. It was in a pile of miscellaneous pictures and envelopes full of old negatives that had fallen behind the stacks of sheets and towels. She pulled it out and opened it, the black paper pages brittle beneath her hands.

The first thing she saw was a picture of her eight-year-old self, dressed in cutoff jeans and a striped T-shirt, posing on a rock, one hand shielding her eyes as she stared off in the distance, a serious look on her face.

She laughed, and carried the album to the sofa. All the photos were from the family's vacation to Yellowstone that year. She smiled at a picture of the four of them posed in front of Old Faithful. Her father, of course, had binoculars around his neck. Del's lower lip was stuck out in a pout. She seemed to remember he was mad because his mother wouldn't let him throw rocks in the geyser.

And there was Karen, standing between her mother and father, a huge smile on her face. She looked so happy.

It had been a fun trip. While her father wandered off to look for birds, her mother took her and Del on a nature hike, bribing them with the promise of roasted marshmallows and hot dogs when they returned. They had climbed rocks, balanced on fallen logs and picked wildflowers, laughing and shrieking with the abandon of children who had spent three days cooped up in the backseat of a car.

Rounding a curve in the trail, they had come upon a grizzly sow feeding in some berry bushes. Sara had screamed and gathered the children about her. The bear had ignored them and lumbered off. Del started crying and Sara tried to comfort him, while Karen stared, fascinated, at the magnificent animal.

Back at camp, she had rushed to be the first to tell her father the news of the sighting. He'd helped her look up bears in one of his guidebooks and they'd read about grizzlies. Closing her eyes, she could still remember the feel of his arm around her as he held her close and turned the pages of the book, the smell of insect repellent and campfire smoke permeating his clothes.

How had she forgotten that moment? Why did she so seldom remember those things now, but rather focused on the disappointments of her youth?

Maybe because those happy times made all the other days seem that much worse. Those good memories were a reminder of what might have been—the ideal they approached, but never really reached.

She was still studying the photos, and remembering, when Sara arrived an hour later. She swept into the house bearing a tower of Tupperware containers. "Leftovers from my ladies club luncheon," she explained as she unpacked the containers onto a plate. "I thought you'd appreciate not having to cook."

Karen admired the array of chicken salad, fruit salad, salmon sandwiches cut in quarters, crusts removed, and a container of vaguely familiar hors d'oeuvre-looking items.

"What are these?" she asked.

Sara made a face. "Sushi. California rolls, I think. They're from Estelle Watson. She fancies herself a *gourmet*."

Karen sampled one of the rolls. "They're good."

Sara made a face. "I suppose. Though why good old deviled eggs or cocktail sausages aren't good enough for her I'll never know." She filled a plate with some of each of the dishes and handed it to Karen. "I'm betting you haven't had lunch yet. Eat."

"Yes, ma'am." Karen carried the plate to the table. Her mother followed and sat across from her.

"Where's Casey?" Sara asked.

"He and Sadie walked down the road to a neighbor's who has a pool."

"Who is Sadie?"

Karen flushed. "Sadie's a dog. A big mutt Del foisted off on us. Casey's crazy about her."

"And you didn't have the heart to tell him he couldn't keep her." Sara shook her head. "You spoil that boy."

"You're one to talk. You never said no to Del."

Sara smiled. "I see a lot of Del in Casey. I suppose there are worse things than having a dog. He might have asked for a motorcycle. Or a drum set." She spotted the photo album and slid it toward her. "What's this?"

"I found it in the linen closet this morning. It's pictures from our vacation to Yellowstone. Do you remember?"

Sara slipped on her reading glasses and opened the album. "Oh, I remember. The bear."

"That's right. We saw that grizzly bear when we were out hiking."

"I was so terrified after that I refused to spend another night in the tent."

"Is that why we moved to the lodge? I didn't think much about it. I was so excited to be able to swim in the pool."

"Children are easy to please at that age."

She ate in silence for a moment. She would never have described herself as *easy to please*. "What was I like as a child?" she asked after a moment.

"You were a very serious child. Frightfully solemn." Sara removed her glasses and closed the album. "I never knew quite what to make of you. You took after your father that way."

"I did?" She had never thought she had that much in common with her dad.

"Oh yes. Everything was so dreadfully important to you, from doing your homework perfectly to dressing just so. If anything went wrong, you would pout or cry." She shook her head. "Del was much easier. He and I knew how to have fun."

Her mother made her sound so…unlovable. "I wish we'd taken more vacations like the one to Yellowstone. That was fun."

"After your father saw all the 'easy' birds in the United States, he wanted to spend his free time abroad. The thought of traveling in remote areas with two children didn't appeal to me, so we stayed home."

"Didn't it bother you, that he wasn't more a part of our lives?"

"It did. And it didn't." She tilted her head, considering the question. "Sometimes it was easier being able to do things my own way, without interference. And men weren't expected to be as involved with their children back then. That was the mother's job."

Karen ate another California roll. "Is that why you waited until we were grown to divorce him?"

"Partly. I don't know if it's hormones, or empty nest, or an awareness of time getting away, but a lot of women in their forties get restless. They start looking for more in life."

"I thought it was men who had the midlife crises."

"I'm not talking crises. It could be something as simple as changing the way you wear your hair or taking up a new hobby." She smiled. "It's a wonderful chance to find out what you're really capable of."

"How old were you when you did all this?"

Sara gave Karen a knowing look. "About the age you are now, I think. Isn't that interesting?"

She looked away. Interesting. And a little unnerving. She had enough changes going on in her life right now without contemplating more. And yet the idea of making some kind of choice for her life, instead of always reacting to whatever was thrown at her, held a powerful appeal.

Did she want things to keep moving along the way they always had been, or was she ready to make some changes? And what kind of changes? She didn't know any other kind of life than the one she'd lived for years as a wife and mother and business partner. There had to be other options out there, but the thought of exploring them stole her breath. Reaching for something new seemed to mean letting go of something old. What if she released the wrong thing, and ended up worse off than before?

9

It's not only fine feathers that make fine birds.
—*Aesop, "The Jay and the Peacock"*

The Great Crested Flycatcher perched on the uppermost limb of the big pine. The compact silhouette gave it away as a flycatcher; Martin had thought it an Ash-throated at first. Then it turned and sunlight highlighted the yellow belly and the distinctive crest.

He glanced at Karen. She was studying the tree intently but had yet to spot the bird. She was looking too low down. He leaned over and tugged at her sleeve, then pointed toward the top of the tree. "Look."

It came out to his ears more like *oog* but she seemed to understand, and elevated her gaze.

"I see it!" Her voice held the excitement of a child spying a prize at an Easter egg hunt. She fumbled with the binoculars, sighting through them, then scanning the treetop, struggling to locate the bird again.

Did she remember nothing he'd taught her? He grunted to get her attention, then demonstrated the proper technique. First, find the bird with the naked eye. Then, without looking away from the bird, lift the binoculars into place and adjust the focus.

The flycatcher leaped into view, the gray throat, yellow belly and rufous tail feathers making identification easy.

"I see it now, but what is it?" Karen asked.

He lowered the binoculars and gestured toward the field guide at her elbow. It wasn't going to do her any good if he identified everything for her.

She picked up the guide and flipped through it, glancing from time to time at the bird, which remained still on the perch, as if posing for them.

Martin wondered sometimes if birds knew they were being watched. It was a frivolous idea, and he was not a frivolous man, but too many times when he'd been unsure about an identification, the bird in question had turned to show some singular marking that answered his question. It made him wonder....

"Is it some kind of vireo? No, that's not right." She flipped through the guidebook, studying the pictures, scanning through the list of identifying features, habitat maps and descriptions of birdcalls. "A flycatcher, then. The size is right." She looked at him for confirmation and he nodded.

"All right, then. I can eliminate the ones that don't live here." She hurriedly flipped pages, impatient as she narrowed in on identifying the sighting. "That one's head isn't right.... That one doesn't live here.... That one's wrong...." She stopped and studied the illustration of the Great Crested Flycatcher, then checked the bird above them through the binoculars again.

Obliging of it to sit still so long, Martin thought. Most of the time in the field you were lucky to catch more than a passing glimpse. He'd have to teach her to make a more rapid assessment. She needed to learn to note features such as the presence or lack of wing bars, the shape of the beak, colors and their pattern, eye stripes or rings, and a dozen other distinguishing characteristics, all in a matter of seconds.

He'd long felt that birders would make excellent witnesses

in the event of a crime, provided they were focused on the villain, and not some more interesting feathered quarry on a nearby telephone wire.

"It's this one." She held the book out in front of him and pointed to the painting of the Great Crested Flycatcher.

He nodded and waved a shaking hand toward the notebook in her lap. "Mark." Which came out *mar* but she understood.

She carefully noted the time, day and location of the sighting. "That's three new ones this afternoon," she said. "I'm afraid I have a long way to go to catch up to you."

She never would catch up, of course. She had no serious interest in being a big lister. Which suited him. He hadn't worked this hard to make records that would be easily broken, even by his own progeny.

It was enough that she wanted to sit here with him now, to learn a little of what he had to pass on to her. She'd surprised him when she'd come to his office a few days ago and asked him to teach her about birding. For forty years she'd shown little interest in his avocation, and now that he had lost most of his mobility and practically all his powers of speech, she wanted to share this with him.

"I just thought, as long as I was here, it would be a good time to take up a new hobby," she'd said.

A more morbid man might have suspected she wanted to learn his secrets before he carried them to the grave with him.

"It's very peaceful here, isn't it?" she said, focusing on the tree once more. It rose thirty feet into the air and in its branches Martin could hear and see dozens of birds, mostly the chickadees, nuthatches, titmice and sparrows common to backyard feeders throughout the United States. Bright red Northern Cardinals and blue-and-white Eastern Jays rounded out the local hoi polloi. Karen had added all these to her list in the first two days of their birding together.

She'd impressed him with her ability to sit quiet and still, observing. Before, she'd struck him as a woman plagued with the need to be busy, like her mother, who had once protested that fidgeting had been proven to burn calories, so she saw no need to give it up.

Maturity had brought a settledness to Karen he appreciated. Maybe she did have some qualities from his side of the genetic helix.

"Is that what attracted you to birding? This sort of zen quality to it?"

There was nothing zen about the compulsion he felt to list birds. It was as if the more time he spent finding birds and adding them to his list, the greater his chances of understanding their ethereal nature. Plus, he wanted to accomplish something few men had accomplished. Not blessed with great brains, brawn or ability, he'd sought to see more birds than anyone else in the world.

But he had no way of expressing this so that Karen would understand. Instead, he shrugged, and scanned the tree once more. Silence settled between them again, a stillness void of the awkwardness he'd felt too often in her presence. Birding had given them that, at least. Something they could do together without the need for conversation.

Except that Karen was in the mood to talk. "Do you remember when I was a little girl and you taught me about birds?" she asked.

He would not have called his few attempts to share his passion with his children a success. They grew impatient with sitting still so long, though Karen, at least, had had a good memory for names and details. He nodded.

"I think I probably spent more time picking wildflowers and collecting pretty stones that I did actually seeing birds on our expeditions." She lowered the binoculars and turned to him. "Mostly what I enjoyed was getting to spend time alone with you."

He blinked, startled that she had such positive memories of what, for him, had been frustrating outings. The boundless energy and short attention span of his children when they were small overwhelmed him, and he had never felt he was really getting through to them.

"I found a photo album the other day, with pictures from that vacation we took to Yellowstone, when I was eight. Do you remember?"

He nodded. He'd seen Trumpeter Swans and Whooping Cranes during that trip, and Sara had been frightened by a bear. He also remembered that Karen had not been afraid at all. She'd been eager to tell him about the grizzly. Together, they'd looked through one of his nature guides, and read about the great bears. He had a sudden memory of eight-year-old Karen standing in the circle of his arms, listening raptly as he read to her from the guidebook. The realization that he had had a part in creating something as perfect and precious as this child had overwhelmed him. Affection and wonder and pride left him speechless, and terrified that he might do or say the wrong thing and lose her altogether. When Sara called Karen to wash up for supper he was almost relieved to have the chance to school his feelings into a more comfortable reserve.

He studied the woman beside him, looking for signs of that girl. They were there, in the dimple to the left of her mouth, and in the way she tilted her head to one side and smiled at him now. "That was a fun trip, wasn't it, Dad? I wish we'd taken more like that."

He nodded, and blinked away stinging tears. Regrets were a poison he wanted no part of, but now, speechless and immobile, they worked on him with painful intensity.

He grabbed up his own binoculars and raised them to his eyes, pretending to search the treetops once more. He was almost grateful he'd been robbed of the ability to speak. In the best of times, he'd never known what to say to his daughter. There were no words to explain this paradox of wanting to reclaim a closeness he had forfeited long ago, and the fear that the price he owed for such a privilege was far too dear.

Karen had turned to birding as a way to connect with her father, but she was surprised by how much she enjoyed looking for birds, watching their behavior and trying to determine their identity. She had no desire to count and categorize species the way her father did, but the solitary, out-of-doors nature of the activity made for a lot of time to be alone with her thoughts.

Her life up till now hadn't had much room for contemplation, and the nature of some of her thoughts surprised her. There was the usual litany of worries about the boys, Tom, their landscaping business and her father's health. But once she'd gotten all that out of the way, she found herself remembering things that hadn't come to mind in years—ambitions she'd had as a girl, old hurts and triumphs long since put aside, beliefs she'd held that hadn't proved true. In those hours spent on the front porch or out back by the pond, eyes trained overhead and heart turned inward, she felt like an archaeologist removing layers of refuse and artifacts to reveal clues about her life as it was once lived, secrets she'd once told herself and then forgotten.

She was sitting in a lawn chair by the pond, watching a Golden-fronted Woodpecker trace a crooked spiral up the trunk of a half-dead yellow pine when Casey found her one late afternoon. Sadie ran ahead to greet her, tail wagging. Karen ignored the dog and jumped up from the chair. "What is it? Is Grandpa okay?"

"He's okay. He's taking a nap." Casey bent and scooped up a pinecone and hurled it toward the pond. "I came out here to see what you were doing."

"Bird-watching." She held up the binoculars, feeling a

little foolish as she did so. To a teenager, watching birds must seem about the most uncool thing a person could do. "I'm trying to figure out what your grandfather finds so fascinating about it."

She sat once more and Sadie sat next to her and put her head on Karen's knee. Karen absently rubbed her ears and was rewarded with a steady drumming of the dog's tail. It amazed her how quickly the dog had insinuated herself into their lives. How quickly she'd come to seem, even to Karen, like part of the family.

"What have you seen so far?" Casey came to stand beside her chair.

She flipped to the front of the guidebook, where she'd been keeping her list. "This afternoon I've seen an Eastern Wood Pewee, two Killdeer and a Golden-fronted Woodpecker. Others, too, but those are the ones that are new to my list."

He sat on the ground beside her chair, long legs folded up like a grasshopper, knees sticking up. When was the kid going to stop growing? He'd need all new pants before school this fall. She frowned at a hole in the toe of his right shoe. "Why is there a hole in your shoe?"

He stretched out his leg and examined the hole. "I guess my toe rubbed through. These shoes are a little tight."

"We'll try to get you another pair one day this week." She added it to her mental list of things to do. Later, she'd transfer it to the running tally she kept in a notebook in her purse. *Her brain,* she'd jokingly dubbed the notebook. The thing that enabled her to keep all her plates in the air.

"That'd be good." He gazed out over the small pond, silent for a moment, then said, "When we were little, Grandpa would bring us out here after supper to fish. He'd put worms on our hooks and we'd toss our lines in, and while we waited for the fish to bite, he'd teach us about birds."

"He would?" She searched her brain for some memory

of such a tender familial scene and found none. "I don't remember him spending that much time with y'all."

Casey scratched at a mosquito bite on his arm, then leaned back, propping his weight on his hands. "It was that summer I was nine. Matt and I stayed here with Grandpa and Grandma while you and Dad went on that cruise."

How could she have forgotten? It was the first vacation she and Tom had taken together since the boys were born. They'd spent a week in the Caribbean, drinking fruity drinks, soaking up the sun and making love every afternoon in their tiny cabin. They'd dubbed it their second honeymoon, and vowed to make it a semiannual tradition. But they'd never found the time or money to go again.

Sadness washed over her at that thought. Why had they denied themselves that chance at closeness, that opportunity to remember what made them a couple? If nothing else, this time spent apart had opened her eyes to all the little things they'd left out of their relationship, things maybe they both needed.

"So do you think Grandpa decided to be a petroleum engineer so he could travel all over looking for birds, or he started watching birds because his job took him all over the world?" Casey glanced up at her.

"The former, I think. I seem to remember he started birding while he was still in high school." She looked down at her son, at the cowlick at the top of his head. It delighted her that all the carefully applied styling gel in the world couldn't tame that little-boy curl of hair. "I guess he was lucky to find a job that allowed him to indulge his passion."

"I think it's cool when you can earn money and still do what you love." He plucked a piece of grass and twirled it between his fingers. "Like Uncle Del. He owns the oil-change shop, but he takes off whenever he wants to go fishing and stuff."

She struggled not to let her dismay show. Her brother as role model was not an idea that had ever crossed her mind. "Casey, look at me," she said.

He turned his head to her. The end of his nose was peeling with sunburn, and blond peach fuzz showed on his upper lip. She supposed he'd be shaving every day soon. She didn't know if she was ready to admit how much of a man he'd become.

"Your uncle Del can be a really nice guy," she said slowly, wary of painting her brother too black and therefore making him that much more attractive to a teenager. "But he hasn't always made the best choices in his life. Financial or personal."

"Well, yeah, but he's got a great girlfriend now, and a cool truck." He looked at her sideways. "A fancy house isn't everything, you know."

She stifled a groan of aggravation. Of course a sixteen-year-old would think a great girlfriend and a cool truck were the height of personal success, but could she help it if she'd hoped for a little better perspective from her son?

"I'm not saying a fancy house is everything. And neither is a girlfriend and a truck. What's important is to spend some time right now, before you have to make choices, deciding what you want to do with your life. If you start on the right path when you're young, you'll save yourself a lot of grief."

She said the words with only a twinge of guilt. What did she know about choosing the right path? Almost nothing she'd set out to do in life had turned out quite as she'd imagined, from her choice of vocation, to the kind of marriage she'd have, to the relationship she'd have with her parents and her children. She was over forty and still trying to get things right. Who was she to preach to Casey, except a mother who hoped he'd do better at figuring things out than she had?

He tossed the blade of grass to the side and plucked another one, and began tearing it into tinier and tinier pieces. "Yeah, that's what everybody says, but really, what's so wrong with making mistakes? You learn things that way."

"But you aren't the only one your mistakes affect."

He dusted his hands together and stood. "You don't have to worry about me. I'm not going to end up a bum. But if I did, at least I'd be a happy bum."

She made a face. "Those aren't exactly comforting words to a mother's ears."

He picked up the binoculars she'd dropped and focused them on the pond. "Parents worry too much."

"Children don't worry enough." She studied him, seeing Tom in the strong curve of his jaw and the fullness of his bottom lip. But she was there in his face, too, in the narrow nose and high forehead. She wanted so much for him—money, love, good health and freedom from worries. But most of all, she wanted him to be happy. "Isn't there anything you've thought about doing for a living? Anything that interests you?"

He lowered the binoculars. "I think I might like to be a writer."

"A novelist?"

He shrugged. "Maybe movies or plays. Or nonfiction stuff. Articles. Things like that. But I'd like to travel around some first, you know, to gather material."

She had a sudden recollection of a summer day when she and Tammy were working on their tans on a bluff overlooking the Trinity River. They'd been sharing deep thoughts and Karen had suddenly announced that after graduation, she was going to join the Peace Corps and work helping people in Africa. Where this sudden burst of altruism had come from, she couldn't have said, and after a few months, her noble ideals had died a quiet death. She'd gone to work for the hospital, met Tom, and so the rest of her life had played out.

But what would have happened if she'd held on to that impulse? How might her life have been different? She stood and put her arm around her son. "I think you'd make a great writer."

He flushed. "You do?"

"I do. You're smart and you have a good heart." Important things to remember when worry got the best of her. Maybe those things didn't add up to the kind of success she always envisioned for her children, but they surely couldn't hurt.

As for the mistakes she'd made, who was to say any of her other options would have turned out any better? It was nice to imagine she could have been a world traveler or a great humanitarian or a more devoted daughter or more passionate wife, but would any of those things really have made her any happier?

Was the answer, instead, to appreciate more what she had, or to reimagine her fantasies to closer fit her reality? Like the good memories of her childhood she was only beginning to unearth, maybe there was more to her life than she thought. Maybe the restlessness she was feeling now was only the beginning of discovering she was better off than she'd imagined.

Mary Elisabeth agreed to sit with Martin one afternoon so that Karen could take Casey to buy new shoes. No one consulted Martin about the arrangement; Karen presented it to him as a *fait accompli*. He said nothing about it one way or another. It was a sad thing when a grown man had to have a babysitter.

But he could do worse than this young woman. Whatever else he could say about Del, he couldn't fault his taste in women. This one was designed to make a man think about sex, from her thick-lashed dark eyes to the fall of brown curls around her shoulders to the breasts that swelled her too-small

T-shirt to the tight round bottom scarcely covered by her cutoffs.

She wore too much mascara and a ring in her navel, and he'd caught a glimpse of a butterfly tattooed over her left breast. In his younger years she'd have been deemed *fast* but he supposed nowadays she was just a normal young woman. They didn't try to pretend these days that they weren't as interested in sex as men always had been. There was something to be said for that kind of honesty.

Just as well she couldn't read the thoughts in his mind. It would probably shock her to know a man his age still contemplated such things. To her he was merely a dried-up husk in this wheelchair, incoherent and harmless.

Not that she'd have anything to fear from him even in his prime. He'd always been a man more inclined to thought than action, at least when it came to women. And he had enough dignity left not to make a fool of himself over a woman young enough to be his granddaughter.

"I thought maybe we could listen to some music," she said, looking through the bookshelves in his bedroom. He'd managed to get himself out of the bed and into his chair before she'd arrived, but he hadn't yet made it into his office when she swept in on a cloud of floral perfume. She flipped through the stacks of cassettes, then looked back at him, eyes wide. "These are all birdcalls."

He nodded. He would have liked to explain how he used the tapes to lure birds to him, but complex sentences were beyond his powers of speech at the moment.

"I guess you use these to learn all the different calls." She straightened and looked at him. "I'm here to keep you company, so what would *you* like to do?"

"Office." The word came out slurred, so he tried again, concentrating on shaping his tongue to make the correct sounds. "Of-fice!"

"Karen said you like to spend a lot of time in your office."

She took hold of the wheelchair and maneuvered him through the door and down the hall. The dog joined them, tail wagging, tongue lolling. Apparently Del had talked Karen into taking in the animal. Martin had never approved of dogs in the house, but as with everything else in his life these days, he had little say about it.

"Is over here by the desk all right?" Mary Elisabeth asked, parking the chair in front of the computer.

He nodded, and shifted onto his left hip. He'd lost weight and sometimes it felt as if his backbone was trying to poke through his skin. Mary Elisabeth noticed him fidgeting, and worry lines formed on her perfect forehead. "You need a pillow at the small of your back." She plucked a small pillow from the love seat by the window and arranged it behind his back. "And if you raise this footrest just a little…" She bent and adjusted the footrests, then straightened. "That will help take some of the pressure off your spine."

Skeptical, he settled back in the chair, but found that he was, indeed, more comfortable. He looked at her. "How?" How had she known this?

"Oh, my mom was in a wheelchair."

"Why?"

"She had MS. Multiple sclerosis. I can hardly remember when she wasn't in a wheelchair."

"Hard." Hard on a kid to have a parent who was crippled that way.

"Yeah, it was hard sometimes. I used to wish she was more like other kids' moms, until I figured out they all had problems, too." She shrugged. "Life is what it is. You have to make the best of it."

It was the kind of trite advice that usually annoyed him, but coming from her, it had the ring of truth. He studied her again. Her hair was pulled back from her face with tiny clips shaped like butterflies, and she wore half a dozen rings in each ear. When she smiled, dimples formed on either side of her mouth. No one looking at her would ever guess she was anything but carefree, even frivolous. "Your mom... alive?" he asked.

She shook her head. "She died when I was sixteen."

Too young. "Casey's...sixteen."

"Yeah. Kind of a tough age for a kid. You're trying to figure things out."

Plenty of people spent most of their lives trying to figure things out. For instance, he couldn't figure out why he'd been felled by a stroke in the prime of his birding career, or why his children too often seemed like strangers to him. Del hardly spoke to him, and Karen's words didn't always match the expression in her eyes. All his years spent observing wildlife around the globe hadn't prepared him for dealing with his adult children. When they were small, he'd told himself he'd be able to relate to them better as adults. They'd be more like peers, less dependent on him, less needy.

Yet now they accosted him with a whole different set of demands, still bound to him by blood and obligation, expecting to be treated as more than peers, needing him in a different way than they had as children, but seemingly needing him no less.

His eyes met Mary Elisabeth's. "Miss her?" He meant her mother.

"I do. It sneaks up on me sometimes. I'll be doing something and I'll wonder what she would have said or thought, or I wish she was with me. But I knew for a long time before she died that she probably wouldn't be around to see me grow up. It was hard, but it also made me appreciate the time we did have."

"Life...short." Her mother's life, but so many others, too. And the older you grew, the shorter your life ahead became. He had never contemplated such things before his stroke; now there were days when such thoughts blotted out everything else.

"It's a cliché, but true." She took hold of his hand and held it in hers. She had cool fingers with neatly manicured nails, painted shell-pink. "Enough morbid talk. You're going to be around a long time yet. And your talking is getting better. I don't have any trouble understanding you now."

She understood a great deal. Lessons some people never learned.

"So tell me about your bird-watching. I see all these awards on the walls." She turned to look at the plaques. "But why do you do it? Is it that you just like birds, or is there more to it?"

Yes, there was more to it. The fact that she got *that* made her rise another notch in his opinion. He wrinkled his face, trying to think how to explain. But his limited powers of speech failed him. He turned to the computer and typed.

Birding is a challenge. Something I can do others can't.

She nodded. "Like people who climb mountains or run marathons, or things like that."

Yes. But it is about the birds, too. They fascinate me.

"They are fascinating. And there are so many of them. Always more to discover." She turned her attention to the map that bristled with pins marking all the places he'd recorded bird sightings. "Look at all the places you've traveled. All the countries you've seen." She smiled over her shoulder at him. "I'd love to travel that way—to see all kinds of people and cultures."

He didn't tell her he'd spent most of his time in those countries away from people, searching for birds. Other than those he associated with through his work, he hadn't gotten to know the natives of the countries he'd visited.

Except one time.

Perhaps it was being here with Mary Elisabeth that brought the memory back to him, sharp and bright. He'd been in

Thailand, ostensibly to do research for his employer, but he'd made sure to allow time on either end of the business trip to look for birds. At the airport alone he'd added three new birds to his life list.

A meeting had ended early and he'd gone to the beach near his hotel, thinking he might find a few shore birds to add to his list, bringing the total to 2,027.

He had found no birds, but had met a young woman. She was Polynesian, but she spoke softly accented English. She had approached him, and struck up a casual conversation. He'd decided she was a prostitute, but didn't discourage her company.

He had ended up spending the evening and the night with her. She had been like Mary Elisabeth, with much more depth than her appearance had led him to expect. They talked about everything—nature, politics, books, life. Sitting with her he'd felt something come alive inside him. She had awakened him to things that might be missing in his life.

He'd returned home later in the week determined to pay more attention to those around him. The possibilities had excited him. But it was too late. His attempts to connect with his wife and children were met with indifference. He had waited too long and they had learned to live without him. Rather than try to overcome their resistance, he had slipped back into his old ways, focusing on his work and his lists of birds, self-contained and unemotional.

He was like a man who had stood by a campfire and enjoyed its warmth, but when the fire had died down, he'd been content to sit in the coolness. The warmth had been nice, but maybe it wasn't for him.

"What should we do now?" Mary Elisabeth perched on the corner of the desk.

"Music." He clicked the appropriate icon on the desktop and a Haydn concerto swelled from the speakers. It was too loud for conversation, allowing him a convenient excuse to retreat once more to silence. He was comfortable here, if a little cold.

A few days after his shopping trip with his mom, Casey called Matt and asked him to sell the guitar Casey had gotten two Christmases ago and send him the money.

"Why?" Matt asked.

"Because I don't like being broke." He leaned back on the sofa, feet dangling over the edge, phone cradled to his ear. "I hardly ever play the guitar anyway."

"Why don't you get a job?"

"I can't. I have to stay here and help Mom with Grandpa." He could hear some kind of machinery running in the background behind his brother. A wood chipper, or maybe a chain saw.

"How's he doing?"

"Okay. He can talk some now. He's not as grumpy, so I think maybe he feels better."

"How's Mom?"

"Okay. She looks tired. And kind of sad." He drew his knees up and wedged his toes beneath one bottom sofa cushion. "I don't know if it's because her dad is sick, or because she misses you and Dad and Denver."

"We miss her. Dad especially. The office is a mess without her."

"So what's it like, being a foreman?"

"Okay. Some of the older guys gave me a little grief, dissing me because I'm the boss's son, but I showed them I can work as hard as they do and I'm getting a little respect."

He hunched his shoulders against a stab of envy. He didn't think anyone had ever respected him, least of all his dad. "So is Dad pissed that I'm not there?"

"He was at first. He hasn't said anything lately. I guess it's good Mom's not down there by herself. He says he might try to take off a few days to come see y'all."

"That would be cool." He wasn't anxious to see his father if he was still upset with him, but Mom would probably appreciate a visit. "Hey, we got a dog."

"A dog? I thought Mom hated dogs."

"She doesn't hate dogs. She just never had one. She thought they were all dirty and everything, but this one's nice."

"What kind of dog?"

"I don't know. Part golden retriever, but something else, too. She has long gold hair and floppy ears and she smiles a lot."

"Dogs don't smile."

"This one does."

"What are you going to do when it's time to come home?"

"Bring her with us, you goof." It wasn't like they could leave Sadie here with Grandpa. Besides, Casey was her favorite person. The way he saw it, she was really his dog. "So will you sell the guitar?" he asked Matt.

"Why don't I just send you the money? You can pay me back later."

"You'd do that?"

"Yeah. I mean, you're a screw-up sometimes, but you're the only brother I got."

He swallowed around the lump in his throat. "Thanks."

"Yeah. You just remember you owe me."

"Right." When he got back home, maybe he'd quit charging Matt for using his hair gel. He'd even volunteer to clean Matt's side of the room for a week or so. That ought to be enough.

He didn't want to take this brotherly love thing too far.

10

I hope you love birds, too. It is economical.
It saves going to heaven.
—*Emily Dickinson,* Life and Letters of Emily
Dickinson

"I stopped by to see if you and your father have managed to kill each other yet," Sara announced as she entered the kitchen one afternoon the first week in July.

"Why would you think we'd do that?" Karen asked.

"I spent a good part of the last years of my marriage wanting to strangle the man, and I have no doubt he felt the same about me." She deposited her purse on the counter and checked her hair in the reflection from the microwave door.

"You're exaggerating."

"Not by much." She sat at the table and looked around the room. "Never underestimate the ill will two people who were once in love can harbor against one another. Do you have any coffee?"

"I was just about to make a pot." She'd taken out the coffee canister as soon as Sara walked into the house. Her mother lived on caffeine, martinis and deli salads, which perhaps explained why she still wore a size six at age sixty-nine.

"Where is my ex, anyway? I should say hello."

"He's working with the occupational therapist."

"He doesn't have an occupation, so what's the point? Though I suppose they could work on holding binoculars and typing on the computer."

"I believe they're doing something called 'fundamentals of daily living.' She's teaching Dad to dress himself, brush his teeth, maneuver his wheelchair, plus some speech therapy." It was depressing to think of a seventy-year-old man having to relearn how to tie his shoes, but the alternative was more horrible to contemplate.

"How's he doing with that?" Sara asked.

"All right, I guess. He gets frustrated and impatient, I think." Just last week, he'd thrown a shoe at the therapist, Lola.

"Martin can be a bear when he doesn't get his way, but then, can't we all?" She checked the coffeepot, then studied her manicure. "I saw your brother last night at Kelso's. He bought me a drink."

Kelso's was the local watering hole, a bar with pool tables upstairs and a big-screen TV in the main room, where matrons gathered for cocktails alongside beer-drinking truck drivers. Her brother and mother were both regulars. "What's Del up to?" Besides fishing, playing pool and avoiding responsibilities.

"The manager of his oil-change shop quit and the poor boy has been working himself near to death trying to keep things going." She took out an emery board and began filing her nails.

"I seriously doubt Del is in danger of working himself to death. Not as long as he has time to drink beer at Kelso's."

"Now, as a business owner yourself, you should know the kind of stress he's under. Nothing wrong with letting off a little steam." She put away the emery board. "Is that coffee ready yet?"

"I'll fix you a cup." She poured the coffee into an oversize mug, and added sugar and milk, reminded of mornings when she was a little girl when she'd beg for the privilege of fixing her parents' coffee. It had seemed such a grown-up thing to her then, and she always felt proud when they praised her for getting it "just right."

She served the coffee and sat down across from her mother with her own cup. "I've taken up bird-watching," she said. "Dad is teaching me."

Sara made a face. "Please tell me you haven't inherited his crazy obsession with birds."

"No, but I'm enjoying it. It's very relaxing. Contemplative."

"That must be why I never cared for it. Of course, I never liked yoga, either. I'd much rather *do* something than sit around meditating or whatever."

"Do you think if you'd shared Daddy's interest in birding, you'd have stayed together?"

Sara leveled a stern gaze at her daughter. "I never waste time contemplating what might have been. And your father and I had problems that went beyond common interests. The man is incapable of developing an emotional attachment to anyone."

The harshness of her words stung. "You make him sound like some kind of sociopath," Karen said. "Granted, he's reserved, but that doesn't mean he doesn't have feelings."

Sara's expression softened. "I hope you don't think taking up this hobby is going to give you some kind of instant spiritual connection to the man. Or that he'll suddenly grow all warm and sentimental."

"No, of course I don't think that." She shifted in her chair. If she couldn't have warm and sentimental, she'd settle for some sense of…closeness. Some sign that he was proud to have her as his daughter. That he loved her.

"You should get out of this house more. I've signed up

for ice skating lessons at the rink over in Nacogdoches. You should join me."

"Ice skating? Mama, are you crazy? You could fall and break something."

"If I do, I know I can count on you to look after me."

Karen's heart stopped beating for a minute and she sucked in her breath, a vision filling her head of her mother lying back in a hospital bed, issuing orders left and right.

"Don't look so horrified, dear." Sara laughed. "Oh my, I can see that would be your idea of hell—playing nursemaid to both of us at once." She sipped her coffee. "Well, don't worry. If I get sick I'm going to find some handsome male nurse to wait on me."

Except what were the odds of that happening? Her mother had no money, really. Not enough to pay for private care. There was no one else but Karen to come to her rescue. What she'd told herself would only be a few months' inconvenience could become years of being caught between the demands of her parents and her husband and children. The idea wrapped itself around her like a python, strangling her breath.

Lola emerged from Martin's bedroom, shutting the door softly behind her. "That's all for today," she said as she joined them in the kitchen.

"How did it go?" Karen asked.

"He didn't throw anything today, if that's what you mean." She grinned. She was a small, round woman with olive skin and almond-shaped eyes, her black hair cut very short all over and sticking out in all directions like quills on a porcupine.

"Would you like some coffee?" Karen asked, already reaching for a cup.

"That would be good." She set her bag of equipment on the floor. "Make it about half milk so I can drink it fast. I can't stay long."

"Have a seat." Sara nodded to the chair next to her. "I'm the ex-wife by the way. How's the old man doing?"

"He's making progress. Slowly. His speech is a little clearer, but there are things he needs to work on." She accepted the cup of coffee with a grateful look. "He's stubborn, which can be good and bad when it comes to therapy. It's good when they're determined to get well, bad when they resist going through the steps needed to get there."

"I can guess which kind of stubborn Martin is," Sara said. "He always hated being told what to do."

"I've dealt with worse." She smiled. "I can usually convince them to do things for their own good."

"So you think he's doing well?" Karen joined the women at the table. "I mean, well enough that he'll be able to talk again and do things for himself?"

"That's hard to say." Lola cradled the cup in both hands.

"What she really wants to know is, will he be able to live on his own again?" Sara said.

Lola shook her head. "At this stage, there's no way to know the answer to that. These things have to be taken in baby steps. Martin may never get back to the way he was, but the goal is to improve his quality of life and give him as much independence as possible."

Karen swallowed hard. "What will happen if he can't look after himself?"

"Then you may want to consider some sort of assisted living facility."

"A nursing home," Sara said.

"There are worse places to be," Lola said.

"I doubt my father would agree."

"The ideal situation would be for family to continue to look after him, but that isn't always possible." Lola drained her cup and set it on the table. "I'd better go now. I have one more client to see this afternoon."

"Thank you for everything." Karen walked her to the

door. "I'll talk to Dad, see if I can't get him to be more co-operative."

"I'm sorry I couldn't give you a more definite prognosis, but I don't like to raise false hopes."

"I understand."

"Try not to worry." Lola patted her arm. "Whatever his final prognosis, you'll figure out what to do. Families always do."

Sure. She didn't bother telling Lola, but she'd ceased being the woman with all the answers six weeks ago somewhere between here and the Denver Airport.

Martin's body ached too much to let him sleep. Lola had been a tyrant today, demanding he bend and stretch and lift until he was in agony. She'd shown no pity, telling him over and over again that he had to challenge himself, to teach his dormant nerves and muscles to work properly again.

His spirit was bruised as well, from the shame of failing over and over at such simple tasks as buttoning his shirt correctly or cutting up food.

Lola had the grace not to comment on his fumbling, except to correct his mistakes and urge him to try harder.

It hadn't helped any that he'd gotten e-mails this morning from no less than three people in the birding community, crowing about their planned trips to Arkansas to look for the Ivory-billed Woodpecker—a species that until recently had been thought to be extinct. To add one to their personal list was now the holy grail of every birder. And Martin, though he lived only a few hours from the place where the wood-peckers had been found, was stuck, unable to move.

Sara had stopped by for a few minutes not long after Lola left. "How are you doing?" she'd asked, with real concern.

He'd shaken his head, and refused to say anything, his bad mood making conversation unwise. Though they'd been divorced for years, he still felt close enough to Sara to forgo politeness, and let her bear the brunt of his ill will, as he had too often in the latter days of their marriage.

"It's hell getting old," she'd said sympathetically. She patted his shoulder lightly, then sat across from him, on the side of the bed. "The therapist says you're doing pretty well for a stubborn old coot."

He'd always wondered how old men had come to be associated with a large black waterbird. As far as he knew, coots weren't particularly cantankerous.

"When this gets to be too tough, just remember it's not forever," Sara said. "I've found I can get through a lot of things that way."

He nodded. Had she gotten through their marriage that way? Maybe toward the end. In the early years they'd both believed in till death do us part. Only later did they realize how difficult, even impossible, that was sometimes.

"I won't wear you out chattering on. Just wanted to see how you're holding up." She stood, then bent to kiss his cheek. "Hang in there. You really are looking better."

He listened to her high heels clacking on the wood floor of the hallway as she left. Even at sixty-nine she still insisted on wearing heels and makeup and having her hair and nails done. "A high-maintenance woman" one of his coworkers had labeled her, and it was true. But he'd never minded. Throughout his marriage, and even now, he hadn't lost his amazement that Sara Ellen Delwood had agreed to marry him.

When Martin was a teenager, he worked for a time for an old rancher, doing odd jobs and helping with the cattle. The old man had seen it as his duty to pass on advice to his young helper. On marriage, he'd been succinct: "Find the prettiest girl in town who will agree to sleep with you and stick with her," he'd said. "Unless you've got money or looks—and trust me, boy, you don't have neither—then you won't go wrong with that philosophy."

The first time he met Sara Delwood, Martin thought she was the prettiest girl he'd ever seen. He was too shy to ask her out, but she'd turned the tables and approached him first. "I was thinking about going into town and getting a hamburger and a malt," she'd said late one Friday after school. "Would you take me?"

He took her, and continued to escort her around all that summer and through their senior year. The night after graduation she'd turned to him and said, "Everybody thinks we've been dating so long we should get married. What do you think?"

So Sara had dragged him along with her into marriage and buying a house and having children and all the trappings of a conventional life. The only thing unconventional was his constant pursuit of birds. Eventually, the thing that had brought him the most peace and satisfaction in his life separated him from the family he'd acquired through no real effort of his own.

When she'd asked for the divorce, he hadn't argued. He had never completely lost the feeling that she deserved more than he could give her. He missed her for months—at times missed her still. But there was relief in being on his own, too, freedom from the guilt that he was letting someone else down when he focused on his passion for birds.

He was counting on that passion to get him through this rough time, as well. "You should set some goals for yourself," Lola had said. "It's good to give yourself something to aim for."

Goals. His goal was to get out of this bed and this house and back in the field. He wanted to go to Arkansas, and most especially, he wanted to return to Brazil. He had to find the Brown-chested Barbet. That one omission on his list loomed over his career like a dark cloud, overshadowing his other achievements. To be within a single species of cleaning up an entire country and not achieve that goal felt like the most ignoble failure.

How would he get there? He'd need help, obviously, though it pained him to admit it. A guide, then. Not one of those professional birding guides others hired to locate and point out the species for him. That wasn't true birding to him.

No, he needed someone to provide transportation to the area where the barbet would most likely be found. Someone to carry his bags and help him communicate with the natives.

Ed Delgado knew some people down there. Tomorrow Martin would e-mail and ask him for the names of some reliable guides. He wouldn't have the stamina he usually did; he'd have to allow for shorter days. He could go out early in the morning, then rest during the day and return at dusk, taking advantage of the prime hours for bird activity.

He'd have to be able to get around on his own more. He couldn't maneuver a wheelchair in the jungle. And he'd have to be able to talk to his interpreter. Lola had said with effort, and practice, he could do this thing. "Bar-bet." He tried the name on his tongue. To his ears, it sounded like *Ar-eth*.

"Bar-bet." He pressed his lips together to shape the *B*. Better that time. "Bor-ba." The name of the province he'd need to visit. "Ma-pi-a." The river where he'd be most likely to spot the barbet. The syllables were clumsy on his tongue. He repeated them over and over, mumbling to himself, trying to make the sounds as clear as he heard them in his head.

He fell asleep in a few moments, exhausted, birds darting through his dreams, elusive and always just beyond recognition.

Determined to force Del to do *something* to help her and his father, Karen knocked on his door one hot early July morning. As soon as he opened the door, she said, "The yard needs mowing. When can you do it?"

He looked over her shoulder at the overgrown yard and rubbed his chin. "It doesn't look that bad to me."

"Del, it's up past my ankles. And it looks terrible."

He shook his head. "Nobody around here really cares. The neighbors haven't complained."

"*I* care. I'm asking you to please mow it."

He sighed, the sound of a greatly burdened man. "All right, sis. I'll get around to it as soon as I can."

"That's not good enough, Del. I want you to do it today." Even as she listened to herself talk, part of her realized the unreasonableness of her request. Why should Del do anything she asked? Why should he try to please her now when he never had before?

But she couldn't stop herself from trying to berate him into behaving—just once—in the manner she thought he ought to behave. She wanted him to be the thoughtful, helpful brother she needed him to be right now. If he wouldn't do it voluntarily, then she would do her best to nag him into it.

"Can't. I've got plans."

"Then change them."

He stood back a little and looked her up and down. "Your problem, sis, is that you're too uptight. You need to learn to relax and go with the flow."

"Uh-huh. And while I'm relaxing, who's going to do all the work that needs doing around here?" How many times had she said that before—begging the boys to clean their rooms or nagging Tom into catching up on his share of the paperwork at the office.

"Maybe some of it won't get done." He shrugged. "It won't be the end of the world." He stood up straighter. "I've got an idea. Why don't I take you out Saturday night? Casey can look after Dad for a few hours. Take your mind off your worries for a while."

A night out with Del? "Where would you take me?"

"Oh, you know. Just around."

She shook her head. "I don't think so."

"Why not? Are you afraid you might have a good time for a change?"

She flinched at this dig. "No, that's not it. I just don't think your idea of fun and mine are the same."

"You know what they say—when in Rome... I think you're scared you might find out the two of us aren't so different after all—that you're not as smart and sophisticated as you like to pretend, and that I'm not the dumb hick you make me out to be."

Ouch! He made her sound so snobby. "I've never thought you were dumb." Lazy, immoral, dishonest and sneaky, but never dumb.

"Then I dare you to go out with me. Just once. Don't be afraid to have a good time." He winked. "You might even find out I'm not so bad after all."

His smile made her remember the Del who had been her childhood playmate, the one who had always been able to make her laugh—the one she still loved. Maybe this was his way of extending an olive branch, offering them the chance to be friends again. "If I go out with you, will you mow the lawn?"

"You bet. First free day I get."

It wasn't the answer she wanted, but she sensed it was the best she was going to get. "All right," she said. "I'll go out with you." Who knows, she might enjoy herself. Or even learn to enjoy her brother again.

11

You cannot fly like an eagle with the wings of a wren.
—*William Henry Hudson,* Afoot in England

The interior of Del's truck reminded Karen of a frat house she'd visited once, with the same crushed beer cans and pizza boxes on the floorboards, the same odor of stale pot clinging to the upholstery and—she could have sworn—the same black silk thong hanging from the rearview mirror.

She stepped gingerly over the trash and settled into the seat. "Don't you ever clean this thing?"

"I was in a hurry." He leaned across her and swept all the garbage out into the yard.

"Del, you can't just leave all that trash lying there."

"I'll get it when we get home."

She frowned, knowing he'd never remember. Which meant she'd be out there in the morning, cursing him for being a slob.

She took a deep breath and leaned back in the seat. She'd promised herself she wasn't going to get into a fight with her brother tonight. She was going to take his advice, relax and have a good time.

"Where are we going?" she asked as she pulled on the too-tight safety belt that had her pinned in her seat.

"Somewhere you wouldn't be caught dead in by yourself,

that's for sure." The headlights of oncoming cars illuminated his face. He was grinning, the look of the bratty little brother who'd just put a frog in his sister's bed.

Actually, it had been a lizard, which had remained hidden until ten-year-old Karen switched off the light and crawled into bed. Five minutes later she stood in the middle of the bedroom, screaming at the top of her lungs while the lizard clung to her long brown hair like a kid on a wild carnival ride. Del stood outside her door, bent double with laughter, while her father bellowed at them to all be quiet and her mother chided Karen for being hysterical.

She liked to think she'd grown out of that kind of hysteria. If this evening proved to be the adult version of the lizard-in-the-bed, she'd get through it without losing her cool. And when she got back to the house, she'd start plotting her revenge.

"How's the dog?" Del asked.

"The dog is fine." Somehow, Sadie had found a soft spot in Karen's heart. Whether it was the dog's liquid brown eyes, or her habit of resting in the evenings with her head against Karen's feet as Karen watched television, or Sadie's obvious adoration of Casey, Karen no longer thought of her as a dirty beast to be tolerated, but as another part of the household, like Mary Elisabeth or Lola.

"I knew she'd grow on you. Dogs have a way of doing that."

"Then why don't you have one?" she asked.

"I did. A chihuahua named Max." He laughed. "Can you believe that—me with a little nothing of a dog like that?"

"What happened to him?" she asked, almost afraid to hear the answer.

"Sheila took him with her when she split. Said she didn't trust me to look after him."

Karen made a snorting sound. She'd always known Sheila had good sense.

Del switched on the radio and the plaintive voice of a country singer moaned about his sorry lot in life. Karen looked out the side window of the pickup, at the seedy taverns and ramshackle houses that dotted the roadside, each one illuminated in the rosy glow of a mercury vapor light, like tawdry jewels on display. "I never should have let you talk me into this," she said.

"But you did. Couldn't hardly believe it myself. Now relax. If you let yourself you might even have fun tonight."

"I don't want to have fun."

He chuckled. "There's your problem in a nutshell."

He, on the other hand, never wanted anything but fun.

He turned off the road into a gravel parking lot. Karen stared at the sprawling, squat-roofed building before them. The Bait Shop, proclaimed the red neon sign over the door.

"I would have thought this place would have burned down by now," she said as Del shut off the engine.

"Nah, it'll be here when your grandkids are looking for a place to party."

She followed him across the gravel lot. Local lore held that the original owner of the bar had named it so that local husbands could go out drinking while truthfully telling their wives they were headed to the bait shop.

Gleaming Harleys and dented pickup trucks crowded the small parking area. Inside, most of the light was provided by a dozen or more neon beer signs. Cigarette smoke fogged the air, and the clack of pool balls provided a staccato counterpart to Aerosmith on the jukebox.

"Don't wrinkle your nose that way," Del said. "It's unattractive." He grabbed her elbow and pulled her toward the back of the bar. "Come on, let's play some pool."

They found an empty table. Del fed in three quarters and began racking up the balls while Karen selected a cue.

"Hey, Del, who's your new honey?" A short man

with the most freckles Karen had ever seen came up to them.

"Lay off, Eddie. This is my sister, Karen."

Eddie sobered and tugged on the brim of his gimme cap. "Nice to meet you, Miss Karen." He grinned. "Never would have thought an ugly old cuss like Del would have such a pretty sister."

She flushed in spite of herself. Of course, Eddie was spouting hot air, but it had been a long time since a man had told her she was pretty.

"Pay attention, sis. It's your shot."

She bent over the table, trying to remember everything she'd learned as a teen, in the hours spent wielding a pool cue in the back room of the convenience store/bar a few blocks from the house. She aimed carefully, and missed.

"Out of practice, are you?" Del moved to make his next shot.

Eddie was still standing there, staring at her in a way she found unnerving. "How do you know my brother?" she asked.

"Eddie works for me at the oil-change shop," Del said, moving around to make another shot.

Eddie nodded. "Been there a year now. Best job I ever had."

It dawned on Karen that Eddie was what they used to refer to as *slow*. Not the brightest bulb in the chandelier. "That's nice. So Del's a good boss to work for?"

Eddie's grin broadened. "The best. A few months back, my trailer was broke into and the thieves made off with my television and stereo and everything. Wouldn't have been so bad, but my wife was seven months pregnant and the doctor had put her on bed rest. Watching TV was the only entertainment she had. Next thing I know, Del's over there hooking up a fancy thirty-inch color television. Said it was an extra one he had around the house and he wanted us to have it."

Karen glanced at her brother, who was at the opposite end of the table, frowning at a difficult shot. "Del did that?"

"Yeah. And come to find out, it wasn't no spare set at all. It was his own television." Eddie's voice wavered and he looked at the floor and cleared his throat. "I never had nobody do nothing like that for me before."

"Don't pay attention to him, sis. He exaggerates." Del clapped Eddie on the shoulder. "Why don't you go ask the waitress to bring us some beer."

When Eddie had left them, Karen turned to Del. "Did you really do that? Did you give him your TV?"

He shrugged. "It's not like I'm home much to watch it, anyway. And I did have a little set in the bedroom until Sheila split and took it with her." He nudged her arm. "Now go on, make your next shot."

She managed to sink two balls in a row before missing one. Eddie returned with three beers and handed one to each of them. "Thanks," she said.

Two more men, Troy and Frank, joined them. They'd been friends with Del since high school, and it surprised her a little to see the gawky teens she remembered grown up into muscular men. "Nice to see you, Karen," Frank said, nodding to her. "Del says you've been working hard, looking after your dad."

She still found it hard to believe Del had been saying nice things about her to his friends. She certainly never went out of her way to speak highly of him.

More people came in, all hailing Del, clapping him on the back, offering to buy him a beer. Karen would have said he was the most popular man in the place. But why? What was it about him that made people like him so? And what did it say about her that she couldn't see it?

She had her back to the main bar, focusing on making her next shot, when a woman's voice cut through the jumble of conversation around her. "Delwood Engel, does that floozy you've been sleeping with know you've got a new one on the side?"

Karen straightened and turned to see Sheila, the former Mrs. Delwood Engel, headed toward them, fire in her eyes. The crowd around them pulled back like a receding tide, leaving Del and Karen alone under the pool table light.

"You need to have your eyes checked, Sheila," Del drawled. He picked up a square of chalk and began chalking his pool cue. "Don't tell me you've forgotten my sister, Karen."

Sheila stopped short, and stared at Karen. Then a smile broke across her face and she held her arms wide. "Karen! Hon, it's so good to see you." She surrounded Karen in a crushing hug, then drew back to look at her again. "I knew you were in town but I never dreamed I'd find you here with that skunk of a brother of yours."

"Del talked me into taking a night off," she said weakly. "Casey's watching Dad."

"How's that little boy of yours doing?" Sheila asked. "Although I guess he's not that little anymore, is he?"

"He's sixteen and six feet tall," Karen said.

"I wish I could see him. Tell him his aunt Sheila said hello." She kept one arm around Karen and turned her away from the pool table. "Let's find a spot to sit and visit a little."

Karen always had liked Sheila. And the chance to hear her side of her split with Del was too tempting to pass up. She turned and handed her pool cue to Eddie. "Take over for me, will you?" she said. "I'm not very good at this anyway."

Sheila led her to an empty booth within sight of the pool tables, but far enough away they wouldn't be heard. "So tell me what you've been up to," she said. "How's your dad? And Tom and the boys?"

"They're all good. Well, Dad's been better, but he's recovering. Making progress every day."

"You know if there's anything at all I can do, I will. I felt terrible about not getting over there to the house as soon as I heard, but my lawyer told me until the divorce is final, it'd be best to keep my distance."

"So it's not final yet?" Karen asked.

"We finally have the court date, in a couple of weeks." She fished in her purse and took out a pack of cigarettes. "Mind if I smoke?"

Karen shook her head. Sheila shook out a cigarette and lit it from a red lighter that matched the red of her long nails. She had bleached blond hair piled high on her head, and a long face, deep furrows on either side of her mouth. Not the beauty Mary Elisabeth was, but she'd stood by Del longer than any of his other wives or girlfriends. Karen had to think there'd been some real feeling between them at one time. "If you don't think I'm being too nosy, what was the delay?" she asked.

"Del owed his lawyer money, so the lawyer wouldn't file the right papers until he got paid." Sheila waved cigarette smoke away from them. "But I guess he found the money somewhere and finally paid the bill, so things are good to go."

So Del had been telling the truth about why he needed the money from their dad. "I was sorry to hear about y'all splitting up," Karen said. "But I can't say I blame you."

"Best decision I ever made," Sheila said. "I don't know why I didn't do it sooner."

"It's not easy to decide to end a marriage," Karen said. "Especially when you love someone."

"Yeah, but after a while it wasn't so much love as habit." She took another long pull on the cigarette, the end glowing red. "It's easier to stay with what you know—even if you're miserable—than it is to cut loose and face the scary things you don't know." She shrugged. "I don't think I realized how miserable I was until I left him and started living on my own."

"I'm glad you're doing well."

"Honey, I'm doing great!" Sheila's grin lit up her face. "I married my first husband when I was seventeen, and pretty much went straight from his house to Del's. I'm living on my own for the first time in my life. I can cook what I want for dinner, when I want to, watch what I want on TV, have a whole bathroom to myself without tripping over his dirty clothes or wet towels." She stabbed out the stub of the cigarette in a glass ashtray. "Except for the having kids thing, which I never did, I don't know why any woman would bother with getting married these days. There's just so much more freedom in being single, you know?"

Karen nodded, though she didn't know. Not really. She'd gone from her parents' house to Tom's and never thought much about it. What would it be like to have only herself to answer to? Lonely. Then again, she might find out she was pretty good company for herself.

"Gawd, here I am going on and on about myself. What have you been up to?"

"Taking care of Dad and Casey." And before that, she'd been taking care of Tom and the two boys, and looking after their business. She didn't even have any interesting hobbies to talk about.

"You still in the landscaping business up there in Denver?"

She nodded. "It's doing really well. Matt is working for us now, too."

Or rather, he was working for Tom. The business was really Tom's. Karen had the title of office manager, but she deferred to Tom on all but the simplest business decisions. "Are you still working for the school district?" she asked.

Sheila nodded. "I'll have been there twenty years in September. But I'm also doing sales on the side."

She dug in her purse and pulled out a business card. The

mauve lettering on a pale pink background announced that
Sheila Engel was a Mary Kay representative.

"You need anything while you're in town, give me a call.
Or maybe you can come over one day and let me give you
a free facial. We have some great products I know you'd
love."

Karen nodded weakly. "Thanks."

Sheila checked her watch and jumped up. "I've got to go
or I'm gonna be late." She winked at Karen. "I've got a date.
Real nice guy." She laid a five on the table and weighed it
down with the ashtray. "When the waitress comes by, tell her
that's for my drink." She leaned down and hugged Karen,
smothering her in the scent of Shalimar and cigarette smoke.
"I'll call you sometime, okay. You take care."

She hurried away, leaving Karen to ponder how much she
had in common with her soon-to-be-former sister-in-law,
and how differently their lives had turned out.

She was still sitting there when Del found her. "Sheila get
tired of bad-mouthing me and leave?" he asked.

"She said she had a date."

"Humph. I ought to find out who it is and send the guy a
sympathy card." He looked around the bar. The crowd had
thinned and the jukebox had switched to mournful Hank
Williams. "This place is dead. Let's go find some action
somewhere else."

Karen followed him out to his truck. "I think I want to
go home," she said.

"Home? The night is young." He unlocked her door, then
went around the driver's side.

"I know, but I'm tired. And I don't like leaving Dad at
night like this."

"Casey's with him. He'll be okay." He started the truck
and backed out of his parking space.

"Casey's still only sixteen." And not the most mature
sixteen-year-old she'd ever met. "What if Dad falls?" Her

stomach clenched at the thought. "Or what if he chokes? He still has trouble swallowing sometimes and—"

"What if he does?" Del's voice was cold. He turned onto the highway and sped up. "It wouldn't be the end of the world."

She caught her breath and stared at him. "Del! You don't mean that. He's your father."

He glanced at her, his expression as calm as if they were discussing whether or not the fish were biting. "How much difference is it really going to make to you if he's dead or alive?"

"It will make a difference." Surely it would.

"Not to me it won't. And if he dies, at least I stand to inherit a little dough."

"Del, you don't mean that."

He glanced at her again. "You think I'm the world's biggest bastard for using the old man for whatever I can get, but I don't believe you're any better."

"What do you mean? I've never asked him for a dime. And I put aside everything to come down here to look after him."

"Yeah, but why would you do that? It's not as if you were close to him before. It's not like he'd do the same for you."

"You don't know that—"

"Hear me out." He held up one hand. "You see, I'm thinking you rushed down here because you want something from the old man. It's not about him at all. It's about what you think he's going to give you."

"That's not true!" *Was it?* "Wanting to have a relationship with my father isn't a bad thing," she protested.

"What about what he wants? He was okay with keeping his distance for forty years. Why should he change now?"

"I can't believe he wants to spend the rest of his life alone."

"Some people do. And some of them are perfectly happy doing it. Or as happy as they ever get."

He made a sharp turn onto a side road, throwing her against the passenger door. "Del, slow down!"

He ignored her and punched the accelerator harder. "So see, I'm not the only selfish one in this family. Just because you want something more *noble* than money doesn't mean you aren't using him the same way I am."

She braced herself with one hand on the dash. Why hadn't she had the sense to call a cab from the bar? Del was in no condition to drive. And he had no business second-guessing her motives for being here.

"All right, what if Dad thinks he's content being so distant from his children? That doesn't mean he's right."

Del eased off the gas and slowed the truck. "Haven't you heard the expression, you can't teach an old dog new tricks?"

"We're not talking about learning to sit or roll over. We're talking about communicating. Getting to know each other. We've got time now to try. Time we never really had before."

He shook his head. "You talk like those things aren't a lot harder than sitting up and rolling over." His face had gone slack and he looked tired, and much older. And more like Martin than Karen would have thought possible. "You'd be better off making your peace with the old man, the way I have."

"You mean giving up."

"I'm not beating my head against the wall and trying to change somebody who won't change, if that's what you mean."

"People can change." She'd changed, just in the few weeks she'd been here. She'd started to look at her life and herself differently. To see possibilities she'd never considered before. All these new choices were both scary and exciting.

"Go ahead, then," Del said as he turned onto the road leading to her father's house. "It's your funeral. But stop lying to yourself and pretending you're only here for him."

She closed her eyes and leaned her head back. "All right, I've heard you. You can shut up now." She didn't want to listen to him anymore. What if she was here because she wanted something from her father, and not purely out of daughterly devotion? Was that so bad? Considering how many years she'd spent helping her husband, raising children and running a household and a business, maybe it was time she did something that was purely selfish.

Two days later, having given up on Del, Karen asked Casey to mow the lawn for her. He promised he would, then left to go fishing, taking Sadie with him. So Karen found herself one hot afternoon the next week in the shed behind the house, pouring gas into the tank of the riding lawn mower and cursing the men in her life.

Del should have done this. She wasn't buying any of his excuses. She tossed the empty gas can aside and replaced the tank lid, wrinkling her nose at the sour smell of the gas. This was one more example of the way he slacked off on his responsibilities. Would it have killed him to help her with this one thing?

Her feelings toward Casey were more mixed. She was annoyed with him for not fulfilling his promise before taking off to go fishing. At the same time, she was reluctant to come down too hard on him. How many boys his age would want to spend the summer helping to look after his grandfather and doing chores? He deserved some downtime.

Tom would say she was being too soft on him, that a boy should keep his commitments. And he was right. But Casey was her baby, and he wouldn't be hers much longer. She didn't want to be the bad guy all the time with him. Not when he responded to kindness with smiles and hugs—something she didn't get nearly enough of these days.

She turned the key and breathed a sigh of relief as the motor turned over. Carefully, she backed the mower out of the shed and started toward the house. As she passed the front porch, she waved to her father, who didn't wave back. Maybe he'd fallen asleep. She'd parked his wheelchair in the deepest shade of the porch, and made sure his binoculars and a bottle of ice water with a straw were within easy reach. He was getting better at maneuvering with one hand, though his left side was still mostly useless. At the suggestion of the nurse's aide, she'd hung a whistle around his neck that he could blow if he needed her. She wasn't sure if she could hear it over the roar of the mower, but she figured it was worth a try.

The sun beat down like a hundred-watt bulb in an inter-rogation room. She could feel it burning the top of her head even through her hat. Within five minutes, sweat soaked through her shirt and ran in rivulets to pool between her breasts. Conditioned by years of warnings to avoid the sun in Denver's thin atmosphere, she'd dressed for this job in jeans and a long-sleeved denim shirt, broad-brimmed hat and hiking boots. She didn't have to worry about sunburn, but heat stroke might very well do her in.

When she was a teenager, she'd mowed the lawn wearing a bikini top, cutoff shorts and grass-stained Keds. The object was to work on her tan while doing her chores. It didn't hurt her feelings any when the local boys drove by and honked their horns and whistled as she buzzed the mower along the front fence line.

Come to think of it, the most vocal argument she and her father had ever had happened when she was sixteen and she'd headed for the lake wearing a minuscule crocheted bikini and a see-through gauze cover-up. He'd ordered her to return to the house and put on *real clothes*. His face had turned an alarming shade of red and he'd literally sputtered when he talked. At the time, Karen had dismissed him as a clueless old man out to ruin her life. She smiled, remembering. As a parent herself now, she understood his concern. And it touched her to remember how much he'd cared, even if only about her appearance.

The heat and the steady roar of the mower lulled her into a stupor. Each pass across the yard showed a broader expanse of neatly cropped grass. If only everything in her life was so easily put in order. Maybe that was the real appeal of the landscaping business to Tom. The results of hard work were almost immediately visible and satisfying.

She finished the front yard in less than an hour and drove the mower around back. There was twice as much area to cover here, including the sloping banks around the pond. She shut the mower off and stared at the expanse of overgrown grass, tips burned brown by the sun. The pond sat like a mirage at the far end of the lot, its muddy surface smooth as a piece of slate.

She climbed off the mower and went inside to check on her father and get a drink of water before tackling the rest of the work. Dad was dozing in his chair, shoulders slumped, chin resting on his chest. The electric fan she'd set up near the steps stirred a few strands of his gray hair, and she curled her fingers against her palm to keep from reaching out and brushing it back from his forehead, afraid she might wake him. Instead, she indulged in the luxury of studying him while he was unaware of her presence.

The stroke had aged him, etching new lines on his forehead, deepening the furrows alongside his mouth, which still drooped slightly on the left side. The skin beneath his jaw sagged into jowls, freckled with age spots, testament to the years he'd spent in the sun. His nose was straight and prominent as ever, and his high, domed forehead made her think of the busts of elder statesmen that ringed the rotunda of the state capital in Austin.

She'd have to see about cutting his hair later today. And maybe a shave, too. She didn't like to see him looking like some unkempt old man. Though unconcerned about keeping up with fashion, he'd always been meticulous about his appearance, and even in the jungle wore pressed khakis and starched shirts.

Funny, that she knew so much about him, even after so many years of scarcely talking. It was as if some part of her had filed away every scrap of information about him, until she'd assembled enough to form this image she'd labeled Father.

Did he know as much about her? Were her characteristics and habits as important to him as those of the hundreds of birds he'd cataloged?

She turned the fan to blow less directly on him, and added ice to his water bottle, then went to complete her mowing.

She was making her first pass by the pond when something exploded up out of the grass, startling her. She squealed and rose half out of her seat, killing the mower engine. A bird flew by her, so near she could hear the rub of feather on feather as it turned to make another pass by her. She had an image of a brownish back and white chest with two black bands. A Killdeer.

As she watched, the bird plummeted to the ground and began dragging itself across the grass, one wing trailing behind it. Horrified, Karen thought it must have somehow been hit by the mower.

Then something she'd read in the field guide her father had given her made her relax a little. Killdeer would feign a broken wing in order to lead predators away from their nest.

A nest! She eased off the mower and took a cautious step

forward. There, behind a clump of weeds, she spotted the shallow, dish-shaped nest. The mother bird tilted her head and studied her with one red-ringed eye. Karen was amazed the bird hadn't abandoned the nest with the mower bearing down on her, but instead had left it to her mate to defend her.

But then, that was the essence of mother love, wasn't it—that desperate feeling that you would do anything to keep your young from harm, even exposing yourself to danger for their sake.

Shaken by the thought, she returned to the mower and shoved the gearshift into Reverse. Straining, she pushed the heavy machine away from the nest, waiting until she was some distance away before switching it back on. The rest of the mowing could wait, until she'd made sure there were no other mothers and their young in harm's way.

Back at the house, she found her father awake. "You...through?" he asked, shifting in his chair.

"Not exactly." She looked toward the backyard, then at him again. "Can I take you to see something? Something I found near the pond?"

He frowned at her, then nodded. "Okay." Conversation was limited to one- and two-word answers these days, but it was a step above typing everything on the computer.

It took some maneuvering to get him down the ramp out front (which Del had finally replaced, after much nagging from her and Mary Elisabeth) and around to the backyard. The wheelchair didn't roll well over the rough ground and by the time they neared the nest Karen was sweating and panting. She drew as close as she dared, then set the chair's brake. "It's a nest. In the grass there. Do you see?" She pointed.

He leaned forward a little, squinting. "Kill...deer." He shaped the words carefully, halting but clear.

"I almost ran over it with the mower. The male flew up

in my face at the last minute. The female sat there, never even moving."

"Birds...are...good parents. Most of 'em." He looked at her, his gaze intent. "Better...than some...people."

It was the longest sentence he'd uttered in months, and the effort visibly drained him. He sagged in his chair, slumped to one side. She hurried to prop him up, her arms around him, hugging tightly as she swallowed tears. Was he talking about the job he'd done as parent to her? Or her efforts to raise Casey and Matt? Whether confession or acknowledgment, his words touched her. "People do the best they can," she murmured, her lips against the top of his head, where the pink scalp showed through the thin hair. "We all do the best we can."

12

Hope is the thing with feathers
That perches in the soul,
And sings the tune without the words,
And never stops at all.
—*Emily Dickinson, "No. 254"*

The summer monsoons descended on Denver in mid-July and Tom decided he could afford to take a long weekend away from the business to visit Texas. Karen met him at the Houston airport on a scorching Saturday morning. They embraced at the baggage claim, holding each other tightly for a long moment, until he finally broke apart and looked down at her. "How in the hell do you stand this heat?" he asked.

She laughed, and he joined in. "That's a fine way to say hello," she said.

"I'm sorry. You look great. I've missed you. How's that?"

"Better. I've missed you, too." She'd forgotten how tall and broad shouldered and absolutely *masculine* he was. Standing here next to him, her body was reminding her of all the wonderful things he could make her feel, and that it had been seven weeks, six days and twenty-two hours since they'd last made love. If it weren't for the fact that they'd suffocate in this heat, she'd have been tempted to drive to some deserted forest road and start ripping his clothes off.

They collected his suitcase and walked to the parking garage. "Where's Casey?" he asked.

"He's back at the house with Dad." She looked up at him, searching his face. "He thinks you're still mad at him."

"I'm not exactly thrilled with him, but I'm pretty much over being angry." He glanced at her. "Wouldn't do any good, anyway, would it?"

"Let him know you're glad to see him. It would mean a lot to him."

"What do you think I'm going to do—yell at him the minute I see him?"

"No. Yes." She shook her head. "I don't know. I can never be sure how the two of you are going to act around each other."

"You worry too much. It'll be all right." He stowed his suitcase in the back and took the keys from her hand. "How's your dad?"

"Good. He's talking in sentences more now. He's eating better and he's starting to put on weight. I'm really encouraged."

"That's good." He started the Jeep, then leaned over and studied the dashboard. "How do you turn the air conditioner up in this thing?"

On the drive to the house, Tom filled her in on his progress with various jobs at work, and happenings around the house. Her roses were blooming. Matthew had collected all the paperwork he needed to register for the fall semester at Red Rocks. He and Audra were definitely dating again. The car needed the front end aligned. The temporary worker was making progress with the paperwork at the office.

Karen sat back and listened, absorbing these petty details of her normal life like a dry tree soaking its roots in a flood. This was what she'd missed most, without even realizing it, this feeling of being a part of the minutiae of her husband's and son's lives. Not knowing the little things that affected them had made her feel too much of an outsider.

At the house, Tom parked the car in the shade and followed her inside. Casey met them at the front door, and took Tom's suitcase without being asked. "Hey, Dad," he said. "How was your trip?"

"It was fine." Tom put his arm around Casey's shoulder and pulled him close. "How are you doing? You look like you've grown another two inches since I saw you last."

Casey grinned. "Three."

Karen felt more of the tension ease from her body. All the pieces of her life were slipping back into their familiar grooves once more.

"Who's this?" Tom asked, directing his attention to Sadie, who inserted her body between Casey and his father, her whole body vibrating.

"This is Sadie." Casey patted the dog's head. "Uncle Del gave her to us."

Tom's eyes met Karen's over the top of Casey's bent head. "I thought you didn't like dogs."

She flushed. "I didn't. I still don't. But Sadie…Sadie's okay."

"She's a great dog," Casey said. "And really smart. I taught her to sit and stay and she hasn't messed in the house once."

If you didn't count hair, muddy paw prints and the occasional flea, Karen thought. Still, the dog had turned out better than she'd anticipated.

The creak of her father's wheelchair on the hardwood floor announced his arrival. He emerged from the hallway and looked up at his son-in-law. "Tom!"

Tom moved forward to take Martin's hand. "It's good to see you. I was sorry to hear about your stroke, but Karen tells me you're doing well with your rehabilitation."

"Too…slow," her father said.

Sara arrived soon after that, then Del and Mary Elisabeth, everyone flocking to greet the newcomer. Sometimes Karen thought her family liked Tom better than they did her. Then again, it was probably easier to like someone with whom you didn't share so much history.

The rest of the afternoon disappeared in a rush to prepare food for everyone. She and Mary Elisabeth chopped vegetables, marinated chicken, passed out paper plates and fixed glass after glass of iced tea. Normally she enjoyed playing hostess, but today all she really wanted to do was get Tom alone. They exchanged glances over the heads of the others and she could have sworn she saw the same longing in his eyes.

"While you're here, I should take you fishing," Del said in between bites of potato salad. "I know some great spots."

"Maybe some other time." Tom smiled at Karen. "I'm only going to be here a few days. I want to spend them with Karen and Casey."

"Isn't that sweet?" Sara beamed at them over the rim of her coffee cup. "Karen Anne, what did you ever do to land a man like that?"

"Just lucky, I guess." What but luck could explain how two people who had hardly known each other when they said vows had stayed together all these years?

Luck, or the power of inertia, a voice whispered in her head.

Finally, the last of the potato salad was eaten, the last piece of chicken consigned to the refrigerator, the last of the tea poured from the pitcher. "All right, everyone." Sara stood and gathered up her purse. "Time for us to leave these two alone. I'm sure they've had enough of us all interfering with their reunion."

Karen flushed, but gave her mom a grateful smile. "Don't

do anything I wouldn't do," Del said as he and Mary Elisabeth headed for the door.

"Of course, there isn't much he wouldn't do," Mary Elisabeth added with a wink.

"I'll help Granddad get ready for bed," Casey said, taking hold of Martin's chair.

When they were alone at last, Karen felt as awkward as a girl on her first date. She busied herself tidying up the already clean kitchen. "Everyone was really glad to see you," she said.

"Not half as glad as I am to see you." He took a glass from her hand and set it aside, then turned her to face him. "Come here. We have some catching up to do."

His kiss was urgent, telling her in more than words how much he'd missed her. She clung to him, sinking into the luxury of that kiss, yet wanting so much more.

Scarcely moving apart, they fumbled their way to her bedroom and shut the door behind them. He led her to the bed, already removing his shirt as he moved. She lay back, watching him, grinning. Working outdoors had kept him lean and hard, the kind of man who made any woman look twice. More than once she'd visited a job site and found women admiring him, and had the satisfaction of informing them that he was her husband. "Are you going to do a striptease for me?"

"I don't know. Maybe we should get you out of your clothes first." He knelt on the bed beside her and reached for the top button of her blouse.

She stifled laughter, and glanced nervously toward the wall behind her that separated her bedroom from Casey's. "We have to be quiet," she whispered.

"I can be quiet. Can you?" He nuzzled her neck, setting her to giggling again.

She tried to relax as he began working on her blouse once

more, but it was impossible now that she'd reminded herself they weren't alone in the house.

Tom noticed her tension. "What's wrong?" he asked.

"I can't relax with my dad and Casey just a few rooms over." She sat up and tugged the quilt from around the pillows. "Come on. I've got an idea."

Quilt in hand, she led him out of the room and across the kitchen floor, tiptoeing. Once they were out the back door, she grabbed his hand and started across the yard.

The air was only slightly cooler than it had been that morning, but not as heavy. Dusk bathed everything in silver light and the first stars were already showing against the pale sky. They walked the path around the pond, to the back of the storage shed. "No one can see us here," she said, spreading the quilt on the ground.

He knelt and pulled her down beside him. "We haven't made love outside in a long time," he said.

"We haven't made love at all in a long time." She took hold of the unbuttoned halves of his shirt and pushed them back over his shoulders, and kissed the bare skin along his collarbone. He smelled of herbal soap and clean sweat and tasted slightly salty.

He finished undoing her blouse, then helped her out of her pants, stripping off his own clothes soon after. They came together with heat and urgency, done with waiting. They moved with a confidence born of familiarity, yet with a sense of discovering each other all over again. She delighted in knowing she could still move him, that he remembered where to touch her to make her pant with need, that he could still bring her to a shuddering climax.

When they were spent, they lay together, wrapped in the quilt, looking up at the stars, a dreamlike quality to the moment. A Chuck-will's-widow sounded its mournful call: chuck-will's-WID-ow! Chuck-will's-WID-ow!

"Dad's been teaching me about birds some," she said, her

head resting on his chest. The steady beat of his heart echoed in her ear and she found herself matching her breathing to his.

"I didn't think you were interested in that kind of thing."

"I wasn't. But it gives us something to talk about. And it is fascinating, in a way. All the different birds and their habits. Plus, they're beautiful to watch."

"Yeah. I guess so." His voice was slurred, that of a man fighting sleep and losing the battle. She snuggled closer and his arms automatically tightened around her. It felt so good to be here with him again. She'd known that seeing each other face-to-face would dissolve the barriers communicating only by phone had thrown up between them. Now that Tom was here, now that he could see Dad's condition and how much she was needed, he'd understand why she had no choice but to be here for this little while. Soon, everything would be all right again. She'd be home, the business would be running smoothly, the boys would be settled. Everything would be as it should be and it would be almost as if this summer had never happened.

The idea brought a surge of relief. Maybe all the unsettled feelings she had since coming here were merely a product of being away from her familiar routine. Maybe the only thing she really needed to change was her location. Back among the familiar, everything would fall into place again.

It was a comforting thought, and she drifted off to sleep cradled in Tom's arms, relieved to know this was exactly where she needed to be.

Karen woke Sunday morning with the comforting weight of Tom in bed beside her. She rolled over to face him, smiling, and he opened one eye and looked at her. "So I didn't dream this last night," he said.

"No, you didn't dream it."

He pulled her close and nuzzled her neck. "And that really was you screaming my name under the stars."

She giggled as he nipped her earlobe. "That really was me."

"I think I'm ready for a repeat." He moved closer, leaving no doubt about how ready he was.

She looked at the clock. It was after eight. "I don't know if I have time. I don't usually sleep this late—"

"Sure you have time." He nudged her legs apart with his knee and slipped his hand beneath the oversize T-shirt that served as her nightgown.

"Dad needs help getting ready in the morning," she protested.

"It won't hurt him to wait." He tugged the T-shirt up to her neck. "I came a thousand miles to see you. You can make a little time for me."

"Of course I can." She took a deep breath and focused her attention on him. He was right. A few minutes wouldn't make any difference.

She pulled off the T-shirt and helped him out of his boxers, then closed her eyes and lost herself in the sensation of his mouth on her throat, her breasts, her stomach....

The bell began ringing just as Tom settled between her legs. "What the hell is that?" he asked.

"Dad. He rings the bell when he wants me."

She started to sit, but Tom pushed her back. "He can wait."

"What if he's fallen or something?"

"He hasn't fallen. He'll be okay. Besides, Casey will answer him in a minute."

"You know how Casey is. He could sleep through a train wreck."

Tom nudged her thighs farther apart. "Pretend you're a teenager again, getting away with something right under Daddy's nose. And I'm the bad boy next door."

His grin was wickedly sexy, and she managed a weak laugh. She wanted to play along with his fantasy, to forget about worries and responsibilities in his arms, but the insistent ringing of the little brass handbell bored into her brain.

She lay back on the pillows and squeezed her eyes shut, straining to focus on Tom, but the moment was lost. She felt stiff and uncomfortable, impatient for him to be done.

She went through the motions of making love, saying the right things and making the right moves, but she'd never thought of herself as an accomplished actress, and she was afraid Tom knew her heart wasn't in the moment.

When he'd withdrawn from her, she sat up and threw back the covers. The bell continued to ring. "I guess I'd better go see what he wants," she said with a smile of apology.

Tom frowned and turned away.

Her father was upset at having to wait. He grumbled at her and refused to help as she maneuvered him into his chair, combed his hair and brushed his teeth. When she took out clothes for him to wear, he rejected her choices. He folded his arms and ducked his head, anger etched in every line of his face.

Tom found her kneeling in front of the wheelchair, trying to put socks on Martin's cold feet. The old man kicked at her and swore under his breath. At least, she assumed it was swearing. She couldn't make out the words but his intent was clear.

"What's going on?" Tom asked.

"Dad's mad because I made him wait. Now he won't co-operate."

"Stop acting like a spoiled baby." Tom put his hand on Martin's shoulder and glared at him. "She wears herself out looking after you. If she wants to sleep in one morning, she's entitled."

Karen looked away, afraid she might blush or otherwise give away the fact that she hadn't exactly been sleeping.

"Go...away!" Martin shouted.

Tom took hold of her arm and pulled her up. "Come on, Karen. If he's going to act like that, he can just sit here in his pajamas."

"Tom. He'll get cold."

"It's ninety-five degrees outside. He won't get cold." He pulled her toward the door.

Once they were in the hallway, she jerked away from him. "What's wrong with you?" she demanded.

"I'm not going to stand by and watch him treat you like some hired servant and not say anything."

"He's a sick old man. He doesn't mean anything by it."

"He'd behave better if you made him."

"So now this is *my* fault?" Rage rose in her like lava, threatening to erupt all over both of them. How could she have believed last night that everything was all right between them, when nothing had changed? Tom still wanted her to choose between him and her father. He still refused to understand why he was asking too much. She balled her hands into fists, fighting the urge to beat against his chest. She glared at him, struggling for some way to express her feelings that didn't involve violence or swearing.

"I'm going to make some coffee," he said, and turned on his heels.

The fact that he'd walk away in the middle of an argument enraged her further, but short of running after him and dragging him back, she didn't know what to do. Instead, she headed across the hall and barged into Casey's room.

"Get up," she said, shaking her sleeping son.

"Wha—?" He opened one eye and looked up at her.

"I need you to get up and help Grandpa dress," she said.

"Why don't you do it?" he mumbled and rolled over, his back to her.

"Because I want you to." She jerked the covers off him. "Just do it. Now."

She left Casey's room and went into the kitchen. A fresh pot of coffee beckoned, but Tom was nowhere in sight. He'd left before she had the chance to confront him again about his boorish behavior.

She poured a cup of coffee and sat at the table, exhausted already and it wasn't even nine o'clock. The weight of unfinished business made her chest hurt. She hated fighting with Tom—hated it so much she usually gave in and did what he wanted. Saying what she felt was much harder than letting him have his way.

But years of swallowing words had left her feeling choked, and fearful there were some things that were too broken to fix.

Sunday afternoon, Casey found himself standing beneath a ladder, holding a section of gutter while his dad worked on connecting it to the eaves overhead. It was amazing, really, how his dad hadn't been in Grandpa's house twenty-four hours and he'd come up with a list of things that needed repairing or replacing. That said a lot about the kind of man his dad was. He was a man who fixed things. The kind of man who hated any kind of disorder or uncertainty.

Which was probably why he clashed with Casey so often. The way Casey saw it, the world was all about uncertainty. Instead of wearing yourself out trying to set everything and everybody straight, you were a lot better off taking things as they came and dealing with them the best you could.

"I talked to the counselors at school and they're going to let you take your finals the week before classes start this fall," his father said as he fit a new screw into the tip of the drill driver.

"What if I'm not home by then? Grandpa—" But his words were cut off by the scream of the drill as the screw bit into the sheet metal of the gutter.

"You'll be home by then," his dad answered when he'd shut off the drill. "You can't afford to miss any more school."

End of discussion, at least as far as Dad was concerned. But Casey had more to say on the subject. "I've been thinking. Maybe I could finish school online. They have this stuff called distance learning, where you study at your own pace."

"You don't study now, with your mom and I and all your teachers on your case. I'm supposed to believe you'll volunteer to do it on your own?"

"I don't mind studying if it's something that interests me. The teachers at school make everything so boring."

"I don't see how a computer is going to make math and history and English any less boring. Hand me another one of those screws."

Casey handed up the fastener. "We could try it." Yeah, the subject matter would be the same in the online courses, but he liked the idea of being more in charge. For instance, he could decide whether to do English or math first, and how long he'd spend with each class, instead of having a schedule dictated by others.

"No. I don't see why I should pay for you to take special classes when there's a perfectly good high school not two miles from our house."

Casey could have argued that the high school wasn't all that good, but what was the point? Dad had made up his mind. He was always right.

The thing to do now was to wait and go to Mom with his plan. She at least considered his point of view. Maybe she could sway Dad to let him give this a try.

"I know you think I'm too hard on you, but it's because I know you can do better. And I know life will be easier for you in the long run if you apply yourself more." He leaned back and studied the gutter. "Does that look straight to you?"

"Yeah, it looks good." Casey didn't know what to say to

the *apply yourself* remark. It was one of those clichés parents and teachers threw around, but what did it mean, exactly? If he preferred to focus on things that interested him, how was that not applying himself?

"Your mom says you've been a real help with your grandfather."

The change of subject caught him off guard. "Yeah, well, he cooperates a little better with me on some things. Maybe he's embarrassed because Mom's his daughter." It had freaked him out a little, the first time he'd helped the old man change clothes, or worse, when Grandpa wet his pants and Casey had to clean him up. He didn't do that so often anymore and besides, after the first time it had been sort of routine. He'd gotten into the habit of talking them both through it, making like it was no big deal.

"I'm not happy about the way you ran off without telling anyone, and without finishing school," Dad said. "But I'm glad you're a help to her."

Dad wasn't the type to go around handing out praise left and right, so having him acknowledge that his youngest had done something good for a change made Casey feel about a foot taller. "I'm glad I could help her, too."

"Good." Dad nodded and climbed down the ladder. "That should do it. Now let's see about getting that porch light replaced."

"Right." One job done, time to move on to another. Casey would never understand this kind of methodical approach to life, but he guessed that was okay. He'd just do like he did with Grandpa—keep talking and keep moving along. It saved everybody from a lot of awkward moments that way.

13

My heart is like a singing bird.
  —*Christina Rosetti, "A Birthday"*

Karen returned from shopping to find Tom, Casey and Martin on the back porch, arguing. She followed the sound of raised voices and found the three of them gathered around the back steps, scowling at each other.

"What's going on here?" she asked.

"I'm trying to repair this broken light over the back steps," Tom said.

"Don't want...fixed," her father said, shaking his head.

"Why wouldn't you want it fixed?" Tom's voice was full of scorn. "Do you *want* everything to just fall down around your head?"

"Hurts...birds." Martin's chin jutted out and his eyes were dark and agitated.

"What? How the hell does the light hurt birds?"

"Re-flex." The old man shook his head. "Like mirror."

"I think what he means is, when the light's on, it reflects on the glass on the sunporch and the birds think it's a mirror and fly into it," Casey said.

"You stay out of this," Tom snapped.

"Leave...him...alone!" Martin roared.

"He's my son, I'll—"

"Tom, please." Karen stepped between the two men and urged Tom into the house. Once inside, she pulled him into her bedroom and shut the door.

"What's going on?"

"I'm trying to help the old man and he picks a fight."

"It's his house. If he doesn't want the light fixed, leave it alone."

"It's his house, but you're living here. Not having a light over the back steps is unsafe."

"It's okay. I won't be here that much longer." She hoped. She had a feeling Tom's anger wasn't so much over the lack of a light as it was over her father not appreciating his efforts to help. That, and a continuation of the argument he and Karen had started this morning.

"You won't leave here soon enough to suit me," he said.

"I'm hoping by the end of the summer Dad will be able to look after himself. Or be able to manage with a housekeeper or other help a couple of days a week."

"I don't know why you didn't put him in a nursing home in the first place."

"He's my father. I couldn't do that."

He looked past her, toward where her dad sat on the other side of the wall. "Why not? He's an antisocial introvert who relates to numbers, not people." His eyes met hers again. "You think I don't know how he's hurt you in the past? You can't expect me to be happy you're choosing to look after him, in spite of all that, when you could be home with your family."

When you could be home with me. If that's what he meant, then why didn't he say it that way? She ducked her head, blinking hard. She didn't know if the tears that threatened were because of Tom's outrage over her father's past neglect of her, or the way his words reminded her of those old hurts.

But since coming here, she'd discovered another side to her father. In the hours he'd spent teaching her about birds, she'd discovered a sensitive soul who appreciated beauty for beauty's sake. She'd thought birding was all about the numbers for him; this spiritual aspect had surprised her.

"He *is* introverted. And sometimes antisocial," she conceded. "But now, while he has to depend on me, is the best chance I'll ever have for us to be close." She struggled to find the words to make Tom understand why this was so important to her. "All my life, I've felt like...like I loved my father more than he loved me." She closed her eyes, squeezing back the tears that painful truth brought forth.

"Then you know how *I* feel."

The words floated on the top of her consciousness, like black oil spilled across a pristine lake—dark and ugly and shockingly out of place. She stopped breathing for a moment, stunned. "Wh-what do you mean?"

"I mean our marriage has been one-sided for years." The pain in his eyes forced her to take a step back. "Practically from the day I met you, I loved you," he continued. "I told myself it didn't matter if you didn't feel as strongly about me—that we'd grow into love. But it never happened."

"I *do* love you!" she cried. "You must know that."

"How am I supposed to know it? You never say it."

"I know." Why were three little words so hard to say? She could talk about loving chocolate or loving a song on the radio, but to say she loved her husband seemed too risky—as if saying the words out loud would tempt fate to take away everything she prized most. "It wasn't a word I heard a lot growing up. I took it for granted you *knew*."

He shook his head. "Be honest with me. When I asked you to marry me, did you love me then?"

She swallowed hard, a lie on the tip of her tongue. But pretending things were wonderful when they weren't hadn't made her any happier over the years. "I liked you, but I didn't have any idea what it meant to love someone that way. I only…I wanted to escape the life I had and I saw that you were the best chance I had at another one."

"That's what I thought." The disappointment in his voice made her stomach ache.

"Tom, wait, that doesn't mean I don't love you now."

But he had already stopped listening. He threw down his work gloves and pushed past her, out of the room. A few moments later, she heard the car start, gravel flying as he spun out of the driveway.

She sank down onto the bed, feeling as if the world had just tilted. His words hurt, as he must have meant them to. But his anger at her didn't wound nearly as deeply as her own recognition of how she'd let him down.

She thought she'd done a good job of hiding her true feelings in those early days of marriage. She'd wanted him to believe she returned his love for her right from the first, and she'd fooled herself into thinking she'd succeeded. Over the years, she had grown to truly cherish him, but she had never been one to express her emotions easily. She had thought it enough that she worked side by side with him at their business, kept their home and looked after his children. She hadn't seen the need for words, hadn't realized he felt their lack.

Oh God. Could it be she was truly her father's daughter, distanced from those she loved by the emotional reserve he had passed down to her?

How could she find her way across that chasm? How could she be anything other than the woman she was?

Casey couldn't believe his mom and dad could get so upset over a stupid porch light but then, he'd stopped trying to understand parents a long time ago. Whether it was the disagreement over the porch light or something else entirely, his dad ended up getting Mr. Wainwright to take him to the airport early.

His mom walked around the house for two days with red eyes, insisting she was "fine," in a clipped tone of voice that made it obvious she was anything but. Grandpa retreated to his computer and threw a shoe at Lola again. The physical therapist didn't even blink; she picked up the shoe and threw it back, narrowly missing Grandpa's head. "You see how it feels, Mr. Engel," she said calmly. "Now let's try the arm raises again."

So when Uncle Del called and asked Casey to go fishing, he was thrilled. "Anything to get out of the nuthouse for a while," he said.

Del laughed. "I guess things haven't changed much since I was your age."

He picked Casey up early the next morning. "Is the dog coming?" Del asked as he loaded Casey's fishing gear into the back of the truck.

"Nah. I took her last time and she got bored in about five minutes. Drove me crazy whining and running around." Cradling an extra-large cup of coffee in both hands, he slumped against the passenger door of the truck and studied the road ahead through slitted eyes. The rising sun was a pinpoint of light glinting through the dark pines. "Where are we going?" he asked.

Del climbed in beside him and started the truck. "A place up on the river I know." He glanced at his nephew. "You're not a morning person, I guess."

"Nope." He slid farther down in the seat, knees braced against the dash.

"If you want to catch fish, you have to get up early."

"Why?"

"Because that's when the fish are biting. They wake up hungry and you want to be there with breakfast on your hook."

He wrinkled his nose. "I'd for sure sleep in if I knew breakfast was a bunch of worms."

"Nobody ever said fish were smart." He reached over and switched on the radio. A country singer mourned the girl who got away. Casey shut his eyes and tried to go back to sleep.

But the increasingly bright sun in his eyes and the coffee in his system overcame the last vestiges of sleep. By the time they turned onto the gravel track leading into the woods, he was sitting up straighter, and beginning to feel hungry. "You got anything to eat?" he asked.

"We'll have some breakfast when we get to the river," Del said.

He slowed the truck to a crawl as the road narrowed further. Casey grabbed hold of the door handle as they jostled over bumps and wallowed in ruts. Trees arched overhead, forming a canopy that shut out the sun. It looked like the setting for a creepy movie—*The Blair Witch Project* or *Texas Chainsaw Massacre*. "How did you find this place?" he asked, wincing as they plunged into a deep rut.

"You just have to know the right people."

What kind of people? Casey wondered. Satan-worshippers? Bootleggers? Marijuana farmers? But before he could ask, they emerged onto an open bluff that overlooked the river. Del parked beneath an arched live oak and shut off the ignition. In the sudden stillness the only sounds were the pinging of the cooling engine and the trill of birdsong somewhere overhead.

"Where are we?" Casey asked.

"About five miles down from the power plant dam." Del opened the door and climbed out. "Grab that cooler and we'll head down to the river."

Casey picked up the cooler, which must have weighed about thirty pounds, while Del grabbed the poles, a tackle box and a faded blue backpack. He led the way down a steep path to a wide sandy beach beside the river. An old fire ring sat between two bleached cottonwood logs. Del dropped his gear beside one of the logs and stretched his arms over his head. "Don't you feel sorry for all the bastards stuck behind desks on a day like this?" he said.

"Yeah." Casey opened the cooler and stared at what must have been a case of beer on ice. He looked up at his uncle. "I thought you said you had food."

"It's in the pack." He grabbed a can of beer and popped the top. "Help yourself."

The pack held a foot-long submarine sandwich wrapped in wax paper, a pack of beef jerky and another of corn chips. "This is more like it," Casey said, unwrapping the sandwich.

While Casey ate, Del untangled lines and baited hooks. He handed one of the poles to Casey. "You ready to catch some fish?"

"Sure." He folded the wax paper over the remains of the sandwich and stashed it in the pack, then followed Del to the river.

Sunlight gilded the water to a bright copper color, the reflections of the cottonwoods and pines along the bank showing black in the still surface. "You want to cast over there by that old log." Del pointed across the water. "Let your hook rest almost on the bottom. Catfish are bottom feeders."

He managed to cast into the general area Del had indicated, then cranked the reel until the red-and-white bobber floated on the surface. "Now what?" he asked.

Del sat on the bank and leaned back against a tree trunk. "Now we wait."

They fell silent, the rising heat and stillness lulling them into a half doze. Casey focused on the red-and-white cork bobbing in the gentle current, allowing the rest of his vision to blur. Overhead a mockingbird ran through a repertoire of whistles and clicks, varying the calls for several minutes, then repeating the sequence again. Casey leaned forward, elbows on knees, and felt as if he was sinking into the soft sand of the riverbank, like a tree, rooted in place.

He decided all those people who studied yoga and consulted gurus and tried to learn how to meditate just needed to take up fishing. All those rednecks who spent every Saturday at the river, drinking beer and baiting hooks, probably never realized they were doing something so zen.

After half an hour or so, Del got a strike. He grabbed up the pole and began reeling it in, letting it out periodically, then taking it back up. He hauled in a good-size catfish, hooking a finger through the gills and pulling it up on the bank. "That's a good three-pounder," he said, unhooking the fish and fastening it to the stringer, which he dropped in a deep pool farther down the bank.

"I'm not getting a thing," Casey said.

"Put a fresh worm on and try casting over to the left of that old stump."

He did as Del suggested and they both settled down to watch their poles once more. "Where's Mary Elisabeth today?" Casey asked.

"She's working." Del winked. "My advice is to always find a woman with a good job. If she has her own money, she won't be spending yours, and you can borrow from her if you need to."

"I thought the idea was for the man to support the woman," Casey said.

"You're behind the times, son. Women these days like to be independent. I say we should let them."

"Then what's to keep them from running off with some rich guy?" Personally, he thought Mary Elisabeth could probably have any man she wanted, so why had she picked Uncle Del?

"Because a rich man wouldn't really need them." He sat up straighter. "Women—most of 'em, anyway—like to be needed. They'll devote themselves to a man who needs rescuing from himself."

"Why would they do that?"

Del shrugged. "Who knows? But it's true. You take your mama. She hadn't hardly set foot in this place in twenty years and the minute she heard the old man was sick, she rushed down here to look after him."

"But he's her father. That's different from a romantic relationship."

"Not that different. Trust me. Women want a man who needs them. That whole nurturing thing is in their genes."

Casey didn't think this philosophy painted either men or women in a very flattering light, but he kept this opinion to himself.

"So what's going on at the nuthouse?" Del asked. "Dad giving you a hard time?"

"He's giving everybody a hard time. But I don't blame him. I'd be ornery, too, if I was stuck in a wheelchair."

"Humph. My dad would find something to complain about if he was a millionaire who'd just won a marathon." He looked out across the river again. "What about your dad? He have a good visit?"

Casey shifted. His mom would probably walk across hot coals before she'd tell anyone—much less her brother—about her troubles, but Casey wasn't as reticent. "Not really. He and Mom had a fight and he left early."

"Oh? What were they fighting about?"

He dug a groove in the sand with the heel of his shoe. "I don't know. I think maybe he wants her back in Denver and she feels like she needs to stay here."

Del looked up at the sky. "That's my sister. Always trying to make everybody happy and making herself miserable." He picked up his empty beer can and shook it, then crumpled it. "Time for a refill." He wedged his pole between two rocks, then stood and lumbered over to the cooler.

Casey reeled his pole in, saw the worm had been stolen and set about impaling another one on the hook. He had just cast again when Del returned. "Here." He tapped Casey on the shoulder with a beer. "Drink up."

Casey took the beer without comment and cracked it open. It tasted good going down, so cold it made the back of his throat ache.

"I'm not trying to be hard on your mom," Del said as he settled back against the tree trunk once more and opened a beer. "She's a good woman. Probably too good. She's got it into her head that if she does right by the old man, looking after him and everything, he's going to appreciate it. I'm here to tell you, it ain't gonna happen."

"What makes you say that?"

Del looked at him a long moment, as if trying to decide how much to share with his nephew. "Martin Engel cares more for a bunch of birds with funny names than he ever did for his own family," he said after a moment. "I could have been the worst juvenile delinquent in the history of Tipton, or the class valedictorian, and it wouldn't have made a bit of difference to him, as long as I didn't interfere with his plans to fly to Africa or spend two weeks in the Galapagos trying to see the Blue-footed Booby or whatever."

He spoke the words matter-of-factly, but the lines on either side of his jaw deepened, and his eyes reflected bitterness.

"I don't know." Casey wedged his rod between his feet and leaned back on his elbows. "I think he would have cared."

Del shook his head. "I've known him a lot longer than you have. I'm his son and every time I walk into that house, it's like I'm a stranger. I bet he couldn't tell you today what's going on in my life."

"I bet he could. He pays attention to stuff." Casey rose up and drained the last of the beer, then reached for another. "I think he has really deep feelings about stuff. He's just one of those people who doesn't know how to show his emotions. Like…like he never learned how, or something."

"What makes you think that?"

He shrugged. "I don't know, just…when he looks at birds, the way he talks about them…for him they're like poetry, or music. Something so beautiful and special…I don't think somebody with no feelings would see them that way."

"Maybe he's like that with you. He isn't that way with me. Hey, looks like you got a bite."

They began catching fish in earnest, then. In between baiting hooks and casting, Casey drank more beer. He began to feel a pleasant buzz. This is how life should be—no hassles, no worries. Just take life as it comes….

Karen wandered restlessly about the house. Dad was asleep, worn-out from his morning therapy appointment. Del had picked up Casey hours ago and taken him God knows where. Fishing, he'd said. Something they both loved. Something she hoped would keep them out of trouble.

She took out her notebook and consulted her list. There must be something on here that would occupy her, at least for a little while. But every item she'd written down was neatly crossed through. Tasks completed.

She ripped out the page, crumpled it and tossed it toward the trash. It bounced off the side of the can and rolled under the sofa. She let it lie, half-afraid if she lay down on the floor to retrieve the paper, she'd stay there, weeping, until Casey came home and found her.

She stopped in front of the phone, staring at the silent receiver, willing it to ring. If only Tom would call her. They could talk. Find a way around this horrible silence between them.

She shook her head and turned away. And what would she say? *I want to be different. I want to be the wife you want, but I don't know if I have that in me.*

Is it so wrong for me to want you to love me in spite of everything I'm not?

She passed her bedroom and heard a snuffling noise from beside the bed. Investigating, she found Sadie lying on the rug. At first, she thought the dog had one of the rawhide chew toys Casey had bought her, but as she drew closer, she recognized one of a pair of leather sandals she'd bought for herself on her recent shopping trip with Casey.

"Sadie!" she shouted.

The dog jumped up and attempted to dive under the bed, but she was too large. So she simply lay there, her head shoved under the bedspread, the rest of her sticking out. It would have been comical if Karen hadn't been so furious.

She grabbed the dog's collar and dragged her out, gathering up the mangled shoe with her free hand. "Look what you did," she said, shaking the shoe in the dog's face. "These were brand-new. How could you?"

Sadie's eyes rolled upward and she attempted to duck her head. Karen could have sworn the dog's bottom lip trembled. The dog began to shake and whimper pitifully.

"Stop that." Karen released her hold on the collar. "I'm not going to beat you. What kind of a person do you think I am?"

The kind of person who couldn't tell her husband she loved him. The kind of person who wasn't even sure what love meant anymore.

Sadie whined and shoved at Karen's hand, her nose cold and damp, an icy jolt to the senses. Karen felt hot tears slide down her cheeks and dropped to her knees beside the dog.

Sadie gently licked Karen's cheek, and nudged her hand again. She stared into Karen's face, eyes filled with concern. When was the last time anyone had cared so much what she, Karen, was feeling? Was that because no one cared, or because she was so careful to hide her emotions from others?

She had spent so many years being the strong, practical one in any group, she'd forgotten what it meant to be vulnerable.

Sadie moved closer, into Karen's lap, and licked harder at the tears, her whines more insistent. Karen put her arms around the dog, surprised at how comforting hugging the furry beast could be. "I'm a mess," she said out loud.

Sadie whimpered, whether in agreement or sympathy Karen didn't know. Karen hugged her more tightly. "We women have to stick together," she said. "We're outnumbered in this household."

The dog's tail thumped hard against the floor, a steady rhythm. Like a heartbeat.

Karen laid her head alongside the animal's soft side. "I never had a dog before," she said. "So I'm new at this whole relating to animals thing. Then again, I haven't done such a great job relating to people." She drew back, and looked into the dog's soft, understanding eyes. "Maybe you can teach me a few things, huh, girl?"

Sadie barked and wagged her tail more wildly. Karen shut her eyes, squeezing back more tears. How pitiful was it to be over forty years old, and taking lessons in love from a stray dog?

But she had to start somewhere. And she could trust Sadie not to judge her efforts too harshly. If only she could show the same compassion to herself.

Casey thought he must have fallen asleep. The next thing he knew, Del was standing over him, nudging him with the toe of his boot. "Wake up, boy. Time to head back to the house." He held up the string of fish. "We'll get Mary Elisabeth to cook us up a mess of catfish."

Casey shoved into a sitting position, then fell back, the world spinning crazily. He groaned. Dell's face loomed closer, distorted, like the view in a shiny hubcap. "You're not drunk, are you?"

"Nah, I'm not drunk." He sat up more slowly this time, steadying himself with one hand on the ground. "I jus' need to wake up."

"Well, come on. Mary Elisabeth will be home from work soon. She and your mom will be wondering where we disappeared to."

Somehow he managed to stand and carry the now-empty cooler up the slope to the truck. Once there, he slumped in the seat and closed his eyes. "You okay?" Del asked. "You're looking kind of green. I don't want you throwing up in my truck."

"I'm fine." He turned his face to the window, the cool glass against his cheek.

When Del started the car, Casey aimed the air-conditioning vent toward him. The cold air revived him some, and he sat up straighter. "Thanks for inviting me to come with you today," he said. "I had a great time."

"No problem. You're not bad company. You want to stay for supper?"

He was tempted, if only to see Mary Elisabeth, but decided against it. "I'd better get home. Help with Grandpa."

"It's your funeral."

14

No bird soars too high if he soars with his
own wings.
—*William Blake,* The Marriage of Heaven
and Hell

Del dropped Casey off in front of Grandpa's house, then drove over to his trailer next door. Casey climbed the steps to the front door, holding on to the railing for support. Maybe he shouldn't have had those last few beers. Or had more to eat than part of a sub sandwich for breakfast.

He was hoping he could slip into his bedroom without being seen, but Mom met him at the door. "How was your fishing trip?" she asked. "Did you catch anything?"

"A few. Mary Elisabeth's going to cook them." But the words came out jumbled, more like "Few. Mar-liz'beth's gonna cook 'em."

Mom's eyes widened. "Casey Neil MacBride, are you drunk?"

"Nah. Only had a few." He tried to push past her, but her hand around his forearm was like a blood pressure cuff pumped up to full pressure. When did Mom get so strong?

"What did you have to drink?" she asked.

"Jus' beer." He blinked, trying to steady his vision. When

he looked straight ahead, her hairline swam into view. Hey, he was taller than her now. Sweet.

"Del gave you beer?" Her voice rose to a squeak. She still had a hold of him, fingers digging into his skin. He wanted to ask her to let go, but all of a sudden he was feeling a little queasy. He didn't want to risk opening his mouth.

"How many did you have?" she asked.

He shrugged. They'd been talking and drinking and fishing. He hadn't counted. All he knew was the cooler was full when they started and empty when they headed home.

"So many you can't remember." She released his arm with a shake. "Go to your room. I don't want to see you again until morning. And I hope you have a hell of a hangover."

He knew he should apologize to her for coming home in this condition, but all he could manage was a groan. His stomach rolled and churned, like a restless sleeper. He lunged past her, down the hall and toward the bathroom.

He almost made it. Instead, he ended up on his knees, puking up his guts just outside the bathroom door.

His mother loomed over him again. "You clean that up, then go to bed."

He looked up at her through bleary eyes. From this angle she looked about six feet tall. "What are you gonna do?"

"I'm going next door to give your uncle a piece of my mind."

He nodded, and used the wall to climb back to a standing position. The stench of vomited beer almost made him heave again. He edged around it and found a couple of old towels in the back of the linen closet. Being stuck here cleaning puke wasn't the very worst thing he could imagine doing right now.

The worst thing was being Uncle Del when his mom lit into him.

Karen had to grant her brother one thing: the man wasn't dumb. He must have known how furious she'd be with him, so he hadn't stayed around his place long after dropping off his nephew. He'd probably gone to Mary Elisabeth's or to one of his no-account friends who'd be sure to take him in. She stood on the steps of his trailer and stared at the empty carport where his truck usually sat. Cold chills overtook her as she realized not only had he gotten her underage son drunk, he'd driven him home while Del himself was almost certainly feeling no pain.

She sat down on the top step and hugged her arms around her knees. In a minute she'd go back and check on Casey, make sure he wasn't still vomiting or blacked out or anything.

"Thief! Thief! Thief!" The sharp cry of a Blue Jay drew her attention and she looked up to see one eyeing her from the top of the crepe myrtle bush beside the steps. It turned its head and fixed one black-rimmed eye on her and fluffed its feathers. *"Thief! Thief! Thief!"* it repeated.

"Do you know the thief who stole my little boy and replaced him with…with that drunken man throwing up in my hall?" she muttered. Casey was taller than her now, and the arm she'd grabbed was wiry with muscle. That as much as seeing his eyes glazed and hearing his slurred speech had frightened her. Somewhere in the last few weeks or months he'd transformed. He wasn't her child anymore. He was his own, independent person, one with secrets and dreams and dirty deeds she'd never know about. She'd known this would happen. She'd already been through it with Matt, but she had imagined she could hold on to Casey, her dreamer, a little longer.

One afternoon with Del and he'd gotten away from her.

She stood and headed back toward the house. Tomorrow, she'd deal with Del. Right now, she needed to find the aspirin, and check on her wayward boy.

The next morning, Karen was over at Del's as soon as she saw his truck pull into the driveway. She intercepted him as he inserted the key in his front door. "We need to talk," she said.

He gave her a sour look. "Not now, sis. I'm busy."

"You're not too busy to talk to me." She followed him into the house and stood between him and the bedroom door, in case he got any ideas about retreating there and locking her out.

"You're mad about Casey." He tossed his truck keys onto the kitchen counter, wincing when they clattered against the tile top. He looked about as rough as he must have felt—his hair needed combing and whiskers stuck out a quarter inch all over his chin.

"You took a sixteen-year-old and got him drunk!"

"Hey, I didn't pour the beer down his throat. And what's wrong with him having a couple of beers? It didn't hurt anything."

"It was more than a couple. He was sick all over the floor as soon as he got home."

Del made a face. "He'll learn to hold his liquor better when he gets older."

"I don't want him learning that kind of lesson."

"Learning that lesson is part of growing up. Deal with it." He sank onto the sofa and rubbed his temples. "Now that we've had this little discussion, could you leave me alone?"

"No, I won't leave you alone. We're not through talking." Anger and frustration pressed at the back of her throat, sending words rushing out of her. "You may think it's all right to waste your life sponging off other people and playing the charming rogue, but I want better for my son. I don't want him to be like you."

Del narrowed his eyes. "Yeah, I know. You want to make him into some uptight worker bee, someone who keeps his nose clean and *contributes* to society and does his mama proud. It's really all about you, isn't it?"

"It's not about me." What was wrong with wanting to be proud of her child? Or wanting to know that he was financially secure and successful? "It's about Casey growing up to be the best he can be." All he needed was a way to channel his talents, something that would interest him enough for him to focus. He wasn't going to find that sitting on a riverbank, drinking beer with his uncle.

"Then quit trying to force him into a mold you've made for him. He's his own person." Del sat forward, his gaze burning into her, his voice a menacing growl that made her take a step back. "He's more like me than you'll ever admit. The sooner you accept that and let him be, the happier we'll all be."

"I won't accept it." She pushed back a wave of panic and took a deep breath. "I'm his mother. My job is to help shape his life. There's nothing wrong with that."

"There is if you can't be happy with him the way he is. Keep trying to make him into what he's not and you'll drive him away for sure."

"That's not true."

"What would you know about it? You've spent your whole life trying to be whatever anyone wanted you to be. And it didn't make you any happier, did it?" He sagged back on the sofa and closed his eyes. "Get out of my house. Before I throw you out."

She ran from the trailer, gasping for fresh air, trying to clear the ugly images his uglier words had conjured: of Casey growing up to be like Del, and of herself as some ever-changing chameleon, trying to please people—her father, Tom, even her boys—who could never be pleased.

The idea made her cold. Was she that way? Maybe, but was it so bad—to want to make the people you loved happy?

But what about making yourself happy? The voice in her head was quiet, but clear, and the question repeated itself over and over, a mantra she couldn't shake.

Karen had calmed down some by the time Casey shuffled out of his room shortly before noon. When he saw her, he ducked his head. "You don't have to say anything. I know I messed up."

"Good. Then you've saved me the trouble of hauling out my lecture on the evils of underage drinking." She folded her arms across her chest and studied him. He was still wearing the clothes he'd had on yesterday, and his hair stuck out in all directions. He looked like some homeless person—or a typical teenage boy, depending on your perspective. "I don't want you going off alone with Uncle Del anymore."

"Aw, Mom." He frowned at her. "This wasn't his fault."

"He brought the beer. And he didn't do anything to stop you from drinking it. If I know Del, he probably encouraged it."

The guilty look on his face told her she was right. "He's supposed to be the adult," she continued. "But he certainly didn't act like one."

He shoved his hands in his pockets. "I like Uncle Del because he doesn't treat me like a kid."

"But you are a kid." She looked him up and down. "Not a little one, but you're not an adult yet, either. And I don't even want to think what could have happened if there'd been an accident on the way home. Del certainly wasn't in any shape to be driving."

"But nothing happened."

"Nothing happened this time. I'm not willing to risk a second chance. I've already spoken to Del. He knows how I feel."

He shuffled past her to the refrigerator, where he took out a Coke. "So what's up with Dad? Why'd he leave early?"

She winced. Leave it to Casey to change the subject to something even more upsetting to talk about. Her first instinct was to try to get the conversation back on track, but that was the easy way out. The one that didn't require her to be honest about her feelings.

She took a deep breath. How much harm had been done

already by never revealing how she truly felt? "He thinks I should put Grandpa in a nursing home and come back to Denver right away. I'm not ready to do that yet." That wasn't the only problem, but the only one she was willing to share with Casey.

"Uncle Del thinks Grandpa doesn't care about anyone or anything but birds."

She sat at the table and stared at her folded hands. "Sometimes it seems that way."

Casey sat across from her, long legs stretched out in front of him. "I told him I think Grandpa cares about a lot of things. He's just not one to show his feelings." He took a swig of soda. "Maybe he doesn't know how to show them."

She wanted to hug him then, but the fear she'd break down altogether if she did so held her back. "Emotions can be scary things," she said, choosing her words carefully. "People have different ways of showing them."

He nodded. "I know." He leaned over and awkwardly patted her hand. "Dad will come around. He just misses you a lot. When you're back home again, he'll understand you couldn't just run out on Grandpa."

She nodded, unable to force any words past the knot in her throat. If only it were that simple.

Casey stood and tossed the empty Coke can into the trash. "I think I'll take a shower."

She watched him go, thinking about the things each generation passed on to the next. Casey had her hair and her nose, and his father's eyes and chin. But he had an emotional openness she'd never known, and a tolerance for others' differences his father certainly didn't possess. Something outside of them had shaped his character. It gave her hope he'd avoid the mistakes she'd made.

Mistakes she was still making. She looked back toward her father's office. He was in there, exchanging e-mails with his birding friends and making plans for his next expedition.

She hoped before too many weeks he'd be able to look after himself, or at least get by with the help of a housekeeper and maybe a visiting nurse.

She stared at the closed door of the office. All these weeks she and her father had tiptoed around each other's feelings. They talked, but never said anything too important. She'd been waiting for him to make the first move—for him to apologize for his distance over the years, to thank her for caring for him now.

She'd been waiting for him to tell her he loved her. As if a man who'd been silent about his feelings for seventy years would suddenly find words to express them.

Oh, she was her father's daughter all right—keeping her emotions locked away where no one could ridicule or reject them. Which left her like a child standing outside the door, waiting to be invited into the party, but too afraid to ring the bell.

No one was going to ring it for her. No one could break this family curse but her. On shaking legs, she stood and walked down the hall, to the door of the study. She waited a long moment, then raised her hand and knocked, holding her breath as she listened for an answer.

and what is a bird without its song? Do we not wait for the stranger to speak? It seems to me that I do not know a bird till I have heard its voice; then I come nearer it at once, and it possesses a human interest to me.
—*John Burroughs,* Birds and Bees, Sharp Eyes and Other Papers

"In!" Martin commanded. His voice was much stronger now, though he still favored one- or two-word sentences, the minimum number of words to make himself understood.

Karen entered and dragged a chair around to sit in front of him. "We need to talk," she said.

He looked at her, eyes alert, like a crow waiting to snatch the fragments of a picnic lunch. She smoothed her palms down her thighs. "When you had your stroke, and Mom asked me to come look after you, I didn't want to at first."

He nodded, expression unchanging, as if this information wasn't new or surprising.

"But then I thought, I should do it. Because… because you're my dad and…and because I thought this might be our last chance to really get to know each other." She looked at him, silently pleading with him to help her out here. Meet her halfway. "You were gone so much when I was growing up. And even when you were home, I—I never felt like I was very important to you." Her voice broke on the last words, and she choked back a sob. *Oh God, please don't let me break down.*

She snatched a tissue from the box on the desk and blew her nose loudly, then took a deep breath, determined to get through this. "You were the one person I most wanted to love me. To *like* me. But I never felt that. So I thought, this is our second chance. But now that I'm here—all these weeks..." She shook her head. "Has it made any difference at all?"

He looked away from her, down at his lap, his expression as unreadable as ever. Her spirits sank and she bit her lip to keep from crying out, drawing blood, which tasted like the tears she refused to shed. They were a pair, weren't they? Crippled by reticence, hearts encased in protective shells that distanced them from everyone else, even each other.

His hand trembled as he reached for her, but his grasp was surprisingly strong. "I'm...sorry," he said, his voice gruff. "I...care. Took...for granted...that you knew." He squeezed harder. "I don't know how...to say things...right." He shrugged, and met her gaze, his eyes glossy with tears. "This is how...I am...too old...to change."

"I know." She leaned forward to embrace him, the strength of his arm around her conveying as much as his words. "I just had to hear it. Once." She patted his back, and rested her head on his shoulder, his bones feeling fragile as a bird's against her cheek. "It's all right now."

She'd wanted more, but would take what she could get. He was probably right, that he was too old to change. But was she? Was she too old to find a way to break this family curse that held her feelings hostage behind brittle walls?

After a long moment, Martin pushed away. He picked

up his binoculars from the desk and rolled his chair to the picture window. He raised the glasses to his eyes and scanned the scene outside, looking for birds.

Looking away from her. Always looking away.

The intense exchange with Karen left Martin drained. He retired to his room and lay down, pondering the rare moment of intimacy with his offspring. He was filled with the same feeling of privilege and elation he had when he had seen a rare bird. Karen was like a bird in that respect—he had moments when he felt he truly saw her and understood her, but these moments were all too fleeting.

As the air-conditioning hummed against the late-afternoon heat, he drifted to sleep, and dreamed of the jungle. The air was thick and heavy in his lungs, his vision obscured by tangled vines and leaning tree trunks. A bird darted past, and his heart pounded as he recognized the chunky silhouette of the Brown-chested Barbet.

He took a step forward to follow, and found himself falling through the air. He opened his mouth to scream, but no sound emerged. No one would know when he died here, alone.

But as the ground rushed toward him, he was suddenly caught, as if at the end of a string, and he began to rise again, soaring under his own power. He was flying! He had no wings, only his arms extended in the manner of a child playing airplane. Yet miraculously, he was held upright, floating on a current of warm air.

Exhilarated, he searched for the Barbet and spotted it ahead. It seemed almost to be waiting for him, hovering in the air. He zoomed after it, coming so close he could see the feathers lying along its back like scales. Then it raced ahead.

Effortlessly, he pursued it, swooping and gliding, laughing out loud with joy. He had never felt so weightless. So free. Warm air blew his hair back from his face and pressed his clothes against his body. His fingertips brushed the velvet petals of orchids, and he breathed deeply of their rich perfume. A pair of long-tailed Capuchin monkeys eyed him curiously from their perches in the trees.

The Barbet flew ahead, always just out of reach. Martin followed, not caring where they ended up, delighting in the moment. Why had he never done this before?

The Barbet landed on the end of a branch and began to preen, thick beak ruffling its wing feathers. Martin slowed, and readied for a landing beside the bird, instinctively knowing how to bank and aim for the branch. He stretched out his legs, ready to make contact, some small part of his brain wondering if the narrow limb would really support his weight.

He woke with a start, eyes opened wide to the sun streaming through his bedroom window. He shut them again, willing the dream world to return, but the orange glow of sunlight against his closed eyelids told him sleep had escaped him. He spread his arms, remembering the feel of flight, but his left side remained leaden and unresponsive.

Tears of frustration spilled from beneath his closed eyelids and rolled down his cheeks, wetting the pillow. After the freedom of flight, he felt imprisoned in his damaged body, bereft as a child who has lost the only source of happiness in his world.

Casey decided he'd better try to make it up to his mom for coming home drunk the other day, so he offered to finish mowing the backyard.

"You can't," she said. "There's a Killdeer sitting on a nest near the pond."

"Not anymore. Grandpa and I checked it out the other day. The babies are grown and flew away."

"Already?" She checked the calendar. "It's only been two weeks."

He shrugged. "I guess that's all it takes with birds." He slipped on his sunglasses. "Anyway, think I'll go mow."

"Be careful. It looks like a storm is coming up."

He glanced out the window. The sky did look dark in the distance. "I'll have time to finish before it gets bad," he said.

"Okay." She looked a little dazed. Maybe she was shocked he'd volunteer to do a chore. So maybe he wasn't that crazy about work—who was? That didn't mean he couldn't do it when he needed to.

He was filling the gas tank on the mower when Mary Elisabeth wandered over from Uncle Del's trailer. "Hey," she said, stopping beside the mower.

"Hey yourself." He grinned at her. She was wearing Daisy Dukes and a sleeveless denim shirt that tied under her breasts. The ring in her navel glittered in the sunlight. "What's up?"

"I heard about your fishing trip," she said.

He flushed. "Yeah, Mom's pissed at Uncle Del. Nothing new about that, I guess."

"Smart people do dumb things sometimes."

"Yeah." He set the gas can aside and screwed the cap back on the mower. "I told her Uncle Del didn't mean any harm."

She poked him in the shoulder. "I'm not talking about Del, I'm talking about you."

He stared at her. "You think I'm smart?"

Her smile could have melted chocolate. "Of course you're smart. I bet you make As in school."

He made a face. "You'd lose that bet. I hate school."

"Why? Because it's boring?"

He nodded. "Yeah."

"Just suck it up and get through it." She shrugged. "You have to do that sometimes."

"I don't see why. I mean, why not do what makes you happy, as long as you're not hurting anybody?" He figured she could understand that philosophy.

"But sometimes you end up hurting yourself." Her expression was serious now. If not for the whole short-shorts and navel ring thing, she might have looked like somebody's mom. "If you don't finish school, how are you going to support yourself? And what if you meet someone and want to get married and have a family? Then you'll need to support them."

"Whoa. I'm not thinking about supporting anybody right now. I can deal with that when the time comes." What was it with women? Did they all have this mom-thing inside their brains? Something tripped a switch and this perfect mom-speech came out? It was wild.

"The choices you make do affect your future," she said. "Realizing that is part of growing up."

Was she saying she didn't think he was grown-up? He stared at the ground between his feet. "I guess sometimes it's more fun to stay a kid."

"Yeah, we all feel that way sometimes."

She nudged his shoulder again, the smile back in place, and he relaxed a little. "Do you feel that way?" he asked.

"Oh, sure. I bet even your mom feels that way every once in a while."

"Mom? No way. She was born grown-up."

She laughed. "No, I bet she sometimes thinks of ditching all the responsibility and just doing what she wants for a change."

This idea was both frightening and intriguing. His mom, a free spirit? He shook his head. "If that's the way she feels, why doesn't she?"

She leaned against the mower and crossed her arms under her breasts. "Maybe because it's too scary. Or maybe because she loves you all too much not to keep looking after you."

He fiddled with the gearshift knob on the mower. "Mom's not one for a lot of mushy talk. I mean, I know she cares about us, she just doesn't say it all the time. Not like some women. I have this one friend, Joe—his mom hugs and kisses him and tells him she loves him every time he leaves the house. Like he's going to forget or something." He shuddered. "I always feel kind of embarrassed for him."

"Some people are more expressive than others," Mary Elisabeth said. "It doesn't mean they love any more, they just like to talk about it, I guess."

"If something's the truth, I don't think you have to keep saying it."

"Yeah, but you should say it every once in a while, just to remind yourself."

He fiddled with the gearshift some more, watching her through half-closed eyes. He got the feeling something was on her mind. "So did you just feel like giving me a bunch of advice today?"

"No, silly." She looked at him sideways, almost shyly. "Actually, I came to say goodbye."

"Goodbye?" His heart hammered in his chest. "Are you going away?"

"Yeah. My sister in California invited me to come out and stay with her for a while. I think I'm going to do it."

"What about Del?"

"Oh, he'll be all right. A man like him never goes long without a woman around."

The casualness of her attitude bothered him. He'd thought she really cared about his uncle. "Aren't you going to miss him?" Wasn't Del going to miss *her?*

"Sometimes. We had fun." She straightened. "But I'm not ready to get serious about someone right now. And he isn't, either, which I guess is why things worked for us. Maybe I'll hook up with a surfer dude in California."

Too bad Casey wasn't a surfer. And about ten years older.

"So what about you?" she asked. "Are you going back to Denver soon?"

"At the end of the summer, I guess." He looked toward the house. "Grandpa's doing better."

"He is. I'm glad. He's an interesting guy."

"I guess he is." He glanced at her. "Most people are interesting, if you get to know them a little."

"I like the way you think." She brushed off her shorts. "I guess I'd better be going. I told my sister I'd leave in the morning and I still have packing to do."

"Thanks for stopping by." He wiped his hand on his jeans and offered it to her. "Have a good trip."

"You, too." She took his hand and held it in both of hers. "Remember, you can get through anything if you have to. Even boring school."

"Yeah." Though he still wasn't so sure about that.

She surprised him then, by tugging him toward her and stretching up to kiss his cheek. Then she was gone, walking across the yard without looking back.

He put his hand to his face, still feeling the soft brush of her lips against his skin, her flowery perfume filling his nostrils. He felt warm all over, and as if his feet might not be touching the ground.

Wow.

Karen watched Casey and Mary Elisabeth out the kitchen window. The young woman had already stopped by the house and said her goodbyes. Karen wondered how Casey would take the news of her leaving. She was pretty sure her son had a crush on his uncle's girlfriend. What teenage boy wouldn't? Mary Elisabeth looked like a *Playboy* centerfold come to life.

Karen was surprised by how much she was going to miss the younger woman. Mary Elisabeth was the kind of person who calmed the atmosphere just by being in a room. Dad was less argumentative when she was around, and even Del could be pleasant under the influence of his younger girlfriend.

She envied Mary Elisabeth, too, for going off on her own, the way Karen never had the courage to do. She'd had big dreams of traveling and making her way in the world, but in the end she'd stayed right here in Tipton after graduation, leaving only when Tom had provided the opportunity.

Now here she was, her children almost grown, her husband angry with her for not giving more of herself to him, her brother disgusted with her because she'd made the mistake of thinking life should be neat and orderly and people's reactions predictable.

She had done one thing right, at least. She and Dad understood each other now. No, he hadn't been the perfect childhood father she'd wanted, but neither had he been the horrible one her selective memory sometimes made him out to be. He'd done the best he could with what he had in him. Something she'd tried to do for her boys, too.

She left the kitchen and wandered down the hall to

Martin's study. She was surprised to find him, not at the computer as she'd expected, but at the window.

"Storm coming," he said. Every day his speech was clearer, though he was still unable to use his left limbs.

"We could use rain," she said. "The weatherman said this is the remnants of a tropical depression from South America."

"Birds get caught in big storms," he said. "Blown off course." He looked at her, his expression charged with anticipation. "Chance to see...birds not seen here...before."

"Maybe we'll both have some to add to our lists," she said, though she doubted there was a bird anywhere near here that her father hadn't already seen. "Casey said the Killdeer chicks are grown and gone already," she added.

He turned from the window again. "They have to grow up fast," he said. "Be ready for...migration."

She picked up a paperweight from the edge of the desk, then set it down again. "What do the adult birds—the mothers—do after the chicks are grown?" she asked. "Do they stay with them or what?"

His forehead wrinkled as he pondered the question. "They go on...being birds." He shrugged. "That's all."

She nodded, the skin on the back of her neck tingling as the idea took hold. Was she like the Killdeer? Could she go on being Karen? Did that mean staying the same, or trying something different?

She'd never thought much about her future—what life would be like when the boys were grown, and beyond that even, to when she could retire from the landscaping business. Maybe she hadn't wanted to think about a time that seemed so scary. She'd spent her whole life being busy, catering to those around her. What would she do with herself when they no longer needed her?

"Dad, can I ask you a question?"

He looked at her, waiting.

"Why birding? What about it made it worth leaving your family, traveling all over the world and enduring so many hardships?" She looked at the awards arrayed on his wall. Surely he hadn't devoted so much of his life to acquiring these pieces of paper. She looked back at him. "I've read all the articles written about you in birding magazines, about how you've walked across deserts and stood in the cold for hours and gotten up in the middle of the night—all to see birds. Why would anyone do that?"

He frowned, the lines on his forehead deepening. He opened his mouth, then closed it again, and moved to the computer and began typing.

She came to stand beside him, and watched the words form on the screen.

I don't know how to explain.

"Try. I want to understand."

When you've waited all night and endured the heat or cold, and finally you see the bird you've been seeking—the feeling is so beautiful, so sweet.... You know then that you've done the right thing. The thing your soul needs you to do.

She blinked, and read the words on the screen again, letting them soak in. *The thing your soul needs you to do.* What did her soul need her to do? Was this restlessness she felt of late a sign that she needed to make changes in her life—find a new job? Travel to another country? Leave Tom and start over with someone else? Or by herself?

She hugged her arms across her chest, as if she could ward off the psychic chill that swept through her. She didn't know if she was as strong as her father, who endured great hardships in hopes of some elusive reward. She didn't think she was as brave as Mary Elisabeth, willing to uproot herself and move across the country for the sake of trying something different. And she wasn't as carefree as Casey, who trusted the future to take care of itself.

That brought her back to the mother Killdeer, and the idea of being Karen. Who was this mysterious woman, and how could she discover her? How could she find the thing her soul needed her to do?

16

If life is, as some hold it to be, a vast melancholy ocean over which ships more or less sorrow-laden continually pass, yet there lie here and there upon it isles of consolation on to which we may step out and for a time forget the winds and waves. One of these we may call Bird-isle—the island of watching and being entertained by the habits and humours of birds.
—*Edmund Selous,* Bird Watching

The storm hit while they were eating supper, rain sounding like gravel against the windows, the tops of the pine trees bent like heavy stalks of wheat in the onslaught. Before he went to bed that night, Martin persuaded Casey to help him position the spotting scope. "Tomorrow...we'll see what blew in on the wind," he explained. He hadn't much hope of adding to his list, but he might be able to point out something interesting for Karen or Casey to add to their lists.

He also had the boy open the window a couple of inches. He lay in bed later with the lights out, breathing in the green smell of wet pine and fertile loam. It reminded him a little of the jungles of Brazil, which smelled of wet and growing things, and the pungent richness of decay.

He fell asleep to the drum of rain cascading off the eaves,

which became the steady cadence of dew dripping from the leaves of rubber trees.

A familiar cry assailed him, and the Brown-chested Barbet flitted into view. It landed on a branch above his head and cocked one eye at him, as if to pose a question or a challenge. Then with a soft flutter of wings it rose into the air and flew away.

Martin spread his arms and stood on tiptoe, a fledgling eager to join in the flight. But gravity held him firmly to the ground. No longer could he fly among the treetops with the birds, though the memory of how that freedom had felt stayed with him, like the scent of a loved one clinging to his clothes though they were long departed.

He clenched his fists and a keening cry of mourning tore from his throat. Why was he trapped here this way, immobile and useless, the things he loved most out of his reach in the treetops?

He woke before dawn, irritable and unrested. The rain had stopped and the sky had lightened to an ashy gray. Restless, he maneuvered from the bed to the wheelchair and rolled to the window, where he checked the spotting scope. Already, birds were awake, scratching for worms and insects in the rain-softened soil, bathing in puddles that formed in the driveway, singing from the tops of the pines, their songs trumpeting the joy of a fresh new day.

A movement in the azaleas caught his eye. He turned the scope toward it and dialed down the focus until he could make out a thick-billed, sturdy bird. He closed his eyes, heart pounding in his chest, then opened them again, sure he must be dreaming.

With its black mask and golden crown, the barbet looked like a bird in costume for a party. The brown band across its chest that gave it its name was clearly visible. It turned and looked right at Martin, bright black eye staring into his as if it knew. *You couldn't come to me,* the bird seemed to say. *So I came to you.*

He held his breath, unbelieving, while the bird remained still, looking at him, as if waiting for an answer. He tried to stand, to move closer to the window, but pain exploded in his head, driving him to his knees. With his right hand, he groped for the windowsill, trying to pull himself up, but his arm had lost its strength. He landed hard on the floor, and lay curled into himself as the world went black.

When he woke, all was bright, the sun warm against his skin. The pain was gone, and he felt light. Light as a bird. Even as the thought came to him, he felt himself rising. Floating. The barbet hovered beside him, beckoning. Wonder filled him as once more he was able to follow the bird into the sky. He laughed, then shouted, as he soared beside it, floating on the wind and a current of unspeakable joy.

A loud *thud* pulled Karen from sleep. At first she thought the wind from the storm had knocked something over, but as she sat and looked out the window, she saw that the rain had stopped, and the air was calm. She strained her ears, listening, but the house was quiet. Still, she couldn't shake the feeling of dread that clutched at her.

She threw back the covers and pulled on her robe, heart pounding. Telling herself she was being silly, she hurried into the hall. Dad might have fallen. If so, she'd have to wake Casey to help her get him back into bed.

She was startled to find her father's bed empty. But when she pushed the door open farther and stepped into the room, she saw his still form lying in front of the window. "Dad!" She raced to his side and turned him onto his back. The eyes that stared up at her were empty and cold.

She sat back on her heels, a single sob escaping before she clamped her hand over her mouth. Shaking, she reached out and closed his eyes. His skin was still warm, though all the color had drained from it. She tried to find a pulse at his throat, then laid her head on his chest, praying for a heartbeat.

Only the sound of her own breathing filled her ears. She reached for Martin's hand and squeezed it. Already it was cold. She stared at his face, curiosity warring with horror. He had always been such a mystery to her. Was there anything here now to help her figure him out?

She was struck by how peaceful he looked. His expression was relaxed, the corners of his mouth tipped up, almost as if he was trying to smile. The thought was absurd. Her father wasn't a jovial man. He didn't laugh easily, and his smiles were rationed out like expensive chocolates.

But something in death had made him smile. A release from pain? Had he seen heaven at the end? A great light or an angel? Or had he learned some secret no one in this life could know?

She sat back on her heels and let the tears fall, eyes closed, shoulders shaking silently. There were so many things she'd wanted to say to him, so many things she'd wanted to hear him say. Yet at the end, they'd found something. Some… connection. A love for each other, as complicated and fraught with tension as the word was. She was grateful for that, no matter how cheated she felt about all they'd missed.

The sun shone brightly through the window by the time she pulled herself together enough to stand. She took the blanket from the bed and covered him, tucking it gently around his shoulders. When she left the room to call the funeral home, a passerby might have thought he was merely sleeping, still and peaceful.

She woke Casey and tried to break the news gently, though he shouted, "No!" and refused to believe it at first. "He was getting better," he said. "He was going to be all right."

"He was getting better. I thought so, too."

"It's not fair."

"No, it isn't."

They held each other and cried, and she thought of Tom, feeling his absence keenly. He would know the right thing to do, the right thing to say. Always, she had counted on him in a crisis.

She called Del next. He was grumpy at first, from being awakened from sleep. She suspected he'd been drinking hard the past few days, not taking Mary Elisabeth's leaving as lightly as he would have had them believe. "Del, listen," she said, breaking into his complaining. "Something happened with Dad this morning. I found him on the floor of his bedroom. He...he's gone."

"Gone? You mean dead?" He sounded awake now.

She nodded, and swallowed more tears. "Yes. I called Garrity's and they're sending someone out." They'd both gone to school with the Garrity brothers, who had taken over the operation of the funeral home from their father. "They'll be here soon if you want to come over."

"I'll be right there."

She half expected him to fall back asleep, but he was on her doorstep in twenty minutes, in khakis and a white dress shirt, his hair combed, his face freshly shaved. He spoke in solemn tones to Mike Garrity, who came with another man to transport her father's body to the funeral home. "My sister will know better what arrangements he would have wanted," Del said.

She stared at him, stunned by his willingness to give way to her judgment, as well as by his belief that she had some insight into their father's mind. "Cremation," she said after a moment. "A man who spent so much time watching birds would want his ashes scattered on the wind." She hoped that was what he'd wanted. They had never thought to discuss such an uncomfortable subject.

Casey stood in the background, sad-eyed and drooping, wilted by loss. When the hearse finally pulled out of the driveway, Del suggested they all go get some breakfast. "I'm not hungry," she said automatically.

"You need to get out of this house." He put his arm around her, his touch surprisingly gentle, and greatly comforting.

Whatever force that had been holding her together left her then, and she turned into his embrace, sobbing. He held her tightly and patted her back. "I know," he said, over and over. "I know."

She believed him, that he *did* know the pain she felt, that his own pain might be even deeper, since he'd never found a way to bridge the gap between himself and their difficult parent.

She raised her head and searched his face, trying to read the expression in his eyes. "He loved you," she said. "I know he did. He just didn't know how to show it."

"You believe that if you want to." He patted her shoulder again. "Did you call Mom?"

"Not yet. I thought maybe you could do that." She wasn't sure she could deal with her mother right now. Sara would no doubt try to cheer her up, but she wanted to mourn awhile longer. Later, she'd appreciate her mother's efforts more.

"Sure. I can do that."

While he called their mother, Karen hugged Casey. "You okay?" she asked.

He nodded, though his face was still pale. "I'm okay." He glanced at her. "You okay?"

"Not the best shape I've ever been, but I'm hanging in there."

"We should call Dad."

"I will." But she wanted to be alone when she talked to Tom. She didn't need an audience for what could be a tense call.

"Mom says she'll be over a little later." Del joined them again.

"How did she take the news?" Karen asked.

He shrugged. "You know Mom. She doesn't let stuff like this sink in too deep."

She nodded. "I guess that's one way to cope."

"Come on. Let's at least go get some coffee," Del said. He looked back at Casey. "You, too."

She shook her head. "I need to call Tom."

"You can call him later."

"No, I need to call him now." The urgency that had engulfed her earlier returned. She need to talk to Tom. To find out what they had left between them. "You go," she said. "You and Casey."

Del raised one eyebrow, and started to say something, then shook his head. "All right. Come on, Case. Let's get the hell out of here."

When they were gone, silence cloaked the house like a heavy blanket. Karen stared at the closed door to her father's room, thinking she should go in there and clean up, but unable to face the task.

Instead, she went into her room and sat on the side of the bed, staring at the phone. Sadie followed, and sat by the bed, her chin resting on Karen's knee, eyes soft with silent support.

What would she say to Tom, after she'd got past telling him about her father's passing? He'd been so angry when he'd flown back to Denver, and she'd felt so empty. They hadn't talked since then. What did he want from her? Whatever it was, did she have it in her to give anymore?

Telling herself it was better to know the truth than to be tortured by guessing games, she picked up the receiver and dialed.

"Hello?" He sounded distracted, and she realized with a start that it was not even seven o'clock in Denver.

She wet her lips and tried to sound calm. "Tom, it's me. Karen." As if he might have forgotten the sound of her voice. "I'm sorry to wake you."

"No, that's okay. What is it? Is something wrong?"

She imagined him sitting up on the side of the bed, raking a hand through his hair and blinking, trying to come fully awake. "Why would you think something's wrong?"

"You sound funny."

Pain pinched at her heart at the concern in his voice. "It's Dad. He…he passed away early this morning." That sounded so much better than *died*. As if he'd passed on to something else. Something better, she hoped.

"I'm sorry. That's really rough."

She nodded. Her throat and jaw ached from holding back tears. "It's bad. But…he looked, I don't know…peaceful. I thought he was getting better, but there was still so much he couldn't do…." She shook her head. "Del came right over, and he was a big help."

"How's your mom?"

"Del called her. She sounded okay. A little shook up, but you know Mom. Nothing gets her down for long."

"I'll be there as soon as I can. I'll let you know as soon as I call the airlines."

"Then you'll come?"

"Of course I'll come. Unless you don't want me there."

"No, I want you here. It's just, when you left here the other day, things were so up in the air."

"We can talk about that later."

"No!" She took a deep breath and spoke more softly. "I need to talk about it now. Before you come back here." *Before I lose my courage.*

"You're upset now. This can wait."

"No. We've waited too long already."

He sighed. The sigh of a man dealing with a stubborn child. The sound angered her. "I've been doing a lot of thinking," she said. "And I've made some decisions."

"All right. What have you decided?"

She thought of her father in the jungle, waiting on birds; and Mary Elisabeth headed to California; and Casey, who saw his future as an adventure waiting to be discovered. "Dad and I were talking the other day, and he told me that sometimes the most difficult thing is the only thing you can do. The thing your soul needs you to do. For him, that thing was birding."

"And what is that thing for you?" His voice was flat, like a stranger's.

"For me—I think it's finding a way to make our marriage work." She'd contemplated leaving. Moving out and starting over. That would be painful, but easier than staying and hashing things out. And it wasn't what her soul wanted. Something in the very kernel of her being told her she still loved Tom deeply, though she hadn't done a good job of showing him. She wanted to stay and do the work necessary to develop that feeling into something big and wonderful.

"I want that, too." The chill in his voice had vanished, and she could almost see his shoulders slumped in relief.

"There's something else, though," she said. "Something else I need."

"What is it?"

"I need to take more time for myself. I've spent so many years looking after you and the boys and the business, I've lost sight of who I really am. I have to do this if things are going to work between us."

"I want us to make them work."

"It won't be easy," she said.

"I've never been afraid of hard work."

She smiled. "That's one of the things I love about you."

"It's good to hear you say that."

"I've been practicing." She held the phone with both hands, wishing she were holding him instead. That plane from Denver couldn't get here fast enough. "If I keep this up, I might actually get good at all this emotional stuff."

"I never meant to hurt you," he said. "I just felt...desperate. Like nothing I could do would get through to you how much I need you."

"I know." She sniffed and swiped tears from her eyes. "When I do get home, let's plan a trip somewhere, just the two of us. We need to spend some time together away from the business and the boys and everything else that gets in the way of just being together."

"That sounds like a great idea."

She cleared her throat, heart racing again at the thought of what she was about to propose. "And I want to take some time just for me, too. Time when I don't have to be the boys' mother or the office manager or any of those other roles. I need to spend some time finding out who I really am, down inside."

"Do you have anything in particular in mind?"

"I was thinking...maybe a bird-watching trip. I know it's a little crazy, but I've taken it up since I've been here and, well, all that time sitting outside, being still and looking at nature—it's very soothing. It gives me time to listen to the thoughts in my head, instead of drowning them out with all the to-do lists I'm used to keeping in there."

"All right. That sounds fair. I was thinking, too—there's a counselor in the next building over. Maybe it wouldn't hurt to talk to her. I mean, we might need some help if we're really going to do things differently."

"Yeah. That's a good idea." She sagged onto the bed, relief leaving her weak in the knees. That her stand-on-his-own-two-feet husband was willing to accept outside help told her how serious he was about fixing their problems.

"We can do this," he said.

"We can." She smiled into the phone. If she was going to start doing things differently, now was as good a time as any to begin. "Tom?"

"Yes?"

"I love you. I really do." That wasn't so hard. With practice, the words would probably roll off her tongue. But she would never take them for granted. Fate was still out there listening, and she had too much to lose if she screwed things up this time.

After she'd hung up the phone, she wandered out onto the front porch, Sadie at her heels. She wanted to escape the house for at least a little while. Pinecones and broken branches littered the front yard, which glistened wetly in the sunlight. Birdsong lent a tropical feel to the setting. She picked up her father's binoculars from the table by the spot where she'd often settled his wheelchair. He would spend hours here, scanning the treetops, never tiring of studying the behavior and habits of the birds.

The binoculars were old, heavy metal with the black paint worn through to silver where his fingers had gripped them so many hours. She fit her fingers over these worn places, and it was as if he was there with her, the way he was when she was small. He'd hold his hands over hers and show her how to bring the glasses to her eyes and adjust the focus.

A sharp cry, almost human, startled her, and she almost dropped the glasses. When she turned toward the sound, she found a crow, perched in the azalea bush beside the porch. It stared at her with one bright, intelligent eye, head tilted to one side, studying her. She held her breath, fascinated, until it spread its wings and jumped into the air. She watched it soar higher and higher.

She raised the glasses and followed it over the tops of the tall pines, feeling her own spirits lift. It was as if her father had given her one last gift—this assurance that she, too, would find what she needed to be whole. That she would discover her own way to soar.

* * * * *

An unforgettable story of family and forgiveness, loyalty and love.

From acclaimed author

LINDA CARDILLO

From her restaurant on Boston's Salem Street, and from her own kitchen, Rose Dante has served countless meals and built a tightly knit community of customers, family and friends. Her daughter Toni tried to create her own life, outside that circle—only to return with her daughter when her marriage failed. Now that Vanessa's nearly grown, Toni must face the bitterness of the past in order to taste the sweetness of the future.

But she can't make such a journey alone. She needs the guidance of a mother, of her family. She needs Rose's recipes for happiness, learned by trial and error over sixty years of marriage. Recipes that are sometimes difficult to follow, but like the perfect *risotto al limone*, worth the effort.

Across the Table

In stores today wherever trade paperback books are sold!

Free bonus book in this volume!

Dancing on Sunday Afternoons by Linda Cardillo
One woman's legacy—two very different loves.

www.eHarlequin.com

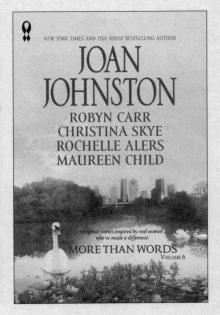

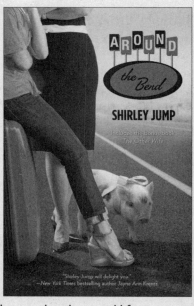